THE
SILVER LION

THE
SILVER LION

Lynn Kerstan

AN ONYX BOOK

ONYX
Published by New American Library, a division of
Penguin Group (USA) Inc., 375 Hudson Street,
New York, New York 10014, U.S.A.
Penguin Books Ltd, 80 Strand,
London WC2R 0RL, England
Penguin Books Australia Ltd, 250 Camberwell Road,
Camberwell, Victoria 3124, Australia
Penguin Books Canada Ltd, 10 Alcorn Avenue,
Toronto, Ontario, Canada M4V 3B2
Penguin Books (N.Z.) Ltd, Cnr Rosedale and Airborne Roads,
Albany, Auckland 1310, New Zealand

Penguin Books Ltd, Registered Offices:
80 Strand, London WC2R 0RL, England

First Published by Onyx, an imprint of New American Library,
a division of Penguin Group (USA) Inc.

ISBN: 0-7394-3835-2

ACKNOWLEDGMENT

Special thanks to Eve Sinaiko for the Italian bits, and to the members of the Beau Monde Chapter of Romance Writers of America, who generously track down and share information about obscure-but-important historical details.

Prologue

1823, India

"But if you catch the Tiger, what the devil will you do with him?" The governor-general mopped his forehead with a soggy handkerchief. "Not that he will let himself be taken. Continue to hound him, and more than likely he'll put you out of his way."

"We'll see." Derek Leighton, Earl of Varden, had been listening to similar warnings since arriving in Calcutta. But it had taken him awhile to realize that the prophets of doom had their own reasons for wanting him to leave their pet criminal alone. "I understand that you dislike interference, especially from an outsider. All the same, the East India Consortium is being bled dry by this outlaw. I mean to stop him."

"What you really mean is that *I* should have stopped him. But it is not so simple as that. He is clever. There is little evidence that will stand up in court. There are no witnesses."

"Of course there are witnesses." Exasperation edged Varden's quiet words. "But half of them profit from his crimes, and the other half fear him. Your government is disinterested because he targets only the Consortium's cargoes."

"This is a large and unruly country, sir. We cannot police every mile of it."

"I understand the difficulties." Varden managed a smile. "My own success is notable only for the lack of it. The time has come, I think, to move beyond commonplace tactics and civilized ploys. To try something a bit more unorthodox."

"What do you mean?" Hands planted on his desk, the governor-general regarded him with dismay. "You don't know Michael Keynes. He is not a gentleman. And I daresay he is the master of unorthodox tactics. No insult, Varden, but you are out of your depth here."

"Your advice is well-meant, and I do value it." *And I am learning to lie without blinking,* Varden thought with a shot of amusement. "I know his brother, the Duke of Tallant. You may be sure that I am prepared for trouble. My advantage is that Keynes won't be expecting trouble from me. Not the sort I have planned for him, at any rate."

"You've found out where he is?"

"I have a lead, from a source I've no intention of revealing. If it all goes wrong, Adam, your hands will be clean."

There was little to say after that, although they drank sherry together before leaving the office and returning to the public rooms at Government House, where an afternoon party was underway. It was someone's birthday, Varden had been told, although he never found out whose. As always, the mamas with marriageable daughters harried him like horseflies, but he made an adroit escape out a servants' door in the back.

Action at last. The trap he had set for the Tiger was about to close.

After leading a series of raids in the Carnatic, Michael Keynes had returned to Bengal. He had been spotted on the outskirts of Calcutta shortly before noon, and word of it came to Varden by way of a message slipped into his hand at Government House.

But having only just arrived, Varden knew better than to hare after his quarry straightaway. Keynes had allies in high places, and if alerted to danger, he would vanish like a ghost.

Leaving the manicured grounds of the British enclave, Varden came onto streets swarming with dust-stained white dhotis and jewel-toned saris as the citizens of Calcutta hurried home in the twilight. Wearing stark British formal dress, he was even more out of place than usual, a raven among smaller, brighter birds that flicked aside to let him pass.

The governor-general assumed he had come to India on behalf of the Consortium and its decimated profits, but he cared nothing for that. And while he did care about bringing criminals to justice, he needn't have come half a world from England to find them. It was the lure of adventure that had brought him here, an escape, however brief, from his pampered aristocratic life. He relished the chance to prove himself more than the sum of what he had been gifted with at birth.

Even so, he could not shake off a distaste for the bribery and deception that had brought him to this point. Nor was an ambush strictly fair play, but that was next on his agenda.

In his belly, a devil of excitement began to stir.

The crowds thinned as he left the bustling city proper and made his way to Clive Street, a meandering oasis lined with scraggly gardens and dry fountains languishing in the pre-monsoon heat. Yellow light glowed from dusty street lamps. Tangy odors of dung fires and dinners cooking over them wafted through the smoky air. Although the houses were unpretentious, it was an expensive place to live because of the space and the quiet. This was a neighborhood for people who wanted to be left alone.

He rounded a slight curve, caught sight of his destination, and stepped quickly behind a withered hedge.

About fifty yards down, isolated in a little cul de sac, stood the narrow two-story house that Michael Keynes had secretly owned for a dozen years. Varden's men had been watching it for several weeks, and finally the surveillance had paid off. Plain, a dirty light brown, the building had no distinguishing features except a staircase along one side to a landing on the first floor. Like a watchtower, it stood dark, silent, and aloof.

Two men detached themselves from their post behind a wall and approached him, taking no precautions to avoid being seen. Swearing under his breath, he beckoned them behind the hedge with his sword cane.

The smaller man crouched a little distance away, watching the street. He looked like a weasel and answered to anything with money attached. The other hireling, a hairy man whose chest and stomach strained against a filthy shirt and faded red vest, swaggered directly up to him.

"Keynes is gone." Dasim threw an angry look over his shoulder at the watchman. "About an hour ago. This one followed, but he lost him within a mile."

"Then we'll wait in the house. Perhaps our friend will join us later."

Frustration blistered Varden's tongue as he climbed to the landing on the first floor, where Weasel had got the door open and was putting away his tools. Inside, a solitary lamp flickered on a table near a narrow bed. He used it to search the sparsely furnished rooms, finding nothing of interest. Then he doused the light and settled in to wait.

Well after midnight, footsteps beat against the wooden staircase. Varden gestured the men to either side of the door and took up his position directly across from it, pistol held at the ready. Fumbling clicks and the grate of a key inserted into the lock. More fumbling and an oath. The door swung open.

A shaft of dim yellow light fell across the barrel of

Varden's pistol. Then a tall, wide-shouldered man filled the doorway.

Keynes erupted into the room and swerved to the right. A swinging kick struck Varden's wrist, dislodging the pistol and sending it across the floor. In a continuous motion, Keynes whirled and jabbed his eye with a hard left, following through with a powerful right to the midsection.

Varden doubled over, came up with a blow to Keynes's jaw, stuck air with his next try. Keynes sent another sideways kick hard at his chest, hurling him breathless against the wall. He began to slide down it.

Dasim caught up with Keynes and grabbed for him. Another kick, a piercing screech. Dasim collapsed into a ball, clutching his groin, and rolled away.

Then Weasel was on Keynes's back, clamping him around the waist with his legs, around the throat with his hands. Keynes drove his elbows into Weasel's ribs. The clinging body dropped off like a singed moth.

Varden pulled himself across the floor on hands and knees, fumbling in the darkness for the gun. His fingers touched metal.

Instantly a booted foot slammed down on his hand. He heard the crackle of splintering bone and his own scream. The gun skittered away.

Nearly blinded by pain, he dragged himself to where he thought it had gone. Sounds of blows and grunts as the other men fought. Something flew past him and crashed against the wall. He heard a familiar slide of metal, the blade being drawn from his sword cane. A shriek. The thud of a heavy body hitting the floor.

He looked over his shoulder. On the other side of the room, Dasim lay on his back, the sword pinning him to the floor through his neck. Beside him was Keynes, knees bent, facing the open door. Footsteps pounded on the stairs, going down. Weasel must have got away.

At last Varden's good hand closed on the gun. He pulled it awkwardly erect and slouched with his back against the wooden bed. "Don't move."

Keynes turned slowly to the sound, arms held out, hands splayed. In the faint light, his eyes glittered.

"Don't move," Varden said again, a little more in control.

Then Keynes dove at him, head-on, straight for the pistol.

He seemed to be moving slowly, as if through water. Daring Varden to shoot. *Wanting* him to shoot. Varden was sure of it.

His finger froze on the trigger.

"Oh, for God's sake." Keynes wrenched the pistol away and shoved it in his belt. "Why carry the damned thing if you won't use it?"

"I don't shoot unarmed men."

"And see where that's landed you. Get up."

Varden's hand felt on fire. The room began to spin. "I . . . don't think I can."

"Then stay there. I'll dispose of the garbage."

Varden fought the dizziness, but his vision clouded. Next thing he knew, he was lying on the bed with his back and head elevated against a bank of cushions. His right hand, wrapped in what looked to be a soft muslin shirt, rested on a pillow at his side.

Several lamps had been lit. He could see that Dasim's body was gone. He thought Keynes had gone as well, until the door opened.

"Done with your nap?" Keynes was carrying two bottles. "I've been to the cellar for refreshments. Archangel or not, I think you need to get stinking drunk."

Varden grimaced at the reference to a nickname he loathed. "You know who I am?"

"You're hard to miss, all that bright hair and luminous self-righteousness. I had you followed the first weeks after you got here, but gave it up as a waste of time. You didn't seem likely to cause me any trouble."

"It appears you were right." Speech came hard. So did thought. The fire in his hand seemed a living thing, torturing the rest of him with glee. Then the bottle was brought to his mouth and brandy poured inside, flowing down his throat like lava. He choked. Coughed. Accepted another drink.

"In fact, I miscalculated," Keynes said. "What you lacked in experience, you made up for with sheer doggedness. Who betrayed me?"

"You can't expect me to answer that."

"I suppose not. Aristocratic honor and all that twaddle. But what the devil did you hope to accomplish with an ambush?"

"I intended to interrogate you."

"Good God. What was I to tell you? The plans for my next attack on a Consortium riverboat? The names of my associates? Not bloody likely. Did you imagine your bully boys could beat a confession out of me?"

"They were to restrain you, that is all. Clearly I should have brought several more of them."

Keynes laughed and gave him another drink. "Well, if it's any consolation, you've opened the lid on some of the government's dirty little secrets. To protect themselves, the authorities will have to stop letting me run wild."

"That's something, then. No more raids."

"Not on the boats or the cargoes. I've no choice now but to carry the fight back to England and the man who sent you here. Just as well. It's past time I disposed of my brother."

Varden began coughing in earnest, sending a blast of pain down his arm. "You shouldn't have told me," he said after a time. "I'll have to stop you."

"You can try." Keynes stuffed the bottle of brandy into the crook of Varden's good arm. "You'll be here alone for perhaps an hour. I don't think you'll be disturbed, but I'm going to lock you in anyway. If you have company, use this." He pulled the pistol from his belt and laid it across Varden's stomach. "I'm sending Hari Singh to play nursemaid. When you see something that looks like a bear with a beard, don't shoot him."

Shadows closed in, and the room began revolving again. "Why are you helping me?"

"Because I'm an idiot. But only this once. Stay clear of my affairs, Archangel. Meddle again, and you'll lose more than a wing."

Chapter 1

January 1824, England

Since the day the women of the Leighton family first gathered around his cradle to discuss a prospective bride for the squalling newborn heir, the Earl of Varden had been plagued by marriage. Not his own marriage, which, to his family's dismay, had yet to occur. But a friend's marriage, an enemy's marriage, even the upcoming marriage of a servant, inevitably found a way to cause him trouble.

In this case, his secretary's wedding and removal to the north of England had left him without assistance just when most he needed it. After eighteen months away from home and an adventure now consigned to his nightmares, he was about to take up his life again, or whatever he could reclaim of it. Unfortunately, that included all the routine matters he'd rather not deal with himself, including a formidable amount of paperwork. Blaine's marriage was also his divorce from his employer, who was having difficulty replacing him.

After the latest rejected applicant had slumped out of the study, Varden turned his attention to the last packet on his desk. Eight prospective candidates come and gone, and the ninth, now waiting in the anteroom, had a nose the shape of a cauliflower.

Not that it made the slightest difference. He had

hoped for someone presentable, but considering his re-
clusive plans for the future, even a pug-face would do.

He sifted through the thick stack of credentials. Impressive indeed, as befitted an earl's private secretary.
The candidate boasted too many skills for one person
to possess, a dozen recommendations from impeccable
sources, and had provided almost nothing in the way
of personal information.

Just as well. He had lost his taste for personal rela-
tionships of any kind.

A tug on the bellpull brought Quill to the door, his
brows waggling with agitation. Staring meaningfully at
his employer, the butler jerked his head in the direction of the anteroom as if robbers had invaded it.

"What is it, Quill? Did the last applicant give up
and go away?"

Lips clamped together, the butler went on jerking
his head. His hands waved Xs in front of him, signal-
ing *No.*

"Am I about to be shot? Speak up, man."

"He is trying to warn you," said a clear, crisp voice.
"About me."

With a sigh, the butler withdrew to admit a slender,
pale-skinned woman wearing a steel gray dress, a
matching bonnet, and darkly smoked spectacles.

Varden had seen her before—the spectacles were
unmistakable—but he couldn't think where. Rising,
his habit in the presence of a female, he watched her
stride purposefully to the desk and stand before him,
her back straight as a lance.

"You were expecting a man, of course. I apologize
for the mild deception, but it couldn't be helped."

"What became of the pugilist fellow I saw waiting
in the anteroom?"

"Finn is my driver. I cannot bear to be idle for any
length of time, so he held my place while I explored
the grounds. Now he is with my carriage, expecting
me to arrive there momentarily. I, on the other hand,

believe you are fair-minded enough to grant me an interview. We have a bet on it."

He rarely encountered that degree of self-confidence outside the House of Lords. "I fear you are about to lose your wager, Miss Pryce. Or is it Mrs. Pryce?"

"I am unmarried, sir. The H is for Helena."

"Well, it appears you have made the journey to Richmond in vain. For all your considerable experience, I require absolute integrity in the *man* who will become my secretary."

"In a good cause," she said, "I have been known to prevaricate, or dissemble, or tell a downright corker. My references introduce me as H. Pryce in order to mislead you. I instructed my driver to pretend he had come for the interview, and when the next-to-last applicant emerged, I entered the house and presented myself to your butler. Had you known H. Pryce to be a female, my lord, I should never have been admitted to your study. Will you deny it?"

"Certainly not. But what made you think that bluffing your way into my presence would secure you a hearing?"

"Regard for your character. Confidence in my abilities. The certainty you would find no one better suited for the position." A little curve, the shape of a parenthesis, winked at the corner of her mouth. "You think me vain. Perhaps I am."

They were still standing on opposite sides of his desk, immobile as pillars, and he realized with a shot of astonishment that he was beginning to enjoy himself. It seemed a long time since he had enjoyed himself.

"Very well, Miss Pryce." He gestured to the chair where the other applicants had sat, nervous and inadequate, which this female was decidedly not. "If you insist on prolonging a futile endeavor, please be seated and tell me about yourself."

She lifted her skirts and sat, with graceful precision, on the edge of the chair, folding her hands on her lap. "All you need to know is contained in the papers on your desk. For the last several years I was secretary to Lady Jessica Sothingdon, but since her marriage, she has required less of my time. In consequence, I have accepted temporary commissions from several clients, including the Duke of Wellington, Mr. Huskisson, Mr. Canning, Lord Philpot, and the Duke of Devonshire. You have their testimonials."

It occurred to him that he should sit down as well. When he did, he found himself looking directly at the spectacles that entirely obscured her eyes. Crafted to cup her eyesockets, they were hinged at her temples to bend back another inch or so. He found it disorienting, the inability to read her thoughts by looking into her eyes. She might as well have been wearing a mask.

"But you seek a permanent position with me?" he said, because it was his turn to speak. She had the unnerving capacity to let a silence drag on.

"Little in life is permanent. I wish employment with you for so long as I find the experience rewarding. I should advise you now that my services are prodigiously expensive."

He bit back a laugh. "You continue to deflect my questions. What is your background? Your education? Your family?"

"I am an orphan, sir, and if I have living relations, they do not know of my existence. I spent my early childhood in London and was sent to be educated at the Linford Sisters' Academy for Young Ladies in Surrey."

"Your age?"

"Eight-and-twenty."

"Where have I seen you before?"

"At Palazzo Neri, most like. I am acquainted with Beata Neri's companion, Signora Fanella."

He couldn't have said why he persisted. None of

this signified. But she interested him, if only because she posed a challenge he could appreciate without having to deal with it. And because she wouldn't be hurt when he sent her away. Miss Pryce, he suspected, had made herself impervious to insult and rejection. For that, he envied her.

"What is wrong with your eyes?" he asked with uncharacteristic bluntness.

"When it comes to seeing, very little. Nothing that impedes the performance of my duties, unless you require my opinion of a sunset or the quality of a painting. I cannot distinguish colors with perfect accuracy." That beguiling hint of amusement. "Not to be overly dramatic, but the world presents itself to me as through a glass darkly."

It often came to him the same way, without the barrier of smoked glass. "Spectacles so encompassing," he said, "are rather out of the ordinary."

"They are designed for protection. I have a rare disorder of the eyes that makes them excruciatingly vulnerable to light. The merest glimmer causes a burning that is all but unendurable. Exposure for any length of time would result in blindness. You will understand, then, why I take care not to remove the spectacles."

"Are they painful to wear?"

The barest pause. "Uncomfortable. But I have grown accustomed to them, as one must when there is no choice."

He glanced down at his leather-gloved right hand, lying flat and motionless on his thigh. "Yes."

"In every other way," she said, "I am in excellent health."

Something had troubled him since first she appeared. "You could not have been sent by the agency, Miss Pryce. How did you learn of this position?"

"My predecessor, Mr. Blaine, is soon to be married, and his bride recently inherited a property in Northumberland. On Monday last, he gave you his notice. Presuming you would quickly replace him, I posted my credentials and, as you see, presented myself for an interview."

My predecessor? After hearing that, it took some time for the rest of her speech to register. "Mr. Blaine's marriage and departure are scarcely public information. How the dev— How do you *know* all that?"

"I have made a study of you, my lord. I am acquainted with your family history, your financial assets, your education and interests, your political activities, and your prospects. After assuring myself it was in your best interest to employ me, I sought an opportunity to bring myself to your notice."

"Well, you have certainly done that."

"I have no doubt you resent my intrusion into your affairs, and I cannot justify what I have done in terms that will satisfy you. On the other hand, I needn't have admitted to investigating you at all. Be assured, Lord Varden, that your welfare is my sole concern."

"Good God. I already have a *battalion* of female relations meddling in my affairs. Was it my mother who recruited you, Miss Pryce? The grandmothers? One of the aunts? My pestilential sisters? Or did the lot of them conspire to inflict you on me?"

The trace of a smile on her wide mouth, so fleeting he could not be sure he'd seen it. "I am here because of my conviction that a gentleman raised in a household of women will have learned to respect the intelligence, determination, and capabilities of the female sex."

"And to beware them as well." Helena Pryce had swept in like a force of nature, and he kept wondering what she would do next. His life was already complicated beyond measure. "Whatever your talents, it would be unthinkable for me to employ a female secretary. The scandal—"

"Did not concern my previous employers. The foreign secretary and the Dukes of Wellington and Devonshire managed to emerge with their reputations intact." She sat forward on her chair. "You have been treated to the edges of my sharp tongue, sir. You have examined my appearance. It must be obvious that I am not a woman capable of enticing a man. The very notion that the Archangel Earl of Varden would pay me the slightest attention is absurd. No one would credit it."

What was he to say to *that*? She had striking features, to be sure—a smooth complexion, high cheekbones, firm chin, a flawless nose. But her diabolical attractions lay beyond the reach of common understanding. Valor. Wildness. Leashed energy pulsing beneath that rigid self-control. She gave no sign of these things, but he felt them. They vibrated in his bones.

They made her dangerous.

With his left hand, he began to fold up the documents and letters of recommendation she had provided. "I am sorry, Miss Pryce, but for all your accomplishments, you do not suit the requirements for this position."

She said nothing. Neither did she look away as he struggled to assemble her papers and slide them into the leather case. From the tilt of her head, he could tell she was observing his every move. Analyzing the means by which he adjusted to having only one workable hand.

But she didn't try to help, or take over the job for him, as he might have expected from such a managing female. Instead, she left him to get on about it. And that, more than anything she had said or done, impressed him.

It changed nothing, though. Approving her, feeling unaccountably drawn to her, made her dismissal all the more urgent.

At the end, he was forced to bring up his throbbing right hand to hold open the case while he slipped the papers inside. It required several tries, but at last he was able to rise and hold out the packet.

She rose as well, took it, and curtsied. For a moment, just before she turned away, he caught his own reflection in the polished glass of her spectacles. Light hair, troubled eyes, a face that struck him as severe and overbred. He didn't like what he saw.

She moved calmly to the door. Her hand was on the latch. A sense of loss, the certainty he was making a mistake, took hold of him.

"There is one thing," he said, "that you might do for me."

She held still for several heartbeats before turning to face him. "A temporary hire?"

"More of a test. I could hardly refuse to employ a secretary who can do the impossible. I wish to purchase a partly restored castle located in the Mendips, but there is some dispute about the title to the land. In consequence, I am willing to settle for a lease and the right to continue the restoration of the castle until the legalities are worked out, at which point ownership must be signed over to me at an equitable price. Can you accomplish all of that, do you suppose?"

Silence, save for the ticking of the clock. Her full lips tightened as she thought it over. "What if I can?"

"Then you may have the position you came here to secure."

"On my terms?"

"On negotiated terms. You must know I will deal fairly, or you would not be considering my offer."

"Yes. But it is not dealing fairly to assign me all the risk. Even if I fail, Lord Varden, I expect to be paid for my time. The price will be high."

He had a mental image of shoveling gold into a volcano. A vivid image of flames rising up to consume him.

"Very well, Miss Pryce. You want to be my secretary, and I want you to buy me a castle. Let us see if you can work miracles."

Chapter 2

The miracle had already occurred, Helena was thinking as Finn guided her small carriage along the elm-lined road that let to the manor house at Longview, the Duke of Tallant's country estate. Lord Varden had set for her a test that she, more than anyone else in England, had a good chance of passing.

She ought to feel a little guilty, she supposed, for withholding from him her connection with the Tallant family. But she didn't. This circumstance was a link in a chain forged by kindness, by people helping other people.

A year and a half ago, Lady Jessica had gone to the very castle desired by Lord Varden in search of a valuable artifact, and was able to spirit it away because Miranda Holcombe, then living there with her uncle, put herself at risk to be of assistance. Later, Miranda had need of help from Lady Jessica. Helena made Miranda's acquaintance at that time and was soon drawn into a tangled web of deceit and murder, where her particular talents proved especially useful. Three women, so very different, all able to provide assistance to the others when most needed.

She didn't know if Miranda, now the Duchess of Tallant, would sign over the castle to Lord Varden. But she would have her chance, and no one should expect more than that.

At the house, a footman in silver-and-black Tallant livery escorted her to a sitting room, where the duchess welcomed her with surprised delight. It was several minutes before Helena could nudge the conversation toward the reason she had come.

"The *castle*?" The duchess sat forward on her chair, blue eyes wide with astonishment. A swatch of platinum hair that had escaped her neat chignon looped over one ear like a comma. "Why would anyone with a grain of sense want that pile of rubble?"

Helena put down her teacup. "My client," she said carefully, "did not provide a reason. Does it signify?"

"I suppose not. But my uncle poured his heart and fortune into restoring the castle, and after a decade of work, succeeded only in making the keep fit for habitation. Barely so. Out of kindness, you should advise your client to look elsewhere for . . . whatever it is he is looking for."

"Why do you assume my client is male?"

"A woman is far too sensible to buy a castle in a poke." The duchess selected an almond biscuit from the tray and nibbled at it, regarding her guest speculatively. "This is not your usual sort of endeavor, Miss Pryce, and if I may say so, you do not seem quite yourself. Is Holcombe's Folly so important to your client?"

"I didn't know it was called that," Helena said with a stilted laugh. When was the last time she had been nervous? Had she *ever* been nervous? "My client's wishes are a mystery to me, but I do have a personal stake in the success of this venture. It is, in fact, by way of an audition. If I pass the test he has set me, the gentleman will employ me as his secretary."

"You seek employment? But we are in need of a dozen people with a score of refined skills, and you alone could replace all of them." The duchess spoke softly, as always, but earnestly. "Would you consider taking a position here?"

Helena had not anticipated this. God in heaven, she could never work in this place, for this family. "You are very kind, but no. The gentleman is in politics, and because his specific interests march with my own, I have some hope of influencing him to take a more active role in reform legislation. But to have that opportunity, I must secure for him your castle."

The duchess gave a throaty chuckle. "The day you begin advising the government, Miss Pryce, England will be fortunate indeed. And were the castle mine to give, it would be yours this very instant. But there are legal difficulties. My uncle willed it to my cousin Robert, and while there is reason to believe Robert died of a fever in India, we have no way to prove it. He fled England because of gambling debts and used false names when he was abroad. A witness who claims to have discovered his body identified Robert by his webbed fingers, but for reasons I cannot disclose, the witness can never give evidence. So you see the dilemma."

"My client is familiar with the problem, if not the specific details." From the floor beside her, Helena picked up her leather case, opened it, and withdrew a folder. "His offer and the terms he is willing to accept are here. Who is empowered to negotiate?"

"My father, I suppose, to the degree he must give consent. Have another cup of tea while I examine the papers."

Instead, Helena rose and crossed to the large windows overlooking a sweep of winter grass. The pasture ended at a lake framed with trees, their bare branches silhouetted against a pale blue sky. On a patch of ground beside a boathouse, two men were scraping the bottom of an upturned skiff.

A peaceful countryside scene, no mark on it of all the terrible things done at Longview in the past century. This ought to be a blighted landscape, blood dripping from the branches, lambs on the grass with their wooly throats slit. A cold shiver ran along her spine. The new duke and duchess would transform the estate and the family, but the past would always snap at the heels of their endeavors. Old sins, she knew too well, cast long shadows.

"Save for outright ownership," said the duchess, "which I am unable to guarantee, we can almost certainly arrange for your client to take control of the castle. And the duke will pull strings, if necessary, to expedite matters."

Helena, shuddery with relief, wandered back to the tea table, feeling like a different person than she was. Her Great Gamble, nearly lost two days ago in the earl's Richmond house, had taken a turn. Where it would lead, she was no longer confident enough to say. But she understood that with each step, she would be forced to recommit herself. Or abandon her scheme, because when you came right down to it, she had a great deal to lose, and nothing whatsoever to win.

"Thank you," she said, too restless to take her chair again. She stopped behind it and placed her hands on the carved mahogany back. "When you are ready to proceed, send word to me at Sothingdon House."

Head tilted, the duchess regarded her with a mischievous smile. "You have been careful not to reveal your client's identity, Miss Pryce. But in order to sign over rights to the property, we really must know his name."

"Of course." Despite a sudden chill along her spine, Helena spoke with her usual clipped diction. "I saw no reason to mention it until reasonably sure the transaction could take place. My client is the Earl of Varden."

Silence. Then a breathy "Oh, dear."

"Just so. I quite understand if you prefer to withdraw from this arrangement."

"No, indeed," said the duchess promptly. "But

Michael . . . the duke will be difficult to bring around, and not only because of the regrettable injury to Lord Varden's hand. There have been other conflicts as well. Of those I cannot appropriately speak, but the animosity, at least on my husband's part, has not abated."

"Then there is no more to be said." Helena straightened, covering her disappointment with a smile. "I had not understood the complications."

"Oh, there are none of any consequence. With me guiding him, the duke will see that handing over the castle rids us of a nuisance and creates an expensive problem for the earl. He'll not be difficult to persuade."

"I have no doubt you can bring His Grace around, but is it wise? Your marriage is new, and—"

"Planted in bedrock." The intensely blue eyes softened. "The duke will grumble, but Lord Varden shall have his castle, and you shall have the position you seek. Our family is profoundly indebted to you, Miss Pryce. There is nothing we would not do for you in return."

Pride strangled Helena's first response, and her second. It must seem she had come here to trade on services she had performed for them. And to her shame, she was doing precisely that. But how could she have guessed that Varden would drive her back into the orbit of the Keynes family?

Her cheeks burning, she came to the front of the chair and sat, reaching for her half-empty cup of tea. She looked down at it, wishing there were tea leaves to be read there. She knew five women who claimed to read the future in tea leaves, but none of their customers strained tea through so fine a mesh as the Duchess of Tallant. And besides, they were all lying.

"It is so difficult," the duchess said, "to seek help. But only consider how many times I have come running to you. You see what happens when you are so generous? Now I have the habit of relying on you to advise me, as I wish you would do now, on a matter of considerable importance."

Helena suspected the duchess was creating a "favor" to spare embarrassment to them both, until she looked up and saw the troubled expression on her pale face. "What is it, Your Grace?"

"You must not tell the duke I have confided in you. He always pretends nothing is amiss in order to protect my fragile sensibilities, of which I have none. But in spite of his reassurances, I believe his life to be in danger. The man who killed his brother has targeted Michael as well."

For several moments, Helena sat in stunned silence. "But the man who killed the Beast is dead. Mr. Phineas Garvey signed a confession before committing suicide."

"That is the official account, yes. I do not believe it. Lady Jessica, who knew him, says that Garvey was a hot-tempered, impulsive man, not the sort to strike with poison or engage in subtle conspiracies. But I have only my suspicions to go by, and no way to investigate. His Obstinate Grace forbids me to leave the estate except under guard, and he refuses to discuss the matter with me. Of course, he is far too intelligent to accept a trumped-up story, and when I insisted, he did urge the authorities to pursue the investigation. But I doubt they will lift a finger."

"So you wish me to find out what has been discovered, and what is being done?"

"Precisely. You have—shall we say?—unique sources of information, and naturally I shall pay whatever bribes are required. Do not take this as an obligation, Miss Pryce. Your duty will soon be to Lord Varden. But if you keep eyes and ears open, you may learn something that will lead us to the real murderer."

"I shall most certainly try. You can help by sending me a detailed accounting of what you know and what you suspect. Have you protection here?"

"Two Runners, and naturally, the duke instructed them to watch over everyone except himself. I thought of hiring other Runners to secretly guard him, but he would twig to them in an instant."

"Perhaps I can help. In future, when you need to employ a new servant, let me arrange it. Stablemen, drivers, and those with an excuse to leave the estate are particularly useful."

The duchess's face brightened. "Half the former duke's servants ought to be dismissed, but I've been letting them go in dribs and drabs. Now I'll—"

"A wholesale invasion of new servants, particularly the sort I will provide, would arouse the duke's suspicions. Continue dribbing and drabbing, but send me a list of posts to be filled and when they'll be open." Helena glanced at the clock on the mantelpiece. It had been her good luck to arrive when the duke was not at home, and she had already made excuses for an early departure. But of a sudden, she felt an urgent need to make an immediate escape. "It grows late, Your Grace. I must go."

"I cannot persuade you otherwise? Norah and Cory will return in time for supper, and you could share with them the latest plans you've made for their journey to Italy." Her gaze clouded. "I should very much like to hear the plans as well. If the uncertainty persists, if the true killer is not apprehended, I shall try to persuade Michael that we should also make the voyage with his sister-in-law and niece. Would Devonshire mind adding us to his party, do you think?"

"He would be delighted. For Devonshire, the more impressive the parade, the better." Helena rose, shaping a false smile on her cold lips, and picked up her leather satchel. "Really, I must leave now. I've an engagement, and Finn was instructed to bring around my carriage at four o'clock. He nags if I keep him waiting."

"Oh, very well," said the duchess, escorting her into the passageway and toward the staircase. "It is astonishing how quickly I have become used to getting my own way. And here you are, to put me properly in my place."

"In most things, you are supposed to have your own way. You are a duchess."

"A very new one. And my birth was common, you know. I've much to learn. Michael has taken easily to being a duke, but then, he is naturally decisive, not to mention autocratic. Oh, excellent!" She looked over with a smile. "He has returned in time to greet you."

Since they were crossing the entrance hall, with only a pair of footmen to be seen, Helena could not fathom what she meant. But when they had descended to the graveled drive, where Finn dutifully waited beside her small carriage, she saw a puff of dust a long way down the road. It gradually resolved itself into a large black horse carrying a large, black-haired rider.

The duke started to veer off toward the stableyard, appeared to catch sight of the two women, and clattered around the circular drive. He dismounted in a swift, athletic motion, his gaze briefly caressing the duchess's face before moving to her own. "I didn't know we were expecting guests. Tell me you are just now arriving, Miss Pryce."

She curtsied, a Rookery oath lodged in her throat, and forced herself to meet his gaze. "Unfortunately not, Your Grace. Being in the vicinity, I stopped to pay my regards. But I am traveling on a matter of business and must be on my way."

"Not far, I trust. It will soon be dark." The transparent eyes, fringed with dark lashes, were the color of water on a cloudy day. A wolf's eyes in a strong face under heavy black hair—the unmistakable marks

of a true-bred Keynes. "And you appear to be alone,"
he added pointedly.

"Not at all," she replied. "My driver is both reliable
and an excellent shot."

"As you see," the duchess said, "His Grace has developed an exacting sense of propriety, but only as it
applies to others. Pay him no mind."

"That's right," he said, entirely unrepentant. "I am
exempt from my own rules. Your employer, however,
is not. He should provide an escort when you travel
for him. Why don't you come to work for me, Miss
Pryce? I'll pay you well, and God knows we need
you here."

"But you would circumscribe my independence,
Your Grace, along with my efficiency. Or you would
try. And then we would quarrel."

"No one takes well to a pious lecture from a hell-
raiser," he conceded with a grin. "So, who is the fortunate individual who has secured your services?"

He was bound to find out one day, but not this
day. And besides, nothing had been settled with Lord
Varden. "At the moment, I am engaged with tempo-
rary work while considering what I wish to do next.
Will you be kind enough to accept my apology, Your
Grace, and permit me to depart?"

"Grudgingly." He opened the carriage door, folded
down the steps, and offered his hand to help her as-
cend. After a moment, she took it. "Like it or not,"
he said, "I'm sending an escort. He'll catch you up
before you exit the estate and leave off following
when he thinks it advisable."

When she was inside and the door had closed, she
heard him provide a description of the Runner to
Finn. Then he went to stand beside his duchess, one
arm wrapped around her waist as they watched the
carriage pull away.

Helena settled back on the padded bench, her heart
beating at an unnatural rate. The duke would not have

taken such precautions, especially on behalf of someone else's servant, without good reason. The danger was real. It extended to his family, and perhaps to anyone he valued.

But there was little, beyond helping to supply watchers and protectors, that she could do to help. Her heart ached to be so useless, and Jamie's favorite admonition, which she believed without accepting, echoed in her ears.

If you take too many burdens on yourself, they will crush you. And then, what use can you be?

Chapter 3

Heavy fog, yellowed by the murky light of street lamps, curled into the Rookery like a blessing. It obscured the filthy gutters, concealed the shabby buildings, muffled the whimpers of hungry children. Dark figures huddled in doorways and shambled along the cobbled street, stinking of gin. Other odors hung in the damp air—ale and garlic, urine and vomit, rotting garbage. Blood.

Helena, carrying her leather satchel, walked the familiar route with precise steps. About ten yards ahead of her, two men matched her pace, and another man followed close behind. They had taken up their positions shortly after she left her carriage at Broad Street and turned on to New St. Andrew Street, entering Seven Dials.

A dog rummaging through a pile of trash snarled when she passed by. A female called from an alleyway as the two men approached. "Cor, duckies, give a girl a toss?"

"Good evening, Annie," Helena said, crossing the alley.

"Same t'you, Miz Elly," came the good-humored reply.

Along Little Earl Street, the stench was not so great. And when she slipped into the vee-shaped passage that led to Lomber Court, the only light shone behind small windows or filtered under closed doors. The odors of bread, fish pies, and roasting potatoes wafted from the cookshop to her left. From the tavern snuggled next to it, she heard male voices and the clack of platters and tankards. She passed the apothecary shop, closed and dark, and saw just ahead of her the tall, dark-cloaked men. They had stopped and turned to face her in front of the secondhand clothing shop.

"Thank you," she said, doubting her volunteer escort could see her smile. "Is Jamie upstairs?"

"No, ma'am," said one of the Goban twins, she couldn't tell which. "Billy Barnes got took by the watch today. Mr. Carr went to see 'im at Newgate."

A pain in her chest, sharp as a toothache, took her breath. She could not help feeling it, although she had long since trained herself not to dwell on what could not be mended.

But *Billy*? He'd had such promise. Mischief in his blue eyes, sweetness in his smile. Still, there weren't enough tears to weep for all the lost young men, the ruined girls, the sick children, the despairing mothers.

The man who had followed her knocked on the door of the clothing shop, and soon after, a light appeared inside. "I shall remain here tonight," she said. "Will one of you tell Finn to return for me tomorrow morning at seven o'clock? I'll meet him at the usual place. And remind him to bring my portmanteau. He knows where it is."

Before the door opened, all three men had quietly faded into the foggy night. She didn't even know who it was had been following her.

Mr. Gibbs, who had lost the power of speech or chose not to speak—no one knew for sure—raised the lamp so that she could pick her way through the cluttered merchandise. Clothing of every sort, from fashionable gowns to frayed livery and scullcry garb, made its way here. She passed shelves crammed with lace, ribbons, gloves and shawls, bonnets and scarves and neckclothes, nightwear and shoes and chemises and garters. Wigs and swatches of human hair to make more wigs. Bolts of fabric—likely stolen—stood beside folded greatcoats, cloaks, muffs, and tippets. There were drawers full of corsets, dressing gowns, knitted stockings, shirts, frockcoats, and unmentionables. Great ladies and fashionable gentlemen sometimes presented their castoffs to favorite servants, who sold the garments here. Nearly any sort of costume or disguise could be contrived from the materials in this shop and in the attics, where excess merchandise was stored.

At the back of the shop, she entered a passageway and proceeded to a staircase that zigged and zagged all the way to an exit through the roof four stories above. Years of work had merged five adjoined buildings into one, although nobody looking at it from the street could imagine what lay beyond the rough exterior. She mounted swiftly to the third level and carried the lamp Mr. Gibbs had given her into the bedchamber that had been hers since she was eight years old.

As she tried to do at least once every week, she had come home.

The room was tiny, furnished with a narrow bed, a dressing table, a writing table, a bookshelf, and a stand of drawers. She hung her cloak on a hook and her bonnet on top of it, adjusted her hair, and removed several packets from her satchel. Stacks of banknotes, wrapped in paper and tied up with string, went into one oversized pocket, and several parcels of sweets barely fit into another pocket. She used a clean handkerchief to polish her smoked glasses, blurry from the dirty fog, and set out for Almack's.

That's what Jamie called the public rooms that occupied the second floor. Wide openings had been cut through the walls between the adjoining buildings, creating a long room that could be divided with heavy curtains. They were all open when she entered, and as people became aware of her arrival, fifty or sixty heads swiveled in her direction. She smiled, made a gesture, and with a few exceptions, they returned to what they had been doing. The others, new to Almack's, regarded her curiously.

There were always strangers here on trial, replacing members of the clan who had left, or been banished, or got themselves taken by the watch. Only a few men and women who had known her as a child remained, but all of these people, even the latest and least trustworthy arrival, had been brought here by Jamie. And that meant they were her family as well.

After a fashion. She was apart from them, and a little bubble of space surrounded her as she meandered from room to room.

It was work time. Clusters of women stitched remnants of fabric from the clothing shop into quilts. Young boys learned to manipulate stringed toys to be sold in the market. Men and women wove baskets, mended cane chairs, repaired bellows. In the farthest room, children who spent their days scavenging through rubbish piles were being taught to read and write.

Jamie's clan was a haven for those willing and able to better themselves, and his few rules were rigorously enforced. Everyone with a skill must work, and those without a skill must learn one. Loyalty to the clan. Respect for one another. No illegal activities without his express permission.

The other, unspoken rules they all lived by were learned on the streets, in the brothels, in the prisons. These were desperate people, and outside the time they spent at Almack's, their lives were as hers would have been . . . if not for Jamie Carr.

She found a chair near three men who were practicing the music they played at the Covent Garden Market to entice customers to the booths where clan folk sold their wares. A tankard of ale was put into her hand, and in the next hour, several women and one man came by to report on what had occurred since last she saw them. Three of them regularly took orphans into their small homes. Four carried food, coal, and medicines to the sick and elderly. The man, expiating his own guilt, protected women brutalized by their husbands or procurers. To each she gave a wrapped bundle of banknotes and a caution.

"There's extra this time, but you must make it last. I don't know when there will be more."

Nothing any of them did was ever enough. But they had learned not to look into the face of the monster, or discouragement would beat them down.

Helena was deep into her second tankard, her rebellious body pulsing with the music, when a tall man in a black frock coat entered from the far end of the connected rooms and began to make his way from group to group, pausing to spend a few moments with each person.

Handsome and impressive, in his early fifties, with glacial blue eyes and a beaked nose, he carried himself like a judge or a solicitor—two of the many roles he sometimes played. When he drew closer, she saw the lines in his face carved out with weariness, the bleak look in his eyes as he glanced up and gave her a meaningful nod.

She waited a short time before taking her leave, and had been in Jamie's quarters for several minutes before he arrived.

"You needn't be concerned," he said from the sideboard, where he immediately went to pour himself a drink. "It's not the Raven."

When the Raven, as he called it, was on him, Jamie would close himself in his rooms for days and drink himself insensible. Sometimes he vanished for a longer time, and only a handful of confidants knew of the cottage where he retreated to exorcize his demons.

"Did you see Billy?" She lifted the coat from his shoulders and put it in the armoire. "He must be frightened."

"And swaggering to hide it. Pretty boys don't fare well in the common cells, so I've bought him some privacy. He won't be needing it long, I wager. They'll hang him for sure."

"Hang?" A cramp gripped her stomach. "He's only fifteen. What did he do?"

"Pinched a pocket watch off a gentleman, and within the hour, snatched aqua fortis from a chemist shop."

"Oh." There would be no appeal from the penalty for stealing a dangerous substance. "He knows better."

"Showing off for his mates. They cheered him after he slipped away with the pocket watch, and he was so full of his success that his head went empty of sense. Tomorrow I'll take those young hooligans to see what becomes of cocky lads who lose their wits. Don't think on it, Ella. It was Billy tossed his life away for a few minutes of strutting. Except to keep him warm and fed, there's nothing to be done for him now."

Jamie wouldn't let her go to the jail. They had fought that battle many times, and she never won it. He was standing with his back to her, hands propped on the sideboard, wide shoulders slumped in defeat. Each loss tormented him, brought the Wolf closer. But he would fend it off, she knew, for so long as Billy needed him. In the same way, twenty years earlier, he had nursed the woman he loved until her slow, painful death, and taken in the woman's daughter to raise as his own. Helena went and stood beside him, putting a hand over his, resting her head against his arm.

"Well, then," he said after a time. "Has your Arch-angel flown back to London?"

She had not seen the Earl of Varden since the morning she astonished him by presenting a letter of intent, signed on behalf of Edgar Holcombe, which granted Varden a lease to the castle in Somerset. He was also granted permission to make whatever alterations he desired, along with first option to purchase the property outright as soon as the matter of ownership had been finally adjudicated.

He had smiled, but she got the sense he was not altogether glad to have received what he'd asked for. In any case, he immediately honored his agreement, employed her as his secretary, and almost as quickly assigned her to help his mother, grandmothers, aunts, and sisters arrange the come-out of his twin nieces. Then he took himself off to Somerset and had not been seen since. He sent the occasional letter of instructions, of course, and the salary he paid was greater than she had demanded. But for five weeks, she had been little more than a jumped-up maidservant.

Jamie knew her circumstances, and her frustrations. In all the world, he was the only one she confided in.

To a degree.

"He remains in the Mendips," she said. "I gather, from the materials he has told me to acquire, that the property has deteriorated considerably since it was abandoned. What he is doing there is unclear."

"Sweeping? Cleaning the chimneys?" Jamie sliced her a glance. "Perhaps he requires a cottage retreat, Elly. Only, being an earl, he'd want his hideaway to be a castle."

Not for the first time, she wondered if he could read her mind. "It's remote enough to serve that purpose. But he has little reason—"

"Even Archangels fall from grace. There is precedent."

"Well, this one cannot afford the indulgence. He has obligations. Responsibilities. People who depend on him."

"As do I. But you accept my occasional descents

into hell. A few weeks in the Mendips is scarcely cause to suspect him of shirking his duties."

"But we *need* him. Just when he'd begun doing useful work with Peel, he dashed off to India and missed two sittings of Parliament, Now he's about to shrug off a third. Billy will hang, you said. Varden might have prevented that."

"Don't exaggerate. The laws are centuries old and will not be quickly changed. You must be patient."

"I've never been patient. And nothing has worked out as I intended. To earn my position, I provided him the very castle that has taken him away. Now I arrange social schedules, hire decorators, plan a ball, address invitations. I'm a bloody flunky!"

"If you dislike what you are doing, Ella, you should resign."

"I'm positively *obsessed* with resigning." She began to pace the room, which was ascetic as a monk's cell. "Every day that he fails to return, I write a stern letter giving my notice. Then I recall how much he pays me, and how badly the money is needed, and I toss the letter into the fire."

"So we come to it again. You have cut off your ambitions because of a debt you do not owe. If ever you did, you have repaid it a thousandfold. I'll not belittle your financial contributions, my dear, but your truest role for these people is quite different."

Jamie leaned his hips against the sideboard, his drink cradled between two large, rough hands. "They are proud of your success. They live it through you, and are inspired with hope, if not for themselves, then for their children or their grandchildren. All societies, even our little clan, relish watching one born among us soaring to the heights. You imagine you are being generous, but so long as you keep yourself tethered to the Rookery, you shadow their pleasure. And they get so precious little of it. They want more of you than your money. They want your happiness. They *need* it."

"You are the one they love, Jamie. And you are not happy."

Silence. "I might be," he said at last, "if I knew that you were. Everything is different now. You have no reason to hide. Will you not—"

"No." She paused long enough to fix him with her most resolute expression. "It is out of the question. I do not want to change who I am. I'm just now getting good at it. And you must agree, it's better all around to leave things as they are."

"But I don't agree. We've no idea if it's better, and cannot know unless you put it to the test. You needn't do so, of course. The choice is entirely yours. Only . . . be sure your choice is not taken from fear. What might you lose that could not be replaced? Not your pride, surely. Not your confidence. Nothing of value. You will always find a way to make a success of your life and be of service to others."

"You have too much faith in me, Jamie."

"In the long term, yes." His smile acknowledged two decades of exposure to her stormy temperament. "As for the unfortunate earl, will you stomp up to him and launch into one of your scathing critiques?"

"That rather overstates my behavior, even at its worst. But he will probably be treated to something of the kind."

"Is that wise?"

"I expect not. But it is my nature, or a part of it I cannot seem to control. My tongue rushes past my discretion like a racehorse. It will not be stopped until it has won the day."

"And had the last word to boot. He won't give you a letter of recommendation, Ella."

She laughed. "No, indeed. Perhaps I should go down to Almack's and start learning another trade."

"The clan could use a good skittle-sharp. But run along to bed, my dear, and say a prayer for wisdom and discretion. One cannot deal with an earl as if he were a common fellow. Lord Varden won't accept a tongue-lashing from the likes of you."

"I know." She brushed a kiss on his chin. "But what does it matter? Since I am leaving his service, I can say whatever I like on my way out the door."

Chapter 4

After a rainy morning, the March day had turned clear by the time Helena's small coach entered the Mendips on a narrow, rutted road. She lifted the shade with a fingertip to peek out at the rolling hills, lush with new spring grass. Perhaps a long holiday rebuilding a castle wasn't such a daft idea after all.

But by mid-afternoon, with the shadows beginning to lengthen, the carriage came into a landscape ruled still by winter. On a rough carpet of brown stubble, leaf-bare trees stunted by snow and wind stretched their gnarled branches to the pale sun. The earl had chosen a bleak and eerie wilderness for his exile.

She had studied the map given her by the Duchess of Tallant and knew the castle must be close by. Several times she had nearly ordered Finn to turn the carriage around. But her obstinacy, along with a regrettable fancy for theatrics, had trumped her good sense. Now the folly of her intentions was borne home to her. She was salt, and the earl an open wound requiring time to heal. He had every right to solitude. He'd the right to do whatever he wished.

Perhaps she ought to revise her plan. Instead of reading him a lecture, she would explain that her journey was no more than an exercise in good manners, a polite way of severing a relationship that ought never to have begun. She had been blinded by his splendor—she wouldn't tell him that part—and really, even a practical creature like herself was entitled to a mistake now and then.

The castle came into view, perched atop a hill that stood higher than those surrounding it. Sunlight gleamed off the oriel windows and limestone walls of the castle keep, Norman in style like the White Tower in London but half the size. It was the only part of the complex that showed evidence of human attention in the last several centuries. The curtain wall, what remained of it, staggered around the bailey like stumps of rotted teeth. Most segments stood waist high, except for the restored area near the plank drawbridge that lay across a wide muddy ditch. A partly restored tower stood beside the gatehouse.

She winced, thinking how much Lord Varden had paid for this wreck.

When the coach drew nearer, she saw three pony carts full of smooth stones lined up to cross the drawbridge one at a time. An empty cart was on its way out, presumably to collect another load.

Finn, never inclined to give way, guided the carriage onto the drawbridge ahead of the waiting carts, drawing jeers and curses from their drivers. Inside the bailey, he secured the horses and came down to lower the carriage steps. She passed him her leather case, heavy with letters, records of account, and architectural drawings.

To her right, several men engaged in roofing the stable house paused to stare—as everyone did—at the spectacles. She addressed a boy holding the pulley rope that raised buckets of shale tiles. "Where can I find Lord Varden?"

Laughter from the men on the roof, stopping abruptly when Finn stepped up beside her. The boy gestured to the far end of the compound, beyond the keep and a considerable distance from where other groups of men were working.

Satchel in hand, she marched in that direction. When she came around the side of the keep, she saw a lone figure at the farthest curve of the curtain wall, what there was of it. Fragments no more than a few feet tall remained, flanked by fallen mounds of stone. Only one section, shoulder high, stood intact. More accurately, under *repair*, by an aristocratic stonemason.

There was little of the Archangel to be seen in this ungroomed male with shaggy hair, lightly browned skin, and stubbled whiskers. Like a common laborer, he wore heavy brown trousers, worn boots, and an open-necked shirt with sleeves rolled up above his elbows.

He was standing in profile to her, an implement of some sort in his hand. At his left, a tripod held a flat pan, and beside it, a wheelbarrow was piled with stones. Holding to the shadow of the keep, she watched him slice the tool through what she guessed to be mortar and slather it on a portion of the wall. Then he set the tool in the pan, stooped to select a stone, and put it in place. The work, done the way he was compelled to do it, was slow and painstaking.

All these weeks, she had puzzled over what he might be doing to keep him so long at the castle. Not once had she imagined *this*.

Suddenly he held still, head lifted, like an animal scenting danger.

She recognized her cue to step forward. By the time he turned, she was striding toward him with her efficient woman-of-business demeanor, an uncurious expression sculpted on her face.

Today she would give him an opportunity to keep her. She doubted he would take it.

When she arrived at the spot she had chosen, a discreet professional distance about five feet from where he waited for her, she set her satchel on the ground and curtsied.

Rising, she saw that his eyes, which had flashed with anger while she closed the distance between them, showed only mild curiosity. He had donned his diplomatic mask, the way she had seen him do a score of times at Palazzo Neri. "Lord Varden," she said, meeting his gaze.

"Miss Pryce." A pleasant tone, deceptive as a fishing lure. "You will pardon my failure to welcome you properly. I forgot I had sent for you."

"I have brought papers to be signed," she said, ignoring the point he had scored. "And letters from your family."

"Begging me to return to London?"

"I do not read private correspondence, sir. But that has been the primary topic of conversation in your household."

"I cannot help but wonder, given your duties relating to the come-out of my nieces and the usual obligations of a private secretary, how you found time for this excursion to Somerset."

"Efficiency, my lord. I could spend a fortnight in Paris before you or your family caught up with the preparations I have already made and the contingencies I have provided for."

"But what of emergencies?"

"The nearest we have come to a catastrophe is a shortage of Belgian lace and ostrich feathers."

"You are here, then, not of necessity, but because you are bored? Even in this backwater, Miss Pryce, the post is regularly delivered."

"I am here to consult with you on a number of matters. For one, the architectural plans devised by Old Holcombe have been located. I thought you would wish to have them."

"Again, I remind you of the postal delivery system."

She ignored his uncharacteristic sarcasm. "In addition, I have consulted with architects capable of designing and supervising the restoration of this castle.

It seemed advisable to inspect the property before evaluating their plans and proposing which of them you should interview."

"My lamentable memory. When was it I requested the services of an architect?"

"When you expressed your intention to restore this property. The need for an architect was surely implied, or so I believed at the time. I failed to understand that you meant to piece together the castle single-handedly."

"A single hand indeed," he said, picking up the trowel. "This is a slow business, as you see. I had better get on with it."

Remorse sent heat to her face. She was glad he had turned away, dismissing her, although she'd no intention of leaving. Not yet.

For a time she stood quietly, watching him work. His movements were repetitive and efficient. Dip the trowel, spread the mortar, put down the trowel, select a stone from the wheelbarrow, set it in place—all done with his left hand. The section of wall he'd completed, about twenty yards in length, stood like an island amid the empty places and the rubble.

The outdoor work had put color on his face, on the exposed neck and vee of chest, on his well-shaped forearms. There were new lines at the corners of his extraordinary eyes. The nails of his ungloved left hand were broken and dirty.

Over the years, observing him from a distance, she had nearly got used to his remarkable beauty. She'd learned to see him without catching her breath, to speak to him without being distracted. Well, not overly distracted. But always he had been the model of elegance, the quintessential aristocratic gentleman.

Now she was utterly transfixed by the well-defined muscles working in his back and shoulders and arms. The breeze riffling through his untrimmed hair. The strength of purpose in this simple labor. His sheer male vitality sent forbidden thoughts scurrying through her head. Mouth dry, thighs moist, she closed her eyes and reminded herself in no uncertain terms who he was, and who she was, and why nothing she was imagining could ever come to pass.

"May I inquire," she said, to turn her thoughts where they belonged, "why you are doing this?"

A brief hesitation, stone in hand, and then a slight shrug. "Fresh air, exercise, the strengthening of my left arm and hand, which must now do the work of two. A wish, for a time, to be alone."

Dip. Slap. Smooth. Set the stone. Dip. Slap—

"I meant, why go to such trouble, and spend so much money, to acquire a relic? What will you *do* with it?"

"I'm thinking of stashing impertinent females, related and otherwise, here to keep them out of my way." He shot her a glance over his shoulder. "There's a dungeon."

A joke, but in her position, she could not openly enjoy it. "The effort to restore the castle, sir, has already cost one gentleman his health and fortune. You see how little he accomplished."

"Less than I was given to expect when I bought the property. According to the documents you provided, the keep was in reasonably good condition and the curtain wall about seventy percent reconstructed. Neither is the case."

"In this matter," she said, "I have failed you. Instead of examining the property myself, I relied on the assessment taken shortly after Old Holcombe's death, and the price was set on that basis. But it seems that with no caretaker keeping watch, the previous Duke of Tallant scavenged everything of value from the keep, and the locals carted off what was left, including every stone they could pry loose. They use them to build their homes and barns."

"Good God." Varden turned, an arrested expression on his face. "All this time, I've been buying back my own stones?"

"I'm afraid so. The moment I arrived, I understood that you had paid a third more than the property is worth. But I believe that once the situation is explained, the contract can be renegotiated. I shall see to it."

"There is no need," he said after a moment. "That would rather defeat the purpose."

The last part was spoken to himself, and had she not been watching his lips form the words, she'd not have made out what he was saying.

"What *is* the purpose? While you put stone upon stone, your family requires your presence. Members of Parliament devise strategy for the upcoming session, and you are not there. With your position come duties, and they are neglected."

She had overreached, by miles. She saw white knuckles on the hand gripping the trowel. Color flagging his cheekbones. His eyes . . . For the first time, she could not meet them.

It hurt, more than she had calculated, to sever herself from this man she had so long admired, to let go the thready bond she had worked so hard to forge. They could have accomplished much together, her efficiency and skills linked to his rank and charm and influence. With him she would have thrived. Like a mushroom growing in rich soil, to be sure, and her season would have been brief. But . . .

Never mind. It was done now. And with nothing left to lose, she felt the tight rein she had been holding on her temper slipping from her control. "Does responsibility mean nothing to you, sir? How can you *waste* yourself in this place when there is so much of value for you to accomplish?"

"My activities are none of your concern, Miss Pryce. Nor will I tolerate a presumptuous servant. Consider yourself dismissed." Icicles practically formed on his words. "I shall pay your salary through the end of the month, but the termination is immediate."

"Then we are agreed, sir. Among the correspondence and documents I have brought, you will find my letter of resignation."

"You came here to give your notice? But not, unfortunately, before taking the opportunity to read me a lecture." He set the trowel in the mortar pan. "I have never encountered anyone quite like you. Notable skills, impeccable recommendations, uncommon arrogance. Unfailing insubordination. Am I an exception, Miss Pryce, or do your employers generally permit you to scold them?"

"There is rarely the need. But you are quite right, sir. I do not conduct myself like an ordinary servant, and there is no reason for you to put up with my behavior. Neither am I inclined to change my character to suit your expectations. My habit of plain speaking is tolerated by discerning employers, in the way a gentlemen will put up with an ill-tempered horse if it wins races for him."

A short laugh. "But you expect me to change my character to suit *your* expectations?"

"Not your character. But you have veered off course, my lord. You squander time and misuse your considerable gifts."

"Perhaps. The situation is temporary. And surely I am entitled to direct the course of my own life."

"Not when Parliament is sitting. Not when you can help better the lives of those who have no one to speak for them. Before departing for India, you had worked to reform the laws that unfairly afflict the poor and desperate. Now the home secretary has taken up that cause, but instead of supporting him, you have left the field."

He was regarding her with a speculative look. A decidedly *suspicious* look. "And what interest," he said too smoothly, "would a proper young woman

have in the sentencing of criminals? Have you an in-
discretion in your past?A relative due for a hanging?"

"Not at present." What did he *know*? "But in a
country that executes a father for stealing a pie to
feed his children, or a boy for robbing a shopkeeper
of a length of cloth, who among us is safe? Well, you,
of course, and your peers who make the laws and see
them enforced. But under your rule, the jails are a
disgrace, the laws are unjust, and the punishments do
not fit the crimes. You are a good man, Lord Varden,
with influence and the respect of your fellows. If you
will not see right done, then we must, all of us,
despair."

"You place far too much credit in my ability to
effect change. Robert Peel—"

"The home secretary is a splendid administrator
who lacks the ability to win over his opponents. You,
on the other hand, are universally admired—"

"Not by you."

"Not at the moment. But you have the ear of the
king, who is sentimental. With proper handling, he can
be swayed by the plight of the helpless. You have a
gift for smoothing waters and reconciling opponents.
The women in your family have taught you how to
do battle in a graceful manner that leads, finally, to
compromise and agreement. But here you are, in the
back of beyond, building a wall. Is it meant to close
yourself in?"

"Or the world out. Perhaps I merely want to build
something for myself. You would be surprised to know
the satisfaction I take in this stretch of mortared wall,
unstable as it probably is. And from across the bailey,
workers are no doubt eyeing the stones, waiting for
the opportunity to make off with them again. Nothing
endures, Miss Pryce. We simply make do."

She understood, then, for the first time, that he was
well and truly lost. Not forever, like the fallen angel he
so resembled, because his strength of character would

eventually win out. But for now, this was a time of self-indulgence. Of licking his wounds. Of sulking in his tent. To a degree, she sympathized.

But mostly, she wanted to slap him back to his senses.

"Do you imagine," she said, a touch of malice in her voice, "that if you rebuild this broken-down relic of the aristocracy, you are in some manner reconstructing yourself?"

He stiffened. His gaze shifted to his gloved hand. She felt in her bones the effort it required to control his anger.

"Well, never mind all that," she said briskly. "I must be off. The letters and documents will be left for you at the castle keep."

She'd got about ten yards before he responded.

"Miss Pryce!"

Two syllables, hammered out in steel. They brought her to an involuntary halt.

"Within the hour, the sun will set." He came up beside her, moved a little past her, speaking in a tone of absolute command. "The roads are treacherous, the weather uncertain, and there is no inn or posthouse where you might safely take refuge. You will remain here for the night."

Her automatic "no" lodged in her throat. She had never heard him speak, not to anyone, in just that way. And when he turned to look at her, she saw a stranger.

"Do you mean to quarrel with me about this?" he said.

"No, my lord."

"Very well." Her capitulation was accepted as if he'd expected nothing else. "There are no provisions here for guests. I'll instruct the housekeeper to prepare a room and provide you a supper tray, but it will take some time. Can you occupy yourself until arrangements have been completed?"

"Certainly. May I explore the grounds and the buildings?"

"If you like, but keep clear of the workmen. Your driver can stay overnight in the gatehouse. And as a courtesy, you will not venture to the upper story of the keep, where I have my quarters. Under the circumstances, it's best that we not meet again while you are here. I shall trust you not to depart before sunrise. If the weather is bad at that time, we will make whatever adjustments are necessary. Do you accept these conditions, Miss Pryce?"

She couldn't help wondering what he would do if she declined, and had to fight the temptation to find out. But she recognized an iron will when she saw one, and knew that his strength—when he chose to exert it—was more than a match for her own. "They are perfectly reasonable, sir. Thank you for your hospitality."

The barest glint of humor in his eyes. "You won't be so grateful when you see the accommodations."

He went off then, leaving her to cool her heels for the next hour or two. She didn't mind. After studying the architectural drawings, she knew quite a lot about the castle, and the stories she had heard from Lady Jessica and the Duchess of Tallant made her curious to see what they had described.

But first, she went back to the wall Lord Varden was rebuilding.

The workmanship, for an amateur, was excellent. She doubted he ever did anything without bringing to the task all his attention and whatever skill he possessed. Like her, he was a perfectionist, except that he didn't have to work so hard at being perfect.

After making sure he was out of sight, she chose an especially smooth, well-shaped stone from the wheelbarrow. Then she took up the trowel, applied mortar to the next spot on the wall, and carefully set her stone in place.

This once, in this small way, she and Lord Varden had built something together.

Chapter 5

While daylight remained, Helena dealt with her disappointment the way she always dealt with a setback. She thrust it firmly from her thoughts until she had scraped up a bit of perspective and detached herself from her emotions.

Unruly, incorrigible, *exasperating* emotions. They had never served her well. But after the initial flood of mindlessness, she was generally able to bring them under control. All excepting her temper. *That* had a life and a will of its own.

For a time, she exorcized her anger with an energetic walk in the hills. Varden, she saw from a distance, was back at his wall, and when she returned to the castle, she gave it a wide berth. He never looked up.

From Mrs.Culworth, the plump housekeeper, she learned that her room was not yet ready. Something about linens, mold, and smoking chimneys. Still restless, she took a lantern and inspected the keep from top to bottom, or nearly so. Reaching the third story, she cast a look at the staircase that led to forbidden territory, felt a sudden pain in the vicinity of her heart, and threw herself into a meticulous examination of damp, dirty, mostly empty rooms. They looked as if they'd been pillaged and abandoned centuries ago. Dust coated the few pieces of tatty furniture that remained. Chimney pieces had been ripped out. She saw empty niches and watermarked outlines on walls where pictures had once hung.

All the rooms and passageways were dark, save for a single torch burning in a wall sconce beside each stairwell. When she came to one of the small windows overlooking the bailey, she spotted the earl in the same place he had been before, now working by the light of a quarter moon and a pair of lanterns.

On the second floor, she saw a maidservant inside a small room, beating at bed canopies with a broom. Dust billowed out like dandelion seeds. With a shudder, Helena kept moving.

When she reached the ground floor, she encountered Finn, who had been seeing to the horses and plying the workmen for information. "Nothing of use," he said in a low voice. "They all go home at night, saving the two who keep watch at the gatehouse. None of the outbuildings are good for quartering servants until the roofing is done, but they think the earl will give up before then. He's a good fellow, pays well, keeps to himself. That's all they have to say of him."

"Some of the doors are locked," she said. "What is he hiding?"

Finn shrugged. "I brought your portmanteau and left it with Mrs. Culworth in the kitchen. She says you're to have supper there in an hour. Anything more I can do for you, Miss Elly?"

"Just be ready to depart at sunrise. I wish to be gone without any fuss."

It was off to the dungeons after that, lantern in hand, a candle and a small tinderbox in her pocket in case of trouble. Lady Jessica had described a secret passage that led to a hidden dungeon, and after a time, Helena located the entrance. But it was ribboned with cobwebs, which meant spiders. Spiders in a dark, enclosed place. She turned back.

The light wavered as she stood at the foot of the cellar stairs. Her hand was trembling. From exhaustion, she thought, recognizing the slight dizziness, the sense of cotton wrapping around her brain. She could drive herself for a considerable time, several twenty-hour days in a row, but eventually she became unreliable. She started making poor decisions, or letting others make them for her.

Nothing of the sort had occurred in the past two or three years. She had taught herself to be careful. But now . . . Well, too late now for taking care. Perhaps it was for the best. Perhaps tonight she would sleep right through the aftershock of quarreling with Lord Varden.

She knew how it would be in future. She was not significant enough for him to dislike or ignore. If they chanced to meet, he would produce a distant smile, speak a few polite words, and move on. She must remember not to be hurt.

And the pain struck again, like a blow to her chest.

Telling herself it was hunger, she made her way to the kitchen where Mrs. Culworth had set a place for her at one end of a trestle table. She slumped onto the bench with a sigh, looked down at the mutton stew and brown bread provided her, and realized she wasn't hungry at all. But she ate a little, to avoid giving offense, and tried to draw the housekeeper into conversation.

Mrs. Culworth was laying out dishes on a tray that must be intended for the earl. "Not my concern," she replied to Helena's questions. Or, sometimes, "Humpf." Likely she'd been warned by the earl to say nothing.

But Helena persisted, determined to learn why the earl was obsessed with rebuilding the castle. "Did you know Old Holcombe's brother? Mr. Edgar Holcombe, I mean, and his daughter, Miranda?"

"Oh, aye." Mrs. Culworth brought Helena a pottery mug filled with strong, steaming tea. "Poor gentleman. Miss Holcombe took right good care of her father. I felt bad, leavin' her here after her uncle died. But she told the servants it was best we all go. She got out, too, afore the duke they calls the Beast come after her. First, though, she brought me her cats to care for. I wanted to write her they be doing well, but I never knew where she went to."

"If you like," said Helena, "I can carry the message. We are acquainted."

For the first time, the housekeeper's expression softened. "Will you tell her? I don't write more'n a few words. The gray dropped a litter last month. She's the one with the long name I can't get my tongue on. We calls her Andy now."

The maid appeared just then, her aprons streaked with dirt, to say the room was as ready at it would ever be.

There were a pair of rooms, Helena discovered when Mrs. Culworth escorted her upstairs. She set down her portmanteau and looked around. What was once a large chamber had been divided into two by a brick wall with a door at one side. The tiny bedroom opened onto the passageway, and she had to pass through it to reach the larger room, which had two small windows, a working fireplace, a battered table, and two badly upholstered chairs. The bedroom contained only a large canopied bed and a narrow dressing table with a stool. There was a fireplace as well, but it must be the one that smoked. No fire was set there, and the room was exceedingly cold.

Mrs. Culworth carried a tray with a basin, two pitchers of water, some biscuits, and the refilled mug of tea into the large room and placed it on the table. "Polly is fetching extra blankets, towels, soap, and candles. Then we be off for home. What you need after that, you can look for in the kitchen or the pantry. His lordship won't mind what you take, but he don't like to be disturbed."

Helena suspected that Mrs. Culworth had been told to provide that warning. Fine with her. She had no intention of disturbing his lordship, no indeed, nor of taking anything at all without paying for it. Not even the night's lodging and her supper, or Finn's, or the horses'. In the morning, she would leave the money she owed on the same table near the front entrance where she had placed the letters and papers, including her terse letter of resignation.

She had already decided not to undress. And if she slept, it would be in a chair in the back room, fully clothed and coifed. She always took precautions when she traveled, or when she stayed anywhere except Sothingdon House, where locks and a suite of rooms designed to her specifications put her beyond fear of discovery. Her bedchamber there was the only place she ever slept well.

For a time, snuggled in a blanket and curled up on a chair by the fireplace, she read one of the books she always carried when she traveled. Herodotus, she had to keep reminding herself by looking at the title page. None of the words were sinking in. For a longer time, she gazed into the fire, trying not to think. So much had depended on her establishing a close working relationship with Lord Varden. She had thrown all her resources into the effort. All her hopes as well.

Now her greatest goal was stillborn, and she didn't know what to do with herself. Lady Jessica no longer needed her. She would have to take another temporary job, and another, and another. Varden had been right about one thing. No gentleman, except perhaps the one she could never approach, would employ her on a long-term basis. That left the women, but so few engaged themselves with business or politics. She had admired the ladies of Varden's family, but they had taught her she had no patience with the usual affairs of females.

She was *thinking* again. And to no purpose. Few options were open to her at the moment, and besides, she was demonstrably incapable of making a sane decision. Look what happened when she bet everything on Lord Varden, only to watch with horror as he pulled out of the race.

Rousing herself, she went over to a narrow window and gazed outside. What with the thick, dirt-streaked window glass and her own dark spectacles, she could see nothing but her own reflection. Until she turned her gaze downward. Three long rectangles of golden light, broken into smaller squares like a chessboard, stretched out over the black ground.

She had noticed those tall windows when she wandered the grounds, but heavy curtains had prevented her from seeing inside. It must have been one of the rooms she later discovered to be locked.

The earl was surely in there. She drew out her pocket watch and checked the time. Nearly one o'clock. What could he be *doing*?

The impulsive streak in her character broke free of its chains with a vengeance. Even as her good sense chanted *no no no*, she was already digging through her satchel for the architectural drawing of the keep. As always with important papers that came into her possession, she had made a copy for herself.

A few minutes later, candle in hand, she made her way along the passageway and down the stairs to the first floor, where she took a left turn, then a right, and finally came to a low, narrow door. Inside this room, marked on the sketches as storage, she ought to find another door.

It was right where it ought to be. This was the discreet passage used by musicians to enter the minstrel gallery.

Extinguishing her candle, she took a few deep

breaths, dropped onto her knees, and tried the latch. A dull clink. She opened the door a crack, the hinges protesting, and peeked through. At the far end of the Great Hall bloomed a mushroom of golden light. A little of it reached the ceiling directly above, but the rest of the Hall was cloaked in darkness. Blessedly, that included the gallery, jutting out midway between the two-story-high ceiling and the floor.

From the doorway, she could see little more than the ceiling and upper walls. Nothing for it but to make her way to the railing, keeping low, and peer through the carved wooden balusters.

With the rusty hinges squealing like stuck pigs, she opened the door only wide enough to let herself slip through and pulled it gently closed again. Then she crawled to the balustrade, sat with her legs curled under her, and looked out.

Mirrors? Good heavens! There were five of them, tall cheval mirrors lined side by side in a gentle arc at the farthest end of the hall. They reflected a dozen candle stands arranged at intervals to create an island of light. It shone on a rectangle of polished wood, about twenty feet long and half that wide, that had been laid out over the stone floor.

There was no sign of the earl. Wishing she'd brought a blanket to sit on and another to wrap around her, she settled in to wait for his return.

About ten minutes later, almost directly beneath her perch, a door opened and closed. Then Varden appeared, carrying a long wooden case and moving toward the circle of lights and mirrors. He had changed from his workman's clothes into a loose white shirt, biscuit-colored knee breeches, stockings, and slippers. As always, he was wearing the black leather glove, but his other hand was bare.

The light embraced him as he entered it, gleaming off his pale hair, limning his perfectly shaped body. He set down the case at the edge of the flooring, removed his slippers, and approached the mirrors. Pausing a few feet away, then stepping to one side, to the other side, and forward, and back, he appeared to be examining his image. Now and again he adjusted the angle of a mirror. Then he returned to the case and crouched beside it.

His back was to her, and from where she sat, she couldn't see his reflection in the mirrors. He opened the lid, removed something. A flash of silver. When he rose, there was a sword in his hand.

She released the breath she hadn't known she was holding. So obvious, especially to her, but she hadn't guessed. Lord Varden had set up a fencing studio.

For a few moments he appeared to be adjusting his grip. He slashed the foil back and forth, shook his head, realigned his fingers. It finally dawned on her, dull-witted as she was this night, that he was working with his left hand, training it to do what his right hand had once done with grace and ease. Even the simplest act, like gripping a sword, had to be relearned.

When satisfied, he went back to the mirrors and, after the slightest hesitation, stood in profile to them, his legs straight, his feet at right angles with his left heel positioned directly in front of his right. He appeared to be instructing each limb, one by one, where to put itself.

He broke the position and assumed it again, more smoothly this time. Once more, and then once more. On the last attempt, he continued directly into the *en garde* stance, extending his left arm and bending it, his elbow the proper six inches from his hip, his forearm and foil in an unbroken line. The tip of the sword pointed at where an opponent's eyes would be.

Adjustments, several of them, as he checked his stance in the mirror. Then he brought his right arm into place, the upper arm in a horizontal plane, the forearm perpendicular. Adjustments yet again, to the curve that brought his hand toward his head.

His shoulders were out of alignment. He saw it, made the correction.

As she watched, he repeated the entire procedure several times, each motion taken separately. Then he attempted to put himself *en garde* in one fluid motion.

She winced. Watched him try again. Five times. Ten. His body kept wanting to move the way it once had moved, thousands on thousands of times. Clearly he was—had been—an experienced swordsman. But now he had do everything from the opposite direction, and his training and instincts were operating against him.

What she witnessed was painful to see, and beautiful as well. Her own body, without moving, echoed his motions, mirrored them as the real mirrors captured his image and cast it across the room. Her muscles tensed and flowed into the lines his body was forming, as if the two of them had become one being.

Even in her imagination, she had the same difficulty he was having, a right-handed fencer addressing an opponent from the left. Given his obvious frustration with minor flaws in form, the first awkward stages must have been excruciating for him.

Next he practiced the advance—start from toes, land first on heels, feet barely clearing the floor. Not bad, she thought. His retreats were not so good. His lunges, the first twenty she saw, were terrible. Too many moves to be made simultaneously, or one move a fraction of a second ahead of the next, most of them to be executed with a snap.

He paced for a minute or two, wiping his forehead with his sleeve, anger rising off him like steam. Then he was back at it, a few more lunges that were worse than the ones before.

What was he expecting? Did he forget that he had worked all day on his idiotic wall?

As if he heard her, he gave up on the lunges and turned to recoveries for a while. Then he moved to simple forms, engaging an imaginary opponent, his attacks hesitant, his parries awkward.

For an ordinary swordsman, he was more than adequate. But she knew he would never be satisfied with ordinary, each imperfection driving a nail in his pride.

Of a sudden, she could not bear to spy on him any longer. Nor could she leave, not until he did. She looked up, watching the shadows play across the ceiling as his movements stirred the air and the candle flames. Even that was too intrusive. She closed her eyes.

And saw him in her imagination, alone in a circle of light, ferociously doing battle against his demons. Against himself.

For nearly an hour her legs had been curled under her on the icy floor, and while her attention was directed toward the earl, they had gone numb. Now, as she tried to think of something other than him, she became aware of sharp pins and needles in her feet. Her calves were beginning to seize up, first with mild cramps, then with cold knives stabbing into the muscles. As gently as she could, she eased her legs out from under her, moving a little sideways to straighten them and rock her feet backward and forward.

It didn't help. Teeth clenched, she tried various motions to shake out the cramps, but they had taken root. Tears of pain sprang to her eyes. She wiped them away with her fingertips, let her eyes open, and gazed up at the ceiling. Pale golden light washed over it like a winter sunset, smooth and still.

No shadows. No flickers! Perhaps he was gone, and she could make her escape. She lowered her head and peered through the balusters to where he had been. It was all a little tear-blurred, the circle of candles and mirrors, and he was not inside it. She nearly wept again, this time with relief.

Turning a little, she pushed up onto her hands and knees. Then she saw him

He was standing at the edge of the wooden flooring, his head lifted toward the gallery, his sword pointing in her direction. The Archangel Lucifer, luminous with anger, had caught out a rat.

"Come here, Miss Pryce." A soft, masterful command. "Now."

She never considered disobeying. But it took some time to get there, starting with a crawl across the gallery. In the adjacent room, she dragged herself upright and stomped back and forth to shake out her taut, agonized muscles.

More tears, maddening tears. She mustn't let him see her like this, weak and limping and weeping. He would never believe it was all down to cold floors and stupid leg cramps. He would think she feared him. Or felt guilty. Which she did, but he needn't know that. In a few hours she would be gone and there would be an end to it.

But beforehand, a scolding.

Was it only that afternoon that she, a servant, had scolded him, an earl? Well, irony had always appealed to her, and a good thing, too. She was about the swallow a heavy dose of it.

When her legs consented to do her bidding, she made her slow way downstairs and to the heavy, iron-studded doors that had been locked that afternoon. They were wide open, and straight ahead of her, waiting for her, stood Lord Varden.

He was exactly where he had been, but relaxed now, the sword point blessedly touching the floor next to his stockinged foot. He was too far away for her to read anything in his expression.

Her woman-of-business stride had no place here. She kept herself from slinking across the wide space between them, which seemed to her a great accomplishment, and was pitifully glad that he couldn't see her eyes.

A curtsy would be out of place as well, she decided,

halting just beyond sword's reach. She stood there for a moment, arms at her sides, chin lifted. Let him have at her, then. She would endure the assault with grace and dignity.

No assault. No change in his calm demeanor. He simply looked at her, the way he might look at a mildly interesting bug that had scuttled into the room.

"You wish an explanation, I suppose" she said when the silence became unbearable.

"Not at all. I recognize prying. You were meddlesome, disrespectful, insolent, ill-bred, incorrigible, and rude. Have I left anything out?"

"Foolish," she said. "Presumptuous. Pigheaded. Oh, a score of disparaging adjectives, all of them quite accurate. I am ashamed, sir. You have my most earnest apology for intruding on your privacy."

"Nicely spoken." He didn't seem in the least impressed with her display of humility. "Now, how did you get in here? And how long were you up there in the galley, snooping?"

"I've a copy of the papers I brought you. Old Holcombe's sketches of the castle. But I never meant to use them to spy on you, my lord. It was you insisted I stay here tonight. I couldn't sleep, and when I looked out the window, I saw light coming from the windows of the Great Hall, which had been locked up earlier, when I tried to—"

"How long, Miss Pryce?"

"Since shortly before you came in with the sword case."

His jaw tightened. "And you remained all this time?"

"I've an interest in fencing, sir."

"You saw precious little of it. Or are you entertained by watching an amateur stumble around, making a great fool of himself?"

"I saw nothing of the sort." She felt starch gathering at her spine, stiffening her will. "I saw an expert right-handed swordsman training himself to work with his left hand, and going about it in all the wrong ways. Well, some of the wrong ways. You require a fencing master."

"No doubt. But in the Mendips, fencing masters are not thick on the ground. The one I employed in London set me to the exercises you observed, and while you may not credit it, there has been progress, if only a little, in the last few weeks."

"A tribute to your patience, my lord. Might I ask how you discovered me?"

In response, he led her to the mirrors and positioned her directly center of them. "Lean slightly forward, Miss Pryce, and look into the second mirror."

"Oh. At this angle, it reflects the gallery. But in the dark—"

"You moved. There was a distinction, impossible to see with you no longer there. And now, young woman, you may as well toddle off to bed. The performance is over."

This time she did curtsy, a great sorrow pressing her down, making it difficult to rise again. On leaden feet she moved back the direction she had come, to the edge of the gleaming floor where the wooden case lay open. Inside it, she saw the twin of the sword he was holding.

Stopping, she took a deep breath and looked back at him. "I could show you."

"How to fence? I'm not sure, Miss Pryce, that it would be wise to put a weapon in your hand."

"I've not held a foil for nearly a decade, sir. Even if I wished it, I could do you no harm. But perhaps I can demonstrate why you are having so much difficulty. If you will only change your methods, progress is sure to be rapid."

"You are a menace." The sound of weary resignation. "And devilish hard to get rid of."

"I've been told that before." She lifted the sword

from the felt bed on which it rested. "This grip is unlike any I've used. Italian?"

"The fencing master recommended I try it. The crossbar provides a firmer grip and ease of manipulation, which I require for my left hand. It lacks the strength and flexibility I enjoyed with my right."

"So far. It will improve." She fumbled with the unfamiliar guard. "I think you must show me how to hold this."

When he failed to come to her, she crossed into the light, searching his face for his mood. She saw only a polite aristocrat enduring a temporary unpleasantness. But he stowed his own sword under his right arm and beckoned her closer.

"Like this," he said, hooking the first joint of her middle finger over the crossbar. "The thumb flat, just here."

She barely noticed his instructions, all her senses focused on where he touched her, and on the beauty of his hand. Long-fingered, slightly browned and roughened by work, it was at once graceful and wholly masculine. When he laid it over hers, to curl her fingers around the sword grip, her skin went on fire.

Helplessly, inadvertently, she looked up. He was looking back at her, eyes glinting with an awareness that matched her own, although he surely couldn't tell. Not through the glasses. But her face was flushed, she knew, and her lips, of their own accord, parted.

She snapped them closed. Bent her head, studied the sword grip while he placed her index finger in position.

"This provides support from underneath. Your thumb and index control the foil. The others provide a firm grip. How does it feel?"

Like I am dissolving.

But he had stepped back, meaning her to try the sword, so she obliged him by swishing it back and forth. The feeling, like all the other feelings clamoring for her attention, was unfamiliar. At least she had a little control of the sword. Unlike her body, which had begun galloping off in every direction.

"What is it, then, you wish to show me?"

She dragged together a few thoughts. Saluted him with the foil and smoothly went *en garde.* He was a second behind her, no more, moving without hesitation or thought.

Simple attacks. Straight lunge in his fourth line. Cutover in his sixth line. Moving slowly at first, she proceeded to compound attacks. Feint with direct thrust, and against parry of fourth, deceive and lunge. Press in sixth, extend, lunge.

Then she stopped announcing her moves and simply went from one to the next. He parried easily, made the expected counter, disengaged. After a time, he inaugurated an attack, and then another. Nothing complex, for she was long out of practice, and he was not yet ready to attempt an advanced pattern.

As they circled, she sometimes found herself looking at six Lord Vardens, the real man and the five reflections, all of them graceful, sophisticated, and intense. They were dancing, she thought, a courtly minuet, their swords an extension of their hands, their gazes locked on her.

"You were right," he said, pulling back for a moment. "The motions, after the first two or three times, come almost automatically. Why?"

"Before, you were trying to direct your body with only your mind and will. Now, by watching me, you have another cue to give it. Your experience has taught you to anticipate and meet your opponent's moves. With your eyes and instincts joined to your mind and will, you can overcome the body's wish to move as it formerly did."

"And how did you know this would happen?"

"It seemed logical." She gave a small shrug. "I was guessing."

Another of those looks from him. It felt like a touch.

"*En garde*, Miss Pryce."

She barely countered his attack, retreated, and found herself defending against a series of attacks against the blade, nonthreatening but assertive. He had got back his confidence, and if his form lacked the elegance he would achieve with practice, it didn't seem to matter. It was the precision he sought, the mastery.

She circled, fending him off, a little breathless with exhilaration. No minuet for them now, no refined dance. Like gypsies around the fire, sheened with perspiration, they clashed and recovered and clashed again, the metallic beat of their swords resonating off the stone walls and ceiling.

He was smiling a little, toying with her. She tried to disengage, but he was quicker, forcing her to retreat. Then their swords met again, his on the inside, forcing her arm back, his gaze intent on her face. She knew better than to yield. He pushed, not hard but inexorably, until both sword arms were extended to the fullest degree.

She thought it was over, that he would permit her to withdraw. Instead, in a motion so unexpected she hadn't a chance to react, he stepped forward, wrapped his right arm around her waist, bent her a little backward, and brought his lips to hers.

A bare, quick breath before his mouth covered her mouth, before his breath became her breath. Her sword clattered to the floor. His sword came up behind her, cool against her back, hard against the back of her head. Imprisoned, unresisting, she felt his unshaven chin press her cheek as he slanted his lips, slid his tongue between her lips and over her tongue, an intimate fencing match that set her blood roaring in her ears.

"I want you," he said on a breath, and claimed her

mouth again. His body covered hers. If he released her, she'd have fallen. But she was safe in his arms, protected by his determination, by a possessive embrace that demanded more of her. A new dance altogether, and she was not unwilling.

It astonished her, even as he engaged her mouth with kisses. She had never imagined receiving such attentions from this man, so far above her station, infinitely beyond her reach. Whatever it was she represented to him this night had exploded into passion, like fireworks. Within a short time, it would blaze out and be gone. She knew it. Didn't care. An hour, perhaps a few hours, in his arms, his body joined to hers. For that, what would she not surrender?

Her arms were around him as well, drawing him closer, telling him without words that she consented to everything he wanted.

He knew it immediately. Lifting his head, he brushed his gloved fingertips along her cheek. "You must be certain."

"I am. A time out of time, for joy and pleasure, with no expectations and no regrets. On those terms, my lord, I am very sure."

Disengaging, he set down his sword and held out his left hand. "Come with me, then."

She shook her head. "It must be in darkness. I don't wish to wear my spectacles, or fear they will become dislodged. My room is small, but I shall require time to prepare it. And myself. Will you come to me there in half an hour?"

"So long?" He gave her a frustrated smile. "Where will you be? And what if you change your mind in the interval?"

"I won't. The room is on the second floor, to the left when you come out of the stairway, and then around the corner. I'll mark the door in some way. But before you knock, you must extinguish any light you carry."

"With you there are always lectures and rules." His smile melted into sweetness. "I shall obey, in the beginning. And then, you will obey."

That sent her rocketing out of the room and to the kitchen for what she must have to protect herself. She would give to him everything he asked. Everything he demanded. Just to imagine it fueled the burning at her breasts and between her legs.

But when he was done with her, when he was gone, would she ever find herself again?

Chapter 6

It had seemed to Varden, watching Helena leave the Great Hall, that when she was gone, whatever had seized possession of him would loosen its grip. His flesh would return to the control of his mind, if only he let himself think a little. Then he would accept the unsuitability, the impossibility, of yielding to this insane desire for a female he had met only three times.

But it felt as if he had known her for centuries, the way a root sprouting from a seed knew to plunge itself deep into the warm, wet earth. And she, eternally female, would unfurl her fragile leaves and open herself to the sun's bright heat.

This was primal. Irresistible.

Desire had been simmering in him from the moment she strode purposefully into his study at Richmond. He had never met a woman like her. Plain clothing, unflattering hair arrangement, stiff posture, those odd spectacles . . . She might as well have been wearing a sign that said, "Do Not Touch." And here he was, longing to touch her. Chaffing at the delay.

Waiting for his brain to begin functioning again.

She was a virgin. She had to be. And a servant. If her reputation was lost, she would find employment only with men who wanted to take advantage of her. Men like . . . well, himself.

He laid the swords in the case, closed it, and went

from candle stand to candle stand, snuffing the flames.
All but one lit candle, which he took with him up the
four flights of stairs to his Spartan quarters. Five minutes gone, twenty-five remaining. She vibrated against
him, as if already in his arms.

Not that he would really go to her bedchamber.
Twenty-five minutes was plenty of time to come to his
senses. Soon the edge of his lust would wear down,
for lust invariably declined without stimulus . . . even
for a man who had not touched a woman for a very
long time.

Didn't it?

After nearly two years of abstinence, he wasn't altogether sure. He had always been selective, perhaps a
little fastidious. He preferred a steady relationship
with an intelligent, companionable, realistic woman. If
he was fortunate, she was also lovely and possessed
of an inventive streak. Never had he indulged himself
with a prostitute or yielded to a passing fancy for an
enticing widow. Never *ever* had he imagined himself
feeling as he did on this night, for this woman, for no
intelligible reason.

He was not going to her bed. But he ought to clean
up a bit before going to his own, if only for the sake
of his sheets. And shave, perhaps, and certainly brush
his teeth.

An interior clock ticked off the seconds and minutes. He groomed himself as if for his wedding day . . .
assuming he was to be married in a wasteland. Sponge
bath. Rough shave with country-made soap, not the
French-milled variety he was used to. Clean shirt and
trousers. Leather slippers. Clothes he was putting on
so that she could remove them.

Who had he been trying to fool? He was going to
her. The lust had not abated.

He was cleaner, though, and more in control of himself, if only a little. If she still meant to have him, he
would give her everything she wanted. Beata, bless

her devious heart and experienced body, had taught him how.

Taking up his candle, he made his way to the second floor and turned left, as she had directed. It was only after he'd examined a long series of doors for the marker she had promised that he realized her directions were given for a man arriving from downstairs. Blood that ought to be fueling his brain had clearly taken its business elsewhere.

At last he found the door, marked with a bit of ribbon around the latch. That surprised him. He had never seen Miss Pryce in the vicinity of a ribbon, or any other female adornment. Perhaps she wore, beneath her stern dresses and functional footwear, lacy chemises and frilly petticoats and silk stockings.

He was looking forward to finding out.

When he extinguished the candle flame, the passageway was plunged into darkness. He set the candle against the wall, took a deep breath, and rapped on the door.

A pause that seemed to him infinitely long. Then her voice, barely audible. "Come in, my lord."

An invitation that resonated to the soles of his feet. With a hand not altogether steady, he fumbled for the latch, found it, and pushed open the door.

Equal darkness met him. Absolute darkness. And cold, like the heart of winter. The sound of the door closing, the latch dropping, seemed to echo in the room.

Then silence. Pure silence. Where was she?

He became aware of his pulse, throbbing in his veins, pounding in his ears. The sough, like a breeze over dry grass, as he drew in air and expelled it. The faint rustle of his shirt as his chest rose and fell. His body became an orchestra of sounds. He had never before been so aware of himself, of what bits and pieces of him were constantly doing when he wasn't paying attention.

Where was she?

New sensations introduced themselves. Fragrances, sifting through the still air. Wax. Lemon. Soap. Freshly laundered sheets. Vinegar.

And then the murmur of skin against skin—he knew that's what it was. And when it stopped, the air he breathed in tasted like tea. All around him, the unmistakable scent of an aroused woman.

He reached out, found her first with his gloved hand. Then his other fell on her, on the smooth curve of a flank. The tips of his fingers curled around a sleek buttock. She was naked.

A gasp from his throat as he became aware of it. She said nothing. Waited, unmoving, as he began to explore the slopes and mounds, the dips and crevices of her complex, unutterably fascinating body. She made him free of it, not resisting when he drew her closer, her discipline greater than his own.

Her skin, softer than anything he'd ever touched, made him long to touch it with more than his hands. Her breasts were fuller than he had expected, with nipples that went hard when his thumbs passed over them. He sent a hand gliding along her back, down the swell of her buttock, around her thigh, and felt the moisture already released from her. Moved up, to the swollen core of her, and came upon a thin string.

She knew to protect herself, and how. It explained the smell of vinegar. A piece of sponge, soaked in vinegar, tied with string, inserted deep within her. She had made herself ready for him, ready to accept him.

She wasn't a virgin, then. He should have reckoned it before, when she presented herself like a gift, like every man's secret fantasy of a woman who would reveal her passion only to him. These were the signs of a woman who knew how to entice a man. She was willing. Knowing. More eager even than he.

Relief swamped him. Not an innocent, naive servant after all. They could meet, at least in the bedchamber, as equals.

And if he mastered her, it would be what she wanted.

Darkness. Silence. Feeling without seeing. Her bare flesh now pressed against his clothed body. The experience, mysterious and supremely erotic, consumed him.

She could feel him, he knew, confined in his trousers and straining to break free. Her hips moved against him, out of position because he was taller, but effective nonetheless.

Too effective. He withdrew his fingers from where they had been and fumbled at the buttons on his trouser flap.

Her hand fell on his wrist. "This way, my lord."

She tugged him a small distance, let him go, and then his thighs were pressed against a high bed. She was on it, her legs open, wrapped around his. Her hands went to the buttons and began to undo them, one by one. They brushed, necessarily or flirtatiously, against his engorged cock.

He'd left off his drawers, and when the trouser flap was undone and dropped, he sprang free like a warrior. And there she was, wet and hot and open, her hands now on his hips, pulling him to where he most wanted to be.

He fell forward, hands on the bed near her shoulder, then on her breasts. His cock nudged at the warm folds, found her opening, and there was no waiting now. He drove inside her.

Met a barrier. Swore . . . he couldn't help it . . . and she was raising her hips and pulling on his. And then he broke through. Was inside. All the way, and held there, breathing heavily.

"You should have told me," he said when he could speak.

"If I had, you would not be here."

"I could not stay away, Helena. Sweet Helena. But I would have taken greater care with you."

She moved restlessly under him, sending pleasure through him like a crossbolt. "You did not hurt me. And I don't wish you to take care."

He held still, fighting for control. "What do you want, then?"

"Everything you will give me." She stirred again, her body impatient. "Everything there is."

He was swept away by the urgency of her passion. His own was frantic, without restraint as his hard flesh pumped inside her, his hips rocking in the cradle of hers. She was so tight around him, so warm. He wanted it never to end. But thought fled, and discipline, and too quickly he was gone, his climax so intense that he cried out with it.

When he came to himself again, he realized his feet were still on the floor. His breeches were tangled around his legs. His upper body lay on top of hers, his head nestled in the curve of her neck, her arms around his back. They were still joined.

"I should get undressed," he said, withdrawing gently. "Before I trip over my trousers."

With a little chuckle, she slipped out from under him. "Wait a few moments. Then I shall undress you."

He sat on the edge of the bed, his imagination conjuring pictures from the sounds and scents coming to him in the darkness. The splash of water as she cleaned herself. The brush of a towel as she dried herself. A sudden, sharp whiff of vinegar as she replaced her protection.

She wanted him inside her again!

That was enough to send his thoughts careening through a score of exotic fantasies. Unfair that he could not indulge them all. No more than one, perhaps two—men being less resilient than women. Less enduring. But there was so much left to do. He hadn't even kissed her, not while he was in her. And the devil knew he had brought her no pleasure. Not the sort she had given him, anyway.

His fantasies narrowed to one. A perfect, sustained, glorious orgasm for his splendid lady of the dark castle.

Who was now kneeling at his feet, he suddenly realized, removing his slippers. Then she was tugging at his trouser legs. He raised his feet and the trousers slid off. He heard them land across the room, where she must have tossed them.

He thought she would next remove his shirt, but she had more intimate and practical intentions. A brief pause, and then a wet cloth moved up the inside of his thigh. It was removed, and rinsed, and brought to his other thigh. He could almost see better in the darkness, guided by sound, than he could see by light. It was the focus, he thought, looking forward to her next move. The absence of distractions.

By the time she brought the cloth to his testicles, they were already tight with anticipation. He planted his palms on the bed to support him as the cloth swirled around the heavy globes. More rinsing, and then she laved his penis, which was not yet ready for another bout—it was too soon—but ah, it felt good. Her soft hair drifted over his thighs as she worked, taking her time as an artist would.

How was it this amazing, inventive, experienced female had remained a virgin? Where had she learned what she knew?

She left him, briefly, and when she returned, she made a dance of removing his shirt. By the time she had drawn it over his arms and head, she had touched every part of him above the waist. Not long enough. Only a promise.

"Will you stand, my lord?" she said.

He did, and heard her working behind him, doing something with the bed. It occurred to him for the first time that he had felt something beneath her hips, perhaps a layer of toweling. He nearly laughed aloud.

Only Helena, efficient Helena, would think of preparing a place to receive her virgin blood.

"Are you cold, sir? Should I draw down the covers, or do you prefer to . . ."

The touch of uncertainty struck him to the heart. She was not so sure of herself as he had thought. "I'm somewhat overheated," he said truthfully. To think the bedchamber had been frigidly cold when he first entered it. "And I like the freedom to move about."

"So do I," she said. "I like it when you move about. Will you join me here on the bed?"

Barbarians assaulting the castle could not have stopped him. Turning, he lifted himself onto the high mattress and pulled himself up. Lay next to her on his right side, to keep his left hand free for exploring. She was on her back, probably expecting another onslaught like the first one. But this time was for her, and he would take it slowly. Take her slowly, with all the skill he possessed.

He began with a gentle command, because if she touched him, he would not have the control to finish what he was beginning. Her body lay before him like a map, and he would travel, with hands and lips, through all the fascinating landscapes that made her who she was.

"I am sorry for the glove," he said at one point. "Does it feel too rough?"

"It feels exciting." Her short breaths, all she had produced for the last minutes, gave the amen to her words.

He felt her quivering, forcing herself to keep from reaching for him. And the longer it took, and the more difficult it was for her to resist, the more thrilled he was with her responses. Wait until he got to her breasts. To her mouth. To his goal.

But first he had to enjoy the wondrous places on her legs, so beautifully curved, and her arms, soft but strong from work. Her neck. He could write a symphony to her neck, and the curve of her chin, and the delicacy of her ears. Wherever his hands went, his lips and tongue were not far behind. He marked her like an animal marking its territory, leaving no spot that did not bear his claim of possession.

Finally, because it was Helena, he spent a long time kissing her. Deep, wet, exploring kisses, and possessive as well. She was so independent. He admired that. But he craved, inexplicably, to curb her separateness by putting himself in all her feminine hiding places. Making sure she would never forget he had been there, making sure she would want him there again.

When at last he gave his attention to her breasts, she could no longer refrain from moaning. When he suckled them, her hips lifted and fell with invitation. She tasted like sugar and salt. Like hot brandy and clear water.

He was running out of time now. Had been hard for too long without release. But this was for her, so he arrowed his concentration on leading her to what she had never experienced.

His hand slipped between her legs. His fingers ghosted up her thighs, the left and the right, approaching and retreating until she was shaking with need. But before he gave her what she hungered for, he wanted to feel the inside of her.

Without his help, her legs had already spread apart. Now he lifted her knees slightly. She made a little sound in the back of her throat that nearly undid him. *For her. For her.*

"Only one," he said, sliding his forefinger inside. The warm, moist folds enveloped it. Squeezed it as her body demanded more. "Very well, then. Another, since you want it." And she did, he could tell when his middle finger joined the first. He played with her for a while, careful to stay away from the swelling nub that would bring her to climax.

"Will you have three?" His tongue slipped into her ear as he ended the question.

"Y-yes." When he waited, she added, "Please."

"Let me know if you want me to stop," he said, withdrawing his fingers, adding the third, and bunching them to reenter her.

"I never want you to stop. It feels so good. And when you leave me, I feel so empty. Ahhh. Yessss. Like that."

He was swirling them around, the heavy moisture of her welcome easing any fear he might be hurting her. She might even have taken a fourth finger, because she had already taken him, and he was large. But he wanted her to climax when he did, or close to, and with his body inside of hers.

He withdrew his hand, found a pillow, and lifted her hips onto it. Then he covered her and slowly, slowly entered her. Her knees came up higher. His lips went to hers, and his tongue into her mouth.

She was so ready, as he had been the first time, that she fired off before he could begin moving in her. So he waited, savoring the vibrations of her orgasm, waited until she subsided. And then he moved, with long, deep strokes, taking his time, leading her to a new and more intensive height. When she was nearly ready again, he freed himself to drive to his own pleasure, and when he reached it, she was there to meet him.

They lay for a while together, silent and replete. He didn't want to leave her body, and she didn't seem to want him to.

After a time, a soft hand stroked his hair, and she said, "May I discover you, my lord? The way you discovered me?"

"By all means." He kissed the tip of her nose. "What do you wish?"

"That you will first lie on your stomach, and then move as I direct you."

"Mmmm. I don't much like being directed."

"You will like this," she said. "While I am about it, think of me as an instrument of your pleasure. Be imagining what you want to do with me, no matter how adventurous. And when I am finished, I will give myself into your hands, and you may have me any way you wish."

Excitement surged through his veins. Immediately he put himself in the position she ordered, and let her spend an hour with his body, leading him to the brink of every delight he could imagine. And dragging him back from it before it peaked, so that she could prolong what she had promised him for this night. Joy and pleasure.

By the time she knelt before him on the bed, head bowed, and gave herself over to his will, he was possessed of such vigor and endurance that nothing seemed out of reach. He took her as she begged him to take her, in one position after another, and felt her excitement grow with every adventure.

The finish, when it came, left them both drifting in a place of soft breezes and bright stars. He opened his arms, and drew her closer, and knew nothing more.

Dawn was creeping over the horizon when Helena finished dressing. She was in the room next to the bedchamber, working by the bare light of dying coals in the hearth. Her portmanteau stood ready by the door.

With the discipline perfected in her childhood, she had emptied her heart of feelings and her mind of distracting thoughts. For all that they had done together, nothing had changed between them. She was departing, as she had told him she would, at sunrise.

She would not insult him by leaving payment for her lodging as, in a bad temper, she had earlier resolved to do. Nor would she write a note of explanation or farewell. What could she say that would not offend him?

More than likely, he would be relieved to awake and find her gone.

She had nothing more to offer him. Last night she had given all of herself, and lost herself as well. Just as she had feared, she would likely never be whole again.

But regrets? Oh, no. Offered the same choice a thousand times, she would make the same decision a thousand times.

And expectations? She had entered this with none, and left it with none. What expectations could a daughter of scandal have from the Archangel Earl? He had already showered on her more blessings than she could ever have dreamed of.

Now, the night of joy and pleasure, the time out of time, was over.

Taking up her portmanteau, she opened the door into the bedchamber. And just then, sunrise sent a wash of light across the bed, across his body, naked and so beautiful that she could not help but pause, commit the vision to memory, and carry it with her into the cold, empty morning.

Chapter 7

"Come to your senses, have you?" The voice, iced with a French accent, resounded through the entrance hall.

Varden, divested of hat, greatcoat, and gloves by the butler, strode to the staircase and bowed to the small woman glaring down at him from the landing. "Good afternoon, Grandmere. You are looking exceptionally fine today."

"Flummery." The Dowager Countess of Varden, his father's mother, gave a loud snort. "We are in the drawing room. Unless there is somewhere else you'd rather be."

Wincing, Varden slowly mounted the stairs while the thump of her cane on the floor announced his arrival to the others. He wondered how many were gathered to pounce on him.

"The prodigal returns," announced his other grandmother when he reached the door. Ensconced on a Sheraton chair, Lady Hetty raised her lorgnette and examined him from his newly trimmed hair to the toes of his polished boots. "Not as bad as I expected after a month of pottering about in an old ruin. What do you think, Jane?"

Hetty's daughter—his mother—regarded him critically from an adjacent chair. "He's far too brown. Just when he had started to fade after that India nonsense. We require you to be fashionable, Varden."

"We also require you to be *here*," put in Ann, his eldest sister. "The girls are depending on it."

He glanced over at the golden-haired twins, Chloe and Penelope, named during Ann's unfortunate Grecian period. They were perched side by side on a love seat, looking deceptively demure. "My complexion may not be fashionable in London," he said, "but it's all the thing in the Mendips."

"I quite like it," Chloe said. "Bronze is exotic. I wish to be exotic as well, but Mama says I must first have your permission."

"She wants to dye her hair red," said Penelope with patent disgust.

"Indeed?" He clasped his hands behind his back, regarding his nieces with interest. Pert chits, the both of them, eager for their come-outs and impatient with the restrictions of a critical Society. "Red, you say? Well, I don't see why not."

A collective gasp from his mother and grandmothers.

"Are you mad?" exclaimed Ann, putting down her cup and saucer with a snap.

"If a young woman cannot manage the hair on her head, she is not sufficiently responsible to be loosed on the world. Either take the twins back to Westmoreland for another year of indoctrination, Ann, or resign yourself to extending their leashes."

"Uncle!" Chloe leaped up and wrapped him in a hug. "You are trumps."

He had been almost that naive for far too long. "It is a shame, though," he said, guiding her gently to a splash of light near the bay window. "Not that I blame you in the least. The Leighton hair is a curse. We all look the same."

"You don't," said Penelope, always practical. "Your

hair is much lighter, and you have green eyes. Except for Gran Hetty, we all got stuck with hazel."

"People have no trouble distinguishing me because I am the lone male in a gaggle of females. But Chloe is a yellow-haired female in a family of yellow-haired females, and a twin besides. If she dyes her hair, Pen, I'll finally be able to tell the two of you apart."

Chloe plucked at his sleeve. "You said it was a shame. Why?"

"I was speaking of what you will lose, that is all." He twirled a finger through one of her short curls. "Every shade from flaxen to guinea gold can be found here, each shining with its own particular light. But dyed hair, every strand of it, looks precisely the same. The color is flat."

Her brows knit in a frown. "I don't know what you mean."

"Like Gran Hetty's hair," Penelope said. Lady Hetty, on the sunset side of seventy, had dyed her hair since before most of the people in the room had been born. "Flat as the bottom of an iron."

"I shall disinherit you," said Hetty, not for the first time.

A typical family gathering, Varden was thinking. *Except for the ominous undertones.*

"Red is not so flat as black," he said. "Not quite. Its tendency to go brassy gives it a little dash. Of a sort."

"An improper sort!" Ann was becoming agitated. "What kind of females have you been consorting with, Varden?"

"Lately, the kind that milk cows and gather eggs. Let the child dye her hair. Later, you can torment her with 'I told you so.' Or else the young blades will be smitten with her, leaving her blond twin in the dust. Pen will have to confine herself in a convent, and her frustrated mama—"

"Will hang for murdering her insufferable brother."

Chloe, scowling, towed her sister into the light and examined her hair from every angle. Then she turned on her uncle. "That was mean. You made me be wrong."

"My dear, the women of my family have taught me two immutable lessons. No female is ever wrong, nor can I make one do anything she doesn't wish to do."

Penelope's eyes narrowed. "Is that why Miss Pryce gave her notice?"

He had been steeling himself for this moment, had practiced a response or two. But the thoughts that sprang instantly to his mind would have scandalized every woman in the room.

"That will be enough," Hetty said. "You gels take yourselves off now. Chloe, if you persist in frowning, your forehead will become permanently wrinkled. Penelope, you are becoming officious. That is my role in this family. You may have it after I turn up my toes."

When the door closed behind the twins, Varden, already resigned to the inevitable, put a mild expression on his face and waited for the barrage. Out of sympathy for the injury to his hand, the women had not pressed him overmuch on his return from India. They were too pleased to have him back, and too worried about him. But he could practically hear the barred doors clanging shut as his reprieve came to a close.

"If only to get it out of the way," said his sister, "what did you do to poor Miss Pryce?"

Poor Miss Pryce? He nearly laughed. "I paid her an exorbitant salary to do very little work for me, and rather a lot of it for you. But while she holds you all in high regard, it seems she is disinclined to arrange wardrobes, social calendars, and balls."

"Nonsense." That was his mother. "She gave no sign whatever of dissatisfaction. She was perfectly . . . well, perfect. More to the point, under her supervision, the twins behaved themselves. We want her back for the Season or until both girls are betrothed, whichever comes first. You will see that she returns."

"That will not be possible. Miss Pryce has made her intentions quite clear. And the lot of you are capable of managing two or three small countries while paring your nails. Let Miss Pryce get on about her business, whatever it may be."

"That proves it," Ann said, fixing him with her sternest look. "You are responsible for her departure."

"We can tell," Hetty explained, "because you protest too much. And your cheeks are flushed."

"Not from concern about a servant, I assure you. If you want that one back, fetch her yourselves. My apprehension, and I confess to a degree of it, has to do with what else you plan to throw at me during this inquisition. Might we move directly to the rack and thumbscrews? I have an engagement this evening."

The silence that followed that pronouncement clapped like thunder in his ears. When had he ever spoken so to them? The House of Ladies, they called themselves. The Parliament of Four, entrusted with the welfare of the younger Leighton sisters, the husbands they married, and the children they bore. But their primary responsibility, embraced ferociously by them all, was for the male scion in whose loins resided the continuation of the centuries-old earldom.

He understood their passion. He loved them. He wanted to be anywhere but here.

"You were such a perfect child," said his mother in mournful, guilt-inducing tones. "You never misbehaved. There were no tantrums. You did exactly as you were told. I should have known you were storing up common childish behavior for your adult years, when most we rely on you to do your duty."

"Cut line, Mary." Hetty disliked theatrics, unless they were her own. "The boy was entitled to indulge himself a bit, and he has done so. If the India voyage turned out badly—" Up went the lorgnette again. "You never did explain that to my satisfaction, Varden. What the devil happened out there?"

"What I told you, Gran." With effort, he kept his voice steady. "An accident, caused by a misjudgment on my part. No more than that."

"But you are doing well now?" His mother looked sincerely worried. "Does the hand pain you still?"

"Barely a twinge, and only when rain is threatening. You needn't, any of you, cosset me. What I can no longer do with my right hand, I am learning to accomplish with my left. Quite soon my black glove will be regarded as a charming affectation."

From the relief in her eyes, he knew he had convinced her. For the time being, at any rate. After losing two infant sons, she could not be blamed for overprotecting the boy who had survived, especially since his difficult birth meant she could never bear another child. When that became clear, when the family knew he was the last hope of the Leightons, they had closed around him like an affectionate Imperial Guard.

They imprisoned him, these women, with their love and their need. But who was *not* in prison, one way or another? The corpulent king enwrapped in too much flesh and afflicted with poor health, holed up in Windsor and sustained by flattering cronies. Lady Hetty, age closing in on her, gout confining her to the house six days out of seven. Miss Pryce behind her smoked glasses, her brilliant mind constrained in the body of a woman, never able to rise to the heights her talents merited.

He could have taken her a little of the way.

But he had . . . Well, never mind. In the last eighteen months, he had done little else but make mistakes. Perhaps his mother was right. Perhaps he had stored up all his failings like gunpowder, waiting to ignite them just when he ought to be fulfilling the family's expectations.

He glanced up and found himself looking out the window. He didn't remember turning, putting his back to the ladies, focusing his gaze inward. *Inward*, where it had so rarely been before. He had thought that, by coming home, he would find the man he had used to be. Instead, he rather hoped he would not find him.

"I wish you would tell us what is wrong," Ann said in a gentle voice.

"I'd prefer to know why he bought a derelict castle in Somerset," said Grandmere, her accent more pronounced than usual. She prided herself on the practicality of her French ancestors, who had saved their money while their peers squandered louis d'or and francs like dandelion seeds. "What must it have cost? And the expense to repair the place will be outrageous. Do you intend to pursue this extravagant folly?"

"You can't mean to live there!" his mother said in renewed alarm. "I won't permit it."

He looked across the stretch of lawn that reached down to the river. The boat he had taken from the city to his Richmond house was tied up beside the water gate, bobbing as the wind picked up and the tide began to turn. Nearby, the oarsmen sat beneath an awning, protected from the drizzle that would soon transform itself to rain. He would be expected to stay here the night, and on any other night, he would probably have agreed to do so.

"The castle is my new hobby," he said. "I had thought to restore it, but as amateurs will, I underestimated its problems and overestimated my ability to deal with them. At present, I am not sure how much attention I will devote to the place. Not much, I expect, until the Season is over. And I do not foresee living there for any extended period of time. Is that satisfactory?"

A short silence. Then, from his mother, "I worry about the money."

"Don't!" snapped Hetty before he could reply. "He does not gamble, nor is he known to spend lavishly on women and the usual ramshackle pursuits of young men about town. Or has that changed, Varden? Are you throwing your money to the wind?"

"I spent rather too much to buy the castle," he said, "and will doubtless spend too much to restore it. Otherwise, my habits remain much the same. And I beg you to remember that I have funds of my own, for the most part wisely invested. I'll not bankrupt the family."

"It's a harmless enough indulgence, I suppose." His mother sounded dubious. "But if you intend to remain in London for the Season, why are you not residing here, in your home?"

"More accurately, I am in London for the sitting of Parliament, and it is not convenient to stay in Richmond. I have leased a small house in Great Ryder Street."

"But you *will* escort us to the important social events?" Ann said. "We must launch the twins in style."

"I presume you'll give a ball, and of course, I shall attend. But do not rely on my presence at other times. I expect to be occupied with matters of state."

"Keep in mind," Hetty said, "that England will be a good deal safer when the twins are wed. Now as to the main issue at hand—"

"I have all the traditional arguments committed to memory, Gran. There is no reason to trot them by me again." He turned, heartsick and resigned, to give them what they most wanted. "I have decided to marry."

The dumbfounded silence and open mouths might have amused him, except for the mourning bell tolling in his head. With five words, he had accepted the inevitable. The death of his hopes. The confinement of his lost love to a small place inside himself, a secret grave he would visit now and again, in solitude.

But he had just made his family very, very happy. He mustn't spoil it for them. Time to smile.

He did, and the four of them started talking at once. The sounds washed over him, the words expected and meaningless. His mother rushed up to embrace him. Grandmere bounced on her chair. He glanced at Hetty and quickly looked away. She was regarding him closely through her lorgnette, and always saw more than he wished to reveal. Especially now.

"Have you someone in mind?" she said, her words slicing through the general excitement. "Not that Italian woman, the one you took up with before going out to India. She's buried three husbands here in England, and the devil knows what she was up to beforehand."

He detached himself from his mother, brushed a kiss on her tear-streaked cheek, and faced the canniest of his relations. "I doubt Beata Neri would have me, or any other man with interests and obligations not directed at her. But oblige me by not insulting the lady. For the time we were together, we suited each other well enough. Our friendship endures."

"No insult intended, so long as she don't come into the family. Who else, then?"

"There is"—he had to swallow before he could say it—"no one. I was gone for nearly a year and a half. By now, most of the young women I knew will have found husbands."

"Not that you paid them any mind at the time. But there are the leftovers from last year's Season, and a new crop about to spring up. Plenty to choose from."

He imagined a field overgrown with Penelopes and

Chloes. Eager young girls on the lookout for a wealthy aristocrat who would buy them presents and . . . Dear God. What had he got himself into? But it had been the same since first he went on the town. Only then, there was no hurry. Plenty of time to find the *one*. To fall in love with her. To court her, and because his life had always been perfect, to rejoice as she fell in love with him. A love match had seemed inevitable. All his sisters had managed it.

". . . and we'll help you," his mother was saying. "I know all the unmarried young women. They're not all *leftovers*, as Mama would have it. Some are careful. Selective. At least three quite desirable candidates come immediately to mind, and when I have reviewed the possibilities—"

"No," he said. "On this point, I am resolved. My wife will be of my own choosing. And because I do not wish to make a selection while under siege, you will—all of you—oblige me by telling no one of my intentions. That includes husbands, sisters, children, and your nearest friends. Nor will you thrust eligible ladies into my company. Let me handle this my own way, or I shall withdraw my declaration."

"The boy is right," Hetty said. "We'll not serve him up like a roast pig on a platter."

"Thank you, Gran. But may I add one thing? While you have known me from my infancy, you don't appear to have noticed that I've now reached the advanced age of thirty-three. For the sake of my shredded dignity, will you strike 'boy' from any sentence referring to me?"

"You have my apologies," Hetty said promptly. "I am grown dotty in my old age. Anyone under fifty years seems to me positively green."

"But do you really mean it?" said his mother, doubt knitting her forehead. "Every year since you turned twenty, I have hoped that you would select a bride."

And nagged him to do so. But then, she had actually

met the reputedly loathsome heir presumptive. He knew only that distant cousin Walter Leighton had fled to the Continent years earlier, in debt up to his eyebrows. No one wanted to see him return as head of the family, which meant that the Earl of Varden was obliged to breed a son, and preferably two or three more to be held in reserve.

"You may safely rely on this," he told them quietly. "I give you my word of honor. Before the end of the year, I shall be wed."

Chapter 8

Varden arrived at Palazzo Neri just ahead of the rain. The villa, a Mediterranean fantasy of whitewashed wood and hand-painted tiles, spilled along the grassy, tree-lined acres that sloped from Paradise Row to the Thames, its windows and courtyards ablaze with light. At this time of year, with people gathering in London for the upcoming Season, it became the center of business, politics, and pleasure for the select company who had met with the owner's favor.

He had met with her favor, and a great deal else besides. Beata Neri, whose Italian origins remained obscure, had arrived in England twenty years earlier and found herself an aged and wealthy husband. He was succeeded by two others much like him, none of the three surviving the marriage ceremony for more than a few years. With their fortunes, the widow built for herself an extravagant jewel box where she played hostess to statesmen and aristocrats, gamblers and scholars, poets and painters, and anyone else who captured her interest.

Varden had done so at their first meeting and held it for longer than most. But he'd known from the first that his credit with Beata was rooted in the cachet he brought to her and the Palazzo. Before their long affair began, she had been relegated to the fringes of Society. Afterward, people who wouldn't think of inviting her to their homes made free of hers, enjoying the gaming, gossip, and lavish entertainments she provided.

Others came for more serious purposes. Determined to make her Palazzo the meeting place of choice, she had devoted one wing of the sprawling villa to rooms of assorted sizes for businessmen, politicians, and intellectual societies to assemble. He was headed for such a meeting tonight, a planning session for Tory leaders called by Lord Gretton.

But first, he must pay his respects to Beata. A servant directed him to the largest parlor, the Sala dei Medici, and after pausing to greet acquaintances along the way, he finally stepped through the wide double doors. And came to an immediate halt.

Across the room, extravagant in a hunter green gown of Lucca velvet adorned with blond lace, Beata Neri held court from a complexion-flattering position between two wall sconces. Beside her, javelin-straight in a plain gray gown with high neck and long sleeves, stood Helena Pryce.

His lover of two years, in company with his lover of one night.

As if sensing his arrival, they simultaneously looked over at him.

He crossed to them, smiling at Beata, noting the stiffening of Helena's already rigid posture and the slight flush on her high cheekbones. She was not so indifferent as she wished to appear.

"Ah," said Beata, leaning forward to brush a kiss on his cheek. In the presence of other women, she always marked him as her possession. "I began to fear, *caro*, that you intended to remain in the wilderness."

"Only for a brief holiday. The Mendips are lovely this time of year."

A little sniff to his right, barely perceptible.

"Mah! But I forgive you for departing without a farewell, because you have done me a kindness. By making yourself objectionable to the splendid Miss Pryce, you have freed her to assist me during this busiest of times. Under her direction, my hospitality will be unsurpassed. You will see. After your meeting, come have supper with me."

Beata never took well to a refusal. And with sources of information that bordered on the supernatural, she had an uncanny way of knowing what had happened almost before it happened. If he dined with her, he might discover what she knew, what she guessed, and what she suspected of his brief entanglement with Helena Pryce.

"I would be delighted," he said, kissing her hand, wishing Helena weren't watching all this calculating flirtation. "Unless the meeting runs overlong."

"Oh, it will not. Gretton has suffered an injury that would make a long meeting inadvisable. But I shall leave him to explain the circumstances. Until later, *caro*."

He met her amused gaze, returned the smile she was expecting, and turned politely to the lady whose masked eyes had been scorching him all this time. It was only the reflection from the wall sconces, of course, their flames dancing on the smoked glasses like Maenads. But he knew the heat behind them, the blazing passion that had erupted in his arms. Anyone glancing over at her now would see a starchy, self-contained young woman. He saw a banked fire, an explosion inviting a sulphur stick to ignite it.

"Miss Pryce," he said with practiced manners. "The family would wish me to convey their regards. I hope you will accept mine as well."

"Thank you, Lord Varden. I see that Mr. Peel and the Duke of Wellington have already left the room. You are about to be late for your meeting."

And so she got the last word, he was thinking as he made his way to the south wing. In point of fact, she had effectively dismissed him. But what had he expected? That because he had done as she wished by returning to London and reengaging himself in politics, she would again throw herself into his arms?

It astounded him, how greatly he wished she would do exactly that. Even a smile would have warmed him. But for all the recognition she gave to his sacrifice, he might as well have announced that he'd bought a new pair of boots.

Straight ahead, inside the brightly lit meeting room, a dozen men were taking their seats around an oval-shaped table. At each place, atop a blotter, Beata had provided pens and a penknife, ink, paper, and a Moroccan leather folder. There were goblets, decanters of claret, and platters with thinly sliced bread, roast beef, and cheese.

He took the vacant chair between Wellington and George Canning, as he was expected to, and made the usual polite remarks while wondering what had put Lord Gretton's left arm in a sling.

Gretton, a pleasant, unpretentious man in his late forties, was standing behind his chair, looking pale and determined. He was perhaps the most influential man in England, although he took care not to draw attention to himself. Quietly, expertly, he manipulated the king's decisions, refusing the honors and appointments offered him in order to maintain his reputation for impartiality.

That reputation, along with his popularity and keen grasp of the issues, placed him at the head of meetings like this one. He waited until everyone was settled, nodded to a servant who left the room to stand guard beside the closed door. Then he gave a mildly embarrassed smile.

"Gentlemen, some of you have heard this tale already. I beg you to endure it once more, that the curiosity of the others can be put to rest before we proceed with the business of the evening. Last night, on the road from Windsor, my carriage was intercepted by a highwayman. Or so I thought him to be at first. But instead of stopping the coach and demanding money, he rode alongside, positioning himself to take a shot at me. I was working on some papers, and the interior lamp was lit, making me a perfect target. He was masked, wearing a wide-brimmed hat that shadowed his eyes. I had a glimpse of dark hair, and then I saw the pistol aimed at my head."

He pulled out his handkerchief and wiped it across his forehead. "It was," he said after a moment, "somewhat terrifying. I felt a jolt as the carriage wheels hit a rut. At the same instant, there came a flash and a loud report. The bullet struck low, passed through my arm, and lodged in the squabs. There appears to be no permanent damage, except to my new leather upholstery. If you wish further details, such as they are, I'll be glad to share them at another time. For now, Mr. Canning is first on the agenda."

Gretton sat, a little gingerly, the foreign secretary rose, and the meeting was underway.

Varden had been to others like it, but not for the better part of two years. Much had changed while he was gone, and the issues addressed were unfamiliar to him.

For the next three hours he took notes while the others argued about recognition of former Spanish American States, now liberated. He learned that only a few weeks ago, the President of the United States, Mr. Monroe, had warned European nations not to intervene in the affairs of the American continents, nor to establish themselves in unoccupied areas of those continents.

There was the Greek revolt against the Turks and the potential interference of Russia to discuss. The problem of Portugal. Daniel O'Connell and the Catholic Association in Ireland. Slavery was touched on, but by then, Gretton was sagging in his chair, white-faced and breathing heavily. Wellington stood, brusquely called an end to the meeting, and suggested Gretton take himself home before he had to be carried.

Not once, Varden realized as he tried to stuff his barely legible notes into the folder, had anyone addressed domestic problems. Robert Peel, the home secretary, had spoken little more than Varden did and only perked up when the subject turned to abolition. He was the first to leave the room, followed swiftly by most of the others. Canning and Huskisson escorted Gretton at a slower pace.

"Well, then," said the duke. "Little enough came of this meeting. A tot of brandy, Varden, before I go out into the rain?"

A few minutes later, when they were seated in wingback chairs before a fire in a small parlor, Wellington came quickly to the point. "You have been out to India," he said. "It's near twenty years since I was there, and one day, I should like to hear what you have to say of the place. But being gone, you've missed what is happening here. That gives you a perspective the rest of us don't have. What think you of the attack on Gretton?"

Taken aback, Varden gave it some thought. "An assassination attempt, I suppose. Fairly inept. So long as the horseman was going to the trouble, why not carry two pistols? On the other hand, he knew when Gretton would be on the road. Windsor to London is a well-traveled route, but he was able to pick out a specific coach in the dark."

"Yes. All of that. Gretton might have been killed, of course. Sheer luck that he wasn't. The point I'm making isn't particular to this incident. It's that so many incidents of one sort or another have occurred in the last several years, most involving men of rank. I have found one link common to several cases, but it may be mere coincidence. I've a mind that looks for patterns, and on occasion I see them where they do not exist."

"What exactly have you seen?"

"Evidence of extortion. Money to be paid in exchange for silence about one's misdeeds, real or fabricated. Over the years I have received more than one such threat, and I deal with them all in the same fashion. Publish, say I, and be damned. These serpents have only to get their teeth in you to bleed you dry. Look at Castlereagh, poor fellow."

"But he committed suicide, did he not? Shortly before I left for India. It was said the strain of office became too great for him."

"That was the surmise. When last I saw him, he was delusional. Raving about enemies on his heels, about horses waiting outside to carry him to safety, except there were no horses. On my advice, the doctor and servants removed every instrument with which he might harm himself. But they overlooked a small penknife, and a few days later, he used it to slice through his jugular."

Wellington took a drink of brandy. "Straightforward enough. But he had been troubled for a considerable time. Was heard to babble of entering a brothel, and of a crime not to be named. More of his delusions, it seemed. But a few of us have since learned the truth of his situation, and I wish to tell you of it."

"You may, of course, rely on my discretion."

"I rely on your judgment. If you think it advisable, by all means use this information. I do not give it you without purpose." An expression of sorrow passed over the duke's face. "A gang of extortionists, reputedly led by a man named Jennings, had laid a trap for Castlereagh three years earlier. They arranged for him to encounter a woman on the street, and when he had taken her into a brothel and was getting about his business, he discovered that the female under him was, in fact, male. The shock of it all but overcame him. At that moment, the extortionists broke into the room, acquainted him with the consequences of his error—

a capital crime, sodomy—and began a long persecution that ended only with his death."

"Good God. He told no one?"

"He held himself responsible, I believe. Guilt disordered his mind, and shame kept him silent. Castlereagh has been the most notable victim to date, but other peers have fallen inexplicably into debt and bankruptcy. Some fled England, some took Castlereagh's course. I'll provide names if you require them."

"Are you expecting me to conduct an investigation?"

One brow went up. "I thought you might wish to. You were, I understand, consulted in the matter of Beast Tallant's murder. When that odd fellow—I forget his name—confessed before swallowing the same poison he used to kill the duke, he wrote that Tallant had ruined him with an extortion scheme."

"So I heard. But I was not involved in that phase of the investigation. Are you suggesting that Tallant was behind the other crimes as well? What about Jennings's gang?"

The duke shrugged. "Independent operators, perhaps. But I suspect they were being run by Tallant, or someone else with access to information about the victims. Since the duke is no longer in the picture, it is possible his schemes died with him."

"Meaning the attack on Gretton is unconnected to the other incidents. But you don't think so. You are wondering if Tallant had an accomplice."

"It is possible." Steely blue eyes fixed on Varden. "For the time being, I am in favor with the king, and he expects me to keep company with him at Windsor. I cannot follow up on my hunch."

Well, that was clear enough.

He had been given an assignment, unofficially, by the Duke of Wellington. Find the new mastermind of extortion plots, if there was a mastermind, and if there were plots. Do this just when Helena wanted him engaged with the poor and disenfranchised. Just when his family was counting on him to make the social rounds in their company. Just when he was expected to select a bride.

"I'll look into it," he said, fairly sure the duke had expected his consent. "But I'll require all the information you have, or that you can point me to."

"Done." Wellington put down his glass, most of the brandy still in it, and rose. "Now I'm for a long cold ride back to Windsor, and if I am not mistaken, you are for a warm supper with a warmer lady."

Warm? Varden smiled and said nothing. Beata waxed cold or hot, according to her mood. There was no place in her temperament for the in-between passions.

In no hurry to join her, Varden lingered a few minutes, sipping his brandy. Beata had been the most exotic of his lovers, but their affair, like all his affairs, could best be described as civilized. Not discreet, though. Quite the opposite.

When he'd got used to her flaunting him like a prize-winning salmon, he settled into amused tolerance. She had been good for him. For nearly the first time in his life, he had defied convention and done something that shocked his family and friends. Then the gossip died down, the family resigned themselves to the liaison, and life went on much as usual.

In other ways, she had not been so good for him. Beata gave him a taste for adventure, which had led him—was *still* leading him—into one disaster after another. Still, a man who risks nothing makes no mistakes, nor does he accomplish anything of value.

A glance at the mantelpiece clock brought him to his feet. Well after midnight. The evening was just getting underway in the public rooms of Palazzo Neri, but here, the rooms and passageways were deserted. Wall sconces created circles of dim light as he made his way along the corridor. Then, turning a corner, he felt a draft of cold air. To his left, a door leading to a courtyard stood open, and standing beyond the reach of light was the unmistakable silhouette of Helena Pryce.

The lady of dark places. Secret meetings. Unexpected delights.

Cool blood went instantly hot, roaring through his veins.

"Shhhh," she whispered, beckoning him to the dark center of the courtyard, where a circle of potted trees concealed them from view. Then she put careful distance between them, beyond arm's reach. Not that he would have dared touch her.

"I beg your pardon," she said. "I shan't keep you long. You have returned to London. Well, that is obvious. It's only that I wondered if you intend to stay."

Helena Pryce, unsure of herself? Only a little, but still—

"I'm not certain," he said, resisting the temptation to string out his response. "But most likely, I will. You are a persuasive young woman, Miss Pryce. And after a while, mortaring stones becomes devilish dull. On the other hand, much the same can be said of the meeting I just attended. Tell me again why I am suited for politics."

"Because you . . . But, no. It is no longer my concern what you do. You should go now. Beata is expecting you."

"All the discussion was of foreign matters," he said. "I've been so long away that I didn't follow the half of it. How is it you think I can be of use?"

"Oh, for heaven's sake." She made a slashing gesture. "At your worst, you are perfectly competent. Exceptional when you set your mind to an issue. Plead any excuse you like save ignorance or lack of ability, sir. The first is easily overcome. The other . . . well, if you choose to waste your talents, that is your business. All I did was ask your intentions."

She had returned, the Helena everyone knew, strong willed, direct, bristling with impatience. The other Helena, the one she had revealed only to him, had gone to ground. But he felt her, the way he felt his heartbeat, the air in his lungs. He took a small step forward. "What do you want my intentions to be?"

"Have you already forgot? What we spoke of at the castle."

"Legal reforms. Prison reforms. Justice for those without money or influence. Was there more?"

"There is always more. I am glad you have taken up your duty again, my lord. Please pardon me for delaying you."

She turned. He was faster, putting a hand on her shoulder before she escaped. It rose and fell, her shoulder. She was breathing heavily. "Release me, sir. Someone might see you. Us."

"It is perfectly dark. We are alone here."

"I think no one is ever alone in this place." She ducked out of his reach, putting a marble bench between them. "If I am to secure employment, I must have a care for my reputation."

"How so? At our first meeting, you informed me that no one would suspect you of impropriety." Or any man of being enticed by her, he remembered. How wrong she had been.

"Circumstances have changed. The ladies of your family were invariably kind, but they could not help discussing me with their acquaintances. Too many people know I was hired to be your secretary but quickly passed off to your mother and sister and nieces. They know I left your service, and cannot imagine why anyone would choose not to serve in such a notable and delightful household. Attention has been drawn, Lord Varden. I can no longer speak with anyone in your family, most especially you, without notice being paid."

Quickly passed off, she had said. A stab of guilt

caught him unaware. In the rarified Society where she slipped in and out like an eel, practically invisible, she had been marked by him as unsatisfactory. And by his family as superb, of course, but that was no consolation. She did not wish to arrange the social affairs of fine ladies, but thanks to him, they might be the only ones who would employ her. How could he make amends?

"You are a racehorse at the start line," he said, "practically on the run before the pistol sounds. If you will not speak with me here, then where?"

"There is no need—"

"Where and when, Helena? If you need employment, I'll see you get it."

"Don't insult me. I do not require your help"

"Fine. But I require yours."

No riposte. He sensed a change in the air. She had been on the verge of leaving, but now he had her attention.

"I mean it," he said quietly. "You came after me, drew me away from the castle and back to London. I am here to do what you asked of me. You cannot abandon me now."

Silence. The quick breaths of a cornered animal. From both of them, he realized, unclenching his left hand. A pitch-black room, their bodies fencing urgently . . .

That night lay between them, separating them, drawing them together. He wanted her.

"Very well," she finally said. "I am engaged tomorrow, but if you are free in the evening, I can arrange to meet you at Sothingdon House."

"Is that where you are staying?"

"Not at present. Portions of the house are being renovated, and from dawn to sunset, the noise is too great. You must take care not to be seen. Use the back gate, and come to the French windows that open onto the terrace. Will nine o'clock suit you?"

"I am at your service," he said. In every way, if she'd let him. "Ought we to leave here separately?"

"Of course." Exasperation in her tone. "You first. Beata will be waiting. Good night, my lord."

He bowed, doubting she could see it, and set out for the Galleria d'Argento, where supper would be laid out. He was to sit beside the principessa, as she now styled herself, on exhibit, to demonstrate that whenever she wanted him, she had only to beckon.

"A man always wants the woman that other men want," she had once told him. "On occasion, you will oblige me by helping to attract your replacement."

"And what does a woman want?" he had asked, laughing.

"Is it not obvious, *caro*? She wants the man who will want only her."

Chapter 9

Varden set out early the next morning for Number 4 Bow Street, where his request for a meeting with the chief magistrate met with bad news. Sir Richard, it seemed, was not expected until ten o'clock. After some thought about how to pass the time, he went to the office where Runners were employed, examined several packets of credentials, and selected four red-vested men to interview.

The small, wiry fellow he finally chose had a face like a monkey and the quick wits of a sharper. Moreover, he knew the person he was being set to follow. Knew *of* her, at any rate, and probably a good deal more than he was admitting.

"I expect absolute discretion," Varden told him. "She is never to become aware of your existence, nor the identity of the man who employed you."

"If she don't know the first," Tommie Trotter said with a grin, "she can't very well know the last. I been where the lady sometime goes. People thinks nothin' to see me there."

"I had in mind you wouldn't be seen at all."

"That's because you never set foot in them streets. Everyone what lives there knows who belongs and who don't. Nobody comes in unseen, and not many leaves unrobbed. I don't likes to think what would become of you, milord, all rich and golden as you be.

But a cove like me kin trot along to a gin shop or a fancy house and be paid no mind."

"Since you know so much about the lady's activities, perhaps we should spare you the exertion of following her. I'll pay for information, never mind how you came by it."

"What I don't learn workin' for you can't be told. A man's got his honor. Are you suspectin' the lady of criminal activities, m'lord? You should know I won't never lay evidence against her. They'd cut out my liver for that."

"Who, precisely, are *they*?"

"If she meets up with any of 'em when I be on her trail, I can give over their names. Will what I tell you bring her to harm?"

"Good God, no. It's a matter of business. *My* business, not yours. Will you take the hire?"

Trotter, frowning, appeared to be debating with himself. "For one day," he said. "Has to be a Tuesday. That's when she pays 'er calls. Tomorrow, or next week's Tuesday?"

Varden nearly called it off then. He rather thought Charley Trotter had been, in his roundabout way, advising him to do exactly that.

But he wanted to *know*, dammit. Where she went on private time. Whom she saw. What she did. They were dangerous places, from what he had just heard, stocked with dangerous people. The sort of people she wanted him to help, the sort of places she wanted him to improve. How did a refined young woman become acquainted with such creatures in the first place? Why was she permitted to run tame in the sordid alleyways of London?

Reasonable questions. But not the real ones.

Helena Pryce, mysterious in a plain, straightforward way, had become his obsession. Right alongside his other obsession, although no two women could be more different. That he was obsessed at all continued to amaze him. Extreme passions were not part of his nature. He had never before experienced anything like this wrenching turmoil in his brain and belly. And elsewhere.

He glanced up to see the Runner grinning widely.

"Follow her tomorrow," Varden said.

The chief magistrate had still not arrived when Varden stopped again at his office, so he asked to see the files connected with the former Duke of Tallant's murder and the subsequent attack upon his successor. The clerks, aware of Varden's association with the home secretary, speedily obliged, and soon he was settled in a private room with a slew of documents spread out on the desk.

Some he had seen before. Others, new to him, contained startling revelations. He reviewed them all in light of what Wellington had told him and—he was forced to admit—in the light of what he wanted to believe.

Some evidence he judged to be fraudulent. Gentle Miranda Holcombe, now Duchess of Tallant, could not have done what was reported, and signed to, by her husband. The lie cast a shadow over his entire testimony.

The more he read, the more convinced Varden became that the truth of the Beast's murder had yet to be discovered, and that the danger had not been contained. An unknown villain, perhaps more than one, still lurked at the heart of the web, laying traps, plotting extortion and murder, driving victims to despair and suicide.

A rap on the door. "Sir Richard has arrived, my lord," said the young clerk, poking his head into the room. "Will you speak with him now?"

"Yes. Wait there a moment." Varden gathered up the papers he had set aside, leaving the others on the desk. "I wish copies of these," he said, handing them to the clerk on his way out. "When you are done, restore the originals to their proper files and make sure they are kept under lock and key. No one is to examine them without first obtaining my consent."

He didn't have that much authority, but expected he could get it before his injunction was put to the test.

Sir Richard Burnie, not long in the position of chief magistrate, was more than anything determined to secure further advancement. Flushed-faced, solid as a peel tower, he glowered from behind his desk when Varden entered. "Well, well, my lord. I thought you had abandoned those of us who labor in the vineyard. After the lovely young woman you admired managed to get herself exonerated, you appeared to lose interest in the search for justice."

Varden was becoming used to the barrage of criticism that seemed to follow him everywhere these days. "I assumed, Sir Richard, that with you in charge, justice rested in safe hands. But of late, for reasons I am not at liberty to reveal, I have come to believe that a new investigation into the Duke of Tallant's murder may be warranted."

"*May?*" Burnie snorted. "But it's too late. Much as I should like to pursue the matter, it would be a waste of my time."

"Only a little time, to answer my questions and provide your educated opinion. I shall undertake the rest. Perhaps the investigation will come to nothing, but if new evidence is uncovered, the case would naturally be returned to your supervision."

Sir Richard appeared to be thinking it over, but that was for show. "What questions would those be?" he said, a Scottish burr rumbling beneath his words.

"To begin with, who killed the duke?"

"It's all in the record." Sir Richard made an impatient gesture. "Phineas Garvey, shipowner and India country trader until he went bankrupt. Tallant held his debts and had threatened to foreclose on his property.

Garvey's confession, and the fact he killed himself by swallowing the same obscure poison he slipped to the duke, wraps it up nice and tight."

"I mispoke. In your very *private* opinion, who did the murder?"

"Ah." For the first time, Sir Richard looked at him with approval. "You disagreed before, because of the woman, but I hold to my conviction that the victim's brother is responsible. A clever man, the new duke, and as wicked as his predecessor."

Varden agreed with that accessment, to a point. He just hadn't figured out where that point lay. "Go on, then. I've studied the official reports. What do you think really happened?"

"You won't like it." Sir Richard pulled a flask from his drawer. "Do sit down, Varden. I never knew a man who could stand so still for so long."

Like a statue in a church, he had been told. A statue of an archangel. Varden sat, draping his left arm over the chair back to appear relaxed, which he wasn't.

Sir Richard, after downing what he liked to call a medicinal wee dram, leaned forward with his elbows propped on his desk. "I'll use the names they had when the case was underway. From the time he arrived in London, Michael Keynes was heard to make threatening remarks concerning his brother. There was a confrontation at Tattersall's, witnessed by dozens of people."

"He made no secret of his intentions," Varden agreed. "You don't find that strange?"

"I'll get to his reasons for drawing attention to himself. Miranda Holcombe also had a grievance against the duke, who had laid claim to her family home and property because of debts owed him by her cousin. If you believe her story, Beast Tallant accosted her not long before the murder, she drew out a stiletto to protect herself, and he took it from her. That same knife was later found plunged into his heart."

"Old history, Sir Richard. Come to what I do not already know."

"Theatrical stuff, don't you think? And most of it staged in public before the killing. Too many things one would expect to be handled secretively were carried out in front of witnesses. The afternoon of the murder, Miss Holcombe went to the duke's house wearing a conspicuous blue cloak and bonnet. You had just delivered her to Palazzo Neri, but instead of waiting until you were out of sight, she climbed immediately into a hackney driven by a flamboyantly red-bearded chap who would be easy to trace. After reaching her destination, she instructed him to wait for her. She *wanted* to be observed."

Varden's stomach twisted. The facts had always troubled him, but his faith in Miranda Holcombe had never wavered. A man must trust the woman he loves. Whom else is she to rely on, when all the world turns against her?

"You were present at the lady's interrogation," Sir Richard said. "She was uncooperative. Evasive."

"I thought her to be exhausted. And the evidence shows she could not have poisoned the duke."

"The lady was a distraction. A red herring, dragged across our path by Michael Keynes to lay a false trail. His own confession had the same effect. He knew we'd learn it wasn't the knife that killed his brother, and that he, like Miss Holcombe, could not have done the poisoning."

"I take your point. Suspicion was sure to fall on him anyway, as heir to the title and fortune."

"Indeed. So he planned accordingly. In the weeks before the murder, he was often seen to drink excessively, and to take reckless actions. After his astonishing confession, he became the talk of London, and his sudden release fueled the fire. Beginning to end, he made the authorities look like bumblers."

"Perhaps we were. The evidence, when it had been

analyzed, contradicted his confession. We had no choice but to let him go."

"And how he enjoyed the humbuggery. Instantly he became one of those rogue heroes the public takes to its heart. What use is an investigation now? Even with new and compelling evidence in hand, it would be difficult for us to bring charges against him."

"The difficulty is irrelevant. If the evidence leads us to the duke, we shall proceed against him, never mind the public outcry."

"Easy enough for you to risk being discredited. An earl's position does not depend on appointment, election, or political favors. I, on the other hand, would become a laughingstock."

"You mean to sidestep your duty, Sir Richard?"

"I merely point out the price I am likely to pay for it. Keynes and the woman gulled us. They were in collusion from the first."

Sir Richard had expounded that same theory from the beginning, which had given Varden no high opinion of his judgment. Not at the time. But it may have been his own judgment gone missing. "You have proof of collusion?"

"Not enough of it, and all circumstantial. There was plenty of opportunity to conspire, of course, what with their cottages at Palazzo Neri located side by side. And because of your regard for the lady, I will grant you that it is possible she did not willingly cooperate. Keynes was seen to press his attentions on her. He may have threatened her father, or found some other way of coercing her. I've other grounds to substantiate my conclusions, but those, I expect, you would not be pleased to hear."

"I seek the truth, Sir Richard, whatever it may be."

"Noble sentiments, but the truth can be slippery. I expect you recall, because it was you requested my authorization, that Miss Holcombe visited Keynes in the Tower. Shortly after, she vanished. The evening of his release, Keynes disappeared as well. When next we saw them, here in this office, they were husband and wife."

Varden experienced, momentarily, the same shock and rage he'd felt when the new Duke of Tallant looked him in the eye and, with mocking amusement, announced the marriage.

"How did they strike you that afternoon?" Sir Richard said. "Their demeanor? Their dealings with each other?"

Varden could scarcely remember. He had wanted to look into Miranda Holcombe's eyes, to see in them her denial of Keynes's words. But to look at her would have broken him. He had not seen her since that day.

"They were cold," Sir Richard said irritably. "And when the murder was discussed, visibly angry. A clerk who saw them in the street reported that Keynes put her in the carriage and sent her off without him. They had been quarreling."

"That means nothing. It was a difficult time."

"When questioned, a servant at Palazzo Neri said that while they shared a cottage after the marriage, they did not share a bedchamber. Then they went south to the Tallant estate, where they also kept separate quarters. The new duke spent notably little time at the house. For that we have the testimony of the butler, who has since been dismissed."

"I can see why." Blood pounded in Varden's ears. The office went dim. He saw only Miranda, forced to wed, now trapped in a loveless marriage with a blackguard.

"You are starting to believe me," Sir Richard said.

"Perhaps." Varden rose. "The investigation will be reopened, unofficially. You are to tell no one of my interest in the case, or that it is being looked into. When I require information, you must find a way to provide it without arousing suspicion. In exchange, should I find evidence that leads to a conviction, you will receive all the credit."

"Fair enough. But take care. If the duke suspects you are on to him, you could become his next victim."

With a nod, Varden left the office, his mind spinning with what he had learned.

He wanted Michael Keynes to be guilty. Miranda to be innocent, so that he could rescue her. How could justice be done, with so prejudiced an investigator?

But Sir Richard was unreliable as well, ambitious and overeager to prove himself right. And Wellington, who had no horse in this race, had launched the inquiry and then detached himself entirely.

So it was down to him, Varden thought. In honor he had accepted the task, and in honor he must pursue it without regard for his own interest. It would be a test of his integrity, that was certain, and put him at war with his every inclination.

When he reached the street and had got the attention of a hackney driver, he started to wonder where he should go next. The rest of the day stretched out like a wasteland, all the way to nine o'clock and his appointment with Helena Pryce. He realized, with astonishment, that his anticipation of being with her had been vibrating at a low pitch beneath everything he had done since last he saw her.

There was plenty for him to accomplish, of course, but he'd already spent too many mind-numbing hours poring over records and piecing together information. He needed to clear his head. Stretch his muscles. Perhaps he should take advantage of the pleasant weather and enjoy a long ride in the country.

Shortly after two o'clock, Varden arrived at Banstead Downs and began looking for the private road that would take him to his destination.

When he'd gone home to change into riding clothes, it had occurred to him this would be a good time to find out a little more about the mysterious Miss Pryce. Another piece of the puzzle, to lay beside the information Charley Trotter would collect for him tomorrow.

She had attended the Linford Sisters' Academy for Young Ladies, he remembered from their first interview, and the heading on her letter of recommendation from Miss Lily Linford had referred to the village of Woodmanstone in Surrey. No more than fifteen miles from London, with a good road most of the way. He'd decided to pay a call.

A man repairing a fence provided directions, and soon he had made his way along a tree-lined road that passed through well-kept grounds before ending at a large greystone building. About a dozen girls playing some sort of a game with a ball stopped to watch him dismount, pass the reins to an ostler who came out from the stable, and walk up the stairs. From behind him, he heard exclamations and giggles.

It was his bad luck to arrive at a change of classes. A bell clanged, and immediately after, girls of various ages began swarming along the passageways and the twin staircases at either side of the entrance hall where he was standing. With no idea where to go, he could only remain where he stood, the center of their fervid attention, until a plump, gray-haired woman appeared and herded them off with the efficiency of a Border Collie.

When things had quieted down and he had explained the reason for his call, the same woman led him outside again and to a pretty limestone cottage where the elder Miss Linford, now retired, tended her garden and hosted afternoon teas for the senior girls.

"Oh, you are most welcome," Miss Linford assured him, brushing off his apology. "I'm not so dotty that I'd turn a handsome earl from my doorstep, never mind the lack of notice." And then she set him a basin and towel, to wash off the dirt of the road, while she bustled around the kitchen preparing tea.

Miss Linford was much like his mother, he was thinking, but without a brace of servants to do the work. For the next half hour, she all but forced him to sample scones and poppyseed cake and apple tarts while she chattered about the school she and her three sisters had built, little by little, over the last forty years.

Finally he was able to direct the conversation to the reason he'd come.

"Helena Pryce?" Miss Linford looked pleased. "But of course I remember her. She was with us nearly ten years. We asked her to stay on after, as a teacher, but she declined. Just as well. A young woman of her talents requires a larger garden to flourish. But what is it you wish to know? I cannot betray any confidence, although in her case, I have little information. She came from obscurity, and when she left, we heard no more of her, save the letter I receive each year from her at Christmas. It says only that she is doing well, and that she continues to appreciate our kindness while she was with us."

"She has recently taken employment with my family," he said, treading a thin line of truth. "But my position in the government requires that I secure her history and references. It was she who directed me to your school."

"Ah." The lines around her faded blue eyes wrinkled as she smiled. "She asked you to call?"

"She supplied the letter of character you wrote. I am here on my own initiative, primarily because"—he cast about for a reasonable explanation—"because I wish to discover if Miss Pryce has relatives that might prove difficult, were they to appear at some time in the future."

"I shouldn't think so. In fact, her lack of connections nearly caused us to turn her away, as is our policy." Miss Linford wagged a thin finger at him. "You needn't look so disapproving, my lord. There is good reason for it, in cases where the family resides abroad. Should misfortune befall them, as too often occurs where the air and water are bad, then what is to become of the young girl in our care? We cannot throw her onto the streets, but neither can we afford to maintain her year after year. The school does well now, but twenty years ago, when Miss Pryce first came to us, we had quite a struggle to remain open."

"Where was it her family lived?"

"India. Her mother had recently died of a fever and her father, fearing for the child's health, brought her to England, and to us. A tall, well-spoken man, Mr. Phillip Pryce, with a nose on him that one cannot help but remember. Our conversation was satisfactory, and the child exhibited intelligence and excellent manners. But when he told us of his intention to return to India, I explained that we would require legal documents from a relation or temporary guardian here in England, guaranteeing payment of her fees or the provision of a satisfactory home, should that become necessary."

"And he was unable to provide such guarantees?"

"There was no one, he said, to whom he might apply. No family on his wife's side, nor on his. And he could pay only six months' fees in advance, because the long voyage would keep him from his business for more than a year, with a consequent loss of income. I sympathized, of course, but what could I do? My sisters would never permit an exception to be made."

He accepted another scone, since it appeared to please her, and waited politely for her to continue. Miss Linford liked to stretch out her stories, keeping him in suspense so that he would remain a little longer. He recognized the tactic. Grandmere did the same, only in French.

"Although Mr. Pryce was displeased, he made no protest. I remember that he stood and held out his hand for the child to take. She was a weedy girl, all arms and legs, and of course, those odd spectacles. But everything had changed, you see."

Everything had changed. That was something he might have said, directly after Miss Pryce entered or left a room. "How so?"

"I cannot perfectly describe the sensation. She had been well-behaved throughout the interview, and answered my questions with the sort of precise intelligence you must have observed in your dealings with her. But beneath that uncommon self-restraint, she pulsated with energy. With *longing.* She greatly wanted to remain at the school. Later, being refused, she gave no sign of her disappointment. Indeed, she behaved just as she had done before. But inside the room, the air had gone thin. The colors had paled. It was as if her departure would take away all that was vibrant and hopeful. I could not let her go."

"I know how it is with sisters, Miss Linford. Did yours make a great fuss when you put aside the school's policy and accepted Miss Pryce?"

"Indeed they did, although they could not keep it up for long. She came first in all her classes, never got into trouble, and was always willing to be of service. That endeared her to the teachers, as you can imagine, but her fine qualities set the other students against her. Young girls can be quite cruel, Lord Varden. Many of them shunned her, and the mean-spirited ones mocked her appearance. 'Witch-eyes,' they called her."

He did not like hearing this. Did not like imagining Helena, worth more than the lot of them, being mistreated by the other girls. Eton had not been a picnic for him, for some of the same reasons. He had been studious, obedient, and his appearance brought undue attention to his person. No one shunned a wealthy earl-to-be, but the boys had put him to the test. Constantly. Painfully.

"Once," Miss Linford said, "five girls dragged her into the copse beside the river and tried to rip off her spectacles. She screamed and screamed, and fought them like a demon. I was nearby with another teacher. We rushed to help, coming close enough to see her seize a rock from the ground and strike the girl who had one hand on the spectacles. That stopped the fight immediately."

Miss Linford paused long enough to refill his teacup. "Four of the girls were sent down. The other, frightened by what was occurring, had run off when the trouble began. She was put on probation."

"As I understand it," he said, "the slightest exposure to light would do great damage to Miss Pryce's eyes."

"So we had been told by her father. We'd always made special provisions to darken her room, and after the attack, her door was fitted with a lock. But there was no further trouble. Some of the older girls set themselves to protect her, if not befriend her, and she was left to pursue her studies. She craved knowledge of every sort. We had to arrange for her to use the vicar's library, which was more extensive than ours, and the local gentlemen sent over their newspapers when they had finished reading them."

"What of Mr. Pryce? Did he return to England?"

"We never had another word from him, nor were there letters for his daughter. But every six months a bank draft arrived, sufficient for her fees and a meager clothing allowance. The funds did not allow for extras—private lessons in music or art, excursions, the maintenance of a horse—until she asked if we could provide a fencing instructor. She was, I believe, ten years old at the time. It was shortly after the attack. I thought it a foolish notion, but she insisted. 'I might need to fight a duel,' she said. And at that moment, I thought her capable of doing so. We eventually found someone to teach her the rudiments, and later, a retired fencing master agreed to give her lessons. I often wonder if she kept it up."

The image of a slim form, deadly grace, fierce determination. Of her taking care not to insult him, or harm him, as he struggled to wield a foil with his left hand. "I expect Miss Pryce does not easily let go of anything she cares about." He folded his napkin, laid it on the table, and rose. "I beg your pardon, but I must be on the road for London. You have been most kind, Miss Linford, to receive me."

She went with him all the way to the stable, fussing a little because he would be riding back in the dark. "Will you give Miss Pryce my fond regards?" she asked as he swung onto the saddle.

Lying had never come easily to him, even in politics, where it was practically the native language. "In fact, I think she would not be pleased to know I have spoken with you," he said, smiling. "I must compete with others who wish to employ her, so you understand my dilemma."

"She was ever protective of her privacy," Miss Linford conceded after a moment. "Very well. I'll not mention your visit, but should she ever inquire—"

"You must tell her the truth, of course. It is no great secret. I bid you good day, Miss Linford, and thank you again for your hospitality."

The road to London also led him to his appointment with Helena, now only a few hours away, and for the entire journey, he thought of little else. He could not remember, in all his life, when he had looked forward to anything quite so much.

But in between the anticipation, the planning of his strategy and the rehearsal of the arguments meant to convince her to return to him, he thought of the lonely child with witch-eyes, shunned by some of her fellows, tormented by others, and in all those years, never so much as a letter from her father.

Unbearable thoughts. Almost, they made him forget what he had not yet learned to endure—the constant, incalculable pain in his hand.

"You will feel it anyway," the Sikh physician had told him, giving him the choice. "In the wars, I have severed countless arms and legs, hands and feet. It is a mystery, that what vanishes in the flesh remains constant in memory and sensation. But survivors tell always the same unfortunate tale. If I amputate, you lose only the hand. The mind experiences what the hand would feel, were it still there."

So he'd decided he might as well keep the hand and accustom himself to the pain. He would have to, wouldn't he?

Chapter 10

The Earl of Sothingdon's imposing town house in Grosvenor Street, a beehive of workmen in the daytime, stood silent and nearly deserted after dark. On the ground floor, Helena had built a fire in the parlor, set out a decanter of claret, and selected a chair with a view out the French windows to the terrace garden. The curtains were open a few inches so that she could see Varden when he came through the back gate.

The glass of wine meant to steady her nerves sat untouched on the side table. All day she had been on edge, unable to eat, her mood swinging between excitement and dread. She ought not to be meeting him at night. Alone. And in, of all places, the very room where Lady Jessica had once waited for her secret lover. Jessica, of course, had made Lord Duran climb over the garden wall.

That had been nearly eight years ago, just after Helena passed her twentieth birthday. Jessica, a year older and resolved to be independent of her troubled family, had reluctantly moved into Sothingdon House at her father's insistence, although she intended to repay him when she could. Independence, as Helena could have told her from experience, was virtually impossible to sustain without funds. Few positions, save those carried out on one's back, were available to females, and an earl's daughter was not employable in any case. Knowing she would have to create a job for herself, Jessica chose to become a broker of art and antiquities, the only difficulty being that she knew next to nothing about them.

Later, she often said that her first decision, hiring Helena Pryce from an agency to be her secretary, was the best decision she ever made. Working for cheese-paring wages, Helena procured the books they both studied, selected instructors, and created thick volumes of information for Jessica to reference in her work.

They had been friends, after a fashion, and still were. But while the difference in rank never concerned Jessica, Helena always took care to hold a distance from her employer. She had always understood that she would spend her entire life as a servant, if an elevated and specialized servant, and that no position would be permanent.

During the few weeks of Lady Jessica's affair with Hugo Duran, Helena had been sure she would soon be back at the agency, hiring herself out by the day or the week. But then, as swiftly as he came into Jessica's life, Duran vanished without a trace. Bereft and pretending otherwise, Jessica threw herself into her work, eventually making a great success of it. And Helena had profited as well, with Jessica insisting she accept generous bonuses to make up for all the years of working practically for free.

But what Helena had anticipated finally came to pass. Hugo Duran returned, swept Jessica off her feet for a second time, and married her. Their newborn daughter had been named, so they imagined, for the secretary whose services were no longer required, although Helena would always have a place with them. Even her rooms at Sothingdon House were to be maintained. It was pride that demanded that she take her leave. When the workmen had finished the renovation, she would return only to pay the occasional friendly call on her former employers.

For now, alone in their home, she couldn't help reflecting on the lesson she ought to have learned when Jessica, willful and reckless, gave her body and her heart to a man who all too soon abandoned her. On the nights when Jessica was waiting in this room, perhaps in this very chair, for Duran, Helena had been alone in her cold bed, imagining what it would be like to have a lover. She'd hear them walk together up the creaky stairs to Jessica's rooms, hear the soft murmurs and the laughter before they closed the door, and then it was all down to her imagination.

Envy had sucked at her marrow. What man would ever want the unbeautiful, socially unacceptable, sharp-tongued Helena Pryce? Jessica was so lucky, and so very brave, to risk everything for love. Then Duran vanished, and for a few weeks of happiness, Jessica paid with six years of pain and loneliness.

As for Helena, her envy had vanished right along with Duran. If Jessica, the beautiful and spirited daughter of an earl, could not hold the affection of the man she loved, what chance had—

Never mind. She had been granted her own miracle when Jamie took her under his protection and saw to her education. And then she'd been given a night of riotous passion with the most desirable man in England. She mustn't be greedy. Varden, stronger than he thought and more vulnerable than he would admit, had troubles of his own. The last thing he needed at this time was the distraction of a purely sexual affair with a servant. But he did require a compass and a destination, and those she could safely provide.

A sound from outside, a tall figure approaching the French windows. With a flutter of anticipation, she went to raise the latch.

After a small bow of acknowledgment he stepped

inside, mysterious in a black greatcoat, a woolen scarf muffling his neck and chin, and a wide-brimmed hat that hid his conspicuous hair. He propped his silver-handled cane against the wall and reached out his arms.

"Helena." An invitation in his soft, slightly husky tone. A caress.

Temptation in a single word.

Her heartbeat picked up. Backing away, she raised her hands, palms out, as if to fend him off.

He halted immediately, a shadow of pain darkening his face. "Are we not alone here?"

"That isn't . . . the point. This is a meeting to discuss business and matters of—of politics."

"Yes. But that needn't be all. Should not be."

Her mouth felt dry. "It must be all. You have forgotten our agreement. That night was a time out of time, never to return."

"I've not forgotten. If I agreed, it was because you wished it. But I see no reason why we must be bound by that condition now." A small hesitation. "Unless you regret what we did together."

"I . . . No." It would have been easier to lie, but she could not. "I will always treasure the memory of those hours. But they cannot be repeated."

"Why?"

He was relentless. "Because . . . Oh, there are a hundred reasons. We cannot, either of us, afford such self-indulgence. The cost is too high. For nearly two years you have neglected your responsibilities. Now you must turn all your attention to them."

"Another lecture? You have persuaded me to take up my duties, and I am doing so to a degree that would astonish you. But I am not an automaton, Helena. You have stirred in me a desire unlike any I have experienced. Don't ask me to pretend there is nothing between us."

She had not imagined this, or prepared herself for

it. "I was there for your loneliness," she said after a time. "And for your anger, and your impatience with yourself. I roused your temper, that is all."

A curve of his lips. "Not quite all, my dear. Then or now. But if you have retreated into your own castle and pulled up the drawbridge, I've no choice but to remain outside. And, I should warn you, to mount a siege."

"Exactly so, my lord. We must remain apart. But without the siege, if you don't mind." It was the sort of civilized flirtation she heard at Palazzo Neri, undercurrents pulsing beneath the light words with their several meanings. She understood the game, but she could not play it. "Did you come here only for—for that, or might we proceed with other matters?"

"I am yours, Miss Pryce." He removed his hat and scarf, peeled off his greatcoat, and laid them across a table. "Do you wish to put me in my place?"

"Over there." She pointed to a chair across from hers, with a long, low table set between them, and brought a lamp from the mantelpiece to place on it. The light would illuminate his face and leave her own in shadow, which she knew because she'd experimented.

He sat at his ease, one long leg crossed over the other, his arms extended along the padded arms of the chair and his gloved hands draping over the ends. He looked relaxed, save for the brightness in his eyes and a wariness she had come to recognize in him. He knew, as she knew, that they would be fencing tonight. Not with swords, but with words and intentions and schemes. She felt her blood rise at the prospect.

"Last night," she began in a clipped voice, "you indicated a willingness to help advance a number of legal reforms that have languished in Parliament. I thought you might believe there was merit in the bills. Now I wonder if your support was offered in the expectation of payment—of a particular kind—in return."

"I hadn't considered that." He raised a quizzical brow. "Would it work?"

"No." And then she wondered if she might, indeed, trade herself to advance her cause. Or use that as an excuse to— "No," she said again, more firmly. "But you will, of course, wish to be compensated."

"Why do you assume that?" He looked mildly offended. "If the cause is just and the reforms in the interest of the nation, I would support the bills as a matter of principle."

"Yes, but I speak of *active* support, and you won't win friends by it. The most punitive judicial sentences are unmerited and seldom employed, but conservatives in both houses of Parliament demand the right to hang perpetrators of minor crimes in order to make examples of them. People are being executed on a whim, sir. Or when a few shopkeepers complain loudly enough, or because a judge is out of temper that day."

"You needn't convince me, my dear. I will do as you ask, because you ask. But you must direct me to the bills I need to resurrect and provide the information I require to be effective."

"Of course." She felt suddenly light, as if a weight had been lifted from her. *He had consented!* "I have prepared reports, copies of bills, lists of those who support them, those opposed, and those uncommitted. Facts, history, numbers . . . several portfolios of information. If you require anything that is not there, I shall provide it. Should I have the materials delivered to Richmond?"

"At present, I am staying in Great Ryder Street." He drew a slim gold case from an inner pocket in his jacket, removed an engraved card, and placed it on the table near the lamp. "It is too much to expect, I suppose, that you would deliver the documents personally?"

Anticipating a long debate about the political stakes, with arguments lined up in her magpie mind to counter any possible objections, she hardly knew how to deal with instant capitulation. Especially when it carried a sting in its tail. Nothing would pass between them, she was beginning to understand, without an invitation to his bed.

She decided to ignore his provocative suggestion in favor of a question she had been longing to ask. "Might I inquire, sir, what is to become of the castle?"

A slight frown. "I was forced to accept that little can be accomplished this time of year. But a reliable caretaker must be employed to prevent my neighbors from dismantling what has been rebuilt and hauling away the materials. Again."

"Shall I find you one?" A chance to repay him without removing her clothes.

"I wish you would. In fact, I want you to come back to work for me, under the same terms we originally set. This time, I promise, you'll not be farmed off to my family."

"Under the circumstances, sir, that cannot be a good idea."

"Why do you think so? Surely you don't fear I'll lose control of myself?"

More likely she'd lose control of her frail powers of resistance. "It is as I told you last night. So long as attention is not called, gentlemen may employ me without their reputations, or mine, being questioned. But should I return to your service now, after being shuffled off and then dismissed—"

He raised a hand. "I have told no one of your dismissal. As for the shuffling, well, everyone will put it down to the temporary madness that sent me off to the Mendips. You kindly assisted my mother and sister until I returned to my senses, and to London."

And no one will guess you made wild love to me, and that you want to do so again. Even I cannot credit it. She looked down at her hands, folded neatly on her lap, amazed that the storms raging inside her made no waves on the surface.

The money was greatly needed. So many people depended on her. And how easily she could rationalize her way into doing anything he asked. "I shall consider your offer," she said with a snap in her voice. "But before I could possibly accept, modifications to our previous contract will be required."

"A rise in salary, I take it." He looked amused.

"A *significant* increase, with an advance payment in case you decided to hare off again. Rules for public behavior, because when the Season is underway, you will inevitably come under scrutiny. And a secret means of communication must be found. If I work for you, no one must know it."

"Is that necessary? Is it even possible?"

"If you cooperate, yes. I have experience with clandestine affai—transactions, at least in the short term. If it comes about at all, ours will be a temporary relationship."

"So you keep telling me, although you have already written a conclusion to the best part of it. You may assume I will accept your terms, whatever they may be. I am sure you do not intend to exploit my good nature."

"I'm afraid I do." Honesty sat on her shoulder like an annoying cherub, dictating truths she'd rather not admit to. "I shall try to prove worth the trouble I hope to cause you."

"I've no doubt you will. But if I am to pay heavily for the privilege of being exploited, I expect a few concessions as well. While you are always free to speak your mind, and to try to change mine, you will ultimately do my bidding. And there is one service, out of the ordinary scope of your position, that you will provide me several times a week. We shall need to find a place where we'll not be disturbed."

The service wasn't what he wanted her to think, she knew. Or was fairly sure she knew. Since he entered the room, there had been another conversation going on between the words, at the level where she breathed, and where her blood flowed. It was meant to arouse her, which it did. The air tickled her skin like feathers, as his lips had done, and his fingers, before his weight came on her, and his power—

"Helena?"

She looked up at him with burning eyes. "You refer to fencing, of course."

"Of course." A provocative, intimate smile. They both knew where crossing swords had led them. "But time enough to seek our dueling ground after you have come to a decision. Do you still require time to consider?"

She didn't, but thought she had better reserve some on the chance she recovered her wits and decided to be sensible. "Yes. But I'll not keep you waiting long."

Chapter 11

Standing at his bedchamber window, Varden looked out at a gray, wet morning that matched his mood. He had spent a lonely, restless night wishing he were elsewhere, in another bed.

He had not expected Helena to reject him. They had shared something extraordinary, a passion that carried them beyond desire, beyond pleasure, to a realm he had not known existed . . . until she took him there. How could she turn her back on him, as if that night had no significance? As if it were not to be remembered, never to be revisited? Hours of trying to figure it out, of trying to figure *her* out, just left him all the more frustrated.

In the dressing room, Theodophilos Partridge was laying out shaving gear. Varden yawned, stretched, and prepared himself for another round of unspoken servantly disapproval. "I'll not have a shave now," he said. "I'm staying in this morning, perhaps all day. Arrange for breakfast to be served in the study at eight."

Partridge sniffed, as if the day had taken on a strange odor. Then, with the reverence of one bearing the crown jewels, he took the basin and pitcher of steaming water and marched from the room.

Not too bad, Varden thought as he put on a loose shirt, trousers, slippers, and a quilted dressing gown.

He had employed Partridge because there was no more skillful valet in England, and because after a lifetime of obsequious servants, he appreciated the novelty of disdain.

A fire was blazing in the hearth when he entered his study, and coffee arrived moments after, along with a footman carrying a silver tray. On it was a copy of the *Times*, Varden's morning post, and a thin packet, simply wrapped and bound with twine. He reached for it immediately, his fingertips tingling with awareness. From Helena. Her consent to remain in his service. He fumbled with the knot until the young footman took scissors from the desk and cut the twine.

Inside were perhaps a dozen sheets of paper folded in half. He flipped through them, puzzled. There was no mistaking her handwriting, firm and precise, with a touch of feminine elegance. But she said nothing about his offer. This was an index, an annotated table of contents, every item related to the legal reforms he had agreed to support.

"The rest is in a box, milord. It wouldn't fit on the tray."

"Bring it in, then," he said, disappointment rasping his voice.

The box was large and had been delivered shortly after dawn, the footman told him, by a havey-cavey fellow with bushy eyebrows. Varden read over the index while picking at his breakfast. Then he settled in a comfortable chair by the fire, the open box beside him, and began to work his way through the papers.

After two hours absorbed in facts, numbers, history, and analysis, he roused himself long enough to ring for more coffee and make a few circuits of the small room, shaking out his tense muscles. Reading her work, the product—he could tell—of dedicated research, was something like making love to her mind. No substitute for the real thing, to be sure, but it helped illuminate why she fascinated him to so great a degree.

He admired the devotion she had poured into this work, and the dispassion with which she presented it. In her meticulous accounting, English justice was evaluated by standards higher than those commonly found in practice, with no quarter given for rank, privilege, or good intentions. The same evenhanded analysis was applied throughout an invaluable document that no official would ever bother to read, let alone appreciate, because it had been produced by a female.

Helena required . . . well, *him*. Or someone like him, willing to be her voice in places where no one would listen to her. She must have set her sights on him long ago. Picked him out, evaluated him with the same thoroughness with which she approached any project, and watched for an opportunity to insinuate herself into his company.

He thought back to their first interview, and how she had known his former secretary was to be married, and that a position had opened. He ought to have asked her, later, how she so quickly passed the test he had set for her. Helena Pryce redefined tenacity. When he disappointed her by withdrawing to the castle, she came after him. Dared him to take up his responsibilities. Bribed him with the offer of her lithe, eager body, which he had—

No. It hadn't been like that. Or, it might have been, if she were more clever and devious than anyone he'd ever known. Which, come to think of it, she was.

So now, having enchanted him, she withheld her favors to entice him all the more. Wanting her—and heaven help him, he did—what would he not concede in order to have her again? She had manipulated him with devastating ease.

He ought to mind, he was sure, more than he did. But she was what she was, and he desired her.

He realized that he was circling the room like a child's windup toy, his dressing gown swirling about his ankles. With a shrug, he kept going. She might have him twisting himself into knots, but by God, she also made him feel alive.

Why shouldn't he give her what she wanted? It cost him nothing. For a change, he was satisfyingly useful. And it wasn't as if they could ever be more than temporary associates, in business or in bed.

Within three quarters of a year, he would stand before an altar with the new Countess of Varden and surrender what little freedom he had claimed for himself the last two years. In the interim, it would please him to give what time was left into Helena's keeping.

"I was expectin' an earl to be having a bigger house," said Tommie Trotter when the footman ushered him into Varden's study at nine o'clock the next morning. The Runner, swathed in coat and muffler against the snow, was precisely on time.

Varden nearly laughed. "I'm sorry to disappoint you. Did Miss Pryce go on her rounds yesterday, in spite of the storm?"

"A cyclone might stop 'er. Not much else. I wrote out where she went."

Varden took the report, two pages inscribed in pencil, and carried it to the window for examination. Times, places with their directions, the occasional name. It might have been the record of a shopping excursion. "You will have to clarify these locations. What precisely is Teale's?"

"A house, milord, belongin' to one Mrs. Dora Teale. It was used to be a fancy house until she had a Methodist conversion, as she tells it. Now it be a residence for doxies takin' the cure."

"And Miss Pryce's business there?"

"She went in, stayed more'n an hour, and come out again."

Varden tapped his finger against the papers. "This won't do. I understand you could not follow her inside, but clearly you know more than you are telling. Who will hire you when it becomes known that you withhold relevant information?"

The Runner's mouth twisted. "Ought not to have taken this job. Knew it, but figured you'd just hire some fellow what had no respect for the lady. She went the same places she always goes on Tuesdays. I heard she lived for a time at Teale's, back when she were a girl. Don't know it for a fact."

Lived in a whorehouse? He skimmed the list again, saw a name he'd missed the first time. Good God. "And Molly Buttons's establishment? Did she reside there as well?"

"Not that I ever heard. There be three other places like it. You can tell 'em by the names. She stopped in, but only a little time."

Nine Lilies. Tup and Ewe. The Warming Pan. He had never set foot in a brothel, but his virginal lover ran tame in half a dozen of them. No wonder she knew the use of contraceptive devices. He took a moment to still his quick breathing and his anger.

"The Hairy Dog's a tavern," said Trotter. "Puddles be a gin shop, and so be Tom Dick's. Most of the shops got no names on 'em, bein' that only the people what lives in Seven Dials goes into them. The ones you want t'know about be in Lomber Court. I wrote what they are, startin' with the secondhand shop. What's important is what's upstairs. All the upper stories be owned by one man, he what used to be a bishop."

Trotter glanced up, a grin on his face. "That be the man what runs the flash, or his slice of it. A chief of pickpockets, robbers, thieves, bawds, and whatever else he has in his keepin'. Not so much in the games now, is Jamie Carr, but he's got a finger in near every Rookery pie. Miss Pryce keeps a room in his crib, and most times stays there on Tuesday nights."

"If Carr is a known criminal, why is he not in prison?"

"For one thing, he don't do the crimes hisself. And he keeps order where there wouldn't be none without 'im."

"Do you know the man?"

"Aye, to wave a hand to when we pass on the street. A tall drink of a fellow, with a nose on 'im like an ax head. Can pass for a toff, can Jamie, or a man of law. Has the tongue, and the learnin'. Come down from Scotland mebbe twenty-five years ago, and nobody knows what he did afore that."

"I see." He could hardly bring himself to ask. "And Miss Pryce remained in his—his building last night?"

"She went in, and a little after, they both came out. Walked to where the lady left her carriage and climbed in. Rainin' in sheets, it was, and I all but lost 'em. But a hack come by, and I rode up on the box, and we followed 'em to Newgate."

Brothels. Gin palaces. A lair of thieves. A notorious prison. On any given Tuesday, Helena Pryce had more adventures than he'd had in his entire life.

"I found a good place to watch," Trotter said. "They got out and was havin' a disagreement. I couldn't hear the words, but seemed like she wanted to go with him, and he were pointing her to get back in the carriage. She finally did, and he were gone mebbe an hour. The rain had stopped when he come back with a face full of trouble. She run over and he told her somethin' that made her cry. Couldn't see her eyes with them glasses, but she were shakin', and he wrapped his arms around her. After a time, they got back in the carriage. She left him off in Seven Dials and went to the other earl's house what be in Grosvenor Street. I watched 'til midnight, but she never come out."

Varden turned to the window to conceal his face from the Runner. Yesterday, while he had been lounging warm in his study, drinking rich coffee laced with cognac and reading her accounts of English injustice, Helena was getting news about a prisoner. News that made her weep.

It was personal, then, this crusade of hers. She had denied it, even as she traded herself for his influence.

But he was rushing his fences. All he had were a few details from a Runner determined to tell him as little as possible, and his own guesses, which were not altogether reliable.

"Very well," he said, crossing to his desk. "Your assignment is satisfactorily completed. But I shall double your wages in exchange for a little information about Newgate Gaol. How do I go about finding and meeting the person Jamie Carr visited? And how do I keep my interest in the matter confidential?"

Chapter 12

An hour later, flanked by a pair of liveried footmen and rigged out to impress, Varden set forth in his crested coach for Newgate.

Folded inside his breast pocket were banknotes to be used as bribes. He'd committed to memory the names of prison officials and their government superiors, had a general idea of the prison's layout, and in a reluctant gesture of trust, Trotter had confided the false identity Jamie Carr assumed when masquerading as a solicitor. All the rest was up to the Earl of Varden who, Trotter had assured him, could swan his way to wherever he wanted to go with a lavish display of rank and money.

His wardrobe, servants, and lordliness got him through the gate and into the presence of the keeper of Newgate, self-proclaimed emperor of this squalid underworld. Two narrow eyes fixed him with greedy curiosity.

"I am looking for a prisoner," Varden said, "one visited yesterday by his solicitor, Mr. Silas Jones."

"And you be?"

"Varden. The Earl of Varden. I'm afraid I have forgotten the name of Mr. Jones's client. Can you direct me to him?"

"Well, now, I'd have to think on it. Lots of visitors

in and out of here. I might be needing somethin' to stir me mem'ry."

Varden contrived to look befuddled. "I can't imagine what would do that. I've been trying all morning to remember the name Mr. Jones provided me."

"Most times, milord, me mem'ry works best when money drops into me hand."

"Oh." An enlightened smile. "I brought very little, I'm afraid. It may not be sufficient. But I am most eager to visit the prisoner—"

The Keeper accepted a banknote, his gaze on the three others Varden was holding. "Not the Common area, if I recalls rightly. Jones went to the State area, where we house them that can pay for better quarters. I could hire a guide to take you there."

Varden forked over another note. "Will that get me to the prisoner I seek?"

"To him, yes." The Keeper's tongue snaked out to moisten his lips. "But if you crave to speak with him in privacy, that's another thing. Do you require to be in the cell? I can tell you now, that will cost more than you've taken out of your pocket. Ten pounds, milord, to get what you want."

The real thieves, it seemed, were on the wrong side of the bars. And the pimps as well, Varden realized while he was counting out the exorbitant sum. He opened his mouth to correct the Keeper's assumption, but figured it was a waste of time. Why else would an earl be visiting a felon whose name he didn't know? "I require a little information," he said instead. "His identity, the details of his case, family connections . . ."

The Keeper opened a ledger and flipped through the pages. "Here he be. Billy Barnes, fifteen years, no family. Took for nicking a gentleman's silver watch, and for stealing from a chemist shop a quantity of aqua fortis later used in an assault on two women. He's to be brought to the bar at the March Sessions,

Old Bailey, on . . . ah, tomorrow. And Edward Noggins be the judge. Bad luck, that. Noose Noggins, they calls him. No need to tell you why. You want to see another than Billy Barnes, milord? A boy what might be available a bit longer?"

"You are under a misapprehension," Varden said, his jaw stiff with anger. "I have no unorthodox designs on Master Barnes. I am here only to fulfill my Christian duty. The corporal works of mercy instruct us to visit the imprisoned."

"Aye." The Keeper looked doubtful. "It's just that you've not been visiting before now."

"There are rather a number of merciful corporal works. I am working my way through them."

That effectively concluded their business together. No refund was forthcoming, probably because the Keeper didn't believe his story, and to be sure, his motives had nothing whatever to do with Christian charity. He was here for Helena, and keen to make sure she never learned of it. Before leaving the office he made clear to the Keeper what his fate would be, should he breathe a word that the Earl of Varden had set foot in Newgate or inquired about a prisoner.

More bribes were required before a mute keeper with a lantern led him into the bowels of the prison. Screams, oaths, and pleas for help assaulted him from all sides, and the stench forced him to hold his breath until he couldn't any longer. Then he had to fight the urge to cast up his accounts. At last they came to the end of a long passageway, turned a corner, and he was faced with a heavy wooden door. A grate, about eye level and the size of a facecloths, gave him a view of a tiny, dimly lit cell. On a pallet against the opposite wall, a figure lay huddled under several blankets.

It was still in the same position when Varden was admitted to the cell and the door had been closed behind him. He paused to take stock of the accommodations. Stone walls pocked with oaths and messages dug out by prisoners. A rough floor, also stone. A slop bucket in one corner, explaining the stench. In another corner lay a bowl containing what looked to be congealed stew, a ragged chunk of bread, and a mug with unknown contents. Beside the untouched meal, a dirty lamp glowed like a dying coal.

"Master Barnes," he said in a firm tone. "Where are your manners?"

A noise like a frightened animal's cry, a twisting of blankets, and then a disheveled head popped out.

"On your feet, young man."

The boy scrambled up, his straw-colored hair sticking out like fork tines. He was all bones and sharp angles, sunken cheeks and pallid skin. "B-be it time, then?"

Varden was about to ask "Time for what?" when he understood. "Not yet," he said, keeping his voice level. "You haven't eaten your dinner."

Blue eyes glanced at the dishes without interest. "They brought it yesterday, or mebbe some other day. I weren't 'ungry."

"Unfortunate, but unacceptable. You may sit, if you prefer." Varden went to the grate, stuck out a finger to beckon one of his servants, and issued an order. When he turned back, the boy was still on his feet. Teetering a bit, but erect. He had pride. "Very well, Master Barnes, let us get to it. You are accused of stealing a pocket watch. Did you do it?"

"Aye." No hesitation. "And I filched a bottle of aquiforty from the shop, but I don' know zactly what it be. An' I dint know they meaned to squirt it on some ladies, and that it would burn up their clothes. Me mates tol' me to filch it, an' I wanted 'em to think I be clever, so I did it. An' I gived it them, but the watch nabbed me afore I could run away. The ladies wasn't hurt, though. Mister Jamie tol' me so."

"Does that make it better?"

"Not for what I did. Better for the ladies, though."

The boy's nose wrinkled. "I'd have felt real bad if they was hurt. I think about that a lot."

Varden imagined one of his sisters wrapping this skinny, terrified boy in her arms and assuring him that he had nothing to fear. But Billy Barnes had everything to fear. A trial before a punitive judge on the morrow, and within three days, a public hanging. "Did it mean so much," he asked, genuinely wondering, "to be thought of as clever by friends who would injure a woman for the fun of it?"

"No!" The first sign of fire flashed in the boy's eyes. "I never knew they was that sort. I took the aquiforty for the same reason I took the pocket watch. I be small and useless and pretty like a girl. It's hard, when you gots to live in the streets, to be like that."

Other people's expectations dictating one's choices. The treadmill of always trying to measure up. Varden knew precisely how that was. "Yes, it's hard. But you must still do what is right. That's what makes you a man."

"I be no good at it, then. Mebbe as well I be hanged. Mister Jamie says I gots to be, for what I done. He be bringin' t'other lads to see me swing so's they won't do like I done. I's to be an abject lesson. An' he says I gots to be brave, but I don' feel brave. I feels skeered."

"Fear is not shameful. Courage is doing the best you can when you are terribly afraid. But if your body is weak, Master Barnes, your pride will be weak as well. From now until they take you out, you must eat every bit of food given you. Is that understood?"

In reply, the boy untangled his feet from the blankets and shuffled toward the corner where the bowl and its repulsive contents lay.

"Not that," Varden said quickly. "It's gone bad. Are you acquainted with Miss Helena Pryce?"

"Aye." A hint of a smile. "She be kind. I wanted

her to come see me, but Mister Jamie said she be a lady, not meant for this place."

A rap on the door, and the servant's face at the grate. Varden moved aside to let him enter, along with a fellow who carried away the moldering food and the smelly bucket. The liveried servant spread a cloth and laid on it a cheese pie, a pork pie, a wrapped packet of gingerbread, and three oranges. Beside them, he set a jug of lemonade and a cup.

The boy's eyes lit up as if a shower of gold had landed at his feet. "Be this for me?"

"Yes. And you are to swallow every bite. But not all at once, or you'll be sick."

After a moment, the boy picked up the largest orange and held it out to Varden. "I only ever had one o' these afore, but it were gooder than anything. You take this for yerself, sir. Mister Jamie says always to share."

Varden had learned enough in the last few minutes to accept the offering with a smile. "Thank you, Master Barnes. An orange is just what I should most like. Ah, here's your bucket again, all clean, and fresh blankets as well. Now I must go. Keep your spirits up, eat your meals, and say your prayers."

He made a quick exit, his good hand clutching the orange, before he betrayed his own weakness. The boy remained standing, Varden saw through the grate, until everyone had gone and the door had closed. Only then did he sink cross-legged onto his pallet, fold his hands, murmur what must have been a prayer, and begin ripping the peel from an orange.

Varden stood for a few moments, eyes closed, fighting an uncommon desire to strike someone. After a time he navigated his way outside and paused to gulp deep lungfuls of air. A testament to the stench of Newgate that, by comparison, London's air seemed clear and sweet.

Across the street loomed the Old Bailey. Tomorrow, frightened and trying not to show it, Billy Barnes would be taken there in shackles and under guard. The conclusion seemed forgone.

In front of Varden, his shiny coach pulled to a halt. The luxury of it seemed unnecessarily extravagant. Why had he been given so much, when others wept at the gift of a few oranges? He watched his groom lower the steps, glanced again at the Old Bailey, and understood that he was not yet done. "I've another call to make before we go," he said. "It may take a while. Clarkson, come along with me."

With the March Sessions just underway, the Sessions House was bustling with lawyers, witnesses, plaintiffs, visitors, and clerks. He had never been inside, and wouldn't have known where to track down his quarry in any case. While Clarkson went to see what he could learn, Varden found a spot out of the traffic and watched for someone who appeared to know what he was about. Five minutes later, he'd snagged a judge and was being led to where Noose Noggins could be found when he was not in court.

Conveniently, he was at a table in a small office, eating his lunch. A narrow-faced man with weary eyes, Noggins had set off his wig for the occasion, revealing a bald pate with a few tufts of gray hair at his nape. He was not pleased to be disturbed.

He was also, to Varden's surprise, not unwilling to consider a sentence of transportation for Master Barnes. "One example is as good as another," he said, wiping his chin with a napkin. "I can't very well hang them all. If the boy did no violence, he can be off to New South Wales early next week. Mind you, if he can't stand up for himself or pay for protection, the voyage is apt to be worse for him than the rope."

"Is there no alternative? Prison for a short time?"

"We haven't room to house a quarter of the felons and debtors we're saddled with. He hangs or he goes,

unless you can secure him a pardon." A short laugh
and the waggle of his brows. "Is the boy worth that
much to you?"

"What is the going price?" Varden said between
his teeth.

"Oh, I couldn't say. Only His Majesty can provide
what you require, and if he's signing pardons for
bribes, the word hasn't got to me. I was referring to
the difficulty. Once the boy is sentenced, and I cannot
delay his trial, we're in a great hurry to clear him out.
If you've been inside the prison, you understand the
problem. We allow a few days when possible, for the
sake of the family. Don't tell me if he hasn't one, or
I shall be obliged to expedite his departure."

"How long have I got, given the benefit of family?"

"Monday. It could be later, depending on the ship-
ping schedules, availability of space, even the tides.
Best not to count on it, though. If you mean to try
for a pardon, I'll have my clerk provide you instructions. It's always best, I am told, to be well prepared
before approaching the king."

"I'll be grateful for the clerk's assistance, as I am
for yours. You have been most obliging, sir."

"In spite of my nickname, eh? Make no mistake,
I've earned it. But now and again, I find it amusing
to confound expectations." The judge opened a ledger
and scanned a few pages until he found what he was
looking for. "Here we are. Billy Barnes. Oh, dear.
Aqua fortis. Nasty stuff. I'd have given him the noose
sure enough." He took up his pen and made a nota-
tion of some sort. "This is so I don't forget to be
merciful. Will there be anything else, Lord Varden?"

"Where will I find your clerk?"

"Wait here and I'll send him to you. I've to be on
the bench in five minutes." Noggins took up his wig,
plopped it askew on his head, bowed, and left.

Varden's luck, running high all day, ran out when
he attempted to locate Lord Gretton. The best he

could do was the sad-faced Lady Gretton, whom he found in the gaming room at Palazzo Neri.

"He's at Windsor," she said in a wilting voice. "As usual. I think he is to remain there several more days. But perhaps not."

The next obstacle was Beata Neri, waiting to pounce in the Sala dei Medici. "Naughty man," she chided, permitting him to kiss her cheek. "I have not seen you this age."

"Three days is not an age, my dear. And I have obligations."

"So I understand." A sly smile, one that told him he wouldn't like what he was about to hear. "A little bird informs me you have given your word to take a wife before the year is out. Is the bird mistaken?"

If he got his hands on that bird, it would be served up in a pie. Even if it turned out to be one of his grandmothers. "Who is your source, Beata?"

"Should I give up my sources, *caro*, I would soon have none of them. But since we are what we are to each other, I shall assure you that no member of your family has been indiscreet. A servant overheard something, and the news has found its way to me. Is it so great a secret? You must marry. All London knows that."

"I had hoped, during my search, to avoid being swarmed by hopeful mamas and eager young ladies."

"But you have always been swarmed, lovely man. Why should that change now? A shame—is it not?—that Miranda Holcombe got swept away by that great wolf of a duke. When I put the two of you together, I was certain you would make a match of it."

The lead weight pressing down on his heart seemed heavier at her words. He kept thinking that, with time, he would become reconciled to the loss. But so far, the best he could do was put it out of mind for brief periods. It had only been a few months, though. Surely the pain would eventually subside.

"As well that we did not," he said, more curtly than he intended. "This is to be a union of families and fortunes, one that will ensure the continuation of the Varden earls and their status into the next century. It is my duty, and I have always known it, to select a countess from a higher station than Miss Holcombe enjoyed. So tell me, Beata, what it is you expect in return for your discretion?"

She looked, for the first time since he'd known her, a trifle chastened. "Only that you choose a wife who will not forbid you to come here on account of our past relationship. On any account, for that matter. I should miss you more than I could bear."

"I have no intention of being hen-ridden. And that, I am afraid, includes Italian hens. It has pleased you to publically hint at an ongoing relationship between us, although none has existed for a considerable time. The game is harmless enough while I remain a bachelor, but when I am wed, no whiff of scandal is to touch the Countess of Varden. Unless you can persuade me of your benevolent intentions in that regard, it will be *my* choice not to come here."

"You have nothing to fear, Derek." His name sounded exotic the way she pronounced it. "Even if you could not endure the company of your wife, you would remain faithful to her as a matter of honor. Everyone knows it. Such respect is your reward for a lifetime of integrity, which is of value to you and incomprehensible to me. Nonetheless, I shall do nothing to compromise your reputation . . . or tempt you to abandon it."

He believed her, if only because she was so certain she could lure him away if she tried. For Beata, that was equivalent to success, which she needed far more than his presence in her bed. "Then we understand each other," he said with a smile that spoke of early days and pleasurable nights. "And because you are a woman of influence, I rely on you to silence my servant before I am compelled to trace her identity and sack her. Or him."

"Oh, the men do most of the tongue-wagging about courtship and marriage. For women, those are sacred things. Will you stay long enough to share a glass of wine with me?"

"Only if it is accompanied by the use of a writing desk and your silence. I need to send a message."

She provided everything he required, including her absence while he wrote, and shortly the message was handed over to his groom for delivery to Lord Gretton at Windsor. He did not expect a reply. Tomorrow morning he would appear at the Royal Lodge, and if Gretton had not managed to arrange an audience with the king, he'd bully his way inside and have a go at it himself.

By the time he left the Palazzo and climbed into his coach, the sun was low in the sky. He had spent the entire day attempting to preserve the life of a boy he had never heard of until that morning. He would spend all of tomorrow, he supposed, trying to keep Master Barnes off a transport ship.

But if he secured the pardon, what the devil was he to do with the fellow? Not take him into his own household, not after the conclusions everyone seemed to be drawing about his intentions. A safe residence, healthy food, supervision, training or an apprenticeship of some kind. Perhaps one of his sisters. Ann could find a place for him on the Westmoreland farm, although for the favor she would exact a heavy price.

Resigned to playing escort to the twins for the entire Season, Varden arrived home shortly before five o'clock and found a letter from Helena with the news he had been hoping for. She accepted employment, on terms to be specified when next they met, and he was to regard her at his service. A postscript advised him that she would be at Sothingdon House between five and seven o'clock if he wished a fencing engagement.

Varden, his heart lighter than it had been since he could recall, sped upstairs, shouting for his valet.

Chapter 13

"You have been practicing." It was an accusation, tossed at her with a smile as Varden stepped back and wiped his sleeve across his forehead.

"And taking instruction," Helena admitted, a little breathless from the exertion . . . and from his smile. "Only one lesson so far, Monday afternoon, and now I hurt in places that have never before called attention to themselves. But it helped, I think. After ten years, I had forgotten nearly everything I once knew."

"Well, if you continue to study, you will quickly outdistance me. Is that your intention?"

"You can take instruction as well."

"I am doing so. From a master swordswoman."

That surprised a laugh from her, which startled them both. She rarely laughed, and tried never to do so in the presence of an employer. Laughter made her appear vulnerable.

Before he could say anything, she went to the sideboard where she had laid out some towels and brought him one. "I am good only for basic exercises. You should employ someone capable of challenging you."

"You never fail to do that. Especially when you use devious means to distract my attention from your swordplay. Were those breeches worn to entice me?"

"Absolutely not!" She glanced at her reflection in one of the mirrors that lined the Sothingdon House ballroom, making the room appear larger than it was. She had dressed quite properly for a private fencing lesson, if improperly for anything else. Or so she had been thinking when she rummaged through the secondhand clothing store where she acquired most of her wardrobe, including these buff-colored knee breeches and stockings. She'd topped them with a wide-sleeved cambric shirt, a stiff brocade waistcoat, and a silly neckcloth draped to further conceal her breasts, which had a tendency to bounce around whenever she did. Next time, if there was one, she would bind them. Above the whole mismatched assembly were her monumentally ugly smoked spectacles, and the twists of dark brown hair firmly anchored to sausage-shaped forms and pinned in a helmet-shaped arrangement.

Enticing? She thought she looked ridiculous.

He was looking below her waist, to where the knit breeches fit snugly over her hips and thighs. They outlined shapes he'd not been able to see in the dark bedchamber, although he had traced every inch of them with his hands. And his mouth.

Then he looked up. Their gazes met in the mirror. Held for a long, wordless time. Desire became need, became urgent. Became sin.

Eve had not fallen. No indeed. She had *jumped*.

Wrenching herself from the blistering temptation to leap into his arms, Helena retrieved a heavy woolen cape and swung it over her shoulders. "If you prefer not to exercise at a studio, you could bring a fencing master here. I had the workmen refinish the marquetry floor and restore the mirrors. They did well, don't you think? Let me know when you wish to use the ballroom, and I'll see that you are not disturbed."

"You are babbling, Miss Pryce. That is unlike you."

He had no idea, *none*, what she was like. Except in bed, where she had been a surprise to them both. "I thought you came here to improve your fencing, sir.

I wished to provide you a more worthy opponent, which is difficult to do wearing skirts. The breeches were a mistake. When you are gone, I shall burn them."

"No, you won't. I promise not to remark on them again, although I cannot promise to refrain from looking at what they reveal. If you accept employment from a man, Miss Pryce, you must indulge his harmless weaknesses. One of mine is to tease you now and again, in an effort to coax a smile. Or a bit of your elusive laughter. And, yes, take pleasure in the appreciation of a lovely female body . . . even if touching it is prohibited."

He had moved behind her, so close his breath teased at her nape. "Is it still prohibited, Helena?"

She was startled into an admission of her self-doubt. "Is that why you persist, my lord? Because I provide the sort of challenge you rarely encounter? Is it the novelty of refusal that appeals to you?"

"It does, yes."

A gasp escaped her throat. She had never thought he would admit to such a thing.

"A great many things about you are appealing to me. I could make a list, if you like."

Her cheeks had gone on fire. "Don't be absurd. I require no—no *reassurances* from you. And I cannot continue to withstand your advances, which are entirely inappropriate."

"That's good news. The 'cannot continue to withstand' part. Although I don't believe it for a moment. You protect yourself with armor, behind steel bars, inside a fortress." He took a towel from the sideboard and began wiping down the swords. "But I've not given up hope. If you genuinely wished no part of me, you would not have returned to my service."

"You won't think so when you see the rise in salary I mean to demand. My sole interest is money. Besides, there is no agreement between us, Lord Varden. Not until we have negotiated terms."

"Then by all means, let us proceed. Shall we join battle in the parlor?"

"That will not be possible. This evening was for fencing, if you were free to come, but I've an engagement later tonight."

"What time?" He laid the swords in their case and closed the latch. "There are important matters I need to discuss with you. Can you spare me an hour?"

She might have pretended an important meeting, but should he drop by Palazzo Neri, he would catch her sitting quietly with Signora Fanella, softly describing the guests and what they were wearing and what they seemed to be up to. Beata's companion, sharp-eared but blind, liked to be at the center of things.

He was regarding her a little impatiently, waiting for an answer.

"Of course, my lord," she said. "But there is no fire in the parlor. Will the kitchen do? It is warm there, and I can brew some tea."

She was laying out cups and saucers, silverware, a pitcher of milk, and a dish of sugar when he joined her, wearing his polished shoes, a well-fitted waistcoat and jacket, and an impeccably tied cravat. The elegant Earl of Varden in a borrowed kitchen, being served by a nervous female wearing breeches. He propped his shoulder against the doorjamb, folded his arms, and watched her work.

His scrutiny set her nerves tingling. She measured tea into a plain ceramic pot. Using a folded towel to protect her hands, she lifted the kettle from its hook above the fire and filled the pot. Returned the kettle. Put the lid on the pot. Simple tasks, made tortuous by his lucent gaze.

"Have you ever been inside a kitchen, my lord?"

"I'm sure I have. Not for a great many years, though. It makes the servants uncomfortable."

Indeed it does. She took biscuits from a tin, plain ones served to the workmen, and set them on a plate. She had been taught by Jamie to offer food, if she had any, to a guest who might otherwise have nothing at all to eat that day. Rookery hospitality for an earl! What a strange life she was leading these days.

When she had strained tea into the cups, he pulled himself away from the door and gestured her to be seated before he took his own chair at the housekeeper's table. "Have we time for negotiation, Miss Pryce, or may we proceed for now as if we've come to terms? I have business that must undertaken without delay." He gave her a sharp look. "To be perfectly straightforward, you may not wish to accept employment when you hear what I am about. It concerns the Duke of Tallant."

With care, she kept her hand steady as she added sugar to her tea. "You have a grievance against him, I know. But is it wise to pursue it? With the title and inheritance, he has become powerful. And like his father and brother before him, he is reputed to be ruthless."

"A reputation he has earned. I cannot reveal who set me on this course, but you may be sure I am not acting on my own behalf. Not entirely, at any rate. I cannot deny an unseemly desire to see Tallant brought down. And that is precisely why I require someone with no stake in this investigation to assist me."

He ate a biscuit in two bites and picked up another. "I want that to be you. No one else I can think of has your skills, or your readiness to speak with appalling frankness to me. In this matter, I need someone to trust."

He could not trust her. Nor did she want any part of this. But what might happen if she wasn't there to stop it?

He was devouring yet another biscuit, giving her a few moments to prepare for what was sure to come next. She drank her tea, warm and wet in her parched mouth, and refilled her cup.

Get on with it, my lord. I have played these masquerades since childhood. You haven't a chance against me.

"You were supposed to assure me that I can trust you," he said. "But I had forgotten your connection with Tallant. There must be one. How else could you have so swiftly arranged for me to purchase the castle?"

"I did the obvious thing," she said. "I approached the reputed owner and inquired if she was willing to sell the property. But you are correct, sir. I have a slight acquaintance with Her Grace through my former employer. Before she married the duke, Miranda Holcombe asked Lady Jessica to sell for her the antiquities and objets d'art she had inherited from her uncle. I handled most of the transactions, and in the course of business, learned something of the castle and its history."

His jaw tightened. "How amused you must have been when I set you the test of acquiring something I thought to be unobtainable. All the while, you knew it would likely fall into your hands upon request."

"Amused, yes. And a little astonished at the coincidence. But you overestimate my certainty about the result. As I told you, I'd have approached the duchess in any case. That she knew me and regarded me favorably was my good fortune. Or so I thought at the time. I now believe your purchase of the castle to have been ill advised, and I regret the part that I played."

"Even though you would not otherwise have become my secretary?"

She thought—probably imagined—that he looked a little hurt. Everything that occurred between them was touched with poison. For her to work with him meant betrayal. For her to leave him meant he would take on a man in a battle that might well destroy them both. For her to have made love with him meant she would find it impossible to let another man touch her.

There were no solutions. Only guesses, and the surrender of herself to forces she could not control. The Earl of Varden and the Duke of Tallant on a collision course, and no one with the power to stop them. Certainly not Helena Pryce. She'd no illusions about that. But if she stayed as close as the antagonists would permit her to come, she might be able to steer one or the other of them clear of disaster.

While she prepared her next few responses, Varden was clearing the plate of biscuits. She looked up at him with a frown. "Are you hungry, sir? I provided those common biscuits as a courtesy, not expecting you to actually eat them. Would you like something else?"

His face brightened. "*Have* you something else? I'd a busy day, with no time for a bite since breakfast. But I thought no one was in residence here. Have you left Beata's cottage?"

"Not altogether, but I stay here on occasion. The housekeeper comes in every day except Sunday to provide lunch for the workers. Let me see what I can find in the pantry."

She hadn't expected him to follow her there.

"Have you met the duke?" he said from the doorway. "It's important, Helena. I fear my own prejudice will sway me to a misinterpretation of the evidence. If you are connected with Tallant, however slightly, I need to know."

Thank God she was in near-darkness, her back to him. "When I went to Longview to speak with the duchess about the castle, His Grace rode up as I was about to leave. We exchanged a few words. I would say 'polite words,' but he is not a polite man."

She had got her hands on the remains of a cured ham and carried it past Varden into the kitchen.

"Lady Jessica's husband, Lord Duran, is a particular friend of the duke. So is David Fairfax, with whom I am acquainted. My work puts me in the way of many people, but that is not to say I am connected to them. For the most part, they scarcely notice me."

"Give me leave to doubt that." He trailed behind her to the table, and back again to the cold room off the pantry where she located bread and a wedge of cheddar. Then he rested his hip on the table inches from where she set to work "You've had no other meeting with the duke?"

Other than smuggling him out of London under the noses of the men you had set to follow him? But she had only arranged that sequence of events, not participated in them herself. "A few months ago, I encountered him at a tavern not far from the British Museum. He came in with Mr. Fairfax, but they did not long remain."

"You spoke with him?" Varden snatched the first bit of ham she sliced off.

"Mr. Fairfax brought him to where I was seated with friends. There was conversation, yes. I recall that Mr. Keynes—he wasn't the duke then—drank wine. Then they left. I expect I have glimpsed him on occasion at the Palazzo, but I cannot recall another time when we spoke together."

"Thank you. I didn't mean to play Spanish Inquisitor. I simply require to know where you stand in regard to the duke."

"As far away as possible," she said with sincerity, handing him a slab of bread with slices of ham and cheese on top. She'd seen a pitcher of ale in the cold room and went to fetch it.

And a right good servant she was . . . with a touch of Inquisitor in her as well.

On her return, she filled a tankard, watching from the corner of her eye until his mouth was full of bread and ham and cheese. Then she struck. "It is a hard

thing," she said, "for a servant without status or resources to risk the displeasure of a high-tempered
duke. Especially in your company. Am I mistaken, or
does he not regard you as an enemy?"

Varden shrugged. Mumbled what sounded like "A
defeated enemy, perhaps."

She handed him the tankard of ale. "I cannot help
you, sir, unless I know what occurred between the two
of you in India."

At first she thought he meant to deny her. He drank
from the tankard, his expression somber and inward-
turned. Then he made a small gesture of indifference.
"You may as well hear it. But I expect the incident
itself would be incomprehensible without a glance at
what led up to it. This is all from my point of view,
of course. I've no doubt the new Duke of Tallant
would put a quite different slant on the story."

She broke off a piece of cheese and began to nibble
at it, hoping to look interested but uninvolved.

"I should tell you that from the outset, I was responsible for everything that went wrong. Some years
ago, I was asked to become a charter investor in the
East India Consortium, one of several enterprises that
sprang up when John Company lost its monopoly. The
list of investors already committed included a number
of reputable gentlemen. They convinced me that my
participation would attract yet more capital investment at a time when new companies were competing
for funds. It is not uncommon, Miss Pryce, for me to
be pasted onto an enterprise to lend it . . . I'm not
sure what. Legitimacy, perhaps. My family name has
value in such regard."

He lifted himself away from the table and began to
stride around the kitchen, the tankard clutched in his
left hand, his right arm folded behind his back. "I
agreed to join the Consortium, paid a token amount
into the coffers, and occasionally made an appearance
at a meeting if someone urged me to do so. From

what I could tell, the early profits were astounding. Investors rushed to jump on the gravy wagon, and after a while, I was no longer needed as window dressing. Time passed."

He came by her, shot her a look she could not interpret. "In August of 1822, I was summoned to a meeting at the Palazzo. Few of the investors were present, it being high summer. There I learned that the Consortium was on the verge of bankruptcy, due entirely to Tallant's brother, Michael, and his crusade to bring the duke to ruin. That was the first I knew Tallant *had* a brother, or that he held the primary financial stake in the company."

"You did not suffer losses?" she couldn't help asking.

"Not to speak of. I do not gamble on what transpires in India, which is too far out of my control for comfort. Because I had no measurable financial stake in the Consortium, and supposedly because of my skill as an investigator and negotiator, the others urged me to go out to India and put a stop to the bleed of profits. I was given a thick portfolio of information to study on the voyage. Passage had already been booked for me, as if my acceptance were a foregone conclusion."

When he passed in and out of the sparse light cast by the fire and the candles she had lit, shadows danced across his fine-boned face. She knew, of a sudden, that he had never told this, not any of it, to another person.

"Since you had no particular interest in the outcome," she said when he seemed disinclined to continue, "why did you go?"

"Oh, for a number of reasons. No one of them would have sufficed, but added together, they propelled me onto the ship. My two-year liaison with Beata was drawing to a natural close, and in the weeks prior to the meeting, she had urged me to find something useful to do with myself. A civilized way of kick-

ing me out, I expect. And the pressure from my family
to marry had become nearly intolerable. It is an obligation I do not mean to shirk, but at the time, I'd
scarcely ventured from the south of England. Save for
a few weeks in France to escort my sisters on a shopping expedition, my travels had been confined to the
Varden properties and those of my friends."

He made a sound in his throat, rather like a cat
expelling a hairball. "This is ridiculous, Miss Pryce.
You don't want to hear it all."

She could imagine nothing she had ever wanted
more to hear. "It will help, I think," she said, and
began slicing off more ham. Men were invariably
soothed by the vision of females performing wom-
anly tasks.

"I wished for one adventure," he said after a long
silence. "One experience that was not purely English,
purely aristocratic, purely familiar. I wanted to test
myself, to see if I could be more than what my breeding, station, and appearance had stamped out. More
than the Varden heir, the hurry-up-and-get-about-it
sire of the next Varden heir. As it turned out, the
answer was no. But when I strode onto the trader,
confident and excited and determined, the world lay
at my feet. It was the only time"—he glanced over
at her—"the first time, anyway, that I had ever felt
truly alive."

She gazed at him, mute with astonishment and not
a little anger.

*But you have always had everything. How could you
not be happy? What hope, then, can there be for the
rest of us?*

He had already turned away, pacing the large
kitchen while his thoughts roamed the other side of
the world. "India was . . . astonishing. I was entirely
unprepared for it. But in the beginning I dealt primarily with the English, who were busily re-creating the
Society they had left behind. That included the bu-

reaucratic nonsense I was accustomed to dealing with, and yet, I could make no headway. 'Yes,' they would say, 'Michael Keynes is a rascal. Up to no good, we suppose. But it's really none of our concern.'

"In fact, they were neck-deep in concern. Most were engaged in the same commerce—opium for tea—as the Consortium, and when Keynes sabotaged a Consortium cargo or made off with a Consortium riverboat, he struck a blow at their competition and put money in their pockets. No surprise, then, that they withheld evidence and politely evaded my efforts to build a case against him."

"He was guilty," she said, bemused, "but no one wanted him to stop."

"That, and the laws as written made prosecution a venture into the unknown. Is it a crime to stop traders from violating the laws of another country? Treaties come into play, international relations, long-term prospects for commerce, retribution against England for what some of its more adventurous traders were about. For my part, I'd not been aware what sort of trade the Consortium favored. Nearly everyone I encountered thought nothing of smuggling opium into China, but it did not sit well with me."

"Then why did you not abandon the investigation?"

"After spending six months just to get there?" A dry chuckle. "Oh, put it down to obstinacy if you like. I'd been sent to save the Consortium from a scurvy knave, and by God, I was going to do it. But just when several months of beating my head against a wall had me reconciled to slinking home and admitting to failure, a Government House attaché let slip the address used by officials to contact my quarry. So I wrote him a letter."

Helena realized that she was sitting—unservantlike—with her elbows on the table and her chin propped between her hands, wholly absorbed in his story. She straightened her back, lowered her

hands, and neatly folded them. None of this was supposed to affect her.

"A month later," Varden said, "Keynes's reply was
delivered. It consisted of my letter, torn to pieces. And
that is when the affair became personal. I began brib-
ing the native servants at Government House. From
them I learned that Keynes owned a house in Calcutta
and stayed there on occasion, but no one knew where
it was.

"Then a young woman assigned to menial duties
approached me in secret. She'd been a nautch dancer
before a drunken patron slashed her face with a broken bottle. At one time she had performed with
Keynes's mistress, also a dancer, who was unkind to
her. It struck me how often our sins come back to
punish us in surprising ways. The servant provided
directions to the town where his mistress lived."

"And you found him there?"

"That would have been too easy. A beautiful
woman, Priya Lal, but resentful as well. Keynes had
not visited her for several months, although her allowance was regularly paid, and she had no idea where
he could be found. But for a surprisingly modest bribe,
she offered to inform me if he appeared. And a mod-
erately larger bribe secured the directions to his house
in Calcutta."

Varden paused by the table to refill the tankard,
which had been dangling empty from his hand. "It
was not a pleasant transaction. I am unaccustomed to
soliciting betrayal. And while I gave her no cause, she
appeared to believe I intended to replace Keynes as
her protector. Indeed, she was somewhat determined
that I should."

What woman would not be? Helena had never been
a susceptible female, but when the Earl of Varden got
swept up in a fleeting passion, she had been quick to
indulge him.

"Her disappointment meant I could learn nothing

more, so I returned to Calcutta and hired some rather unsavory fellows to watch Keynes's house. He showed up within a week, but by the time I arrived there, he'd gone out again. So with two ruffians, I broke into the house, doused the lights, and waited in ambush."

Varden's pace picked up, as if something were pursuing him. "I meant only to interrogate him. I'd a sword cane and a pistol, not to mention a pair of thugs. What could go wrong? But of course, everything did. Keynes was disinclined to surrender, and within an amazingly short time, one fellow was dead, one managed a painful escape, and I had been beaten to sausage. In the dark, he had no idea who we were, or what we intended. Not unreasonably, he fought like the devil for his life."

Of all possibilities, this was the last she would have imagined. Varden at fault, exonerating his enemy. She kept her head down, fearing that her thoughts could be read on her face. He continued his determined circular journey around the kitchen, paying her no mind.

"You're wondering about the injury to my hand. It happened early on. When we heard Keynes mounting the stairs, I drew out my pistol, expecting that a weapon would prevent a struggle. But he came into the room like a stampeding bull. First he kicked the gun away. Then he began pummeling me. The hirelings rushed him, freeing me for a time. I was on hands and knees, scuttling across the wooden floor in search of the pistol. By feel, because the room was dark. My right hand fell on the gun, but before my fingers could close on it, Keynes's boot slammed down."

Then Varden did look over at her, catching her gaping at him and breathing heavily through her open mouth. "You can't have expected a peaceable story, Helena. The rest is incidental. Well, except that Keynes, having effectively demolished the three of us, sent his Sikh friend to transport me to a physician. By the time I had recovered from the worst of it, both

Keynes and the Sikh were on their way to England. Does all that answer your question?"

To the contrary. It had raised a dozen others. But she could tell, by the taut muscles and the whiteness around his lips, that she ought not to ask them now. Except, perhaps, the most urgent. "It seems, my lord, that you take all the responsibility on yourself. There was provocation, certainly. But your continuing animosity—"

"Is not justified? Is that what you are saying?" His lips curved in a grim smile. "I promise you, no man can abide an opponent who holds up a mirror to his inadequacies. You wouldn't understand, being a rational and enlightened woman. I didn't understand either, for a long time, because I was raised to be civilized. But of late, primitive male instincts have overwhelmed me. I hate a man beyond measure. I desire a woman—you—beyond reason. I scarcely know myself, and I don't greatly like what I do know. The only consolation is that by the end of the year, I shall have drawn in my reins and become again what everyone expects me to be."

"The Archangel?" She regretted the question the moment it left her mouth.

"I'll forgive you that," he said, "so long as it is not repeated. I have never been more than a well-mannered, dutiful man with a deceptively pretty appearance. And while I do not mind trying to live up to high expectations, I dislike enormously the assumption I have already achieved them. Perhaps that is why I so enjoy your company. You are more attentive to my faults than to my virtues, such as they be."

"You want to be *criticized*?" she asked, genuinely surprised.

"Not particularly. But I am profoundly weary of being praised for no reason. You keep me on balance. When you're not throwing me off balance." He shambled to the table and sank onto the chair across from her. "Look. We've fenced long enough this evening, and I have made you late for wherever you are going. Tomorrow, on the way to Windsor, I shall tell you why I am again investigating Michael Keynes, and what I require you to do."

"I beg your pardon?

"Did I not tell you before?" He looked puzzled. And tired. Achingly tired. "I have arranged to speak with the king about . . . on the subject of legal reforms. To solicit his advocacy. You advised me to do that."

"Yes. But *tomorrow*?" Billy Barnes was to be tried tomorrow. Jamie said she was to stay away, but she had resolved to be in the gallery, or closer if she could get closer, so that Billy would know he was not alone.

"If you are to work for me," Varden said, "you must be available when I require your services. Before I go to Peel with a strategy, and to my peers urging them to vote for reform, I must have all my cards in hand . . . including the king."

There was more than that to his spur-of-the-moment trip, she apprehended without the slightest clue what it might be. And she could not escape the images his story had churned up. In her mind, she kept seeing him crawling across a dark floor, bruised and bleeding. His hand falling on the gun. A heavy boot crashing down, splintering bones and crushing flesh.

Oh, my dear lover of one night. You made a mistake, perhaps, but this is too great a punishment.

"I will accompany you," she said. Anywhere he asked, short of his bed. "What time?"

"Be ready at dawn." He stood, plucking a last slice of ham from the platter, and headed for the kitchen door. "We'll take my coach. On the drive to Windsor, you may instruct me on all the proper things to say."

Chapter 14

Varden could not, of course, take his servant into the company of the king. He left her off at a posthouse near Slough, about half an hour's journey from the Royal Lodge, predicting that his business there would be concluded before noon.

Sure enough, his carriage pulled into the stableyard just as the clock in the private parlor where Helena was waiting stuck twelve. From the window, she watched the carriage door, expecting she would be able to read the success or failure of his mission on his face when he emerged. But the door remained closed, and shortly after, ostlers began to unharness the horses. She put down her book and hurried outside.

One of Varden's grooms, heading in the direction of the main entrance, changed course to intersect with hers. "Miss Pryce," he said, withdrawing a folded sheet of paper from the satchel at his hip. "His lordship has been detained. This message is for you, and I am to be at your service until he sends for the coach."

"Thank you, but I require nothing at present. You may as well join the others." She returned to the parlor, scanned the brief note, and slipped it inside her case. Varden apologized for the delay and hoped to join her before very long. But he must not be optimistic about his prospects, she thought, because he had ordered the carriage and horses to stand down. Most likely she had the rest of the afternoon, and probably a good part of the evening, to pass in her own company.

Not enclosed here, though, in the stuffy parlor where she had already spent a long, tedious morning. She put on her pelisse, bonnet, and gloves, wrapped a muffler around her neck, and two hours later, breathless and exhilarated, was standing atop the tallest hill in the area.

Cold wind sliced through her pelisse and woolen dress, but she scarcely felt it, enraptured by the beauty spread all around her. Even in late-winter colors, the landscape stirred the deep places where her feelings were locked away. Country lanes, fields studded with sheep and energetic lambs, leafless copses of mulberry, elm, and oak. And no people. It seemed she had the southern tip of Buckinghamshire all to herself. No one staring at her odd spectacles, no one expecting her to behave properly or perform a service. The city had always been her home, but the countryside was what she dreamed about, on the rare nights when her dreams were pleasant.

Overhead, clouds scudded across a sky that would soon fade into twilight. She had stayed out too long, gone too far. And was glad of it. Delicious irresponsibility, as rare in her life as mermaids paddling up the Thames. First the interlude with Varden at the castle, and now abandoning her post for an impulsive tramp through the countryside, both within a fortnight! She was becoming a willful, wanton female. Who could have imagined it?

No one she knew, except Jamie, and she had no intention of telling him. This latest caprice would go altogether unremarked, unless Varden returned to the posthouse before she did. Gathering up her skirts, she set herself on a run down the hillside. If he caught her out, there would be a polite lecture, which was the worst kind. She ought to have taken one of the grooms as an escort. Left a message for her employer. Not gone out at all.

In fact, she had dutifully told the proprietor of her plans and given him her leather case for safekeeping. But that was only because she was new at irresponsibility. She'd get better with practice.

Burdens melted off her shoulders as she sped along the path to Stoke Poges, took a shortcut through the churchyard, and came out onto a wider path that would lead her back to Slough. The sky was nearly dark now, the wind damp with impending rain. Two miles at least to go, and she'd be wet as an otter when she arrived. Not good for the hair.

She stopped to rest her back against a tree, her breath coming in little pants. It wasn't as if she could just comb it out, like ordinary hair, and let it dry. Perhaps she should inquire about public transportation back to London. A note left for Varden, pleading other obligations. After all, had the king not detained him, they would have departed hours ago.

She was about to set off again when the sound of hoofbeats and a frisson of danger caused her to jump behind the tree. Too late. She heard the horse draw up, heard it snort, and then a voice.

"Miss Pryce, I believe? You may safely emerge."

With a little sigh of relief, she stepped out and curtsied. "Your Grace. Whatever are you doing here? And how did you know me?"

"I saw your spectacles as I came up over the rise. Are you in difficulty?"

"Not at all. I am taking a walk."

A chuckle. "You're alone in the middle of nowhere with night falling and the rain about to do likewise. Where is it you are *supposed* to be?"

She gazed up at the familiar eyes glinting with amusement, the heavy black hair stealing out from a wide-brimmed hat, a pair of imposing shoulders with the capes of his black greatcoat fluttering about them. He was, she knew, as obstinate as she, and held all the authority there was between them. "I am in the area on business, Your Grace, and lodging at a posthouse in the London Road near Slough. It's true about the walk."

"And it's true about the rain." He reached down his hands. "Come along, Miss Pryce. I'll give you a lift."

"But you were going the other direction."

One raised brow was his only response. After a moment, she stepped closer to the enormous black horse and let herself be drawn up in front of the duke. She had never ridden, let alone in this fashion, and found it deucedly uncomfortable. He had planted her in the circle of his arms with her legs dangling over one side and her bottom on the rim of the saddle between his thighs. He draped the sides of his greatcoat over her and set his own hat atop her bonnet.

Moments later the sky opened. The horse took off at terrifying speed, and the wind sent rain over her spectacles, effectively blinding her. If Tallant required directions to the posthouse, he was out of luck.

The journey could not have taken long, but it seemed to her an eternity before he said, cheerfully, "Here we are. I expect payment in brandy, so arrange for it while I stable Loki." Large hands went to her waist, and with a slight jolt, her feet hit the ground.

He had left her off at the entrance. She went inside and removed his hat, surprised at how dry she still was at every point above her knees. Below, her skirts and boots were soaked through.

Varden had not returned, she discovered while ordering the brandy, along with a glass of mulled wine for herself. So far as she could tell, her absence of more than three hours had not been noticed at all. Now she just had to rid herself of the duke before her employer came back and found them together.

When Tallant arrived in the private parlor, she was

standing in front of the fireplace, flapping her skirts to help them dry. "It is peculiar," she said, "that we should both be on the same obscure Buckinghamshire road at the same time."

"In the last year, I've learned not to question the inexplicable." He pulled off his greatcoat, draped it over a hook, and ran the fingers of both hands through his wet hair. "Hari Singh would say that nothing happens without a purpose, which is why I am here in this parlor instead of back on the road. Any guesses, Miss Pryce, as to why we met?"

"So far, Your Grace, it appears you were sent to keep me dry."

"Only that? Good God. And here I've been hoping to repay you for . . . Well, you know what you did, if not how important it all was at a crucial time. Returning a great service in kind would please me enormously. But if keeping you dry is the best I can do, I will travel the breadth of England to provide you an umbrella."

She watched him pour a glass of brandy, look at it for a brief time, and turn his penetrating gaze to her face. "I saw Varden's carriage in the stable. Are you here with him?"

"I came here with him. He is at the Royal Lodge, meeting with the king."

Tallant grinned. "For the first time, the man has all my sympathy. I'm in the neighborhood for precisely the same reason, only my summons was for yesterday. It was a staggering bore."

"His Majesty had business with you?"

"More like a fancy to see a raree-show." He slumped onto a chair, cradling the glass between his hands. "He'd read about me in the newsrags, about the wild younger brother who confessed to the Duke of Tallant's murder, got tossed into the Tower, and got tossed out again. A devotee of scandal and gossip, our monarch, so long as it's not about him. Fortunately for me, he was afflicted with an attack of the gout, drank rather too much laudanum to relieve the pain, and dropped off to sleep about an hour into the interrogation. I had started to think I'd have to confess all over again, just to keep him entertained."

"Are you expected to return? Is that why you are still here?"

"They'd have to drag me back in irons. In fact, I didn't like to travel this far to such little purpose, so I've spent today purchasing sheep for Longview. When I encountered you, I was on my way to see a man about some pigs."

"I believe that most dukes employ stewards and land agents to oversee this sort of thing."

"Yes, well, I'm new at this duke business. The steward my brother employed was worse than useless, but since I tossed him out, I've not found anyone competent to put in his place. Have you a recommendation?"

She ought not. But she couldn't help herself. "Not offhand, Your Grace, but I'll see what I can do. Is there a rush? Her Grace indicated that you might be traveling abroad this spring. Perhaps with Devonshire, when he sets out for Italy. That's in a little more than two weeks, as I recall."

"You ought to, since you made the arrangements. But no, we'll not be going. The duchess wished to and still does, but I have overruled her." He took a swallow of brandy. "She doesn't like it when I do that."

"The drinking or the overruling?"

A bark of laughter. "Both, and a score of other things besides. But she's been ill—"

"Oh, dear. I beg your pardon, sir, for my improper remark." No servant spoke to a duke in this fashion. Even to a disreputable duke. Even to one who looked remarkably cheerful about his wife's poor health. "I hope Her Grace recovers swiftly."

"*Ill* was the wrong word. Most mornings she's been

shooting the ca— That is, vexed with bouts of nausea. Other symptoms as well, of a child-producing kind. Or so she says, when she can permit herself to hope for what she had thought to be unlikely, if not impossible."

"Has she seen a midwife? Or a physician?"

"The local quack, but he's an idiot. I don't suppose you—"

"Certainly. I'll send word when I have a qualified person's name and direction." This was her chance. The question had burned on the edges of her tongue since he entered the parlor. "Might I ask something in return, Your Grace? Only a bit of information. I'm told there was evidence of robbery, or attempted robbery, at the time the previous duke was murdered, and that later, two robbers broke into Tallant House and ransacked it. Do you know what they were seeking?"

"I have no idea."

"But you could guess?"

"Given my late and unlamented brother's interests, I'd expect something used in the commission of a crime. But of what sort, I don't know. I did mount a search, a fairly desultory one, at Longview, but other matters have preoccupied us there. We'll continue to look. In London, Tallant House has been exhaustively searched. The workmen found several hiding places behind the walls and under the floorboards, but they were empty."

"There are other properties, though."

"When I have reliable people to send, I'll have them examined. The duchess is concerned as well." He cast her a speculative look. "Did she delegate you to hound me?"

"Not at all, sir. But I was drawn into the first chapters of this story, and I naturally wish to learn how it turns out. Also, I have a distaste for loose threads."

"So do I. It is my intention to inspect every prop-

erty, but I've been reluctant to go for several reasons."
He rose, stretched, and carried his glass of brandy to
a window. She heard sounds from the stableyard,
voices and rattles and hoofbeats, and wondered if the
duke was watching, as she had been, for Lord Varden's arrival.

What he saw out the window seemed not to interest
him. He turned, frowning. "You waltzed smoothly by
your relationship with the Archangel. I gather you
have taken employment with him, after refusing my
offer. Might I ask why?"

"Perhaps, Your Grace, he needs me more than
you do."

"I daresay." The duke propped his shoulders
against the wall and folded his arms, the brandy glass
dangling from his right hand. "Has he told you what
happened between us in India?"

Varden's right hand could not hold a glass, she was
thinking when Tallant's question hit her between the
eyes. Even standing still, he was like a tiger stalking
its prey.

"What my employer tells me, you will understand,
is confidential."

A pause, somber eyes pinning her to the hearth.
"You are in a troublesome position, are you not, between two men who hold you in high regard, all the
while detesting each other?"

"Not at all," she said with conviction. It was a fla-
grant lie. "Loyalty to my employer is primary, and I'd
not work long for anyone who failed to merit it. I
wonder, though, that you dislike Lord Varden. You
must be nearly the only person in England who does."

"Then I serve a purpose. Universal acclaim, even
for a paragon, cannot be healthy. I repeat—has he
told you what occurred between us?"

"A little. He does not hold you responsible for the
injury to his hand."

The duke laughed. "Well, I *am* responsible. And so

is he, even if the direct cause was accidental. We are now primed for trouble, Miss Pryce. One of us will inevitably ignite the other."

"But why? The sole incident between you happened nearly a year ago, and those circumstances will never recur. Is a reconciliation out of the question?"

"I wonder that this is of such interest to you. It is not unusual for men to take each other in dislike, even without significant cause. And as it happens, I have a number of reasons for wishing him to the devil, not the least being that he fancies himself in love with my wife."

Helena felt the breath rush out of her. "S-surely not. They are barely acquainted. He returned from India only a short time before you were married."

"A matter of days. In Varden's defense, falling in love with Mira requires no longer than the blink of an eye. But that is all the credit I will grant him. The man is a bloody nuisance. Why do you think he sent you to acquire that heap of stones in Somerset? He wanted something that was hers to moon over."

She thought, briefly, that she was going to be sick.

"Are you shocked? I might have done something equally stupid, had she chosen him. But while I comprehend his misery, that doesn't mean I want him drooping about, meddling in our affairs."

She found her voice, said words unconnected to the thoughts tumbling in her head. "You could be wrong about the castle."

"Yes. It doesn't matter." He tossed down the brandy, set the glass on a table, and went to retrieve his greatcoat. "I do not consider him a rival for my wife's affections. She is mine entirely. And I am no threat to Varden . . . so long as he keeps out of my way. If you have any influence, Miss Pryce, see that he does."

She realized, as he opened the door, that he'd left his hat. "Your Grace?" Too late. She grabbed the hat and caught up with him as he was trying to pay for the brandy.

"I have signed personally for that," she said. "Do not insult me. You have forgot your bonnet."

Grinning, he took it and popped it on his head. "I buy them a dozen at a crack," he said. "The same with umbrellas and gloves. You can see why. Come visit us, will you? When Norah and Cory go on their travels with Devonshire, the duchess will want a female to talk with about all the things that make me blush."

Chapter 15

Varden thought he had explored the outermost edges of tedium during his voyage to India, but one afternoon at the Royal Lodge in Windsor Great Park proved unutterably duller than six months aboard a trader.

Lord Gretton, with his usual gracious diplomacy, had arranged for him to meet privately with the king. But what was meant to be a brief audience for presenting his petitions stretched considerably longer than that.

"Wellington won't like it," said His Rotund Majesty, overflowing the chair on which he sat with his gouty feet raised onto a brocade ottoman. "And I'm a Tory now, you know. We're not much for softening up criminal laws."

"That is not our intent. For the most part, the reform bills merely bring statutes into accord with long-term practice. English justice must apply equally to all our citizens, not vary according to the prejudices of individual judges."

"Yes, yes. Well, you may tell those few who still care what I think that your reforms have my support. Better we Tories loosen up a bit at the edges, say I, or the Whigs will be swept into power along with their demmed liberal nonsense. And then where would we be?"

An accurate assessment, Varden thought, revising his estimation of the king's political instincts. They proceeded soon after to the request for a pardon, and Varden was not above playing on His Majesty's notorious susceptibility to emotional pleas. A man who had all his life hungered for approval was likely to feel compassion for Billy Barnes's foolish excesses.

And he did. "But what is the boy to you?" the king inquired after signing the papers with a flourish. "What is to become of him?"

"Master Barnes is distantly connected to one of my servants, who was distressed at the prospect of his transportation. I intend to take responsibility for the boy. He will be placed in the household of a family member and taught a trade."

The king nodded, and Varden thought with relief that he had been dismissed. But when he rose, he was waved back into his chair and treated to a lengthy series of reminiscences by a lonely man who had found himself a new audience for his stories. "Florizel," said the king at one point, his chins jiggling as he caressed each syllable. "That's what they called me, when I was in love with my Perdita. Not so elegant as 'Archangel,' I know, but Florizel has a nice sound to it, don't you think?"

"A splendid sound, Your Majesty." Spoken with gritted teeth, since it was this same royal lover of nicknames who had first dubbed him the Archangel. "Florizel suits you admirably."

If forced to remain overlong, Varden supposed he'd become as bored and obsequious as the Cottage Clique who inhabited this hothouse court. He made flattering comments on cue, pretended he recalled events that had taken place when he was in short pants, and was finally released when the king required to use the royal privy.

But he didn't get far. Lord Gretton corralled him as he was taking polite leave of Lady Conyngham, the king's jewel-draped inamorata, and informed him that he was bid to stay for luncheon.

"It is the *king*," Gretton said with an apologetic smile. "I presume you came here to solicit his favor, and it will be withdrawn if you decline his invitation. He is easily offended, you know."

So Varden remained through a luncheon that seemed to last for a week, smiling at the barbed remarks of the ambassadors and foreign ministers who had become the king's favorites. Once crowned, George IV had perversely reverted to his Hanoverian roots and enjoyed playing the role of influential European prince. Wellington, whose company Varden would have appreciated during the long afternoon, had gone down to his estate for the weekend.

Every few minutes, apparently from habit, someone proposed a toast, and while Varden only sipped at the cherry brandy favored by the king, he was fairly well in his cups before the party adjourned to a parlor for irksome games of patience and ecarte. "I wanted to take you out in my phaeton and show you my plans for a Chinese pavilion at Lake Virginia," whined His Majesty, unhappy when the rain kept them all indoors. Unhappiness meant more brandy, and Varden could not avoid swallowing his share of it.

Well after dark, complaining of headache, the king finally toddled off with Lady Conyngham. The moment the royal backside was lost from sight down the passageway, Varden cornered Gretton and begged for the loan of a horse.

"That won't be necessary," Gretton said gently. "One learns to recognize when His Majesty is near to fading off. I took the liberty of summoning your carriage from the posthouse half an hour ago. Shall we wait in the front parlor, where there is no need to make conversation with the others?"

"How do you endure this?" Varden asked when they were standing together by a window that overlooked the drive. The heavy downpour had dwindled to a light, steady rain.

"It is my calling, I suppose. Or perhaps I have simply found a small way to be of use. I am rather a dull fellow myself, you know. It pleases me that you have taken interest in politics, for what will our country become if it is not guided by the best and wisest of its citizens? You may count on my support, Varden, and I hope you will draw upon what little experience and expertise I can provide."

"Gladly. I'm rather an amateur at this point, especially with nearly two years of political doings to catch up with." He sliced a look at Gretton. "Not to mention the drinking. While I am struggling to stay upright, you seem none the worse for wear."

"Ah." Gretton produced one of his rare, sweet smiles and drew from his coat pocket a slender flask. "This is my secret. I keep it filled with tea. With sleight of hand and a knack for redirecting everyone's attention, I can generally slip tea into my nearly empty glass before a servant refills it with brandy."

"Impressive. Next time, if there is one, I shall sit next to you. You are fully recovered from your wound?"

"Oh, yes." As Gretton flexed his arm to prove it, a nearly undetectable wince passed across his face. "But since the incident, a servant skilled with a rifle rides beside the driver when I travel. You should consider taking similar precautions."

"I do. There have been rather too many incidents of late. Have you learned anything further about the attack?"

"Nothing. A large black horse, a large man, a large gun. Well, I don't know that the gun was particularly large, but it seemed so when the barrel was pointed in my direction. One presumes the scoundrel to have been a highwayman lying in wait for a coach departing the Lodge. Not a bad prospect for a robber, in fact, since most of His Majesty's guests are people of means. In any case, I have put the attack behind me. Shall I expect you to attend the meeting on Monday night?"

"Will Wellington be there?"

"I believe so. Indeed, I hope so, because I have an answer to the riddle he posed at supper last evening. Where, he asked, would someone hide an object that is being sought by his enemies? The others put forward various locations, but since he did not tell us the size of the object, I thought the question muddled. So I asked, and he said it didn't matter."

"Interesting. So how did you answer the riddle?"

"I said, 'In the last place my enemies would look.' And everyone seemed to find that amusing, although I was entirely serious. However, I have thought better of my response. Can you guess what I shall tell him Monday?"

"No. But my answer would be 'In a place my enemies have already looked.' "

"Precisely!" Gretton clapped him on the shoulder. "You have found in a moment the solution that eluded me all of last night. I should let you give it to Wellington and claim the credit."

"I was not in the game. Besides, he may have another answer, a more clever one, in mind. Better that you take the risk and let me know if we were correct."

As he was speaking, Varden saw his carriage draw up under the portico. Gretton accompanied him to the door, where the king's servants waited with his coat, hat, a Moroccan leather folder containing the pardon, and the single glove he'd removed when entering the Lodge. Soon he was settled against the plush leather squabs, his eyes drifting shut as he imagined describing his day—all but the pardon secured for Master Barnes—to Helena. She would be pleased with him, he hoped. He was pretty damn pleased with himself.

His mind floated aimlessly on brandy fumes and satisfaction. He dozed, and woke, and dozed again.

"Hold!"

The shout caused him to jerk upright. Then he was thrown back as the horses sprang into a run. Another shout. The carriage rocked when it swung around a tight curve. Outside, the coach lanterns barely illuminated the trees that lined the road.

He grasped the strap and pulled himself straight. To his right, out the rain-streaked window he saw a horse drawing alongside the coach. A black horse, ridden by a tall rider swathed in coat, hat, and muffler. And a pistol in his right hand. He brought it across his chest and aimed inside the carriage.

Varden dived for the floor. Pain struck his hand. Radiated up his arm. A loud report from the pistol. Glass shattered, raining over him.

Another report almost instantly, this one from the driver's box. He twisted his head, could see nothing outside the window. The carriage slowed and stopped.

Cursing, he dragged himself onto the squabs, cradling his right forearm with his left hand. He'd done some damage when he threw himself onto the floor, no telling how much. The tight leather glove was designed as protection, and for the most part, it did its job. But the pain brought sweat to his forehead. For a moment, black spots danced before his eyes.

The carriage door swung open, and his groom's worried face looked inside. "Were you hit, milord?"

"No. I landed a bit hard is all. Did you bring down the rider?"

A grimace. "I missed. The coach was bouncing around, and he came in my sight just long enough to take his shot. Then he peeled off and headed into the woods. Sorry, milord."

"Bad shooting all around, then. And no harm done. You had better reload, in case he has another go at us."

"Already done, milord, and Pemble sent you down this pistol he keeps in the storage box."

"Thank you. Did you by chance get a look at the fellow? Enough to provide a description, or pick him if you saw him again?"

"I did not. But there was a black horse tied up just inside the posthouse stable for a time. Can't say it was the same one. It was there when we got word to bring the carriage, and still there when we'd harnessed up and left. I never saw who came in with it."

"We'll inquire when we get there. Ask Pemble not to spring the horses, please, unless we come under attack."

There was no more trouble, except for the rain pelting in through the broken window and the fact that his hand was being pitchforked by a legion of devils. This was, he reflected grimly, one hell of a way to sober up in a hurry.

He spent the journey trying to make plans, and when they reached the posthouse about twenty minutes later, he set about issuing orders while they were still lined up in his mind.

The window required covering and the inside of the carriage had to be wiped down.

Were there two men proficient with firearms who could escort the carriage into London? Yes, the stable master told him, but they had to be summoned from their homes. A small delay, but he required the time to see to his hand.

Next an interview with the innkeeper, who described the owner of the black horse that had been in the stable, and told him a few other things besides. Things that made him as angry as he had ever been in his life.

But that, too, must wait for a time. He settled the account, arranged for the temporary use of a small bedchamber and the supplies he needed, and went—

temper in check—to the private parlor he'd hired for the day.

She was seated in an overstuffed chair near the fireplace, her legs curled under her, an open book on her lap. He saw her head turn when he opened the door, and the slight opening of her mouth when she saw him. Immediately she placed the book on a side table and rose. "My lord, I did not know you had returned. What happened with the ki—"

Something in his expression must have conveyed what he'd intended to hide. Her hands took hold of her skirts, let go when she realized what she was doing. But everything about her posture was defensive. An animal cornered, looking for a direction to bolt. God, how had it come to this?

"There was a minor accident on my way back," he said. "It will take a little time to complete repairs to the carriage. And to answer your question, His Majesty has graciously permitted me to drop his name whenever it will help advance the cause of legal reform. Please be ready to depart in half an hour."

He stepped back and closed the door on her thunderstruck face. Why was she so clearly astonished? Had she not expected him to find out?

Perhaps she hadn't expected him to return.

Perhaps she'd expected him to be dead.

None of it made sense to him at the moment, but that was because the pain had taken him over. And the fear. He had never quite believed the bones in his fingers and hand had truly knitted together again, would hold if the slightest force was applied to them. The hand might be useless for anything except balancing an object, but damn it all, he wanted it there at the end of his arm.

Well, his vanity wanted it there. No point denying it. More than ever before, he craved honesty, the purest honesty, even from himself to himself.

As for Miss Helena Pryce, if she didn't have her lies in place by this time, she had half an hour to get them in order.

Not all the pain, he realized as he made a discouraged trip up the staircase, not even the greatest pain, was concentrated in his hand.

How the bloody hell had it come to this?

Chapter 16

Helena packed her book and writing materials into her case, draped her pelisse, woolen scarf, gloves, and bonnet on the sideboard, and returned to her chair to wait. The accident must be responsible for his ill humor. And it had been a long, wearying day—more than twelve hours since they set out from London, with another three to pass on the trip back.

During the drive to Windsor, he had told her about the investigation he'd undertaken into crimes and incidents that appeared to be related, ranging from extortion and suicide to bribery and murder. Suspicion centered on the previous Duke of Tallant, the Beast, who had been accused of extortion by the man who confessed to poisoning him. But since the episodes had not ceased with Tallant's death, it seemed probable his heir had taken up the reins.

"Or that someone else is responsible," she pointed out. "The guilty person might have cast blame on Beast Tallant, whom everyone would be eager to condemn, then transferred blame to his successor, who is virtually unknown. That's what I would do."

Varden had laughed and said he didn't doubt it. Then he outlined her duties with regard to the investigation, and the irony struck her immediately. Not so long ago, approaching her on behalf of Michael Keynes, Lord Duran had asked that she compile a dossier on the Earl of Varden. She had done so, exhaustively, and what she learned about him had drawn her to enter his service. Now, of all things, Varden wished her to compile a dossier on Keynes.

"But he was in India the better part of two decades," she protested. "How am I to acquire information from so far away?"

"His activities there are not pertinent. I might have been able to prosecute him in Calcutta, but in the absence of witnesses, nothing whatever can be done here. We shall confine ourselves to what I suspect he is up to now. Get me information about every property owned by the family, occasions when either of the Tallant dukes last visited them, financial transactions of every sort . . . Well, I expect you know better than I what is needed. My primary concern relates to documents that appear to have gone missing. The Beast's murderer searched his study and removed some papers, although we don't know what they were. Later, Tallant House was ransacked. Most likely the robbers came for the information used by the duke to wring money from his victims."

It had sounded like a guess to her. And it was rather a leap to accuse the new duke of picking up where his brother had left off. When she asked Tallant about the documents that very afternoon, she had got the answer she had expected.

Varden wouldn't believe anything he said, though. And she couldn't explain why she *did* believe him. Not without revealing her involvement in the aftermath of the Beast's murder, the spiriting away of the widow and her daughter . . . all of it. The story was not hers to tell. On the subject of the Tallant family, she tiptoed along a thin line of truth. And what with all the necessary omissions and misdirections, she usually ended up lying like a tuppenny fortune-teller.

A drumming sound drew her attention to the window. It was raining heavily again. Then came a knocking at the other end of the room. He was early, she thought, coming instantly to her feet.

But it was a maidservant, looking overset. "His Lordship asks if you will join him upstairs, Miss. I'll show you the way."

With no little apprehension, she followed the maid to a low-ceilinged room at the top of a narrow staircase. Varden, in shirtsleeves, was seated at a small table laid out with two basins filled with water and chunks of ice, a brace of candles, and a stack of thin towels. Even in the glow of firelight from the candles and the hearth, he seemed pale. Tight-lipped. His right arm was cradled atop his left, in a way that . . .

Of course. In the accident, his hand had been injured.

Behind her, the maidservant closed the door, leaving her alone with the earl.

"Thank you for coming, Miss Pryce." The sharp edge was on his tone again. Sharper than before. "I need to remove this glove, but I can't seem to do it myself. And the maid found herself unable to manage it either, probably because I swore at her. I didn't mean to. Will you give it a try, please?"

There was a rickety chair to his right. She perched on the edge of it, pulled the stack of towels closer so that he could rest his arm on it, and studied the glove. Where it ended, reddened flesh bulged out. She had once sprained her foot and ankle, and the results had been similar. It would hurt him, the stripping of the tight glove from his swollen hand.

But clearly it had to be done. "I will pay no mind to your oaths, my lord. But is there a word we should agree on that commands me to stop?"

"No. Don't try pulling on it from the fingertips. That doesn't work. Start at the top and keep going. You must proceed, no matter what I say or do."

"Very well." She had already decided to be quick about it. Taking hold of the glove on either side of his hand, she began to pull it inexorably down. He made a low noise in his throat. His breathing became harsh. But he held his arm firmly in place and let her get on with it.

It seemed to take a lifetime. The bulges of his knuckles and finger joints were like boulders in the path of the glove. The skin, pale as milk when first exposed, turned quickly red when freed from its shell.

Blood red.

Real blood, smearing the glove and streaming down his long fingers. Then the glove came loose, the sudden release rocking her back on her chair.

Immediately he plunged his hand into the basin closest to him. The water clouded with blood.

"Don't be concerned," he said. "It appears to be a splinter of bone working its way out. That has happened several times in the past, although perhaps not quite so dramatically. If you have tweezers, or can find a pair among the servants, we might be able to remove it."

We, she suspected, meant her. "I've tweezers in my case. I'll request clean water as well, and spirits."

When she returned, followed by a servant with a tray, the bleeding had slowed to a trickle. She sat across from Varden, adjusted the candles, and examined his hand. There were two places, one on the back and the other on his palm, where blood marked the penetration of flesh from the inside. But through her dark spectacles, she could not see what was causing the wounds. "I am not the one to do this," she said after a time. "My vision is obscured. There's a good chance I'll make the situation worse."

"I'd like you to try anyway," he said, picking up the open bottle and splashing brandy over his hand. "As you can see by the scars, other bits and pieces have made their escape. It goes easier when they can be pulled directly out."

The hand was spangled with tiny white scars, prominent because of the swelling. She pulled her chair closer, settled his hand on the towels, and took up her tweezers. Before beginning, she stole a look at his face. He was staring at something behind her, or perhaps at nothing.

Starting with the back of his hand, she gently pressed the area around she spot that had been bleeding. The cut she found was not much larger than the eye of a needle. She brushed the nib of her tweezers across it and met with a slight resistance. The tip of the bone splinter. But to get hold of it, she would have to press harder on the flesh and excavate a little with the tweezers.

"Try not to move," she said.

His hand remained perfectly still.

It was hard going. When she pushed down, the bleeding increased, and she could scarcely see where it was she was digging. She gripped the splinter more than once, but it slipped away again, deeper than before. After a time, her hands were perspiring so much that she could no longer keep a firm hold.

"Calm down, Miss Pryce." His voice was soft, and when she glanced up, he gave her a small, reassuring smile. "It looks worse than it feels. I'll rinse my hand while you take a rest, and then we'll start again."

He was surely lying about how it felt. But she rinsed her own hands, dried them carefully, and found him waiting in position when she picked up the tweezers.

This time, perhaps because she understood he would not give up until she had succeeded, she was able to set aside her fear of hurting him and concentrate on her target. It remained elusive through two more rinses and restarts, and then, inexplicably, the tweezers closed on the splinter and held. A gentle pull, and out it came. She nearly shouted with relief.

"Well, that was great fun," he said, holding out his

left hand for the splinter. She dropped it onto his palm, and he examined it with a frown. "It felt a good deal larger. Ready for the other side?"

This was, in a bizarre way, a more intimate experience than when his body had been inside hers. If he had watched her, she could not have borne it. But he went back to staring at the wall behind her, and she went back to pressing and probing. This time, because the flesh on his palm was less sensitive and easier to manipulate, she pulled the splinter within a dozen tries.

"That's more like it," he said when she held up the half-inch fragment of bone. Another splash of brandy before plunging the hand in a clear ice-water bath. "You may go, Miss Pryce. Someone will fetch you from the parlor when the carriage is ready to depart."

She rose, struck silent by his cold dismissal, and made her way downstairs. Was he embarrassed that she had seen his injury? As if she hadn't seen a few hundred of them in the Rookery, although he couldn't know that. And it was true that men resented any woman who caught them out in a moment of weakness. Even Jamie, who loved her, did not want her near when the Wolf was on him.

Because of the earl's foul mood, she bundled herself up ready to go so that he wouldn't have to wait a single second for her. And while she had decided, after consideration, to tell him of her encounter with the Duke of Tallant, it would have to wait for a better time.

All day, a heaviness had been on her heart. By now, Billy would have been tried and sentenced. How terrified he must be. Varden reported success in gaining the king's support for sentencing reforms, but nothing would help the boys already lost. Jamie said they took condemned prisoners to a special place, held them for three days, and then—

No point dwelling on it now. Tomorrow morning

she'd go directly to Jamie and make him describe the trial. She wanted an image to keep of Billy, standing straight and brave in the docket, accepting his fate with dignity. Even if it hadn't been that way, Jamie would tell her the story she needed to hear.

It wasn't long before a groom arrived to escort her to the carriage, where she saw boards covering the window on the right side panel, just above the crest. Then she spotted the rifle across the knees of the groom seated beside the coachman, and the two riders, one on each side of the carriage, also carrying rifles. The groom led her to the door on the left side, set her case inside, and assisted her up the stairs.

Varden was already there, seated in the opposite corner with a pillow on his lap and his right arm laid across it. His hand, wrapped in what appeared to be cheesecloth, rested on a nest of pouches, the sort usually filled with hot water. From their distorted shapes, these appeared to contain chunks of ice. He wore his dark blue woolen greatcoat and had tied a knit scarf around his neck. His pale hair, illuminated by the lantern suspended overhead, glowed like a halo.

The Archangel Earl, save for his eyes. If fire could be encased in green ice, that's how it would look.

She gave sudden thought to jumping out. But the steps had been raised, the door closed, and as if sensing her urge to flee, Varden lifted his good hand and rapped on the ceiling. Seconds later, the horses were moving.

Chapter 17

As the carriage made its way from the stableyard onto the London Road, Helena sensed an oncoming storm that had nothing to do with the weather. Of all the feelings this man had raised in her, could raise in her if he tried, the possibility she would fear him had never occurred to her. Until now.

He was enraged. And it was directed at her, although she could not think why. That she'd had a conversation with Tallant would anger him, she supposed, but not to this degree. "I gather from the armed outriders," she said, "that what you described as an accident was something else. Highwaymen?"

"One rider, with no apparent interest in booty. He shot at me, but hit only the window. Oh, and the panel just alongside your knee. If there's a draft, I can provide you a handkerchief to stuff into the hole."

She ignored that. "And your hand?"

"I fell on it when I took refuge on the floor. Shall I describe the assassin to you? It is possible you are acquainted with him."

It couldn't be! And yet—

"A tall man," he said. "Black coat and hat. Black horse. Does he sound familiar?"

He knew, then. But there was no particular harm done, except that she wished she had admitted to it straightaway. "I expect you mean the Duke of Tallant, who was at the posthouse about, oh, an hour before you returned. You cannot think *he* attacked you?"

"Why not? He fits the description. Has a reason, probably several, to want me out of the way. And he was in the neighborhood. How did you get word to him, Miss Pryce? I've done the calculations. There was plenty of time, after I told you we'd be coming here, to send a message. But I never mentioned where I would leave you to wait. How is it he found you at the posthouse?"

She could tell already that the truth wouldn't please him. But she'd nothing else to offer. "He found me on a country road in Buckinghamshire, hiding behind a tree."

A sharp crack as his left hand struck the door beside him. "This is not a party game, Miss Pryce."

"It's quite true. I went for a walk—"

"The innkeeper said you were gone for several hours."

"A *long* walk. I have few opportunities to—" But he wouldn't care about that. "I left soon after you sent the carriage back. And of course I should have remained at the posthouse, or stayed close by. But I went out, and was several miles away when the duke chanced to be passing on the same road. When I saw the rider, I concealed myself as a precaution. But he had already spotted me and recognized my spectacles. By then it had begun to rain, so he insisted on taking me to where I was staying."

"Is this the story you concocted between you, or are you making it up as you speak?"

"I am describing what happened. When we arrived at the posthouse, he came inside and we spoke for . . . I don't know. A short time. Then he left."

"On his way to the road I'd be traveling. I presume you told him where I could be found?"

"He saw your carriage in the stable and inquired about you. I said you were paying a call on the king. And he said he'd done the same thing yesterday."

"Which explains why he was still hanging about, rambling along country roads, rescuing truant servants from a rainstorm."

"Buying sheep. He said he was buying sheep. And when he left, he was on his way to buy some pigs."

"I should have guessed. Dukes regularly wander about on their own, purchasing livestock."

There was nothing ordinary about the Duke of Tallant, who made his own rules and did whatever he pleased. Varden ought to know that by now. "Tallant was in company with the king yesterday. That's before you said we would be coming here, meaning I cannot have arranged a meeting."

"Unless you already knew he was to be in Windsor. It seems I provided you an opportunity to set him on me."

"But how could I? You were supposed to return to the posthouse within a few hours. Then you were delayed, and sent back the carriage. I can't have known that would happen."

"But when it did, you set out to find Tallant, who was waiting somewhere to intercept me. He brought you back to the posthouse, waited until my carriage left to pick me up, and followed it."

She had a flash of memory. Tallant at the window, looking out. Sounds from the stableyard. Varden's horses being harnessed, perhaps, and the coach's departure? Sure enough, he'd left not long after that. But perhaps he simply didn't want to be at the posthouse when Varden returned.

It could have been him, she had to acknowledge. He was capable of just about anything. All the Keyneses were. It was in the blood.

I've no doubt you and Tallant are in communication," said the earl when she failed to speak. "The tale you gave me last night, the one describing only two brief encounters and no significant connection between you, was a lie."

What did he know? "I said I'd met him twice. Today we met for the third time."

"Did he send you to take employment with me?"

The question was such a surprise that it snapped her head back. "Of course not."

"But you knew we were enemies."

"All London knew he'd done your hand in. It was general gossip. Look. I had every intention of telling you about meeting him on the road. And yes, it was a . . . an improbable coincidence. I said that to him at the time. And he said that his friend, Mr. Singh, believes that nothing happens without a purpose."

"So he was *fated* to encounter you, and thereby learn of a ripe opportunity to shoot me down?"

Her own temper was on the edge now. A little beyond it. How could he imagine that she would deliberately harm him? "I don't know much about fate, Lord Varden. But I think that if Tallant had meant to shoot you down, you would be dead."

Silence. Then he said, "I've considered that possibility. Perhaps it was his intention to warn me off the investigation. Others know of it, and if I had been slain, they would look first to him as the killer."

"But what if it was some other man? Has it occurred to you that you might be wrong?"

"There is precedent, certainly. If I am wrong, I shall confess it, and apologize, and make amends as a gentleman should. Meantime, you must give me leave to preserve my life, if I can. And because I dare not rely on your discretion, you may expect to be kept on a tight leash."

For a time she just stared at him, fighting to regain control of her temper. But it was already shooting off like a Congreve rocket. "You are *threatening* me? With no evidence, with only your prejudices to bear witness, you accuse me of deceit, betrayal, and entering a conspiracy to commit murder? Do you think me part of the extortion scheme as well?"

"I haven't ruled it out. You move in high circles without being noticed. There is no one better at gathering information."

"Dear God. Even if Tallant were guilty of every charge you've laid at his door, why would I join forces with him against you?"

Varden made a dismissive gesture. "He's a wealthy man. And you have admitted that money is the sole reason you engage in any endeavor."

"One reason. Not the only reason. Whatever you think of my integrity, Lord Varden, it cannot lag very far behind your own. If lies have been told, some of them were yours. Last night, when explaining how you came to pursue a vendetta against the duke, you failed to mention the most important reason of all. That you are in love with his wife."

The fire in his eyes became a conflagration. It felt as if the entire carriage had gone ablaze. But her fear and respect had gone as well. She was done with him now. Only the battle remained, with her pride and rage matched—foil to foil—against his.

Rain battered the windowglass beside her. She heard the thumping of hooves on the macadam road as they came closer to the city. The rattle of wheels. The pounding of her heart.

Finally he spoke, with unexpected calm. "What an interesting conversation you had with the duke. I am surprised he would tell you that."

"Is it true?" She wanted him to deny it, God help her.

"Oh, yes."

She felt sick. "But you could not have known her long enough—"

"A matter of days. Three or four. But I knew from the moment I first looked into her eyes."

"That sounds very like infatuation. She is a remarkably lovely woman, of course, with the sort of beauty that matches your own. It must have been rather like looking into a mirror."

"What a self absorbed creature you presume me to be. Of my own experience, I can assure you that to be sought out for one's appearance is . . . distasteful. Courage, honor, intelligence, humor, confidence—these are qualities I value. And in her, I saw them immediately. I sensed that to know her would be a voyage of discovery to strange and fascinating lands. But how, really, can love be accounted for? It simply *is*."

She stifled an unladylike snort. "How very romantic of you, my lord. But for her, love *wasn't*. And yet you continue to pursue her, although she is married, and to persecute her husband, in good part because he stole her from you."

"Stole? That may indeed be the case. There is evidence that she had no free choice in the marriage. Which is not to say she ever felt for me what I will always feel for her, or that she would have fallen in love with me if the circumstances were different. No doubt you think me a besotted idiot, and to a degree, you are correct. I have behaved that way for longer than even a heartbroken man is allowed to run mad."

He leaned back his head and closed his eyes. "But consider this, Miss Pryce. Females have pursued me since first I set foot at a small-town assembly ball. In all the years after, fully aware of my obligation to marry, I have sought the one woman intended for me, the one I would share my life with. I was not an inexperienced whelp when I met Miranda Holcombe. She was the one I had always sought. There will be no other."

"And so, to preserve a connection with her, you bought that derelict castle and closed yourself up inside it."

His eyes flicked open, pierced her with a look of reproach, and closed again. "Not precisely. That was, I confess, the height of my folly. But the roots of it were deep, and the intentions sincere. You would not be interested in the details."

He might tell her, she thought. Things he would never admit to were they not enclosed alone here, as they had once been enclosed together at the castle. "I am greatly interested," she said carefully.

"And I wonder why, despite my anger, I am inclined to tell you." He gave a small shrug, as if resigning himself to the incomprehensible. "India changed everything. It was for me a stolen indulgence, my last before buckling down to the serious matter of selecting a wife. Love, it seemed, had eluded me, but perhaps it would grow from companionship in the marriage, as sometimes occurs. These things were much on my mind when my travels took me to the town of Agra, following a rumor that Michael Keynes could be found there. I discovered instead the most beautiful of all human creations, a building known as the Taj Mahal. The woman for whom it had been built, Mumtaz Mahal, was the wife of a Mughal emperor, but soon became his counselor as well, inspiring him to acts of benevolence on behalf of the poor and helpless. When she died, he poured his grief into the building that became her mausoleum, and, eventually, his as well. I had never conceived of so transcendent a love. It seized my imagination.

"Not long after came the fight with Keynes, which I have already described to you. The Sikh physician who first tended my hand used few narcotics, but when I came into the care of English doctors, they liberally dosed me with laudanum. I welcomed the relief from pain, but the drug also generated fantastical dreams. In one that recurred several times a week, I was building a monument to the woman I loved, but not of white marble with minarets and onion-shaped domes. My tribute was—you have guessed it—a castle."

She had not expected such whimsy in him. "Do you believe in prescient dreams, my lord?"

"I . . . No. The dream ceased when I forced myself to do without the laudanum, and I gave it no more thought until the last time I saw Miranda Holcombe. She had asked me to arrange a visit to Michael Keynes when he was imprisoned in the Tower, so that she could ask him to release any claim to property his brother had stolen from her family. Once he was executed, she said, the legal complications would take years to untangle. For that reason I helped her, and by doing so, put her into his hands."

Varden was frowning slightly, but his voice remained level. Detached. "Having no assurance Keynes would renounce the claim, I decided to see what I could accomplish on her behalf. That's how I learned about the castle. Then he married her, and there was nothing to be done."

"Except to buy it for yourself."

"Not for me. I intended first to restore the castle, and then to present it to her. I cannot write poetry, or sing songs like the troubadours, but in the tradition of courtly love, I had resolved to give to my unattainable lady a gift."

"Good heavens." Had he taken leave of his senses? "If Tallant knew that, he really would kill you."

"It was a fancy that has passed. A mirage from a laudanum dream. If ever the lady wants her castle back, she may have it."

Her hands had knitted themselves together so tightly they hurt. Until this moment, she had not put the one thing together with the other. Through eyes that felt as if they were bleeding, she looked directly at him. At the golden lashes that veiled his thoughts, that hid the fire burning inside him.

"I had thought you simply wanted a woman that night," she said. "But *she* was the woman you wanted. Your fantasy lover in your arms, in her castle, perhaps in the room that was hers when she lived there. Perhaps in the very bed where she used to sleep."

His eyes snapped open.

"In the dark, in the pure dark, you could embrace her. Kiss her mouth, become one with her body, find your pleasure. In the dark, we all look alike. In the dark, what is real but what we imagine? I wasn't there at all."

"Good God. It wasn't like that. I swear it. When I—" He stopped, sliced his fingers through his hair. Looked confused. "From the moment you strode across the courtyard until the morning you departed without a word, I never once thought of her. Not when . . . not at any time. She was never in that room. There was only you."

She looked into his eyes and believed him. After a fashion. She had not been a substitute after all. Just a female body, present when a man's anger and blood were roused. Which often led to . . . to what they had done together. She had known it at the time. Accepted it.

The only fantasies in that dark room had been hers.

A little ashamed, she nodded. "You must pardon me, sir. I have a bit of vanity under all this starch and wool. Your story is not about me, nor should I have intruded there. Please forget I spoke."

"So long as you understand—"

"I do. Entirely. I was wrong. Let us return then to the issue that does lie between us. Are you pursuing the duke so that if he is found guilty and executed, you may eventually claim his wife?"

"That crosses my mind from time to time. I am not proud of it. But I wish only to protect her from him, and from the consequences of his crimes. When he is found guilty, nearly everything he owns will be forfeit.

He is the last of his line, so unless she has provided him an heir, the title will revert to the crown. I mean to quietly defend her interests, best as I can. There is little chance I will ever have her for myself."

Little chance wasn't *no* chance. He still hoped. He still, in Tallant's words, mooned over his lost love.

Well, let him. She was quite finished with him, and he with her.

She turned her head to the window. Rain shrouded the road. She couldn't tell how far they had come, how close they were to the city. It felt she'd been in this compartment with him for hours, but it had probably been only one hour. Less than that.

Better to close the doors now, before she began making excuses for the both of them. She was not strong enough to bear any more time in his company.

"Taking employment with you," she said, "was inadvisable at the beginning, and the situation has done nothing but deteriorate since then. Shall we consider the resignation delivered you at the castle to be final?"

"Oh, no, Miss Pryce. You'll not pick up your skirts and skip away now. You work for me, and you will continue doing so until I dismiss you."

She swung her gaze to him. "You want me to stay? But you don't *trust* me."

"All the more reason to keep you under my supervision. You cannot be permitted to quit just because you disapprove of me, or dislike how I choose to spend my time. This tendency of yours to walk away when the stove gets hot—"

"The first time, you dismissed me."

"There was some dispute, as I recall, about which came first. In future, I will make all such decisions."

"Rubbish. Even an earl hasn't that much power. You cannot compel me to stay."

"You are quite right. But I can deprive you of a desirable place to go. What is the use of a sterling reputation and singular influence if I cannot manipulate the prospects of a servant? And a female servant at that. You will find no employment of the sort you have become accustomed to. Agencies will send you only to marginal households. No one of status will defy me by welcoming you. No politics for you, Miss Pryce. No aristocratic company. Even modest intellectual and social gatherings will be closed to you. Palazzo Neri, where you have long run tame, will turn you away. Do you think I cannot accomplish this?"

"I cannot begin to think you would be so unkind."

"It astonishes me as well. But your imprisonment will be brief. As soon as I conclude the Tallant investigation, or abandon it, you may bustle off with a good recommendation in hand. *If* in the meantime you have conducted yourself in a trustworthy manner. And obeyed me."

"But how can I prove myself? What duties would you dare entrust to me?"

"Not many, to be sure. Your tasks will be strictly circumscribed and not up to your abilities, let alone your wishes. But under the circumstances, there are plenty of disappointments to go around. You must accept your share."

"And a reduction in salary as well?"

"Ah, the money again. But no. If only to prevent you from complaining, I'll pay you the salary you demanded."

The teeth of his trap were closing around her. "I presume the assignment to gather information about the Duke of Tallant is withdrawn."

"To the contrary. I'll be interested in your report, especially when I have compared it with what I learn from other sources."

Looking for contradictions and lies, no doubt. He was investigating her as well, and didn't mind her knowing it. "You may start with this, then. When we met this afternoon, I asked the duke if he knew anything more about the missing documents, and he—"

"You *asked* him?"

"It is not my habit to waste opportunities. He said that workmen had searched Tallant House during extensive reconstruction and found nothing. As time permits, he will continue to search Longview and the other properties."

"And now he knows the investigation is continuing, and that I am involved." Varden shook his head. "Why am I surprised? You have, of course, told him everything. Shall I expect him to disclose, *as time permits*, that he found no documents?"

"I only convey information, sir. You must compare it with your other sources."

The ghost of a smile. "*Touché*," he said softly. "And now for my dilemma. I cannot trust you with affairs of state. Trivial business affairs can remain in your hands, but I must deny access to anything you might use against me. The fencing will continue, as soon as I am able. And all that adds up to five or ten hours a week. How else am I to keep you busy, Miss Pryce?"

She knew a rhetorical question when she heard one.

"No ideas? Then I suppose the ladies, who were profoundly sorry to lose your services, shall have them again. Try not to corrupt my nieces, will you?"

"You promised me, sir, that I would no longer be compelled to arrange social activities."

"Ah. So I did." His brows lifted, as if he'd just had a splendid idea. "Well, then. Perhaps you should become my mistress."

At first, she couldn't believe he'd said it. Then she decided he was mocking her. But the glint in his eyes wasn't amusement, and the determination that whitened his lips was unmistakable. He meant it. He *meant* it!

She vibrated with fury. "You accuse me of every sort of crime, declare me unworthy of trust or respect, refuse to let me free of your service. You insult me.

Threaten me. And yet you expect me to come to your *bed*?"

"Expect? Sadly, no."

"But how could you even *want* me there? How could you bear to touch me, thinking I conspired to kill you?"

"I don't know," he said at length. "But I do want you. Have never stopped wanting you, in spite of my suspicions, and your rejections, and the impropriety of an affair with a servant."

It was a slap across the face. But what most startled her was that it came from a man who had probably never made a social mistake in his life, or been ungallant to the humblest of his servants. It appeared to startle him as well.

And what right had she to be insulted? From the beginning, this man had sensed the desire she concealed under tightly wrapped hair and drab dresses, behind her dark glasses and a manner as off-putting as she could contrive. And still she would have been safe, so long as she held him at a distance.

But when he called to the passion straining inside her, she had surrendered everything. She became—for one night—what she was born to be. What she had resolved never to become.

Now, stripped of profession, reputation, and pride, she was nothing at all.

"I cannot," she finally said. Her eyes were bleeding again. "I will scrub floors or weed your gardens or beg in the streets before I'll become your whore."

His jaw stiffened. "That is not what I suggested."

"You pay me, I lay myself under you. What else could that be?"

"Desire, tangled up with commerce and our unpleasant circumstances. Or perhaps I intended to outrage you, as your actions have outraged me. It was not the behavior of a gentleman, certainly." He released a heavy breath. "Shall we disengage for a time, let our tempers cool, before I propose a more acceptable task for you?"

She shrugged, and folded her arms, and stared out into the back night. The rain had stopped, but its traces lingered on the windowpane, reflecting light from the carriage lamps.

Mistress to an earl. To the Archangel! How little he knew himself, to imagine he could long tolerate a woman from the stews in his bed. Never mind she'd been a virgin when first he had her. No virginal woman, virginal in her heart, behaved as she had done that night. And if ever he took her in his arms again . . . Well, she did not want to think how she would respond.

Without restraint, that was certain. She knew precisely how whores gave pleasure to men. To jaded men and inept men, to men so repellent only a whore would have them. To aristocrats as well, but only because they sought what decent women would not provide them.

She closed her eyes. No decisions were possible now. Look where impulse and instinct had got her. Where passion had brought her, ripping flesh from bone, reason from dreams.

For the moment, she had only to consent to whatever duties he assigned her. Make a show of doing what he asked, while she made preparations to leave him. And England as well, for she took him at his word. Unless she continued to do his bidding, she would never again find decent work here.

The carriage slowed. She glanced out the window and saw wagons, riders, and a few pedestrians illuminated by street lamps. The outskirts of London, perhaps Hammersmith or a little beyond. Only one day, and so much had transpired, and none of it good.

To distract herself, she began compiling mental lists. People she must speak to. The disposition of her few possessions. Finances. Travel arrangements. She could set out with Devonshire's party and accompany them part of the way, until she decided where she wanted to go.

"I have rarely seen a more calculating expression on a woman's face," Varden said, not unpleasantly. "Might I interrupt long enough to give you a few instructions before we arrive in Grosvenor Street?"

"Of course, my lord. Shall I be required to take notes?"

"I shouldn't think so." He rubbed the bridge of his nose. "All this business with Tallant has distracted me from other matters, including one of surpassing importance to my family. Not long ago, I swore to marry before the end of the year. But now, but with my life under threat, there is some urgency to get on about it. As soon as may be, I intend to wed an appropriate young woman. You are to find her for me."

She felt her mouth drop open. Snapped it closed. After a time, she found one word to say. "H-how?"

Amusement danced with the green fire in his eyes. "Research, Miss Pryce. I didn't mean you should personally select my bride. Simply provide a list of qualified females, beginning with those likely to be in London for the Season. I haven't time to make the rounds of country houses."

"You mean to choose your wife from a *list*?"

"You aren't listening. I've been away for nearly two years. I don't know who is in the marketplace. You are to help me narrow the field, not merely with a list of names but with information about their families, fortunes, education . . . whatever you can unearth. I shall then contrive to meet the leading candidates in circumstances that give no hint of my intentions. A great nuisance, to be sure, but it must be done."

Lizards mated with more sensitivity than this. But he was entirely serious about arranging a speedy marriage. And entertained, she could tell, by the task he'd found for the woman who refused to be his mistress. Was he trying to punish her?

But he had no idea how she really felt. Perhaps he thought she would be relieved to have his attentions directed elsewhere. Perhaps he thought he was doing her a kindness.

And this, Elly, is why you drowned your feelings long years ago. See where caring has got you?

"I beg your pardon, my lord. This is not a duty for which I have prepared myself. Are not the ladies of your family better acquainted with eligible young women?"

"I daresay. But unless firmly restrained, they will fling their favorites in my direction like skeets at a shooter. And when word gets out that I am at last prepared to come to scratch, I shall be besieged from all sides. You will conclude that I want to avoid the melee, which is quite true. But more than that, I wish not to raise hopes and expectations."

With a glance, he raised hopes. With a smile, expectations. He knew what it was to be the object of adoration, as she knew what it was to succumb to the force of his attraction. "Yes," she said. "I see what you mean. Reconnaissance and stealth."

"I've the excuse of presenting my nieces, which will explain my presence at affairs I would not otherwise attend. Which reminds me. I'll provide you a list of my invitations. Do what you can to find out which I ought to accept."

"You overestimate my sources," she said, a little impatiently. "I cannot quiz former employers such as Wellington or Devonshire about *parties*. Lady Jessica would gladly advise me, but she doesn't plan to return to London until late in the Season. I can ferret out the pedigrees of potential brides, sir, and whatever else is contained in public records. But I cannot get hold of invitation lists."

Even as she said that, several means of doing so popped into her thoughts. And when she glanced up at the earl's face, he was grinning at her. He knew how her mind worked. The acknowledgment was like a caress.

Instantly she felt his retreat, and her own.

"What specific qualities do you seek?" she said briskly. "Is there a rank below which you will not look? Would a viscount's daughter do? A baron's? A mere baronet's? Since you are in a hurry, we should eliminate unsuitable candidates before I waste time with them."

"Rank is somewhat important, I expect." He looked as if he'd bitten into a sour apple. "Should her status be lower than mine, marrying me will elevate it. But the Countess of Varden must be prepared to manage a large household—several of them—and take her role in polite Society. If I pursue my interest in politics and diplomacy, I shall require a hostess comfortable with statesmen and foreigners. A wife willing to travel and make herself pleasant to strangers."

The field was narrowing fast. And he was hiring a wife, much the same way he had hired his secretary. But why not? He had loved, and lost the woman he loved, and was convinced he would never love again. Now he was being practical. "Are there physical attributes you favor, my lord? Personal qualities of significance?"

"You needn't concern yourself with appearance," he said, clearly impatient with her questions. Finding the matter distasteful, he wanted it out of his hands and into hers. "She must be of childbearing years. Given the primary reason I am hurrying to take a wife, a candidate from—what is the word?—*prolific* parents would be nice. A woman of good character, from a family of nearly impeccable reputation. Educated. Not silly. I do not require a substantial dowry, and can do without any at all. I'll not settle money on wastrel relatives. What else?"

She didn't answer.

He turned his head toward what should have been a window, met wooden planks, and gave a small sigh. "This will not be a love match, as you know. And I will not mislead her. She'll know I am marrying to provide an heir to the title, and that I expect no more of her than I will bind myself in honor to give. Amiability. Fidelity. Consideration. Respect."

She asked, with no right to ask, "Can you live all your life with only that, my lord?"

"Yes." A pause. "What choice have I?"

A long silence then, as the landmarks outside Helena's window became recognizable. They were nearly come to Sothingdon House.

This time she spoke because she had nothing left to lose. "You love one woman, who is already married to another. You say you desire another woman, who chances to be me. And you will marry, swiftly, a woman for reasons that have nothing to do with love or passion. Should you not take a little time, sir? You may again find passion. Best of all, you may again find love."

"I think you are wrong." Even in the golden light of the lantern, his face was pale. "In all the years of searching, I found only one love. And one woman who set me on fire. And because I can marry neither of them, I must settle on a wife of convenience. They were all supposed to be the same woman, of course, the one I loved and desired and married. It isn't only my hand, you see, that has fragmented into pieces."

Heart aching, she turned her head to look out the window. There was nothing to be said after that. Nothing to do but help him however she could. A few minutes later, when the servant helped her alight from the coach, their silence remained unbroken.

Chapter 18

The books that usually crowded the library shelves at Sothingdon House had been crated up while the floors were being refinished and the walls painted. Helena, swathed in an old apron and sitting on a low stool, rummaged through the boxes one by one, digging out the books she needed and stacking them on a large worktable. Then she began organizing the other books and returning them to the shelves, dusting each one, filling up Monday afternoon with tasks. Anything to postpone the search for Lord Varden's bride.

Eventually, her reluctance was overtaken by her guilt. It was, after all, the last service she would do for him. She should set herself to do it well. Give to her lord a gift, as he had once set out to give his lady a restored castle. She did wish him happy, and if that required her to put a woman in his arms, then she must try to make it the right woman.

By ten o'clock she was well into a preliminary list of young ladies from good families, using information culled from Burke's and Debrett's. Some would have wed since publication, and she had included only the daughters of dukes, marquesses, and earls, but it was a beginning. She was sharpening her pen when a loud knock on the front door startled her.

She hurried to a window and saw in the street a

single horse tethered to the wrought-iron gate. Taking up a candle, she made her way downstairs.

The young man at the door, wearing silver-and-black livery under a black cloak, swept off his hat and bowed. "I have a letter, ma'am, for Miss Helena Pryce."

He thought her a servant, probably just come from scouring the coal bin. "I am she."

His expression, polite from the start, didn't alter as he removed a sealed letter, several pages long, from the pouch slung crossways over his chest. "The Duchess of Tallant bid me, if I found you at home, to wait for a reply."

"Of course. Would you care to come inside?"

"Thank you, but I had better keep watch on my horse."

Nodding, she closed the door and sped to the library, where she read the letter and accompanying schedule, and then read through them again. There was little enough to say in her reply, except that she would do everything she could and write again with more information when she had any. After some reflection, she added a postscript. "It is hard, I know, but you should stay at Longview for now. His Grace would tell you the same."

When the young man was on his way with the letter, she threw off her dusty clothes, washed quickly, and made herself presentable. All the while her thoughts were tumbling like drunken acrobats, but after a while, ideas and plans would begin sorting themselves out. They always did.

To her relief, Finn was in his room over the mews stable. She paced outside while he harnessed the horses, the cold air clearing her head, and soon after, they set out for Varden's leased house. He wasn't there, and the servant who answered the door would tell her nothing of his whereabouts.

She thought she knew, but had stopped by Great Ryder Street because it was closer. On her instruction, Finn set a route for Palazzo Neri, where the inner circle of Tory power generally met on Monday nights.

Robert Peel had the right idea, Varden was thinking two hours into the meeting. Peel had stayed away, which left Varden to field questions and objections from those opposed to the home secretary's reform agenda. For about an hour he was under fire from all sides, and if not for the comprehensive information provided him in Helena Pryce's report, he'd have been lost for answers. Finally the subject turned to second-level cabinet appointments, and he soon lost interest in the proceedings.

Wellington had also let him down, remaining at Stratfield Saye with, Gretton reported, a debilitating earache. Varden had wanted his assessment of Thursday's attack, and in the circumstances, ended up telling no one about it. Not Gretton, who had also been accosted on his way from Windsor to London, although they probably ought to compare notes. He'd not even spoken of it to Sir Richard when he stopped by his office that afternoon to request a new search of Tallant House. For some reason it had felt wrong to speak of the incident, and there was little to be gained by spreading the news.

He had even created a story to explain the condition of his hand, although no one had inquired. After a memorable examination, the physician did not believe any bones had been rebroken, although he could not be certain. Or be held responsible. Or do much of anything if they were. Left to his own devices, Varden had new gloves made in several sizes to allow for the swelling, and for most of the weekend his fingers resembled fat blood sausages. But the pain had finally subsided, as had the swelling, and he was feeling more optimistic.

In part, that was due to one of his few successes—the pardoning and settlement of young Billy Barnes. Ann had agreed to take responsibility for him in exchange for Varden's promise to escort Phoebe and Chloe to virtually every social event of the Season. Master Barnes, released that morning, had been taken to a friend's estate while arrangements were made to convey him north.

All this subterfuge, just to prevent Helena from finding out who had rescued the boy. But Varden wasn't supposed to know of his existence, and he damn well didn't want to explain how he'd found out.

Besides, it gave him pleasure to do her a service, especially without taking credit for it. Not to mention that if he did take credit, she would instantly assume he wanted something in return. A deal-making woman, Helena. She'd do far better in the Lords than ever he would.

The voices droning unattended in his ears had stopped. Realizing it, he glanced up and saw the others looking past him to the door. Turning, he saw Devonshire, his usually pale skin flushed, nodding apologetically.

"I beg your pardon, gentlemen," he said, already backing out the door again. "I've a message to be delivered privately. To Varden."

Alarmed, Varden rose and bowed to his fellows.

Devonshire was waiting for him at the end of the passageway. "She said that only a duke could get in there. What the devil are you all talking about? Are we going to war?"

"You'd be bored senseless," Varden said. "What is the message?"

"Oh, sorry. I don't know. Miss Pryce wishes to speak with you at the same place where you spoke before."

Alarm bells were clanging in earnest now. "Did she seem overset?"

"Miss Pryce? She was as she always is, forthright and determined. As you see, I came for you immediately."

What kind of servant had dukes loping off to deliver her messages? Bemused, Varden thanked Devonshire and made his way to the courtyard.

It was cold there, and dim, lit only with a pair of yellow Japanese lanterns hung in opposite corners. He sensed her before seeing her, drawn to the energy she threw off like rays from a small, vibrant sun.

"Miss Pryce," he said, arriving at where she stood stiff and purposeful beside a potted tree. "How may I serve you?"

A small release of air at the sarcasm, which he hadn't intended. Then she said, "I am sorry, my lord, to have called you from your meeting. I'll not keep you longer than it requires to answer two questions. Have you laid charges against the Duke of Tallant? Have you ordered him taken into custody?"

"No," he said, astonished. "And no. What brings you here in the middle of the night to ask?"

"Do you know where he is?"

"I do not. And I repeat my question."

"At the Palazzo, day is night and night is day. I ask now because *now* is when I need to know. Again, I ask your pardon for disturbing you. Good night, my lord."

Uncharacteristically, she had boxed herself into a corner. She had chosen it, he supposed, because no light reached this far. But unless she chose to clamber over a waist-high box hedge, she would have to get past him on the narrow gravel path where he stood, occupying every inch of it. "What has occurred to distress you?" he said, his voice more calm than he felt. "And to send Devonshire like an errand boy to fetch me?"

"I am not in the least distressed. This is a matter of business and none of your—"

"Cut line, Helena. We'll be here as long as it takes

for you to explain, so you may as well get started. Is Tallant back in the Tower? Chained up in some local constabulary?"

"That's what I was asking you!" A motion, as if she'd started to stomp her foot and thought better of it. "We . . . I don't know where he is. I thought perhaps you might. But if you don't, please let me pass."

"We are at stalemate, then. Except that I am willing to stand here the rest of the night, while you are anxious to be on your way. Shall we proceed directly to the compromise?"

"In my experience, aristocrats compromise by giving orders." She took a deep breath. "Tallant has not returned to Longview. He was expected on Saturday. When he had not arrived by late this afternoon, the duchess wrote to me. Her servant delivered the letter about an hour ago."

"To *you*, who claims to scarcely know the family?"

"She has few acquaintances in London, sir."

She knew *him*. But he, of course, did not wish the duke well. "What is it you plan to do?" he asked, rather sure he knew the answer.

"Go after him, of course." A short hesitation. "I assume you know that he was attacked by two men several weeks after his brother's murder. The man who confessed to the murder before killing himself is thought to have hired them, but the duchess believes otherwise. She thinks the real killer remains alive, free, and dangerous. And knowing of her concern, His Grace invariably writes to her if he is for any reason delayed on his travels. The last message she had from him was sent on Friday. It said he would be home by Saturday evening."

And what, Varden wondered, did a slim young woman, even one with a will of iron, imagine she could do to find him? "The first step, surely, is to employ Runners and send them out looking."

"It might be, except for the delay in recruiting and

dispatching them. In fact, sir, would you take care of that first thing in the morning? And make sure they don't dawdle."

"That will not be possible. If you mean to go haring after Tallant, I shall be forced to go haring with you."

"Out of the question!"

Her mulish expressing and clenched fists told him this was nonnegotiable, and he quite agreed. But he would try a little reason first. "I wish you to consider this without taking insult. If the duke is in trouble, who can best find and assist him? A female to whom no one will pay the slightest heed? Or, the female in company with an earl whose reputation will open all doors and secure all available information?"

"Do you think I haven't taken that into account? But the only earl I know who would go on this search hates the duke and wants nothing more than to see him brought down."

"You believe him innocent of the murder, and of the extortion, and—"

"I think him entirely capable of killing his brother. But not by poison. And extortion is a weaselly crime, not at all in his nature."

"Someone has taken up where the Beast left off, that much we know. If the new duke isn't heir to the crimes as well as the title, he has nothing to fear. Not from me, Helena. You can't imagine I would let an innocent man be prosecuted."

She didn't answer, which struck him, oddly, as a sign he was making progress.

"I don't think chasing around the countryside is of any use," he said. "But if you insist on going, then for God's sake, let us do this together. Believe it or not, I am the one person who can best help him."

Her chin went up, and without seeing her eyes, he could feel her gaze burning into him. "In that case," she said, "he really is in trouble."

There came a point, always, where he could not

continue making demands on her. Leaden-hearted, he turned sideways to let her pass.

She picked up her skirts and swished on by. Then, where the path met a circle of trees at the center of the courtyard, she paused. Turned. "I am going after him," she said. "But first I have arrangements to make. If you wish to come, meet me at the mews behind Sothingdon House in two hours."

"I'll bring my carriage," he said. "What is the use leaving before dawn?"

"To arrive when the sun comes up at our real starting point, which is where he took me onto his horse. That road, such as it is, will not accommodate anything so large as your coach. You must ride, or join me in my carriage. Two hours, sir. I shall not wait for you."

In fact, he was fairly sure she meant to get a two-hour head start. Inviting him along had been a ruse.

Or perhaps not. He wondered, as he followed the path she had taken, if there would ever be a time they could trust each other. Take a risk, a leap of faith, just because—

But there was no reason for trust. One night of magnificent passion had been exactly what she had said—a time out of time. It had no connection to their lives now, or in the future.

When he reached the entrance hall, Beata was waiting there with his coat draped over her satin-clad arm. "A servant told me you were on your way," she said. "Was the meeting so very tedious that you arranged for your own servant to rescue you?"

"Indescribably tedious. And Miss Pryce, who remains a great favorite of my family, brought a message. I am off to deal with a minor crisis blown far out of proportion."

"A family problem, then?" Beata raised a dark, well-shaped brow. "She is still in the employ of the ladies?"

"Of us all." He slid his arms into the coat she held out for him. "The problem could easily be dealt with tomorrow, but I'm using it as an excuse to leave. Politics interests me the most when I am not in the middle of it."

"You are meant to be a diplomat, *angelo mio*. Among swarthy people, I think, like the Spanish or even my own Italians. Then you will be the center of every gathering."

Precisely what he had always wanted. But he gave her the smile she expected, took his hat and gloves from the footman she beckoned forward, and made his second escape of the evening.

Arriving at the Sothingdon mews an hour later, Varden was unsurprised to find it empty. A few lights showed from the house, which did surprise him, to the point he rode around to the front door and knocked.

"You're early," Helena said when she opened the door. "Finn is delivering messages, but I expect him back shortly. Who are those two men on the street? Armed bodyguards? Do you mean to travel with an entourage?"

"No. May I come in?"

She stepped aside, still looking out to the street. "They'll draw too much attention there. Will you direct them to the mews? I'm on the first floor, working in the library." And up she went, all business, after treating him much like a nuisance of a puppy that insisted on following her around.

She was seated at a worktable when he arrived at the library, taking notes from an open book. "I am used to arranging travel," she said without looking up, "but not to the area we'll be searching. I've found maps of Buckingamshire and the surrounding counties that will be of some use, although we shall acquire better information from the residents. I do wish you wouldn't bring servants. On the back-country roads, we shall look like a parade. Or do you think we require protection?"

It was warm in the room. He removed his hat and coat, thinking how he would tell her without making her angry. "The men will leave us when we reach the road to Windsor. One is the groom who fired at the horseman on Friday night. He thought he'd missed, and the rider quickly disappeared into the woodland. But since it is possible his shot struck the man, I have ordered a search to begin from where the attack took place."

She put down her pen. "You believe the duke has gone missing because he is wounded? Or dead?"

"It hasn't been ruled out. But I've little reason to expect my grooms will find anything, unless the rider fell dead close to the site. Rain will have washed away any signs they could follow. Nevertheless they will look, and make enquiries, and possibly discover a wounded man who fits the description and is not the duke."

"They would have to, wouldn't they? If ever the duke decided to attack you, my lord, he would do it face to face. I have called in assistance as well, of a more relevant kind. Finn is delivering messages that will ensure Runners are dispatched. A few less-than-official trackers will be sent out as well. So you see, there is no need for you to accompany me tonight."

"Let us not pluck that crow again. May I be of assistance now, reviewing maps or—" He made a vague gesture. Servants always took care of such matters for him. He'd probably be more trouble than help.

In response, she shook her head and picked up her pen.

He wandered back to the worktable, glancing at the books and papers that had been pushed to one side. Debrett's. Burke's *Peerage and Gentry*. Stacks of ladies' magazines, the sort that featured social gossip. And on one sheet of paper that had separated itself from the others, he saw names. Female names, with ages and snippets of family information. The list of brides.

He felt a little ill to see it. Helena Pryce ought not to be doing this. She had lain in his arms, and he wanted her there again.

Not that he would consider bringing an ineligible female into the family, to be sure. But he had insulted Helena, and mocked his own attraction to her, by ordering her to find the next—and last—woman who would come to his bed. His anger at the time he gave the order was no excuse.

Probably she didn't mind. He had not been in her good graces since he could remember. But once this business with the damned Duke of Tallant was put to rest, he would withdraw the assignment.

"Do you have money?" she asked suddenly.

"Enough to get us through a day or two. I'll draw more at the first bank we find. Are you anticipating extraordinary expenses?"

"No. I'd little on hand, that's all." The first hint of a smile he had not seen for too long. "I had forgot the convenience of traveling with an earl."

Chapter 19

The interior of Helena's carriage had been designed to convert, with a few simple adjustments, into a cushioned platform. Since Varden had elected to ride with his men, she curled up on the small bed and used the solitude to clear her mind. She might even have dozed a little, because she felt groggy when someone rapped on the window to let her know they had arrived at the posthouse.

It was still dark, and a cold wind whipped at her skirts as a groom helped her alight. "Lord Varden is arranging for breakfast," he said, "and a private room where you may refresh yourself. Will you require your portmanteau?"

She could get used to traveling like this, she was thinking as a maid escorted her upstairs, and then to the same private parlor where she had spent the better part of Thursday last. All these people seeing to her comfort, when she had devoted nearly all her life to taking care of others.

Not always successfully, she had to admit when the fallen Archangel looked over at her from the fireplace, where he had been teasing at the logs with a poker. Were there not so much at stake, it might have been amusing, an earl and a servant locking horns. They were so utterly different from each other. So wildly attracted to each other.

But she had stopped questioning their unconventional relationship, preferring to accept it for whatever it was.

Nothing happens without a purpose, Tallant had said. A little sarcastically, as if he felt ridiculous saying such a thing, let alone believing it. She believed nothing of the kind. Yet here she was, still in company with the man she might have loved if everything about her—save her heart—had been different.

While breakfast was being laid out, she showed him the map of Buckinghamshire. "I was on foot, using country paths and stiles for most of the way. If we don't find the road our first try, we'll go to Stoke Poges and approach from the other side. Once we've picked it up, we'll be looking for a pig farm owned by Mr. Silas Bagshot."

"The duke told you his name?"

"The duchess, in her letter. She also said there was a small country house in the Chilterns, owned by his mother's family, that he'd only just learned about. The family died out, except for the duke himself, and the property has been leased to tenants for the last two decades or so. If he concluded his business in time, he intended to have a look at it."

"Ought we not to go directly there? Why bother with a pig farmer?"

"Her Grace does not know where the property is located. The family name was Marleton, but a generation has passed since a Marleton lived there. We'll ask as we go along, of course. And perhaps the duke said something of relevance to Mr. Bagshot, assuming he got that far."

The fragrance of ham, eggs fried in butter, toast, and strong coffee drew her to the table, where Varden held out her chair, passed her the marmalade, and polished off a thick slab of rare sirloin. For a brief time, in spite of her fears for the duke, she was almost happy.

So much good, and so much bad, all in one day. Jamie had sent back a message with Finn that Billy, scheduled to be transported sometime this week, had miraculously been pardoned. He was to be taken north to learn a trade in the care of a good family, and in order to sever all connection with the life that had nearly brought him to the hangman, his destination would not be revealed. She had been relieved to hear he'd won transportation instead of the gibbet, but the pardon was beyond her imagination. She knew of no one taken from the Rookery who had received one.

They were back on the road within a short time, heading north while the grooms turned south. Varden continued to ride, although the day was bitterly cold. She glimpsed him now and again, his posture straight, his gray woolen scarf and the capes of his greatcoat flapping in the wind. Another scarf, looped over his hat, kept it on his head. A sling attached to the saddle held his sword cane.

Almost directly they found the narrow road where she had encountered the duke. It was scarcely wide enough for her carriage to pass, but after a few miles, it ended at a wider road marked with a sign. Varden came to the window.

"A right turn will take us to Uxbridge, and from there, back toward London. To the left is Beaconsfield. I'd expect more pigs in that direction."

"Don't you wish to come inside for a time, sir?"

"Yes. But my horse requires me to keep him warm. Perhaps later."

They reached Beaconsfield not long after, and the second man they questioned provided directions to Mr. Bagshot's farm. It was situated on the edge of a woodland, a neat little establishment with a distinctive odor.

A plump man wearing thigh-high boots emerged from an outbuilding to welcome them, wiping his hands on a towel stuffed into the ties of his oilcloth apron.

"Authority or charm?" Varden asked softly.

The man, his side-whiskers fluffed by the wind, looked friendly as a puppy. She said, "Charm. I presume that means you."

"They both mean me." He stepped forward to greet the farmer.

Silas Bagshot, as friendly as he looked, led them into the house and turned them over to his wife while he went off for a washup. Margaret Bagshot, who looked very like her genial spouse without the whiskers, ushered them into a parlor, directed them to sit side by side on a sofa, and served them cups of tea and a plate of oatmeal biscuits.

A creature of the city, Helena found the farm as exotic as a foreign country. Even the parlor fascinated her. The walls were covered with paintings of pigs, all of them looking very much alike, and attached to the frames were award ribbons. Trophies and engraved plaques covered tables and sideboards.

When Silas Bagshot bustled in, washed and beaming with pleasure, he launched immediately into a history of the great pigs whose likenesses graced his walls, thanks to the artistic genius of his wife. It was several minutes before Varden managed to bring him to the reason for their call.

"Yes, yes, there was a man by that name stopped by—let me see—Friday morning. But he weren't a duke. Leastwise, he never said he were, and didn't look like one neither. Interested in pigs, though. Asked the right questions, but reckoned he didn't want to raise them. He'll buy weaners in the spring for his house. In Kent, I think it be."

"The Duke of Tallant," Varden said, "is a tall man with black hair and unusual eyes. He rides a black horse."

"That be him. Oh, them eyes. Scared me at first.

Not eyes a man would ever forget. And he be a duke?
Fancy that. A duke be buying me pigs."

"We are attempting to find him," Varden said, "in
order to deliver a message. Did he indicate where he
planned to go next?"

"Aye. That he did. Megs, do ye remember the name
of the place what he were looking for?"

"Something to do with beech trees," his wife said
after a little thought. "You sent him to Amersham to
inquire of Mister Lowther."

Helena, who had committed the map nearly to
memory, calculated an hour to reach Amersham. She
put a hand on Varden's forearm to get his attention.
Spelled out the word "Hurry" with her finger on his
wrist.

He gave no sign of noticing, but within a few minutes, they were making the turn onto the road Bagshot
had recommended when she showed him her map.

"Lowther be the man what manages the selling and
leasing of most properties hereabouts," he had explained while his wife prepared sandwiches, pickles,
boiled eggs, and jars of ale for them to take along. "If
he don't handle the beeches property, he knows who
does. You'll find his office near to the Market Hall."

Bagshot had also advised them to keep to the better
roads. "It will snow before evening, I warrant. Can
smell it in the air. The pigs know, too. They be hud-
dling together."

The sky was a clear pale blue when he said it, but
gray clouds were scudding overhead by the time the
carriage turned into the High Street of Amersham,
a town of cobbled courtyards, thatched cottages, and
almshouses. Finn drew up at the Swan Inn. "If you
mean to go on today," he told Helena when she
alighted, "I'll need to hire another pair. These nags
are winded."

"See to it," Varden ordered before she could speak.
"Miss Pryce, it has been four days since Tallant was

sent here by Mr. Bagshot. We don't know that he arrived, or even if the property he's looking for is in this part of the county."

"Are you telling me not to be disappointed if we have reached a dead end?"

"I'm saying only that we're not sure what we are dealing with, and that under the circumstances, we should make no reference to the Duke of Tallant. Nor to our own identities, unless my rank proves useful. Will you allow me to direct the conversation and, if I think it advisable, to mislead Mr. Lowther?"

Not very angelic of you, Archangel. She stopped her smile before it formed. "Of course, my lord. That large building down the way is likely the Market Hall. Shall we go?"

"I never spoke to him," Mr. Lowther said. "My place of business is closed from Friday noon till Monday morning. And it happens we visited my wife's aunt in Tring over the weekend, so your friend would not have found me at home. But yes, I know the property. It was leased to Mr. and Mrs. Cartney for the past several years, but with Mr. Cartney's health failing, they went to live with their son's family in Yorkshire. The house has stood vacant since autumn. Let me find the papers."

Helena, suspicious of land managers, wondered what he had been doing with the rents all these years. Beside her, Varden's expression was calm and pleasant, but that was his usual expression. It meant nothing.

"Ah, here they are!" Lowther pulled a folder from a tall cabinet of drawers and returned to his desk. "Beech Hollow. Not a significant property. It was turned over to me when I bought out my predecessor's business. As he did, I have paid the rents—less my fees—into an account set up for . . . well, I can't recall the name." He flipped through several yellowed sheets of paper. "It seems to come down to the only son of Leticia Marleton, who married the seventh Duke of Tallant. Well, no wonder the rents haven't been claimed. Not worth a duke's bother, I shouldn't think."

"Is it far from here?"

"Not in distance. But the location is remote, the roads poor, and they meander. It's easy to get lost. I was there only last month to decide what repairs are needed before we advertise for new tenants. Is your friend interested in leasing it?"

"I can't say. We're seeking him in regard to another matter. If he asked elsewhere for directions, would he be likely to get them?"

"I expect so. Not necessarily good ones, but he'd have been pointed in the general direction." Lowther paused. Frowned. "I hesitate to say this, sir, but we don't have a great many strangers passing through. Yesterday, one such was discovered not far from here by two sheepmen. They brought him down on a donkey."

Helena's heart gave a lurch.

"He was dead, I take it." For all the emotion in his voice, Varden might have been discussing a deceased squirrel. "Did you see him?"

Lowther let out a heavy sign. "I hope this is not sad news, sir, for the manner of his death was unpleasant. I saw him carried in, but there was a blanket over him. And I heard it wasn't anyone local."

Helena, knees trembling, wished she had taken a chair when Lowther offered it.

"Sad news for someone," Varden said. "I doubt he is the man we are looking for, but if ruffians are attacking strangers, I am concerned about traveling in the area. Especially with a lady."

"He was attacked, that is certain. They found him upright, pinned against a tree by a knife through his throat."

"I see. In that case, I must confess that I have not been altogether straightforward about my reason for being here. Nor have I introduced myself. I am the Earl of Varden, and in association with the chief magistrate, I am investigating crimes that are probably unrelated to this incident. Nonetheless, I must see where this unexpected information leads me. May I deal with you in strictest confidence?"

Lowther's eyes had rounded when Varden identified himself. "To be sure, my lord, although I've little to tell. The authorities have been summoned, but they've to come all the way from Buckingham and won't be in a great hurry about it. Meantime, the body is laid out in the cold room behind the apothecary's shop. Did you wish to see it?"

"Yes. I also want to speak with the apothecary, and with the sheepmen."

When presented to the apothecary, a thin man with wire-framed spectacles and little hair, Varden exerted the quiet authority that Helena had always envied. It got him what he wanted without antagonizing anyone, and usually had people scurrying about, eager to help. After delivering them to the shop, Lowther had galloped of in search of the sheepmen, and now the apothecary was nearly tripping over his own feet leading them to the cold room.

"Perhaps the lady would prefer to wait here?" he said, his hand on the latch.

Varden seemed about to reply. Then he looked over at her, a lifted brow giving her the choice.

As if a child of the Rookery hadn't seen nearly all the horrors that could be. But he didn't know that, and for his respect of her, she found a compromise. "I shouldn't care to look, but I wish to hear the discussion. Might I come in and stand facing the door?"

She might as well have waited outside. The tiny room, lined with shelves that held vials and bottles and jars and packets of medicines and herbs, was cold as an icehouse. She got a glimpse of a figure wrapped in oilcloth and lying on the floor. Too short, she was nearly sure. Not him.

Breathless with relief, she waited until Varden had verified that the dead man wasn't Tallant. Then they all returned to the front of the shop.

". . . nothing to identify him," the apothecary was saying in response to Varden's question. "Nothing whatever in his pockets."

"Could the men who found him have helped themselves to the contents?"

"They're boys, really. Honest lads, from a good family. They might have left him there, and no one the wiser. Took a lot to pull him off the tree, tie him over their donkey, and bring him to town. They had been on their way elsewhere."

"Then I suppose the killer robbed him. What did the boys tell you?"

"Only that it looked as if there had been a fight. They were taking a shortcut down from the hills, on a path fit only for an animal, a horse, or a man on foot. But I'd think that if it had been a robbery, the killer would not have left the knife. A fancy piece, worth a good sum."

He opened a drawer behind his counter, withdrew a square of felt folded double over itself, and laid it in front of them. "See what I mean?"

When he uncovered the knife, Helena felt Varden, standing close beside her, go rigid. "Yes," he said. "A valuable piece. One has to wonder why the owner failed to reclaim it. Is there anything more you can tell us?"

While the apothecary described his examination of the body, she studied the knife. About ten inches long, with a sharp blade and a hilt of silver and onyx, it was as beautiful as it had been deadly. And Varden had recognized it.

"I've been thinking," the apothecary said, "that maybe the chap in the back room has something to do with the fellow who came to my cottage Saturday night. He'd been cut, too, but said he did it himself, butchering a sheep. I stitched him up in the cottage and left him there while I came to the shop for more basilicum and sticking plasters. When I got back, he was gone."

"Not a local man, I gather," Varden said. "What did he look like?"

"Like a chap who makes his living butchering sheep. Rough hands, missing two teeth in the front of his mouth, hair the color of dirt. At that time of night, someone at one of the taverns must have directed him to the cottage."

Varden asked more questions, and by way of thanking the apothecary, Helena purchased a few items for the medical kit in her carriage.

It was snowing when they left the shop, and Lowther, wrapped in a fleece-lined coat and wearing a hat with fleece lappets, was waiting for them down the street. "I didn't know how much to say in front of John Beamer," he said in a conspiratorial voice.

"Good thinking," said Varden as they proceeded along the High Street. "What did you learn?"

"The boys have gone to High Wycombe, my lord. I've drawn a map to the place they found the body, and to Beech Hollow. I have a set of keys for you as well, but you won't want to go up there until the snow's gone."

"I'm afraid we must, or all the evidence—if there is any—will be obliterated. Did anyone examine the location?"

"Not that I've heard. We're waiting for the—"

"Authorities. Yes. Well, here we are. Come inside the inn and let's have a look at your map."

Varden insisted they have a meal before departing,

so they settled at a table over steak and Stilton pies while Lowther explained what he had tried to draw. "You can't take a carriage to where it happened," he said earnestly. "You can get this far on the road"— he pointed to a spot on the map—"and then you must walk to here. You'll know it by the rocky terrain, and by the path that winds its way around boulders and trees. They said he was affixed to an oak."

Helena reached over and marked the spots on the map with the pencil she carried in her pocket.

"If there is nothing else," Vardcn said, "please accept my thanks for your cooperation. After my inspection of the area, I shall file a report with the authorities. Meantime, you are enjoined to silence about everything we have discussed, including the location of the killing."

"There must be very little excitement in this town," Helena said when Lowther had gone. "He enjoyed every minute of your little intrigue."

"It was harmless enough." Varden dug into his pie. "What do we need to take with us, in case we run into trouble?"

"The boxes under the carriage seats are stocked with necessities, but I'll add brandy, extra blankets, and lantern oil." Her feet twitched with impatience. "What do you know of that knife?"

"If it isn't Tallant's, it's identical to one I saw in his hand several months ago at the Palazzo. He'd another as well, also silver and black onyx, but smaller."

"Then you think he killed that man?" She felt some relief at the thought. If Tallant had brought down a rotter, probably a rotter on his trail and up to no good, just as well. But where had he gone from there?

"It seems likely. I didn't witness it myself, but I heard he once gave a demonstration of knife-throwing in the gaming room at the Palazzo, nearly pinning Lord Duran's fingers to a table and his ears to a wall."

"Yes. But Duran told me it was staged to entertain Beata's guests. If Tallant killed the man we saw, he'd a good reason."

Varden put down his fork. "Helena, you won't agree, but—"

"You want me to stay here while you go off on your own. Why trouble to say so, when you already know my answer?" Rising, she picked up Lowther's map. "I'll show this to Finn and make sure everything is ready. Are you intending to ride?"

"Hector has had a long day of it. If you've no objection, I'll take space in a corner of your carriage."

"You are most welcome there. Finish your lunch, my lord. My carriage departs in ten minutes."

Chapter 20

The snow, falling lightly as they made their way out of Amersham, thickened as the carriage wound into the hilly countryside. The hired horses were surprisingly good, Finn had said, deep-chested and strong-legged. They would do well in bad weather.

For as long as she'd known him, all Finn's love had been given to the horses he drove, even those that had been with him only between one posthouse and the next. He had a degree of silent affection for her as well, she suspected, of the sort he'd give to a temperamental mare that refused to run in tandem. She relied on him utterly.

Varden, seated across from her, kept himself busy watching for landmarks. There was no use making plans, since they couldn't know what they would find. And he appeared to feel, as she did, that speculation wasted strength they needed to conserve.

"Do you think Finn can see the road?" he asked at one point. "Perhaps I should ride atop and make sure we don't miss a turn."

"You can if you wish, but he would be insulted. Should he require help, I assure you he'll ask for it."

She refrained from looking at her watch. This search would take as long as it took. She concentrated instead on what little she could see out the window, and on holding herself stiffly in position despite the swaying of the carriage. Varden was seated in the opposite corner, but the space was small and his legs were long. With every bump and curve, his right knee and thigh touched hers, rubbed against hers. Burned against hers.

They were far beyond the explosion of passion at the castle, and beyond the flirtation Varden had later engaged in, hoping to reignite their affair. Nothing would ever again occur between them. And yet, with all their resources focused on the mission they had undertaken, this confinement—this unwelcome intimacy—summoned up images and feelings she thought she had firmly locked away.

The carriage slowed, turned, and began a steeper ascent. Not long after, they entered the stretch of woodland Lowther had marked.

"Any time now," Varden said, flipping open his pocket watch, "there should be a path on the right side. Since you are facing forward, perhaps you ought to slide over and look out this window."

He shifted his knees sideways to let her wriggle by, but she barely had time to worry about how much closer he was than before when she spotted a break in the trees. Finn must have seen it too, because the carriage drew to a halt.

Outside, the snow fell steadily, with no wind to blow it about. Varden walked ahead of her, a dark figure in his greatcoat and hat, the sword cane in his left hand. She followed, stepping where he had stepped, drawing deep breaths of air wet with snowflakes.

They came out of the woods about ten minutes later into a landscape unlike any she had seen before. In some long-ago age, a glacier must have deposited these boulders along a stretch no more than fifty yards wide. Trees had sprung up higgledy-piggledy where they could find root.

The path they were walking ended at the one Lowthor had described. They turned left, as he had directed, keeping watch for the tree where the man had been impaled. The path, steep and rocky, was lined with boulders taller than she. No one had been on it since the snow began, but she detected traces of footprints and hoofprints where the snow had settled into their depressions.

"Here!" Varden waved his cane. He'd got ahead of her.

She hurried to catch him up. He was facing an oak tree empty of leaves, gingerly brushing away snow that had stuck to the bark.

"This is it," he said. "There's the gouge made by the knife. Those darker areas are blood."
He studied the angle of the notch, drew out his sword blade, and slid the tip into the place where the knife had been. "Deep, even with a man's neck between the hilt and the tree. Not a stab from close up. The knife was thrown. Hold this, will you, and keep it the angle steady."

She took the silver handle, made sure the sword point was firmly settled, and waited. From behind her, she heard the rustle of his coat and the crunch of his boots on the snow.

All else was eerily silent. Her breath in the cold air made ghosts that danced on the blade of the sword. Her arm began to ache.

"Come on up if you wish," he called. "I've found the spot."

She propped the sword against the tree and began the rocky climb to a point about thirty yards away. Varden was standing behind a pair of boulders with a narrow vee of space between them. As she approached, he waved her to the opposite side of the boulders, facing him.

"This seems to be the place from which the knife was thrown. Now look to the boulder at your right, about the level of your ear. Imagine a line drawn from there to here and tell me what—"

"Oh!" Something had struck the rock and taken a chip from it. "A bullet?"

"I think so. Helena, there are traces of blood over here. If it was Tallant hiding behind these boulders, something hit him. Perhaps a ricochet, perhaps another bullet. I can't tell which direction he went after that."

She looked at him through a flurry of snowflakes. Frost was forming on her spectacles, and soon she would be unable to see much of anything. "Shall we each pick a direction to look? If he was wounded, he might have fallen close by."

"We can try that tomorrow. For now, better we proceed on to Beech Hollow. Perhaps he took refuge there."

She said nothing. They both knew how unlikely it was they would find him. The events that occurred here took place on Friday or Saturday, and in a short time, Tuesday's daylight would be gone.

They went back the way they had come, pausing only to reclaim the sword cane and take another long look at the surrounding hills, as if they would see something they had missed before.

Finn, huddled under his tarp, looked like a snow-covered boulder on the driver's bench. "We found the location," she said, "but saw nothing to tell more than we already knew. We'll go on to Beech Hollow now."

When she was seated in her corner, Varden climbed in and settled into the narrow space directly beside her. "The warming bricks that kept us cozy from Amersham are blocks of ice," he said. "We'll need to keep each other warm."

She gazed at him in alarm. Seen through her frosted spectacles, he had furry edges, like a white bear. She pulled out a handkerchief and tried to swab the blur away.

"Let me." He took the handkerchief and gently

rubbed the lenses. "Don't worry. I'll not dislodge them."

"My eyes are closed, just in case."

When he was done, she could see more clearly. "There are blankets under that bench, sir."

"You needn't be concerned," he said, draping an arm over her shoulder. "My intentions are entirely pragmatic. We're wet, and we'd get the blankets wet. You can endure my proximity for the next few miles."

She felt resistant as sandpaper. Being held by him was never the problem. It was the letting go that hurt. To affix her thoughts where they belonged, she said, "What do you think happened up there?"

"My assumption had been robbery, since the man who died and the one described to us appear to have been common hooligans. But a remote path used as a shortcut is hardly the place to wait for a victim to come by. Perhaps they spotted the duke on the road, figured him for a good prospect, and followed him up there."

"He would not have been caught by surprise."

"Nor was he. But you are thinking that this is another deliberate attack, like the one that—according to him—occurred not very long ago. On that occasion two men were killed, one of them supposedly by the duchess."

"*Supposedly?* What reason can you have to doubt it?"

"Two arrows that struck deeply and accurately. Tallant's skill as an archer is well-known to those who saw him shoot in matches at Palazzo Neri. But you cannot imagine that Her Grace could fire, with such strength and speed, into a man's back."

"I can well imagine it."

He turned a little, so that he could see her face. "I keep forgetting that you know her. Is she skilled at archery? Physically able to drive an arrow nearly all the way through a large man's body?"

"What I know of the duchess, sir, is based on very slight acquaintance. I have never heard that she enjoyed archery, but people rarely mention their hobbies to servants. There can be no doubt that she is physically strong. As the sole caretaker of her paralyzed father, she lifted him, pushed his heavy wheeled chair, transported him from hiding place to hiding place when the former duke was hounding them. *Of course* she'd be strong. And as you yourself have noted, she is strong in character as well."

After a time he leaned back against the squabs, closing his eyes. "But through a man's *back,* Helena?"

"Was she to stand aside, refusing to engage in anything other than a fair fight? Is that what you would do? Good heavens. A dishonorable opponent, lacking such overnice scruples, would cut you down like a hothouse lily. Were I defending my life, sir, or that of someone I loved, I would do whatever it required. And if the duchess shot a man in the back, it is because he was, at that moment, a danger to someone else. Have you asked her what happened?"

"It . . . hasn't seemed advisable. I am not an impartial investigator."

"I should say not. You have made up your mind on the grounds that a gentle lady would, by her very nature, lack the strength, the skill, and the *will* to do what the duchess apparently did."

"We have only the duke's testimony as to what occurred," he said. "I do not immediately accept it."

"When the English judicial system permits a woman to testify on her own behalf, a great deal more truth will find its way into the records. Meantime, as I suggested, you might consider speaking privately with the lady herself. Or if your emotional state does not allow for that, have someone else—someone respectful—question her."

At this point, for she had not been in the least respectful to him, he ought to be pushing her away.

Instead, after a silence that felt to her much longer than it was, he released a harsh breath and drew her closer.

"Let us not quarrel," he said. "You are right that I need to seek better evidence before drawing a conclusion. And that I am not disinterested where Mir— where the duchess is concerned. Or the duke. I love the one, and I hate the other. Continue to guard me from error, Helena. I'll not punish you for it."

If she spoke then, she would have said too much, and all the wrong things. So she kept silent, and nestled into the warmth of her fur-lined cloak and his arms. At no place did they touch skin to skin. Layers of silk and linen, wool and cambric, broadfine, fur, and leather separated them. When his head bent to rest against hers, it rested against wool, fox fur, and someone else's hair.

There would always be barriers between them. Some could be peeled away, as on the night they became lovers. And if she were not intending to depart England, other barriers would gradually be lowered as well. But only the small ones. Social barriers would always divide them.

Divide? Their differences kept them on opposite sides of an abyss.

She had tossed rather a number of valuables into that abyss. Her virtue. Her ambitions. The life she had constructed for herself and must now abandon.

Her heart.

Beyond the abyss stood walls of every sort, some in part broken down, others acknowledged and left to stand. And there would always remain the secrets that lay in the deepest darkess, so long buried that even she no longer thought of them . . . except to remember, on occasions like this one, why she must *never* think of them.

For now, she thought only of the man slumped beside her, stealing a few minutes of rest before the next task. If the weather worsened, they would be forced to remain in the deserted house. More time lost on a search that grew increasingly hopeless with every passing hour. The men Jamie was to send after them would be delayed as well.

It didn't matter now. If the duke had been injured and failed to find help or shelter, the followers would be most useful combing the area for his body. And there was always the chance he had been hurt, found assistance, and dispatched word to the duchess. He might even be home by now, or well on his way there.

There was no good reason to believe the search must continue, and yet, nothing would turn her back. She was supposed to be here, doing what she was doing. Varden as well, she supposed, because she could not have come nearly so far without him. Little information would have been provided her, no directions given, no keys handed over.

A good team, the whore's daughter and the earl. Who could have imagined it? And for this brief time, this last time, she was sheltered in his embrace.

Closing her eyes, she emptied her mind of thoughts and filled herself with sensations. The soft, even sound of his breathing. The smell of damp wool, male sweat, lemony soap. The throbbing of blood in her veins and the weight of hard muscles around her shoulder. Another closed-off world, like the room at the castle, where he had been hers alone.

Chapter 21

An hour later, after a slow, winding descent, the carriage came to a stop. Helena could see nothing through the frosted windows, but she felt the slight jolt as Finn swung down from the driver's bench.

Varden was asleep. She took hold of his left hand, which lay just where her heart beat too quickly, and gave it a tug. "Wake up, sir. We have arrived."

He sat forward just as Finn opened the door beside her. It was nearly dark. Snow, blowing slightly in a freshening wind, began to dust her skirts.

"No sign of anyone here," Finn said. "There's what looks to be a stable. Better to stay where you are while I get the carriage inside."

Helena used the delay to raise the padded seat opposite her and pull out a few supplies. Lanterns. Candles. Tinderbox. Her hand fell on the parcel of supplies she'd bought from the apothecary and she drew it out as well.

When they were inside the musty stable, Varden ignited a lantern and drew out the keys from his coat pocket. "I'll go ahead and unlock the door."

"Will we be staying?" Finn said, gesturing at the horses. "Or should I leave 'em in harness?"

"Leave them for now. Miss Pryce, give me five minutes to look around. If Tallant never made it here, we'll discuss what to do next."

She gave him four minutes, long enough to help
Finn light the coach lanterns and look around the stable. It had been well maintained, but clearly no one
had been inside since the tenants of Beech Hollow
departed several months earlier. She noticed a triangle
of firewood in one corner, useful if they decided to
stay the night.

Finn was rubbing down the horses when she left the
stable, her hands full of supplies and Varden's sword
cane, which he had left in the carriage.

The house lay, as its name suggested, in a small
valley surrounded by beech trees. Three stories tall
and constructed in the half-timbered Tudor style, it
had probably served as a hunting lodge back when the
woodlands ran thick with game. Several inches of new
snow covered the thatched roof and the ground, its
matte surface broken only by Varden's footprints
leading to the front door. Most of the mullioned windows were dark, but on the first floor, she detected a
faint light moving about.

The scene could hardly have been more peaceful.
But there was a vibration in the air, nothing to be
heard or felt, that resonated inside her. Something was
dreadfully wrong.

Rushing into the house, she found herself in a large
room with a beamed ceiling that occupied the entire
front of the house. There were two enormous fire-
places, one with an iron grate affixed inside and a
poker propped against the mantelpiece. She set her
provisions on the only piece of furniture, an old, heavy
sideboard that stood against one wall, and lit her lantern and some candles.

When they were flaming, she could make out the
layer of dust on the floor, with only her footprints to
be seen, and Varden's. No one else had been here for
a considerable time.

Overhead, the thump of his footsteps and the
creaking of wooden floors marked his passage from

room to room. He had gone directly to the staircase, she could tell by the marks in the dust. That left the downstairs for her to explore.

Taking up her lantern, she headed for the passageway that led to the back of the house. It was narrow, with doors opening to rooms that she examined quickly before moving on. All were empty. A wide door marked the end of the passageway and led to a large kitchen with a stone floor, a cooking hearth, an old iron stove, and a butcher-block table. Two of the walls were lined with a series of doors, all of them closed.

Starting to her right, she opened the first door and came into a storage room. Bits of crockery and a few bent pans littered the shelves. The next room was much the same, except that it had once contained linens and kitchen tools. She saw a frayed tablecloth, some crumpled napkins, and nearly concealed under the bottom shelf, a pair of tongs.

The room that followed held large sinks with pumps attached, and there was a window, the first she had seen in the kitchen area. The two rooms that followed had no discernible purpose and only one bit of furniture, a chair with a broken leg.

Everywhere she looked, the dust was undisturbed. She nearly gave up then, thinking to reclaim Varden and return to the coach before the horses grew stiff from standing. But that inexplicable sense of something wrong, something to be found, continued to gnaw at her. With a sigh, she proceeded to the next door and pushed it open.

Cold air—*fresh* air—stung her face. She halted. Lifted her lantern. Saw a window on the opposite wall with its bottom pane broken out. On the floor directly ahead of her were shards of jagged glass frosted with windblown snow. A low, foreboding sound as the wind, much stronger than it had been, whistled through the opening.

She turned and broke into a run.

No one followed. She hadn't expected to be followed. A broken window in a long-deserted house meant nothing. But when she reached the main room, she snatched the sword cane before pounding up the stairs.

Varden was on the second landing, just beginning his descent, when she reached him. "There's a window broken out," she said, panting a little. "In a room off the kitchen."

"Any sign of someone using it to enter?"

"I couldn't tell. We need better light."

He took the cane from her hand, slipped by her, and led the way to the kitchen.

Nothing had changed since she left. The heavy door stood partway open, shuddering when the wind buffeted it.

"Wait here." Varden moved carefully inside, side-stepping the spray of broken glass, and examined the window frame. Then he crouched and began poking gently at the fallen glass with his cane. After a time, he pulled out a handkerchief and dabbed it against a piece of glass and a section of the floor. Finally he crossed to where she stood, speaking in a low voice.

"The window was deliberately broken. Someone came through it. I saw traces of what looked to be blood on the frame, and there is blood on the floor. Not fresh. Between the wet snow and the warmth of my hand, a little of it could be lifted away." He held out his handkerchief.

She saw only black smudges, their true color imperceptible because of her dark, smeared glasses.

He crouched again, this time to examine the gray stone floor of the kitchen, worn with centuries of use. "Dust is not so apparent here. I can't tell if anyone has crossed this floor. But I'm sure no one has been in the other part of the house, so we're left with the ground level. Have you explored all the rooms leading off the kitchen?"

"I started over there—" She pointed to her right. "This is as far as I got."

"Would you prefer to wait elsewhere, Helena? There may be nothing to find, or there could be something unpleasant."

In response, she strode to the first of the three remaining doors and raised the latch. This was clearly a pantry, with droppings on the floor from rodents and other scavengers come by to enjoy whatever the former tenants had left behind.

Varden had proceeded to the next door, and after a few moments, he was back again, drawing her deeper into the pantry. "Someone has been in the adjacent room." This time he was whispering. "It's much like this one, but inside there's an entrance, low to the floor, to something else. I've not been inside many kitchens. A root cellar, perhaps?"

"Or a cold room, or an ice house." She whispered, because he did. "We may as well look."

Aloud, he said, "This is useless. Let's go." Then, under his breath, "Argue a little, but come along."

"Why not finish?" She followed him back across the kitchen and down the passageway.

"Because the weather is worsening. If we are to get safely home, we have to leave now. We'll send someone to board over the window."

When they reached the main room, he led her quickly to the door. "Whoever broke in is probably long gone. But just in case, I'm going back to make sure no one tries to leave before we search the last corners of this house. Bring Finn."

The wind was stronger and the snow heavier, obliterating the footprints she and Varden had left only a short time earlier. Guided by lantern light filtering from the stable, she trekked across the ankle-deep snow, already planning arrangements for spending the night in the house. There was firewood. Straw and blankets for pallets. The basket of food Mrs. Bagshot had provided them, not much but enough to get them by. Finn should have most of it, since he would have to drive them out in the morning.

She was still making mental lists when she entered the stable, quickly pulling the door shut before the wind caught it. The horses shuffled at the disturbance, rocking the carriage back and forth. They seemed restless. Uneasy. She paused, smelling something she couldn't identify. And where was Finn?

Wary now, she backed toward the door. The flickering light from the coach lanterns sent shadows darting around the enclosure. "Finn? Where are you?"

A whicker from one of the horses. The scuffing of hooves on straw. Nothing more.

Perhaps he had fallen asleep. She crept forward, looked through the carriage window. Empty.

Inside a stall, then. There were four of them, two on each side of the rectangular stable. "Finn!" she called, not too loudly because of the horses. A large brown head lifted, the eye she could see round and accusing. And frightened.

She turned, meaning to go for Varden, and then turned back. The awareness of danger that had prickled on her skin inside the house left her untouched here. She felt only a profound sadness, and a warning.

There could be no stopping now. Teeth gritted, she strode directly to the first stall at her right and stood on tiptoe to peer over the neck-high gate. Old straw and a feed bin.

Nothing in the next stall, not even straw. The horses appeared to be settling, she thought, making no disturbance when she went past them to the other pair of stalls. Then she heard a whicker. The creak of leather. The jangle of metal. From the stall ahead of her!

Looking up, she saw a large black horse lift its head over the gate. A scream caught in her throat.

The horse, saddled, bridled, and damp from melted snowflakes, had not been there when they arrived.

Her thoughts, galloping like her heartbeats, hit a wall. Another sense, stronger than her fear. The scent of blood was thick in her nostrils. She knew, before she opened the gate of the last stall, what she would find.

Finn, his stocky body spread-eagled facedown, was sprawled at her feet. A heavy rake lay beside him, its metal prongs gleaming with undried blood. His head had been bashed in.

Clutching her belly, she willed the nausea to pass. It had to wait. Everything here had to wait.

Don't rush, Elly. Think. Plan.

She sucked in a few deep breaths, found a prayer. Needed a weapon.

Finn's gun. She clambered onto the carriage and located the pistol in a leather sling where it would have been easy for him to reach . . . had he been driving.

For all her resolution, tears burned in her eyes. She got tangled up in her skirts and cloak when she descended, but the horses held blessedly still. On the ground again, she went to the stable door and stopped long enough to consider how she ought to proceed.

If Finn's killer had seen her come to the stable, surely he'd have dealt with her already, before she could warn Varden. He had to be looking for a way into the house, or be inside it.

Not through the front door, though. He'd not have missed her leaving the same way. So he would have gone around the back. Found the broken window.

She had no idea where to go next. Had never fired a gun. All she knew came to one thing. If she rushed in, put herself in jeopardy, she might become a weapon to be used against Varden.

Stealth, then. She removed her cloak, because it billowed in the wind and made too great a silhouette. Tossed it inside the empty stall, in case the killer returned. There was a slim chance he hadn't seen her and didn't know the carriage had brought two passengers.

Only one way out of the stable, though. To open the door again would be like flashing a rectangle of light at anyone looking this direction, but extinguishing the lights would draw more attention in the long run. Better to take a chance now. She cracked the door open, slipped out, shut it quickly, and darted around the side of the stable.

Holding to the rough wooden wall, she studied the house. The sixty-yard expanse she'd have to cross seemed a mile wide. Beyond it, through the fall of snow, she saw a window marked out by yellow light from the candles she'd left burning on the sideboard, and from the lantern she had left by the door.

The broken window was clear the other side of the house. If she got across the break unseen, she could steal around to the back in darkness and . . . and guess what to do from there.

In the killer's place, she'd have gone into the trees that surrounded the house on three sides. From there he could find a way into the house, or simply wait in ambush. She studied the ground, looking for evidence of his footprints. Nothing. Perhaps when he came out of the stable, he had turned right instead of left.

She hurried around the back of the stable and came up to the corner opposite where she had been. She studied the ground, but there was no light, and the snow adhering to her spectacles impaired her vision. She removed them, crouched to get a better view, and looked for indentations filling with snow. In the darkness she could not be sure what she was seeing, but directly to her right, the snowfield looked different. A darker broken line, possibly drawn in her imagination, appeared to reach from where she was standing to where the trees began.

Her breathing nocked up. Assume he went that way, then. Ought she to follow, or go around from the other direction?

Or . . . wait here, concealed by the stable. Varden must be wondering why she had not returned with Finn. He might come looking for her.

She debated her choices as she went back to where she had first hidden herself, and where she could not be seen if the killer returned the way he had gone. As she came up to the corner, she looked toward the lighted window. And saw Varden.

He was standing against the opposite wall, hands clasped behind his neck. Facing him was a tall, wide-shouldered man wearing a caped greatcoat and moving sideways, his right arm held in a way that told her he was pointing a gun at Varden. She couldn't see it. She saw only the back of him—the man who had murdered Finn—and his thick black hair. She felt Finn's pistol, heavy in her hand. And then she was flitting across the snow, arcing right so that he wouldn't see her if he turned a little and glanced out the window.

But through a man's back? Varden had asked her.

She was to the right of the window now, next to the house. Two steps to the left and she would be entirely visible to anyone looking out. Then she must act swiftly.

To defend the life of someone I loved, I would do whatever it required.

She put the gun between both hands to hold it steady. Placed a trembling finger on the trigger. Moved left. Saw the broad back directly ahead of her. Raised the pistol, sighted down it as best she could.

Even kill my brother.

She pulled the trigger.

Chapter 22

After Helena departed, Varden went to the window and watched her cross the wide plane of snow. Despite the bitter wind, her posture was javelin straight, her pace that of a soldier on the march. Intrepid female. No man, not even a warrior in battle, had ever been blessed with a more valiant companion. Smiling a little, he returned to his post in the kitchen.

The door to the room with the broken window had blown shut and was slapping against the frame with every new gust, its unoiled hinges shrieking in counterpoint. He gazed at the door he had closed and latched, the one that led to the small room with the waist-high door on the outer wall. Probably not outer. There must be something beyond it, something added on. Tempted to get started, to have a look, he had to remind himself that Helena would demand why he had not waited for her. So he waited, and waited longer, and began to grow concerned. She might be delayed for a commonplace reason, of course, like a call of nature or Finn doing something for the horses. But nothing of importance was happening where he was, so he lifted away from the kitchen wall where he had been leaning and headed again for the front room.

He was halfway down the passageway when a voice spoke from directly behind him.

"Halt." The voice was deep. Commanding. "I've a

gun at your back." In case there was any doubt, he jabbed the point of the barrel between Varden's shoulder blades. "Put down the lantern. Carefully."

After a few seconds to consider, Varden obeyed. The longer he delayed here in the narrow passageway, the better. He could shout, or make a fuss of some kind, when he heard Helena and Finn enter the house. "Have you been here all along?"

"Just long enough, milord. And if you are expecting help from your driver, he won't be coming."

Finn dead or incapacitated. And Helena? Did the man know about Helena? While Varden was absorbing the implications of what he'd just heard, the sword cane was plucked from his hand. "Who the devil are you?" he said, to keep the man talking.

"My name is of no consequence. When I do business, as I am doing now, they call me Reiver. We have met before, after a fashion. I was not paid to kill you, not then, but I intended to do some damage. It appears I failed."

"The Windsor highwayman," Varden said, unsurprised. "And no, you didn't fail. I had been counting myself lucky to be wounded instead of dead, but you got what you wanted. Might I ask why you were on that road, and how you knew I would be there?"

"I was paid, and paid well. But I'm not here to satisfy your curiosity. What brought you to this house?"

"I'm thinking of leasing it."

A hard blow across the back with his own cane. "Try again."

"It's quite true. Family business brought me to the area, so I took the opportunity to inspect a property, one of several I have been considering. I didn't anticipate snow, or being stranded here."

"You broke in through the window?"

"I came in through the door, using the keys given me by the leasing agent. Are you saying you didn't break the window? That you haven't been lying in wait?"

"I'm saying I don't believe in coincidences. You are here to meet the Duke of Tallant, or you are searching for him."

"Tallant?" Did Reiver know this house belonged to the duke? "I've nothing to do with him."

"I'm told you hate him. I'm told you want to see him hang."

Varden shrugged. "Yes, on both counts. But I can prove nothing against him, and I cannot fight him with one hand. If you are expecting him to come here, and if you mean to kill him when he does, I'm the last man in England who would try to stop you."

"Almost you convince me. Not that it matters what I think. Tallant is known to be in the area. Two men were following him, but he twigged to them and killed one not far from here. Wounded the other. That one reported back to me, and then I cut his throat. Competent help is hard to find, Archangel. I'll have to see to the duke myself."

"I wish you success. But why would he come here?"

"He may have been shot. May have broken in, looking for shelter. I know he's close by. Saw his horse not an hour ago, but it ran off when I got too near."

The gun barrel, or the tip of his cane, prodded Varden in the back. "Move ahead. Slowly."

Varden did as he was told. By now Helena would have come upon Finn, and she had the sense not to come running back into the house. While he kept Reiver occupied, she would have a chance to hide herself and any evidence she was ever here. Better, she would make her escape. "Why did you attack me on the Windsor Road?" he asked, genuinely curious. "To make it appear Tallant had done so?"

"It's a little more complicated than that. But this is no longer your concern. You've worn out your usefulness, milord. If I find Tallant, I'll make it appear you killed each other. At the least, your presence here will muddy the waters. Keep going. Over there, by the wall. Stand with your back against it and fold your hands behind your neck."

The spot he pointed to was halfway between the fireplace and the sideboard. Varden took his position as directed. Reiver was staging a scene, and he had been cast as a corpse.

Reiver, the pistol steady in his hand, set Varden's cane on the mantelpiece before moving toward the sideboard. Not too close, but near enough to spot the keys on their brass ring. He smiled. "So you were telling the truth. In part, at least. But why the lack of servants? The plain carriage?"

"Narrow roads. And when I travel in my crested coach, hooligans shoot at me though the window."

Laughing, Reiver placed himself directly in front of Varden, beyond arm's reach, the pistol never wavering. He really did resemble Tallant in size, build, and coloring, more than enough to fool anyone from a short distance.

"You will have realized we are drawing to a conclusion," Reiver said. "It is unfortunate. I like you. And I dislike killing when I am not being paid to do so. But you have seen me. Now all that remains is how you are to die."

"Let me guess. You intend to shoot me."

"And I'm an excellent shot. I'm also less stupid than you have assumed. Tell me what you know of Tallant's whereabouts and you die cleanly, without pain. Keep lying and I'll put a bullet in your gut. That means what you are thinking it means."

"Dirty and painful." Varden spoke calmly. Felt calm. "But I haven't a choice. Tallant's whereabouts are unknown to me, except that he cannot be in the house. I have examined every room and cubbyhole, to determine how much I should pay if I decide to purchase it. Why would you have found me wandering about alone, if I had stumbled across a duke?"

"I suppose you've no reason to protect him. But damned if I don't sniff aristocratic honor in the air. Had enough of it in the army, I did, taking orders from high-born amateurs. But you weren't among them, so I'll let you go quiet." He raised the pistol. "My apologies, Archangel, for spoiling your pretty face."

Varden was moving before he heard the gunshot. It wasn't loud. Glass shattered, a bullet whizzed by. From the corner of his eye he saw Reiver turn toward the window. Then his hand was on the silver handle of his cane. Good for once to be left-handed. He swung around, whipped the cane at Reiver's arm.

The pistol flew out of Reiver's hand, hit the floor, skittered toward the sideboard. Not far enough. Varden leaped between him and the gun, pulling his sword from the casing.

Reiver was smart enough to go the other direction. He looked to be running back the way they'd come, but he spotted the poker, swept it up, and whirled to face Varden.

The slender blade couldn't withstand an iron poker. Reiver took a swipe. Varden ducked and retreated. A quick look by Reiver at the broken window. Whoever fired might be reloading. Varden used the split second to improve his position.

Then Reiver was at him again, his face contorted. "Now!"

As Varden swerved to one side, the poker struck a glancing blow against his right shoulder.

One chance, he thought, retreating quickly. They both knew a shot might hit either of them, making it dangerous for a Varden ally to fire. Reiver had a little time to get past his enemy and to the gun.

Varden was near enough to kick it under the sideboard, but he left it there as bait. One chance. Draw him in. Attack. Feint. Strike.

He shot a glance at the window, let his eyes widen as if he'd seen something. When Reiver's gaze followed his to the window, Varden came in for the attack. The poker swung at the sword, which wasn't there. A feint to the left, Reiver following it with the poker. If the blow had struck Varden's head, it would have killed him. But expecting Varden to retreat, Reiver swung wide and long, putting him off balance.

Holding ground, Varden lunged low, under Reiver's arm, and thrust the point of his blade into Reiver's upturned throat. It went deep.

The poker hit the floor as Reiver grabbed the sword with both hands, trying to pull it out. Blood streamed from his hands, sliced open by the blade. Varden held on. Pushed harder. But he was the one off balance now, one knee bent, the other straight out behind him, with a tall, heavy man trying to wrench the sword from his hand.

He let it go. The release of tension sent Reiver reeling back, still holding the sword, blood frothing from his neck and mouth. Varden went for the poker, then for the pistol.

But the blade had done its work. Staggering across the room, Reiver made it nearly to the passageway, the sword still in his throat. He stopped, teetering a little, hands dropping to his sides. His legs bent. Then he toppled, landing facedown, driving the sword deeper yet. The point of the blade showed at his nape.

For the first few moments, Varden bent nearly double, sucking in deep breaths of air. Pain from the blow to his shoulder made itself known. When he could drag his head up, he looked to the window, then over to the door. It was open. On the threshold stood Helena, arms at her sides, a pistol dangling from one limp hand.

Her gaze was fixed on Reiver. As Varden watched, she began to tremble.

Reaching behind him, he laid the poker and the pistol on the sideboard. Then he crossed to her, and wrapped his arms around her, and drew her close against his chest.

She was shaking in earnest now. Saying something he couldn't make out. He held her, one hand rubbing her back, his chin pressed against the side of her head. "Brave girl," he murmured. "My brave, gallant girl."

After a time, a long time, her tremors subsided, Her breathing steadied. She lifted her head a little, looking again, he suspected, at the man on the floor.

"I missed," she said. "I c-can't shoot."

"You did all that was needed," he said. "Created a distraction. Gave me a chance."

"Finn is dead. He killed Finn."

"I know. I'm sorry." He reached down, took the gun from her hand.

She continued to look at Reiver. "Who—who is it?" The words, dark and fearful, seemed to come from a cave.

"He gave me a name, but I don't believe it's his real—Helena!"

As if she'd melted, she slid from his embrace, ending on her knees. He hunkered in front of her, studying her face anxiously.

"I am well," she said, her voice shaky. "It was just . . . finding Finn, and seeing that man about to shoot you, and missing with my own shot, and being so sure he would kill you. And there was nothing I could do then but watch, and think where I might go so he didn't find me. So I could tell what happened and describe him. But I could never see his face. I k-kept watching, but I couldn't *see* it."

"You needn't ever see it." Snow was blowing into the room, sifting over them like sugar. "Come inside, Helena. Let me close the door."

But when he helped her rise, she sank into his arms again, clinging as if to an anchor in a storm. He would not have expected this, not from her. He had fancied her beyond the reach of weakness, of fear, of dependency. But she depended on him now. Only a little, and for a short time, but to his shame, it made him glad.

The trembling stilled, became more of a low vibration that resonated throughout his body. He held her, and her spirit invaded him. Was welcomed by him, a communion beyond reason or words.

Too soon, he realized that she had begun to come about, to retake control of herself, to sever the connection between them. Before her muscles went taut, before she put her hands on his arms and gently separated them, she was already gone.

Back to Olympus, he thought with mordant humor, his imperious goddess of anything she chose to rule.

Next he knew, she had closed the door and picked up the lantern sitting just inside, the one she'd left there when she went to the stable. Years ago, it seemed to him. "What shall we do now, sir?" she said.

She understood that all other questions could wait. He looked around for his own lantern, remembered he'd been ordered to set it down in the passageway. "Reiver—that's the name he gave me—came here looking for Tallant. Hired by someone, he wouldn't say whom, and in league with the two men who wound up at the wrong end of Tallant's knives. He also said he'd seen the duke's horse nearby, running free. What with the broken-out window, there's a good chance that Tallant was here for a time. He may be gone—"

"Or in one of the rooms we haven't searched." She started briskly for the passageway, skirted Reiver's body, and was out of sight before Varden thought to move.

Chapter 23

Grown cautious now, Varden reclaimed the gun and the poker from the sideboard before following Helena to the back of the house. When he caught up with her, she was inside the small room, a warning finger held to her lips.

He moved to her side, looking to where her finger now pointed. On the waist-high inner door was a latch, and just above it, a hole had been drilled through the wood. Dangling from the latch was a small length of rusty wire. Below it on the floor lay a longer, broken-off piece of wire. The apparatus designed to permit the door to be opened from the inside had failed.

He took her arm, drew her out of the room, and gave her the poker. "Your voice will be more welcome than mine."

"Is anyone here?" she called. "It's Helena Pryce. Make a noise so I can find you."

At her first words, he returned to the small door and bent down to listen. Nothing. He made a gesture that told her to try again.

This time, when she finished, he heard an indistinct sound.

The hell with caution. He was too tired to think anything through, and if Tallant was there, he must be desperately weak by now. Time was running out for all of them. Varden raised the latch and pulled open the door.

The smell caused him to choke and back away. Mouldering vegetables, human waste, stale air. He took his lantern, set it just inside, and bending double, passed through the door.

A long shape, bundled under burlap sacks, lay shivering at his feet. He saw black hair matted with blood. "We need to get you out of here," he said. "Where are you wounded? Is anything broken?"

"N-nothing." The head turned. The fathomless, water-clear eyes fixed on him. "The picturesque earl. I knew this was hell."

"Not yet, Your Grace. Had you forgot? I'm an Archangel."

"So was Satan, once." His words were the barest mumble, as if his tongue was swollen in his mouth. Tremors seized his body. His head dropped again.

Then Helena was there, lifting away the sacks. "Are you able to pull yourself out? We can help."

"Try. S-soon." But he didn't move, except to wrap his arms around himself against the shaking and the cold.

"We need blankets," Varden said to Helena. "And something for him to drink. Why is it so bloody cold in here?"

"It's supposed to be." She raised her lantern. "See that trap door? It will lead down to an icehouse underneath. Some of these bags contain turnips and potatoes. He's been eating those, I expect. But he appears to be ill. We need to drag him out of here."

The struggle lasted several minutes. Tallant had gone limp, probably unconscious, and Varden couldn't grip him with his right hand. It took Helena on the other side to get the duke aligned with the low door, and then they had to maneuver him through it. By the time he was lying on the kitchen floor, Varden and Helena were panting.

"I'll go," she said, untangling the duke's coat, which had twisted around his legs. "Find something to raise his head off the floor."

Varden thought to retrieve some of the burlap bags, but changed his mind. They were filthy. After closing both doors to seal off the odor, he removed his greatcoat, folded it up, and stuffed it beneath the duke's head.

Long black lashes flicked up. "Why are you here" He sounded more coherent than before.

"Getting out of the snowstorm." Varden examined the blood caked in the duke's hair. "If we're to help, you have to tell me exactly what's wrong with you."

"Beyond being the idiot who got himself locked in a closet? A bullet parted my hair. A fleabite, but it bled a lot, and knocked me out for a time. Devil of a headache. I'm thirsty. Hungry. No turnips, please. The good news is an attack of malaria."

"How is that good?" Varden said, trying to remember what he'd learned of the sickness in India.

"Without the fevers, I'd be an icicle. Back and forth, chills and fevers. They're w-worse now. One more round will finish it."

"What do you need, then? There's an apothecary in Amersham."

"Cinchona. Not likely to be in Amersham. Hari Singh, if you can. At B-Birindar's." The duke was shaking again. But as always, his eyes mocked Varden. "You are hating this, aren't you?"

" 'Of all men else I have avoided thee.' And you're hating it as well."

"Beyond measure. 'But get thee back. My soul is too much charged with blood of thine already.' "

"Oh, for heaven's sake," said Helena, arriving at the door with her arms full of blankets. "If you must play Shakespeare, make it a comedy."

A small laugh from the duke, swallowed up in a bout of shivers.

With crisp efficiency, she unfolded the blankets, all but one, and cocooned the duke inside them. Then she withdrew Varden's greatcoat, gave it back to him, and placed the last blanket where the coat had been. "The food provided us by Mrs. Bagshot is under the rear-facing seat of the carriage. And bring the maps as well, please. We have to get him some help."

Despite the urgency, Varden took a moment inside the stable to locate Finn. They would have to leave him here for now. There was nothing with which to cover him, nothing they would not require for the journey, so he drew out his handkerchief and laid it gently over the driver's head. "God give you safe pasture," he murmured, "with horses to care for."

By the time he returned, Helena was sitting on her heels and using her own handkerchief to apply some sort of tincture to the side of the duke's head. The parcel of items purchased at the apothecary's lay open at her side. "It's a slight wound," she said. "I wish I'd something to help with a fever. He's becoming unnaturally warm."

"It's malaria," Varden told her. "There is only one treatment I know of. He wants us to take him to Hari Singh at something called Beer-in-Darce. Is he awake?"

"Sometimes. Like a door opening and closing. I'll try to get a little of the ale into him, with moistened bread from one of those sandwiches. You should eat something as well, sir. It's you will have to drive us out of here." Her head lifted. "You *can* drive?"

"I used to drive a curricle. Perhaps I should take one of the horses, maybe Reiver's, and ride for help. We could build a fire here before I leave. Tallant didn't seem to think so, but the apothecary in Amersham might have cinchona. It's a bark of some sort used to treat malaria."

She looked down at the duke. Put an ungloved hand on his forehead. "I think we will have one chance only. We must take him where help can be found. Let me go arrange the interior of the carriage while you feed him. When he's a little stronger, we'll try to find out where Beer-in-Darce is."

While she was gone, Varden broke pieces of bread from a sandwich, dipped them into a jar of ale, and brought them to Tallant's lips. After some choking and coughing from the duke, Varden realized his head required lifting. He sat crosslegged and raised the blanket and the duke's head onto his lap. Things went better then, although more ale was spilled than swallowed. It dribbled into several days' growth of black beard on Tallant's face. His hot face, as the fever began to take hold.

It required a great effort, Varden could tell, for the duke to repeatedly try to swallow what was fed him. He knew it was necessary. He knew, better than Varden or Helena, what he was dealing with. Malaria, Varden recalled from stories told him in Calcutta, was a recurring illness. "I always travel with Jesuit's bark," one East India Company official had told him. "Nothing else turns the trick when the fever is on me."

If they could catch the duke's horse, Varden thought, they would probably find a supply of the bark in the saddlepacks. But there was little chance of tracking the horse at night, let alone getting hold of it. And besides, he'd no idea how the bark was used.

"What is Beer-in-Darce?" he said when the duke's eyes opened for a brief time.

"House. North from L-London. Near Finch—Finchley. Walls. But—" A hand punched at the blankets, got loose, seized the lapel of Varden's coat. "D-don't risk her. You said . . . storm. Don't take chance. I sh-should be dead already."

"But you're not. And you're not going to be." Varden unclasped the large gloved fingers from his coat and returned the hand to the warmth of the blankets.

"Miss Pryce won't have it. Save your strength to do as she says."

She returned a short time later, overflowing with plans. On her orders, Varden ate a sandwich and a boiled egg while she used a handful of snow to wipe the duke's face. Then she got more bread and ale down his throat.

It did seem to help. When she tried to sit him up, he managed to hold the position. Then she told him he would have to walk, with Varden's help and hers, to the front door. Or crawl. Or they'd try to pull him atop a blanket, but that would be difficult.

"Crawl," said the duke, to Varden's astonishment. "If I fell, I'd take you d-down with me."

"In that case," she said briskly, "Lord Varden can go ahead of us and bring the carriage around."

Varden, taking with him the items she put into his hands, understood that Tallant would not wish his enemy to see him crawl. And for that matter, Varden didn't want to see it either. Back in the stable, he unsaddled Reiver's horse, gave him a small share of oats, and stowed the saddlepacks in the carriage for later inspection. Then he found the jar of oil and re-filled the carriage lanterns, as Helena had instructed. He eventually figured out the new arrangement of the carriage interior and located the panel that let him store things underneath. Getting Tallant up the steps and onto the bedlike platform would be a trick and a half.

The horses, munching on hay and oats supplied them by Finn before he was attacked, appeared to have calmed somewhat. They came along peaceably when he led them outside, with the resigned determination of soldiers forced into a long, uncomfortable march. They would probably endure his ham-handed effort to drive them as well, although it would help if he knew where the devil they were going. The snow fell steadily, and when he walked to and from the stable, he was ankle-deep in the accumulation on the ground.

He had taken his time, to allow for Tallant's slow progress. But when he had wrapped the reins around a post near the front door and entered the house, the duke was already sitting on the floor, back against the wall, covered with blankets. Kneeling beside him, Helena was holding an open map in one hand and a small pencil in the other.

"There you are," she said, looking over at Varden. "Beer-in-Darce is the name of a man who owns the house we are going to find. I've been pointing at spots near Finchley on the map of Middlesex, and His Grace indicated the approximate location. I've circled it. Our destination looks to be about twenty-five miles from here, but that does not account for the jigs and jogs along the way. You must study the route beginning here in Buckinghamshire, through a corner of Hertford to the Rickmansworth Road, and from there, follow the roads I've marked. You'll have to memorize the way, I'm afraid. If the maps get wet in the snow, they will become unreadable."

He glanced down at Tallant, who was gazing back at him. "Last t-turn is left, between two pillars. Walled house near River Brent. You need not d-do this."

"I'll handle my bit," Varden said, "if you'll help get yourself into the carriage. Miss Pryce, will you open the door, let down the stairs, and climb inside, ready to pull if need be? Tallant, I'm going to lever you up and haul you out there. Move your feet if you can."

He stripped away the blankets, hunkered down, got his left arm under the duke's right arm and around his back, and towed him upright. For a few moments, the unresisting weight of his burden nearly brought Varden to the ground. But Tallant found his feet, straightened his legs, and applied the stubborn determination Varden had seen in him before.

The carriage was only a few yards away. Tallant stumbled along at Varden's side to the stairs, where he propped his hands on the side of the carriage and dragged himself up. The carriage rocked, throwing him off balance. Varden was there to block his fall and help lift him to the next step. From there, out of strength, the duke pitched forward, his upper body sprawled across the padded platform. When Varden was sure he wouldn't slip down again, he went to the other side of the carriage and joined Helena as she pulled the limp body the rest of the way inside.

"He's burning with fever," Helena said, sounding alarmed for the first time since they had found him. "There were pans in one of the rooms off the kitchen. Fill them with snow, please."

She went to fetch the blankets and the other things they'd left in the house that might prove useful. Finally, with everything stowed, she gave Varden Reiver's pistol, still loaded, and two of the blankets. "We'll be warm enough," she said when he began to object. "Did you bring Finn's tarp? Good. It's all to you now, my lord. Take us as far as you can. But remember, there is no fault in stopping if you must."

"It's mostly to the horses," he said. "If they have to stop, we will. Use the cane against the roof if you need to get my attention. And if he becomes delirious—"

"I shall manage him." Her spectacles, fuzzy with snowflakes, were turned to his eyes. "Did I tell you, my lord, that my heart was in my throat when I watched you fighting Mr. Reiver after my bullet failed to hit him? Your tactics were beyond splendid, and your performance exemplary."

"Desperation lends inspiration, I expect." He brought his fingertips to her cheek for a brief caress. "And I have an excellent fencing master."

They lingered for a few moments, the snow swirling around them, each willing confidence and strength into the other. Then Varden took her hand, helped her into the carriage, and closed the door.

Taking the reins, he mounted onto the driver's box, arranged the blankets and tarp around him, and addressed the horses with a great deal more assurance than he felt. "Walk on!"

They did, seeming to know the proper direction. He knew only that the narrow road leading to the house had been lined on both sides with trees. When they came to a wider road, he remembered to turn right. It, too, was marked out by woodland on both sides, and a good thing, because there was no other way to tell they were on a road. The blanket of snow stretched thick and smooth ahead of them.

As time passed, Varden understood he had little to do but hang on to his place and keep watch for the next turn. The snow grew lighter as they came down from the hills, and by the time they drove through the slumbering town of Ricksmansworth, it had transformed itself into sleet. That meant he could see the road, for a time. But when the wind picked up, it drove needles of ice into his face. He had wrapped a woolen scarf over his mouth and tied another over his hat, but the sleet pelted his nose and eyes. He'd no choice but to lower his head and trust the horses to slog ahead.

After Rickmansworth, there would be no turn for six or seven miles. He could no longer feel his hands or feet. Carefully, so as not to confuse the horses, he wrapped the reins around his hands, two on the left and two on the right.

All for Tallant. *You are hating this,* the duke had said. And then he had quoted *Macbeth* back at him, a line that sounded almost like an apology. "My soul is too much charged with blood of thine already."

If he could honestly blame Tallant for what happened in Calcutta, he might have been able to accept an apology. But there could be no reconciliation until he had come to terms with himself, and that he had not been able to do. Only his anger kept him from gnawing at his own mistakes, as though he could chew them off and spit them out like a wounded foreleg. There was no escaping the trap that was himself, the flaws he'd discovered when confronted with obstacles and challenges. There had been few difficulties in his life before then, and he had not guessed how ill equipped he was to deal with them.

Tallant, damn his black soul, had pinpointed every one of his antagonist's failings. Marked them out for sarcasm and the mocking jibes that peppered their every encounter.

There would be no others. He took a vow, on that icy road in the middle of nowhere. When he had delivered Tallant into the house of Beer-in-Darce, there would never again be contact between them.

His resolution lifted his spirits, helped him endure the next several miles in spite of the blasting wind. The nightmare journey was taking them through a wasteland. Theirs seemed to be the only vehicle in the universe. The horses took their own steady, plodding pace, and he remembered to go left at the crossroad near Harrow Villa.

Five hellish miles later, the route got complicated. He did nothing but trace it again and again in his thoughts, because to miss one of the turns meant he would never find the way again. His lashes, clumped with ice, had nearly sealed themselves together. Cold seeped through him like acid. He couldn't have said his name, if asked. Saw a posthouse with lights in the windows, and let the reins go limp. If the horses needed to stop, he decided, they would turn into the stableyard. He wouldn't stop them. He didn't think he could.

They kept going. So did he, then, because he was at least as willful as a pair of hired nags. He resolved to buy them and settle them in lush pastures for the rest of their lives. Taking control of the reins again, he guided them to the right on what he hoped was the road from St. Albans to London, then took a left turn shortly after.

Not at all sure where he was now. There should be a hamlet within a mile or so. Dark still. Cold. Sleet. The wind screaming in his ears. This night had been a year long.

His thoughts went to Helena for the hundredth time, and once again he snatched them back. She had become a torment to him, more than all the other torments. He didn't know why. At least he needn't worry about her, except that he did. When she'd let him hold her after his fight with Reiver, he could not mistake the vulnerability at the core of her. The loneliness that she preserved with temper and bristled words.

It wasn't like the night she gave her body to him, and took his body into hers. That had been a joining of equals. Shared passion. A measure of his disordered mind that he now thought of it as transcendental. He had never spoken that word, or written it, but it seemed, as he reflected on it now, that he had once experienced its essence.

So he was thinking of her after all, and must not. How could he be numb to the marrow of his bones and still feel pain? Be so hell-bent to get somewhere, and yet not care if he made it? Ice had enclosed his heart and his will.

Drifting. He was drifting on a raft atop a lake of ice. Could see nothing now. Might as well cover his eyes and hope the blankets thawed the ice that sealed his lashes together. The horses wouldn't mind. They'd keep going, although a child could walk faster.

Had they come to the hamlet? Hendon. Herndon. Something like that. He wouldn't have seen it. But the warmth was having an effect on his eyes. His lids burned like they were afire, but they could also move. Open.

He stuck his head out from the blankets and met the gaze of a rider.

The man, going in the opposite direction, had taken hold of the reins and drawn the carriage to a halt. "Are you in difficulty, sir?"

After three tries, Varden managed to say, "Finchley."

"You've passed it. There's a private road just ahead, to your left between two columns. If you turn in there, and if your horses are trained well enough to back out, you can reverse course to your destination. Would you like me to help you?"

Through the mist clouding his thoughts, Varden sensed a memory just beyond his reach. He no longer knew where he was going. Why not there? Wherever it was.

"Thank you," he said, barely producing a sound. "That's the turn I was looking for."

"Are you sure? A compound of foreigners at the end of the road. Nice enough fellows. Good builders. They put up my new barn."

"I'm sure." Varden was sure of nothing. "You were kind to stop. If you will lead me to the turn . . . I cannot see well. The ice."

The short exposure to the wind had blinded him again. He felt the horses start up, felt them make the turn, and the man must have stayed with them, because next Varden knew, there were sounds. Voices.

The carriage had stopped. He peeled away the blanket and scarves from his face. For the moment, at least, he could see in a blurry way. Light, of the kind that preceded dawn, overhead. Lights, small ones, rushing toward him like fireflies. A wall in front of him. Iron-studded wooden gates swinging open.

Small figures leading the horses. They were inside the walls then. Stopped near a large, low building.

He tried to let go the reins and could not. His fingers, curled around them, had petrified. Then someone was beside him, sawing through the leather with a knife. Helping him to stand. From below, a man's voice directed him where to put his right foot. He couldn't hear very well. Leaned over to hear better. Heard a shout, and nothing more.

Chapter 24

Varden came awake slowly, with the pleasant realization that he was alive, warm, and comfortable. But when he began to stretch, he quickly thought better of it. From scalp to toenails, his body ached as if a giant had put him in a sack filled with rocks and given the contents a hard shaking.

He tried another stretch, this time expecting the pain, and found that everything moved as it ought. But his eyelids felt sealed together. Had been sealed, he recalled, for much of the journey. They opened when he applied all his will to them, and his gaze met a ceiling where firelight and shadows writhed in a silent dance.

The room was dark, save for the fire in the hearth and in the braziers ringing the low bed on which he lay. It had been, he thought, nearly dawn when he . . . Well, he remembered nothing after deciding he should climb down from the driver's box, and very little of what had happened before that.

Tallant! He sat up. What had become of him?

Struggling to his feet, he realized he was wearing a loose dressing gown belted at the waist, and nothing else. He padded over to a wide, knee-high divan where clothing was laid out for him—his own clothing, taken from his portmanteau. He managed to insert himself into a pair of trousers and a soft woolen shirt before he required to sit for a minute or two with his head buried between his knees.

When the dizziness passed, he looked around for his boots and discovered a pair of soft, embroidered leather shoes lined with fleece. But it hurt too much to bend and pull them on, so he went on bare feet to the door, thinking to find a servant and get some information.

A boy sitting cross-legged in the passageway jumped up, steepled his hands beneath his chin, and bowed. "*Namaste,* Varden-Sahib. It is welcome to see you. Stay, please. I will bring Birindar."

Varden went back into the room, located a mirror on a stand, and took stock of the damage. Eyelids a little swollen, windburn on the flesh around them, a two-day growth of pale gold beard, hair tousled like a small boy's. And now he thought on it, the boy in the passageway had looked remarkably cheerful. A good sign, that.

Shortly after came a knock at the door, and the scratchy response from his sore throat brought into the room a distinguished man of middle age and height, wearing loose trousers and a knee-length tunic.

As the boy had done, he steepled his hands and bowed. "I am Birindar," he said, "and this is my home. You have restored to us our friend. All that I have is yours."

"The duke's health—"

"After a long night of uncertainty, we are now assured that he will recover." Birindar stepped closer, his dark eyes evaluating Varden's appearance. "It seems you will recover as well."

"I fell off the carriage, didn't I?"

"Indeed. Two men were below, preparing to assist you, and all three of you went down together. Do you require a physician, Lord Varden? What may I provide for your comfort?"

Varden realized that Birindar was chaffing to pay a

debt that wasn't owed. "What is the time, please? And I should be glad of something to eat. Also, I cannot seem to find my boots."

Birindar appeared disappointed at the simple requests. "It is just after six o'clock, my lord. The young woman—Miss Pryce—is waiting in the south room to answer your questions. I shall have a meal served to you there. Your boots, I am afraid, are still drying and being stretched. Will you, in the meantime, accept the shoes my wife has provided?"

"Gladly." Varden felt heat stealing up his neck. "But I was unable to put them on. My movements are . . . restricted."

"Will you permit me?" Birindar fetched the shoes, dropped to his knees before Varden, and, with reverence, slipped the shoes, one after the other, onto his feet.

"I've never worn anything so comfortable," Varden said as Birindar rose, smiling.

"My wife measured your feet while you slept. You will honor her by accepting the shoes and the garment she has provided in place of your jacket, which is being mended. When you are ready, Lord Varden, simply open the door. Balvan will take you to Miss Pryce."

Helena, seated on cushions in front of a large square table little more than a foot high, was making lists when the door at the far end of the room swung open. It was a long way from where she was, half the length of the enormous house, and all the light was concentrated in the fireplace behind her and the tall stand of candles at each corner of the table. But she didn't have to see him to know that Lord Varden had come in.

A long, wide-sleeved gown, open at the front, swayed as he walked slowly toward her. When he drew closer, she saw that it was dark blue velvet, embroidered on the shoulder-to-floor lapels with golden thread. Beneath it he wore wheat-colored trousers and a lighter shirt, laced at the throat.

Because it was necessary, she uncoiled her legs, stood, and curtsied.

He didn't like that, she could tell when the candle-light washed over his face. In response to her formal gesture, his smile vanished. He had understood immediately what she was telling him. The bond established between them during their shared ordeal was now severed. They had become, again, what they must always be in future—servant and master.

He gave her a bow of acknowledgment. "Miss Pryce. May I hope you are well?"

"You may be sure that I am, sir."

A gesture of frustration. "What is wrong, then? Have I in some way offended you?"

Remorse burning in her throat, she kept on the road she had chosen during the hours of waiting. Chosen long before that, in fact, but always she had found reasons to change course . . . or gone looking for them. It was unfair to Varden, her inconsistency. It made everything more difficult for them both. "You are a great hero to everyone here," she said, "including me. I am weary, that is all. And my nature is off-putting at the best of times, as you very well know."

"Did you have no sleep?" he said, concern in his voice.

"I had the opportunity. But there was much to do."

"While I slumbered like a kitten." He spun around and began to pace the length of the room. "Why did you not call me?"

"There was no need. The few matters I dealt with required no great effort." She resigned herself to a small confession. "Mostly what I did was worry, about you just a little, and about the duke, who had passed into unconsciousness before we arrived here. Once he had been brought into the house, I was banished from his company. And from yours as well, because of the baths."

Walking toward her now, he passed again into the light. "Tell me everything that has occurred. And do be seated, Miss Pryce. I am tromping about because I require a bit of exercise."

The slight petulance of a disappointed and frustrated male. He resented the physical weakness, as he thought of it, that had kept him absent while she was tending to business. In truth, she had spent most of the day pacing, as he was pacing now, or withdrawing to the privacy of her bedchamber, where she had curled up and wept like an infant.

She lowered herself onto the cushions and folded her hands. "Because he burned with fever, the duke was put into a bath of cold water. And because you were seized up with cold, there was a warm bath for you. Mr. Singh, who had been at the home of the young woman he is to marry, arrived and took over the care of his friend. We waited through the day for his reports, which came every hour or so. His Grace was extremely ill. The reports were . . . difficult to hear. But by mid-afternoon, Mr. Singh was more optimistic, and around four o'clock, he believed the danger had passed." She felt a touch of pride at her own detached report. Perhaps she would, after all, skate through this without being discovered.

Before she could continue, a parade of women came in and began laying out plates of food on the table. The eldest of them, her sleek black hair streaked with gray, her figure slim and elegant, approached Varden and gave to him the traditional bow of greeting.

"I am Nageena Kaur," she said. "Birindar's wife. Our home is yours, and all that is in it. Will you honor us by taking this humble supper?"

As the table filled up with platters, Helena moved her writing supplies out of the way and watched Varden slather charm over his hostess. Oh, very well. He was behaving as he always did . . . to everyone but her. Never mind that when he did set himself to charm her, she turned him away.

When the women were gone and Varden was seated to her left, regarding the array of platters and saucers with some awe, she told him what little she knew about the colorful dishes. "They provide so many," she said at the end, "in the hope your English palate will find something to like. You are not expected to eat them all."

"Well, that's a relief. Although I'm ravenous enough to give it a try." He began filling his plate with whatever was closest to it. "It seemed rude to ask Mr. Birindar or his wife, but who in blazes *are* these people?"

"They are immigrants from the Punjab. Members of the family have been filtering over for three generations, working on East India Company traders until they accumulated enough money to have a try at settling here. Some failed, of course, but a small community has taken root. Birindar is the patriarch of an extended family, many of them living and working in London, others buying land in this area. Most are builders and carpenters."

She helped herself to a fat date sprinkled with sugar, holding it between thumb and forefinger while she finished her explanation. "His Grace is dear to them because he fought in the Punjab for several years after first going out to India, and because he is friend to Hari Singh, a distant cousin of someone in the family. They call him Syr, which means 'tiger.' I mention it so you'll know of whom they are speaking." After a moment, deciding not to continue with what else she had learned about the duke and this house, she bit into the date.

"This is all delicious," Varden said, refilling his plate. "Please distract yourself from my poor manners by telling me what arrangements you have made.

There must be at least a few wheels already turning at your hands."

"Yes. But I only acted on your behalf, doing what you would have done in my place. Birindar sent riders and a wagon to Beech Hollow, where nothing had been disturbed since we left. Finn has been carried here, and they will bring him on to London after I have made arrangements for his burial."

Thinking of it, and of the hour she had spent at Finn's side while the women cleaned him and anointed him with oils and spices, she took a few moments to regain her composure. Seemingly aware of her distress, Varden put down his fork and sat quietly.

"They also found the duke's horse," she said, adopting the clipped tone she used as a shield. "It has been trained in the way Punjabi cavalrymen school their mounts, so they were able to get near enough to calm its fears and bring it in. They brought Reiver's mount as well. I am no judge of horses, sir, but they do look very much alike."

"Chosen for that reason, as was Reiver for his resemblance to the duke. What have you done with him?"

She released a heavy breath. "I asked them to place his body in the ice house at Beech Hollow until you decide how we should proceed. Two men are waiting to intercept the Runners and the other men directed to follow us. Assuming they find their way to the house, they'll be sent back to London."

"With what explanation given them?"

"That there had been a misunderstanding, which is of some embarrassment to those who overreacted to a false rumor. They knew only that they were to follow us, sir. The men I employed will say nothing out of loyalty, and the Runners were chosen for their discretion."

"Neatly done, Miss Pryce. All of it. And as you have long since determined, secrecy is now our primary concern. We can best keep our quarry off balance by pretending nothing is amiss, which means that Tallant must remain here, out of sight, for as long as it takes to solve this mystery. Any idea how we can persuade him to do so?"

And now they were come to it. The news she had withheld because he would so dislike hearing it. "I cannot," she said carefully. "And you most certainly cannot. But I believe the duchess may be able to do so. We sent for her straightaway, and she arrived about an hour before you awoke. She is with him now."

After a silence, Varden took a drink of the tea that had long since cooled in his cup. "She is in danger as well, you know."

"Yes. My letter, carried by a messenger, instructed her to take every precaution. She arrived in a carriage protected by four armed outriders and the two Runners who have been keeping watch over her at Longview."

"And if she was followed?"

"A risk, I know, but not a great one. The duke lay near to death for most of the day, sir. She had a right to be told, and to come here if she wished. Birindar will keep the house well guarded. The Runners have been told to remain. You must decide if the coach and outriders should return to Longview as a diversion."

"The greatest diversion, I expect, will be me going about my business in London without an apparent care in the world. No mention of the attack on my coach, or of traveling for any reason other than family business. That will give me some time to find those blasted documents. They are the key. I am sure of it."

"You no longer believe the duke is guilty of any wrongdoing?"

"I was meant to think so, and I *wanted* to think so, which made me fair game. Now I must undo several things I have set in motion. If Birindar will lend me a horse, I'll set out for London within the hour."

"And I as well, then." She scraped up the courage to ask him straight out. "Or are you going to tell me my services are no longer needed?"

He glanced over at her in surprise. "Is that why you are in a temper? Because you imagine I intend to dismiss you?"

"I think you will do so in a misguided attempt to protect me."

"Ah, yes. Well, I should like to do exactly that, but I need you too badly. We shall, however, take precautions to—" He looked up.

At the other end of the room, the door opened. Silhouetted by the light from behind her was the figure of a woman, her bright hair glowing like a nimbus. The Duchess of Tallant. She sailed across the room, arms outstretched, her gaze on the earl.

He stood immediately and went out a little way to meet her, just beyond the edge of the table.

Helena, who had first started to rise, pulled herself away from the light and made herself small. She felt small. Felt herself breaking apart.

When the duchess reached Varden, she stood for a moment, simply looking at him. Helena could see her face, most of it, and Varden's right profile, illumined with candlelight.

Tears like liquid glass streamed down the duchess's cheeks as she reached out and took Varden's black-gloved hand between her hands. Bowing, she brought it to her lips and brushed a kiss on each finger. Then, raising her head again, she gazed into his eyes.

"You have brought my beloved to safety, and returned to me all the joy in my life. You have given to the babe I carry its father, and to our family the man who is our foundation stone. The cost to you has been great, I know. But it is God who must repay you, for I have nothing to offer but my gratitude. If you will accept it."

He kept himself motionless, in the way he had of remaining a quiet center in a time of crisis. And for him, Helena knew, this was the greatest ordeal of all. The woman he loved, honoring him with everything save what he most longed for, and what he could never have. He had made sure of it, by returning her husband to her.

Helena wanted to weep for him. She had wept more on this one day than in all of her life before. Wept for her brother, and for the man she loved, and for herself, and none of it had done any of them the least bit of good.

She deliberately closed her ears to Varden's murmured reply, softer even than Her Grace's whispery voice, and heard only a remark at the end about lacking a handkerchief to offer her. A gentle laugh from the duchess as she removed her hands from his and drew out her own handkerchief to dab her cheeks.

Then he said, so that Helena would be sure to hear, "Can you spare us a few minutes, Your Grace? Miss Pryce and I were discussing what must be done next, and it is possible you have information that would be of use."

"I hope that I do," said the duchess, lowering herself on the cushions to Helena's right, directly across the table from Varden. "But I can't imagine what it could be."

Varden took his seat as well, moving stiffly. "The danger, I am sure you realize, has not passed. Someone—perhaps a woman or several people, but let us refer to the guilty party as a man—has gone to great lengths to discredit your husband, and then to kill him. The fortunate demise of a notorious blackguard would spare everyone the nuisance of a trial and hanging. More to the point, His Grace's death would likely preclude a serious investigation into his offenses."

"Good riddance to bad rubbish." The duchess folded her damp handkerchief and set it on the table. "So the villain fears that an investigation of the duke would expose his own crimes?"

"That is my conclusion. What is more, he fears the duke—if he is permitted to live—will at some time come across the documents concealed by the Beast, and that what they contain will lead us to him. Clearly we must find those documents before any more harm is done."

"The duke had Tallant House and Longview searched. There are several other properties, of course. You are free to inspect them."

"That may become necessary. But I hope to narrow the search by tracing the former duke's travels in the weeks preceding his death. It stands to reason he would keep documents used for extortion fairly close by, especially if working in league with others. But the return of his brother from India may have caused him to change his practices."

"Oh, it changed everything. The confrontation was certain to end with the death of one of them, and should it have been Michael, the duke would have come under intense scrutiny. It makes sense that he'd choose a new hiding place for the documents, and I doubt it was the usual sort, like a bank vault. He trusted no one, and thought himself more clever by far than any opponent."

"Do you know of a property he may have visited during that time"

"Only one for certain, a small farm in the Scottish Highlands. He took his wife and elder daughter there and left them in the custody of two men who were almost certainly meant to see they met with an acci-dent. When the ladies escaped back to London, Miss Pryce helped us to hide them."

Hearing her name, Helena looked up to see the earl and the duchess gazing at her as if expecting she'd a solution to their present dilemma. But her powers of reason had dissolved when the duchess kissed Varden's injured hand. Like a dutiful servant, she lowered her head and let the aristocrats get on about their conversation.

"Before he went north," the duchess said thoughtfully, "I had an unpleasant encounter with the Beast at Palazzo Neri. He suspected me of stealing valuable artifacts from the castle . . . Well, you know all about that. After he left his wife and daughter in Scotland, it was a considerable time before he returned to London. I remember thinking he might have gone by the castle on his way south, perhaps to take a second inventory. But it was only speculation."

"Would he hide incriminating documents in a property he claimed, but did not own?"

The duchess gave a small shrug.

"Where better?" said Helena when neither of them continued. "Who would pay it any mind, once the place had been stripped bare? And who would expect the duke to conceal valuable documents in a run-down castle to which he did not hold the title? Unlike Scotland, it's close enough to London for practical purposes, but it is also remote enough to escape notice."

"And so large," said Varden, "that there is little chance of finding anything hidden there."

"We have the architect's sketches. Her Grace, who lived there for a time, can provide more detailed information. And I, if you will permit me, shall recruit housebreakers and sneak thieves to conduct the search."

They were both looking at her again, Varden with wary eyes and the duchess with approval. "Just the thing!" said Her Grace. "Did you know, Lord Varden, that your secretary has connections with the most amazing assortment of people?"

"Nothing I learn of Miss Pryce surprises me," he said. "I'll give thought to her proposal. Meantime, Your Grace, you and the duke must remain here, out of contact with everyone you cannot trust with your lives."

"I have discussed this with Hari Singh. If need be, he will chain the duke to the wall."

Varden reached under the lapel of his robe, felt around, seemed to realize belatedly that he was not dressed as usual when in company. "I've cards somewhere," he said, "with my direction on them. I'll leave one for you, in case you think of anything else, or if there is something you require."

"You may do me one small service, if you will. My sister-in-law and her daughter are in London, shopping for their trip to Italy. Will you get word to them at the Clarendon Hotel?" Smiling, the duchess untangled her legs from her skirts and rose. "Do not disturb yourselves. If you will excuse me, I shall—"

She came to a stop, an arrested expression on her face. "I just thought of something else. One afternoon, my father and I were in a small room just off the Palazzo's library, difficult to find unless you know where it is. Of a sudden, we heard voices so clearly the speakers might have been standing beside us. They were in an adjacent room, I am sure, but I could not discover the opening in the wall that allowed us to hear them. There were two men, and while I did not recognize their voices, they seemed familiar to me. An hour later, I encountered the Duke of Tallant. That meeting was so unpleasant that I quite forgot the overheard conversation, but now I am persuaded he was one of the speakers."

Varden was leaning forward, his gaze intent on the duchess. "Do you recall anything of the conversation?"

"Well, it wasn't about extortion. I would certainly have remembered that. They were discussing business,

I thought. The man with the quiet voice spoke of staggering losses and gave the duke something to read. After several minutes of silence, the duke, sounding angry, said that when he returned from seeing to a personal matter, he would take care of it. Then he left. Some time later, so did the other man. None of this is useful, I'm afraid. The losses probably referred to the damage Michael had done to his brother's enterprises in India. The other man may have been an investor in the Consortium."

"That is more than likely," Varden said. "Would you recognize the quiet voice if you heard it again?"

"I doubt it. The man spoke only a few words. But I will keep thinking. Perhaps I shall yet find some way to be of help. A sketch of the secret passages in the castle, perhaps? There are several my uncle did not know about, so I expect they don't appear on the architectural drawings."

"The sketches would be of great use, Your Grace." Again he started to rise, and again the duchess waved him back.

"You know where we will be," she said, "until you release us to go home. I have every faith in you. In both of you."

Silence fell over the room until the duchess had left it. Varden watched her go, and unable to bear looking at her, or at him, Helena undertook an examination of her fingernails. She heard the door open and close.

"Let us come to terms, then," said Varden.

Her gaze lifted to his face. What she saw there, solemn and uncompromising, was the determination of a man who had taken charge. From now until she departed England, she would be, more so than she had ever been with this man, his servant.

"You will no longer reside alone at Sothingdon House," he said. "If you insist on coming to London with me tonight, you will stay at my residence. After that, we'll make other arrangements."

"I should return to the Palazzo, if there is still a cottage to let. I'd like to learn more about the spyhole Her Grace discovered. If there is one, there must be others."

"I've no doubt. The servants are notorious eavesdroppers, and Beata thrives on collecting gossip and entertaining her guests with it."

"Do you suspect her of being in league with our extortionist?"

"I shouldn't go so far as that. At least one victim I know of never set foot in the Palazzo. But it's an ideal place to glean information, and servants can be bribed to share what they have learned. So long as you are careful and behave as you always have done, you should be safe enough there."

"What about the castle?"

"I was coming to that. Your idea about setting thieves to look for the documents is a good one, but how can we trust felons to turn over everything they find? Isn't it likely they'd try to sell incriminating evidence, or engage in a little extortion of their own?"

"Ordinary felons might. But the ones I shall provide will be carefully chosen and supervised. What's more, few if any of them will know what it is they are dealing with. Most cannot read."

"Chosen and supervised by whom?" His gaze locked on her face. "Jamie Carr?"

Astonished past speech, she could only stare back at him.

"Yes, I know about him," Varden said. "I hired someone to follow you."

"Follow? How da—" She clamped her mouth shut. Sank back onto the cushions from which she had begun to spring up.

"How dare I?" He looked, for a moment, as sardonic as the duke he so despised. "You investigated me, did you not? I distinctly recall you telling me so at our first interview. It is not so pleasant to be on the other end of an examination, is it? Even when there is no great scandal uncovered, one feels insulted. But if it is any consolation, you were the object of scrutiny for only one day."

"You didn't *trust* me?"

He appeared to think it over. "In fact, at that time I believe that I did. But for a brief period, my curiosity about you got the better of me. You needn't worry. I learned almost nothing, except that on Tuesdays you visit a number of establishments no decent young woman would enter. And, too, you have the acquaintance of a man reputed to be a leader of criminals and ne'er-do-wells. Is it Jamie Carr you would make responsible for the search?"

What to do? What to *do*? Unthinkable to admit Varden into her world. To let him see where she had come from. She wasn't ashamed of it. How should she be? But neither did she want him there, looking on her with pity, imagining her somehow triumphant to have escaped the Rookery and made something of herself.

But how else to discover if the documents were hidden at the castle? And it no longer mattered, really, what he thought of her. She would soon be gone. Perhaps she would create for herself a brand-new identity, begin an entirely new life. That would keep her busy for a while.

"Miss Pryce? Are you plotting a way to wriggle out of this?"

"Not at all, sir." Said with confidence, to her surprise, given how weak the rest of her felt. "Merely considering the logistics. You wish, I take it, to speak directly with Mr. Carr. Where would you like to meet?"

He gave her a speculative look, on guard for a trick. "I'll go to him tomorrow morning if that can be arranged. You will take me."

To argue would make him all the more suspicious.

"Without Finn to deliver it, getting a message to Mr. Carr is not a simple matter. But I shall do my best."

"Of course you will." He rose and came around the table, dropping onto one knee in front of her. "You always do your best. Why are you so angry, my dear? Why are you fearful?"

She struggled to hold her position. He was so close she could see the light shifting over the varicolored strands of his hair whenever he moved. "I am neither of those things, sir. I am just as I have always been."

"A thousand times since we met, I have wished to see your eyes, to read in them your moods and the truth of your feelings about what I have said or what has occurred." His voice, soft and compelling, wrapped around her like wings. "But since you can never reveal your eyes, I have learned to seek elsewhere for the truth. In the tilt of your head, or the stiffening of your posture, or the way you hide your hands when they might betray you. I find messages in the color that steals up your face, beginning here." His fingertips brushed the right side of her chin, lingered there. "In the quickening of your pulse at your throat, just here. Yes. Exactly like that."

When he drew his hand away, she felt suddenly cold.

"You are going to tell me," he said, "that I should not draw inferences from physical manifestations. That your pulse might beat faster from anger, or fear, or enthusiasm. From passion. How am I to interpret these revelations?"

She found her voice, stripped it of all expression. "How indeed, sir? There is no significance to be read in anything you have described."

"Oh, but there is. Your body has a language of its own, Helena. I haven't yet learned to decipher it, not altogether, but I shall. You may be sure of it. And when I do, I'll discover at last all that you take such pains to hide from me."

"Rubbish," she said. But her heart wasn't in it, nor her thoughts, which had flown to what would happen when he began to peel away her defenses. To what he would do when he came face to face with the truth. Perhaps she ought not wait for Devonshire's travel party to set out. She could be gone within a day or two, and Varden none the wiser.

He stood and offered a hand, chuckling a little when she clambered to her feet without assistance. If he could read her feelings by looking at her, what might he learn with a touch?

"Be ready within the hour," he said when they reached the door. "I'm going to make arrangements with Mr. Birindar. Can you ride?"

"No, my lord."

"Then we'll take your carriage, if Mr. Birindar is kind enough to spare us a driver and horses. Those posthouse nags have earned a rest."

She watched him stride away, tall and straight, revealing nothing of the devastation he must be feeling. And he thought *she* took pains to hide her emotions, or pretend she had none. What a nuisance they were, all these boiling passions. If she really cared for nothing, she wouldn't have to run away.

Nearing the passageway that led to her bedchamber, she had to pass by the room where the duke had been cared for since his arrival. She had not seen him, nor did she want to. But in perfect harmony with the bad luck that had been plaguing her, Hari Singh came out of the room just as she was approaching the door.

Turning to her, blocking her path, he regarded her with serious dark eyes and a sweet expression on his bearded face. "You have come to see him, *memsahib*." It wasn't a question. "He is sleeping now, but you may enter and keep watch until I return. It will not be long." Then he held open the door for her, and because she could find no excuse to do otherwise, she walked through it.

The pungent scent of lemons, cloves, and other spices filled the room, wafting from copper bowls set atop the braziers than provided the only light. She moved to the large bed, its hangings drawn back, and gazed down at the Duke of Tallant. Her brother—half brother, to be perfectly accurate—who had no idea his father had produced another child.

He lay on his back, his bandaged head elevated with pillows, his arms loose on top of the quilt. With his bronze skin and muscular body, he was as male as a male could be. But she saw also the counterpart of her long black eyelashes, her straight onyx hair, the high cheekbones that made her own face too strong. And she had seen, many times, the famous Keynes eyes, his now concealed by closed lids, hers nearly always concealed by dark spectacles. They were a dead giveaway, and in her case, quite literally so if her murderous father or his beastly elder son had ever chanced to see her.

She sat on the edge of a chair beside the bed. Michael was so quiet now, unlike the fevered man she could barely restrain for the first hours of their journey here. There were bruises on her arms and thighs and shoulders where his flailing arms had struck. "I know you!" he kept saying. "I know you!"

She had thought nothing could be worse than what was happening, not until his strength had all spent itself, leaving behind a limp, unconscious man barely able to draw one rasping breath after the other. Then she was terrified.

Unable to breathe for him or bring down the fever burning him to coals, she simply held him, murmuring reassuring words, finally singing the old hymns her mother had loved and sung to her when she was frightened. He couldn't have heard her, she knew, any more than he had intended to injure her when the fever raged. And she had thought how astonishing it was that the two of them had come together on that night, while his enemy and her lover drove them through the snow and sleet to safety.

Nothing happens without a purpose, he had told her. Could that be true?

A movement from the bed. She had been drifting a little, not seen the moment his eyes opened. They were gazing at her with lucid intensity. A smile quirked the corners of his mouth. "I know you," he said.

"Yes, Your Grace. Helena Pryce. I am pleased to see that you have suffered no lasting harm."

"I mean," he said, his voice a hoarse whisper, "that I know who you are. Who you must be. I saw you . . . When was it? In a carriage, I think. Saw your eyes."

"That is impossible, Your Grace. I never remove my spectacles. The light would damage my vision." But she *had* done, when his violence threatened to knock them off and break the glass.

Silence for a time. His gaze never left her face. "Don't worry," he said at length. "I'll keep your secret. I'll even try to keep it from the duchess, but no promises there."

She felt frantic, tried not to show it. "You are mistaken. You were fevered. Delusional."

"I'm frequently all of those things." His voice was fading. His lashes drifted shut. "Just the same, sister mine, come to me when you are ready. You will be welcome."

Chapter 25

Shortly after eleven o'clock, when Helena was settled in a guest bedchamber and he had been made presentable by his valet, Varden's coach drew up in front a large town house blazing with lights. Lady Fleming's rout was in full swing.

No social occasion was overcrowded this time of year, but the rooms were nicely full of the people he usually saw when making the rounds. Slipping into a long-familiar role, one he had never disliked, he strolled from group to group, making polite conversation, staying nowhere for any length of time. He was there to be seen, and when everyone had seen him, he would quietly slip away.

The Leighton ladies, excepting Gran Hetty, were in the largest salon, sipping champagne or lemonade and chatting with their friends. He spotted the twins, shimmering with excitement and pretending not to notice the young gentlemen who were pretending not to notice them. Chloe had not dyed her hair.

He went to stand with them for a few minutes, winning a smile of approval from Ann, and it wasn't long before mamas hoping to marry their sons into the Earl of Varden's family began hauling them over for an introduction. He wondered if they would be so eager in future, when he was no longer welcome at fashionable parties.

He spent a little time with his hostess, and then went to find Hetty in the room where she was playing cards with two other dowagers and a deaf baronet. "I could not leave without paying my regards," he said, his speedy departure foiled when she rose and directed him to escort her to a nearby room.

"I was watching you earlier," she said, seating herself on a divan. "You paid almost no attention to the eligible young women you are supposed to be cultivating. How do you expect to choose a bride before the end of the year? Pull a name from a hat?"

He hadn't meant to say anything to the family, but Hetty could pry secrets from a standing stone. And besides, if things went well, he was going to need an ally. "I believe I have already found her." He took a seat beside his grandmother. "Or rather, I have just realized that I love her, which she is not likely to believe. Please say nothing of this, Gran. Attention is the last thing I wish at this time, and in point of fact, the lady may not have me."

"Balderdash! No female worth having would refuse the Earl of Varden."

"You'd be surprised." He smiled. "Will you do me a small service? I should appreciate a straightforward answer to this question, just before you forget I ever asked it. If my chosen wife is not, by birth and breeding, of the sort the family expects me to marry, what will be their response?"

She raised her lorgnette to examine him for an uncomfortable time. "Does it matter?"

"Very much. I do not like displeasing them. And they, of course, will be affected by the gossip and criticism that is sure to follow my marriage. Even ostracism, in some circles, although only the black sheep and his wife will be culled from the flock. The others, you and Grandmere and the rest, will surely be invited back to the pasture. But should I expect the family to repudiate me as well, do you think? And will the rejection be permanent?"

"Can you imagine otherwise? All hopes have rested on you, Varden, since the day you were born. If I say that we would not welcome you and your unsuitable wife, would it change your mind about the marriage?"

"I'm afraid not," he said without hesitation. If Helena lived into her eighties, she would be very like this crusty, opinionated old woman. "There will be plenty of obstacles, I know, with most of them thrown up by the bride. She will take your view of this, insisting I look higher for a wife. And to make sure that I do, she'll firmly send me packing. I may be compelled to take a lesson from Shakespeare and make me a willow cabin at my lady's gate. Write loyal cantons of love, and sing them in the dead of night." He took Hetty's wrinkled, spotted hand and brought it to his lips. "Dearest Gran, you cannot be made to accept her, I know. But all of you will be respectful and polite, or you will answer to me."

"Hoity-toity!" She snapped her hand back. "As if we'd cast you off for falling in love. What must you think of us? Oh, there will be mumbling and grumbling, I suppose, especially from your aristocratic French Grandmere. But if your young woman makes you happy, they will come 'round, and I, as you should have known, will always stand on your side." Hetty's green eyes shone with interest. "Now, my dear, who is she?"

"You'll not have the answer today, Gran. I must first make my feelings and intentions known to her."

"I don't see why. In my day, the elders of the family were always consulted beforehand. You modern lads have no sense of the proprieties. Well, come along, my dear. Help an old lady toddle back to her card table. I was winning, you know."

"That's because you cheat." He took her arm and

helped her rise, feeling considerably more optimistic. Social repudiation was one thing, and he would be sorry if it came, but the loss of the family he loved was quite another.

Half an hour after leaving Lady Fleming's rout, Varden was admitted by a sleepy-eyed servant to the home, and then to the study, of Sir Richard Burnie.

The chief magistrate, clad in trousers, shirt, and dressing gown, rose from the chair behind his desk where he had been working. "Sir, my congratulations!" He was practically bouncing with pleasure. "Your surmise was correct. We have found the documents!"

"Indeed?" What pernicious twist had this story taken now? Varden, who had come for an entirely different purpose, put a bland expression on his face. "And what did they reveal?"

"See for yourself. I have the papers here. Wouldn't do to leave them where a clerk might have a look, eh? In fact, I was just making a copy."

Varden sat, so that Sir Richard could do so, and picked up the top sheet of paper from a small stack—no more than six or seven pages—that was placed in front of him. When he had finished reading them, he sat back and folded his arms. "Where were these located? And who knows about them?"

"They were in a concealed wall safe at Tallant House. The duke's bedchamber, to be precise. I chose the seekers from among my best and most discreet men. The caretaker was distracted on his way back from supper, and a locksmith had made keys the previous night. We needn't fear disclosure, Varden. Not until we are ready. Shall I issue orders in the morning for the duke's arrest?"

"Not yet." Sir Richard, even more than usual, was champing at the bit. "Does it occur to you that these papers contain only sketchy information about individuals who are no longer alive? The report concerning Lord Castlereagh is scandalous, to be sure, but he's been gone since 1822. I see nothing here that a working extortionist cannot easily do without."

"But it is you suggested the documents might be hidden where we had already sought them."

Sir Richard ought to have twigged to the setup by now, but his enthusiasm at the prospect of re-arresting Tallant had got the best of him. "As I am sure you have already determined," Varden said, "these papers were planted in the hope we would find them. We are meant to use them as evidence against the duke."

"Is that what you expected to happen?" Sir Richard looked offended. "Why didn't you tell me?"

"I did not foresee this. Like you, I thought Tallant to be neck-deep in extortion and murder. Happily, you have been both wise and cautious. A lesser man would have thrown Tallant back in the Tower by now." And that was laying it on with a trowel, Varden thought, pretending to look again at one of the papers.

Finally, in a bitter voice, Sir Richard said, "Have you any idea who has been playing us like a pair of trout?"

"I may have. But you will agree that incontrovertible evidence is required before we make our move. Let us presume he is waiting to learn that we have found the papers, which will be confirmed when the duke is taken into custody."

"That sounds reasonable." Sir Richard looked confused. "But since we can't arrest Tallant, what do we do?"

"Nothing for the present. Except . . . I shall see these documents returned to where they were found."

"You'll *what*?"

"Well, I'd prefer to retain the originals, so I'll first try to acquire a forged replica. Only consider. When the duke is not arrested, our extortionist will begin to fret. He'll wonder if the incompetent searchers failed to locate the wall safe. He might send someone to take a look, and if he does, your men will be waiting for him."

"Yes, but a housebreaker's testimony would make poor evidence."

"I'm not trying to catch the extortionist by these means," Varden said. "I'm trying to throw him off balance. Trick him into making a mistake. The duke, I have come to believe, is not involved in extortion, and it is unlikely he murdered his brother. At some future time, I shall be able to tell you what led me to these conclusions."

"You bloody well will!" Sir Richard pounded a fist on his desk. "Two days ago, you had quite the opposite opinion. Unless you were manipulating me, and my staff, and English justice itself!"

"Only stumbling about, I am embarrassed to say, as I have been for most of this botched investigation. You are right to question my judgment. I can only ask that you grant me the confidence I have not merited."

Nothing quite like an earl humbling himself to win over an arrogant magistrate. "Well, well, then," said Sir Richard with unnatural benevolence. "We all make an error now and again. I'll listen to your plans, if you have any."

Varden reminded himself that his upcoming confrontation with Helena would be a thousand times more difficult than this. More-than-there-were-stars more difficult. "What I ask, most earnestly, is your silence. If our quarry gets wind that someone other than the duke is under suspicion, he will go to ground."

"But my reputation—"

"Will be in the rubbish heap if news leaks out, as will mine. Let me proceed on my own, with your cooperation to fall back on when I need it. If I am mistaken yet again, you have my word that all the blame will fall on me. And I shall make sure you have the credit for putting a stop to my blundering."

A fearful, prideful man such as Sir Richard ought not to be given time to reflect. Refolding the incriminating papers with care, Varden slipped them into the distinctive leather case in which they had been found. "I must be off," he said, rising and making his way to the door.

There, he paused. "One more thing. You might hear word of unusual criminal activity in Buckinghamshire. If so, take the information, keep it secret, and do nothing."

Chapter 26

Just before eight o'clock, when a servant had delivered hot water for washing up, cold water for brushing her teeth, a pot of chocolate, and a note from Lord Varden, Helena quickly locked the bedchamber door and removed her wig. She had worn it all night, and her spectacles as well, fearing Varden might decide her presence in his rented house gave him leave to attempt a seduction.

Why she would think that made no sense, even to her. Following their quarrel in Windsor, his playful beguilements had ceased, and since that time, he had shown no interest in her person.

With swift and experienced hands, she combed out her own hair, wrapped it tightly against her scalp, and pinned it ruthlessly. Then she groomed the brown hair that had once grown on someone else's head, secured it around the rollers that gave it shape and made it ugly, and anchored it atop her own hair with another arsenal of pins.

She was wearing the last clean garment she had packed, an unadorned carriage dress of gray wool with a high neck and long cuffed sleeves. Her felt bonnet, a little bedraggled after the past few days, would have to do. Pausing a little breathlessly, she regarded her appearance in the dressing table mirror.

Keynes eyes, nearly colorless save for a dark rim

around the iris, looked back at her. A legacy from her father, like the black hair and the distinctive bone structure, like the temper and the damn-you-all determination to have one's own way. She knew him only by reputation, but she had met both of his sons. In some ways, the Devil's children were all very much alike.

Varden's note requested her to join him for breakfast at her earliest convenience, so she polished her spectacles, put them on, and made her way down two flights of stairs to the small dining room. He rose when she appeared, inquired about her comfort, and continued with a stream of pleasantries until she had been served and he had waved the servants from the room. Then, in a swift transformation, he began to tell her about documents found at Tallant House, how he thought they got there, and what he planned to do with them.

"I know just the man," she said. "His lodgings are not far from where we are going today, if you wish to bring the papers along. May I see them?"

He looked up from buttering a piece of toast. "Take no offense, Miss Pryce, but I feel obliged to keep private the contents of those documents. Suffice it to say there are a number of scandalous allegations about well-respected men who are no longer alive to defend themselves. Their honor is now in our hands."

"I meant only to see how great a task it will be to reproduce them. But of course, Mr. Forker can tell you that."

"Forker the forger?"

"That is not his real name, and he professes to be an amanuensis. He can also produce a series of credible documents proving you heir to the thrones of several small countries. Sir, I should tell you that I did not send your footman with a message for Jamie Carr. It wouldn't have been safe, not at night. We shall have to hope he is at his residence when we arrive."

He put down his half-eaten rectangle of toast, wiped his lips with a serviette, and left the table. "If you will excuse me, I've messages of my own to send before we depart. Twenty minutes should do it. Ought I, do you think, bring along one or two of my larger footmen? A weapon?"

"A walking stick is never a bad idea, sir. But you will be perfectly safe, so long as you are with me."

He gave her a smile that looked almost affectionate. But he was turning away at the time, so she had probably seen only what she wanted to see.

Varden's carriage left them off at St. Giles in the Field, where she spoke to the vicar about arrangements for burying Finn, and from there they walked into Seven Dials. Helena took them along the street where at least one of Jamie's unofficial watchmen was always stationed, and by the time they turned onto the next street, they had picked up a three-man escort.

She could not help stealing glances at Varden. In a greatcoat of rich brown, a curly-brimmed beaver hat on his head, and an elegant walking stick in his hand, he was . . . well, entirely out of place. Everyone they passed, including those already well gone on ginevra before ten of the morning, paused to gawp at him. People leaned out their windows, came out from alleyways, stuck their heads out of shop doors to get a better look.

In any ordinary place, the Archangel was a sight to see. Here in the Rookery, he was a circus parade. But if the blatant scrutiny disturbed him, he gave no sign of it. Without losing a jot of aristocratic aloofness, he looked around him with unabashed interest. Now and again, when they passed something unpleasant—a legless child begging from a shuttered doorway, or the sound of screaming from one of the overcrowded lodgings—she saw a muscle tick on his jaw. Perhaps it was possible after all, what he had told her. Perhaps what a person was feeling could be unriddled from small betrayals of the flesh.

What must he think, to see her at ease in such a place? Was he shocked that she knew these people? That she walked these streets without fear, and knew where she was going? Or perhaps his spy, that treacherous Runner, had told him a great deal more than Varden had admitted to knowing.

This is my home, she kept thinking. I will not disown it. Whatever you see here, you must accept in me, for there is little done in the Rookery that I mightn't have done as well, if not for the man you are about to meet. He spared me the desperation of these people, and the hopelessness, at great cost to himself. At cost to those who had not enough for themselves, but who sacrificed so that I could be decently dressed and properly schooled. If you turn up your well-bred nose at any one of them, I shall *slap* you.

A little thrill of pride rippled through her when they turned into Lomber Court, where Jamie was able to enforce a degree of cleanliness and restraint. No garbage littered the street. The smells of ale, roasting meat, and baking bread replaced the unpleasant odors that had made even her, long accustomed to them, feel ill. Varden wouldn't notice, she supposed, let alone understand the triumph of Jamie's accomplishment.

The escort melted away when they entered the secondhand clothing shop, which seemed to fascinate Varden. She had to urge him to keep going, after getting a sign from Mr. Gibbs that Jamie could be found at Almack's. Then she began worrying about what Jamie would say to him. And why she had brought him here at all. And if she had the stamina to endure this when just being with Varden turned her into a quivering jelly. Eight days until she left the country— and the Archangel—to begin a new life without them.

Only one decision remained. Would she begin that life as Helena Pryce of the wig and spectacles, or find an obscure corner of the planet and make up a new person to be? She had long since ruled out identifying herself to anyone as the Devil Duke's bastard daughter. Not to Varden, because she did not expect to see him after her departure. And not—openly—to her half brother and his duchess, who had a century of Keynes scandal and their own troubled pasts to live down. She refused to make their path even more difficult.

Two of the five rooms of Almack's were closed off, as was usual when most of the adults were plying their trades elsewhere. Jamie sat on a stool in a corner of the middle room, teaching a group of restless boys to write. He looked up when she appeared in the doorway, smiled, and then spotted Varden standing behind her. His brows went up like gothic arches.

The boys had to be given a task before he left them, and meanwhile, several people in the workrooms were moving in for a better view of Elly's Archangel. That was what they called her employer, and the splendid male who had moved to stand beside her could be no other. He was the one, they knew, who had paid for their carpentry tools, pencils and tablets, scissors and needles and thread.

Jamie cut a path through the crowd and, after a gentlemanly bow to Varden, took her arm and led them up a flight of stairs to a room overlooking the street. He was dressed in work clothes today, a plain wool shirt and trousers with a sleeveless felt tunic for warmth.

She looked over at Varden, who was wearing his diplomatic mask. Ought she defer to him? It hadn't, until this moment, occurred to her. Men generally preferred to converse with other men in matters of business, but perhaps that didn't apply to thiefmasters and earls.

She performed an entirely unnecessary introduction, only because no one else was saying anything. Then Varden made a few polite remarks, Jamie made a few sardonically polite remarks, and beneath all the pleasantries, the fencing match was on.

Why did Varden dislike every man who had a fondness for her? First her half brother, in a quarrel that began long before she had ever met either of them, and now Jamie. She'd soon had enough. "Lord Varden," she said crisply, "perhaps you should explain why we are here."

"I'm sure you can do that better than I, Miss Pryce. Please go ahead."

Startled, she watched him stroll over to a widow and stand in a patch of sunlight, wrists crossed behind his back, gazing out. With a shrug of confusion, she turned to Jamie and quickly outlined the scheme to have some of his reformed housebreakers search the castle. She could tell straightaway that the idea tickled his sense of the absurd, but he merely nodded when she was done. It was a noncommittal nod, which told her that Varden had only been making a gesture by letting her speak first. The men fully intended to take up the negotiation themselves, and all the decisions would be theirs. That was borne out when she mentioned their second purpose for coming to Seven Dials.

"Well, then," said Jamie, "why don't you carry yourself over to Forker's shop and deal with that errand yourself? Have you the documents to be replicated?"

"I have them," said Varden, reaching into his jacket and withdrawing a flat leather packet. "But she will require an escort."

"Take the Goban boys," said Jamie. "They're in the tavern. Don't worry, milord. They are there to deal with troublemakers, not to imbibe, and they are both the size of plow horses."

She stood for a moment, stunned at the efficiency with which she was being dismissed. She did not want these two men alone together. God knew what they would say to each other. What they would say about *her*. But nothing she could do would stop this now, so she finally turned on her heel and left.

Varden, suppressing a chuckle, went to the door and watched her flounce down the passageway, thwarted and furious. When he was sure she was not coming back, he closed the door and turned to Jamie Carr. "And you, I take it, are her father."

Carr looked amused. "What, may I ask, led you to that remarkable conclusion?"

"I have spoken with Miss Linford. She described the man who enrolled Miss Pryce in her school."

"Ah." He tapped his prominent nose. "She remembered me honker."

"Among other things. Which is the name you invented—Phillip Pryce, or Jamie Carr? Did you ever live in India or do business there?"

"Never set foot off this sceptered isle. Think on it, milord. The Linford sisters, gracious as they be, would turn away an orphan child brought to their door by the rascally Jamie Carr. Where is the crime in making myself acceptable to them? The ruse was harmless enough, and it got Ella admitted, after which I troubled them no more."

"Ella? Her name isn't Helena Pryce?"

"In this neighborhood, Helena is a difficult name for some to get their tongues around. She was nick-named Ella as a child, and those of us who knew her then still use it from time to time."

"And her parents?"

"Long since departed from this life. I knew her mother, and when she passed, I took the child into my care. There was no one else. And now, milord, I think you must cease this interrogation. At the least, you must cease expecting answers."

Varden recognized a man who had created his own kingdom and ruled it with benevolent tyranny. A mere earl from an adjoining kingdom had no influence here, and an earl come to ask a service ought to watch his step. "I beg your pardon," he said. "Having grown fond of Miss Pryce, I was eager to make the acquaintance of her family. When I saw you, I thought I had found one of them."

"Would you be so fond, if a scoundrel like me had sired her?"

"She did not choose her parents, Mr. Carr. And I do not know you. That is, in fact, the reason I came here. While I can see the wisdom of sending experts to search for hidden documents, my concern is for what might become of them if they are found."

"You think one of my thieves will steal them?" Carr laughed. "Are they so valuable as that?"

"Only to me. I want them in my hands with all possible speed, and I will pay well to get them there. My fear is that some or all of the documents will be taken, or that the information they contain will be copied and disseminated. There is no money to be made in that way, but great harm might be done by a misguided fortune seeker. So, yes, I am worried about releasing a pack of thieves into the castle."

"Is there anything of value there to tempt them?"

"Not to my knowledge. They are welcome to pilfer whatever odds and ends strike their fancy."

"*I'll* not welcome them to do that." Carr's eyes blazed. "Which isn't to say they won't, but I will put them out of the clan if they do. Very well, milord. I accept responsibility for mounting a search, and should the documents be found, for returning them safely to you. Will you wait here a few minutes while I send for my pack of thieves? Most are at Covent Garden, selling flowers or baskets or knickknacks. They will be delighted, you can imagine, to jump back into the auld game."

When Carr was gone, Varden returned to the window. He had a new appreciation for fine weather, and even the sparse sunshine that made it through air thick with coalfire smoke seemed glorious, especially in this grim underbelly of London.

He'd not expected to find the likes of Jamie Carr here. Or to learn that Helena was other than an occasional visitor, one of those charitable ladies who carry alms directly to the needy. Wherever her origins, she had ended up a Rookery bird. The people here knew and protected her. Their leader had raised her as his own.

When he came right down to it, he didn't know Helena at all. He had been her lover, her employer, and her antagonist. Her companion through adventures that led them into hardship and danger. Sometimes, he flattered himself that she considered him a friend. But all along, she had a life entirely separate, completely at odds with the woman he had thought her to be.

He found that absolutely . . . fascinating. Exhilarating. Seductive. The prim, starchy, brilliant woman of business led a secret life, one even more clandestine than their unforgettable night in the castle. He had been resisting, since it was proposed as a hiding place, the strong temptation to mount a search there in company with her, just the two of them. To mount *her* again, night after night, in that enveloping, tantalizing darkness. He couldn't, and he mustn't. But damn his lustful heart, he wanted to.

"They should be rounded up within an hour," said Jamie from the door. "Shall we tinker with the details?"

"How much do you want?" Varden said flatly.

"No wages. Even the poorest among us is called to practice giving. It will be payment enough for these sad fellows to escape the city for a few days. There are expenses, of course, for travel and food and the rest."

"Naturally I'll provide the funds. But how is it to be arranged?"

"Helena will see to everything. We lot deal in cash,

so when you get us the money, we can be off. I am going as well, to supervise. Does that allay your fears?"

"I'm not sure. In some ways, it increases them."

"Then I'll give you my word as a gentleman in spirit, if not in fact, to send you whatever we find without examining it. Does that help?" Carr tilted his head. "No, I can see that it doesn't. What denizen of the stews keeps his word? Knows the meaning of honor?"

"We have an agreement. But I wish you would accept wages."

"You have already paid us, I think. Are you not Billy's angel?"

Varden's heart jumped a few beats.

"It was a miracle, if one believes the lad's tale." Carr's lined, worldly face split in a grin. "Billy Barnes, about to be sentenced to hang for a bit of folly, had a celestial visitation. He awoke in his cell at Newgate to find an angel standing there, more beautiful than any creature he had ever seen. The angel told him to be brave, to eat his supper, and to pray. Then the angel gave him oranges, and I know that to be true because he saved one for me."

Keeping only one of the three for himself. Varden, remembering the boy's delight at having the oranges, was deeply impressed. And angry that Carr had found him out.

"I thought it must have been one of the prison reformers, perhaps Elizabeth Fry, taking pity on a sweet-faced child. But now I think it was an Archangel went to see him, and maybe did more for the wee bairn than that. Not many could secure a pardon from the king practically overnight. Have you nothing to say for yourself?"

"You're the storyteller. I can't wait to hear the end."

"I expect you'll have to tell me that part. But it

started, I think, with Charley Trotter. Helena noticed him skulking about on Tuesday week ago, and he followed us to Newgate. In your service, was he?"

Varden gave up pretending he was uninvolved. "For that one day. Trotter reported that after you emerged from Newgate and spoke with Helena, she was overset. Perhaps in tears. I made it my business to find out whom you had visited, and from there, one thing led to another. If you wish to know where the boy is, I will tell you, but only if you agree to say nothing of this to Hele—to anyone."

"You don't want her to know? Do you fear she'll be after you to rescue all her ducklings?"

"I—" How to explain this without giving himself away? "She was unhappy, and I wished her not to be. No more than that. She needn't take on a burden of gratitude for something she never asked me to do. She carries too many burdens already."

"So she does," Jamie said at length. "I'll not add to them. And now, Lord Varden, would you care to visit your bank?"

Relegated to the role of purse, he waited while Jamie went to gather the bully boys who were to escort him and his money. Then he would go home and wait for news.

And just as that thought scratched through his mind, a whole series of responsibilities came rushing in, as if to remind him of their existence. In the days to come, he had to retrieve his horse from Amersham, settle the intrepid posthouse horses, and see the forged documents returned to Tallant House. Arrange for the other Tallant properties to be searched. Accompany the twins to parties, or Ann would have his head on a platter. See what he could discover about the spyholes at Palazzo Neri. No, Helena would do that. Parade himself where everyone could see that murder and extortion were the furthest things from his mind. Decide how to proceed if the documents were recovered and his suspicions proven to be correct.

And all the while, keep himself away from Helena. Well, not let himself be alone with her. He was on fire with love, steam whiffling out his ears. She was sure to notice.

It could not be now.

Before he would be free to begin the best part of his life, he must put behind him the worst part. Rectify his mistakes. Track down the extortionist. Untangle himself, once and for all, from the Duke of Tallant and his family. Both here and in India, he had misjudged the duke's intentions and actions. Misjudged his own feelings for the lovely woman the duke had married. Made trouble for them both, and for himself. At the height of his lunacy, bought a bloody damned fallen-in castle to prove his undying love for a married woman.

Love that turned out to be a bubble, glorious and fragile and lighter than the wind. It had wafted off between one heartbeat and the next, and he didn't even know when it had happened.

Before he saw her at Birindar's house, certainly. Before she thanked him, and kissed his hand. But that was the moment he understood why he had been so drawn to her. Why so many random occurrences had conspired to bring him to the place where her husband lay near death. He had been meant to give to her a gift, yes, indeed. But he had mistaken what the gift was to be.

"Ironic, isn't it?" he had said in reply to Hari Singh's simple words of gratitude for bringing Tallant to safety. "It's as if we are all tethered together, first to do harm to one another, and then to repair it."

"Perhaps to challenge one another," Singh said gently, "so that we might fail, and learn, and change our lives." He followed with a story about the Buddha, an elephant, and some monkeys, the point of which continued to elude Varden. But at the end, the Sikh added a remark that haunted him even now. "What seems to us coincidence," he said, "is God's way of choreographing a dance."

Varden didn't feel as if he were dancing. But he had been challenged, and had learned a little, he hoped.

And he was assuredly changing his life. Once the Tallants were out of it, he could walk into the future with Helena and never look back.

Chapter 27

Varden, tangled in thoughts of Helena making her Tuesday visit to Rookery taverns, gin shops, and brothels, enclosed himself in his study after a light lunch to distract himself with correspondence. He was having little success. Was she safe without Jamie Carr there to enforce discipline on his clan? Were the men who usually escorted her in position? Were they sober?

Carr and nine of his most talented burglars had left for Somerset on Thursday last, and Saturday's post brought confirmation they had arrived. Since then, not a word. He had also received from the duchess a sketched map of secret passageways and hidden chambers, which he sent to Carr by way of a servant. On his return, the servant said the men appeared to be keeping themselves busy. Mildly encouraging, Varden supposed.

Of Helena, he had seen practically nothing. That was for his own sake, but also because she would be safer if he kept his distance. She was staying at the Palazzo, helping arrange Beata's flamboyant pre-Season parties, such as the masquerade ball being held tonight. He was still debating whether or not to attend. A costume and mask would permit him to look on Helena without his attentiveness being obvious, and he had gone so far as to have one made up. Then it occurred to him that she might not be present.

Last night, after the weekly political gathering, he had roamed around a little, hoping she would waylay him and take him somewhere to talk. But she never appeared, before or after the meeting. He knew, from a note she had sent, that the spying apparatus at the Palazzo defied imagination, so more than likely she was being particularly cautious.

He missed her, though. The little bounce when she walked, as if her mind and will were just that much ahead of her body. The tiny curved lines at the corners of her mouth that winked at him when she smiled . . . or was trying not to. He missed the wry observations, the barbed remarks, the incisiveness with which she cut to the heart of an issue. She had cut to his heart as well, his sharp-clawed lioness, and made a place for herself, and taken up residence there.

He had just dragged his thoughts back to the letter he was writing when there was a rap on the door.

A footman entered on command, carrying a good-sized parcel wrapped in brown sacking and tied with string. He looked a trifle puzzled. "Milord, two trades-men delivering meat and vegetables at the kitchen door asked that this parcel be put directly into your hands. But the cook never made the order for the meat and vegetables."

"Give it me," Varden said, his breath and heart racing like Newmarket horses. "Where are the men?"

"In the kitchen. Should I call for the Watch, milord?"

"No, no. I was expecting this. Wait outside the door for my instructions."

When he was gone, Varden cut through the string with his penknife and ripped open the sacking. Inside was more wrapping, this time brown paper, with a note slipped under the binding string. "Send word if this is what you seek," it said. "We will wait here to learn if the search must continue." The handwriting, in pencil, was neat, and the signature read "PP." After a few moments, Varden got the joke. "PP" for "Phillip Pryce."

Beneath the brown paper was oilcloth, and beneath that, more brown paper. At last Varden uncovered a leather portfolio filled with papers of several sizes and kinds. He didn't have to glance at more than a few of them to know that Carr had found Beast Tallant's stash of documents.

Clearing a space on his desk, he wrote a short letter of acknowledgment, signed it, and was about to affix his seal when he thought to add a postscript. "I am in your debt," it said, which was putting it mildly. Then he went himself to the kitchen, startling everyone there, and made sure the men had funds for the trip back to the castle. They were settling down for a meal when he returned to his study.

There he poured himself a glass of brandy, his hand shaking a little, and took a seat behind his desk. He didn't relish, not at all, the reading of these papers. His most urgent goal was to verify the identity of the extortionist and discover if there were accomplices, but eventually he would have to know what each document contained. At the least, he required the names of the people being squeezed for money, so that he could figure out how to best contain the damage and end their torment. He might also discover criminal behavior, and would have to decide if he ought to turn over the relevant documents to the authorities.

He hadn't asked for such a responsibility, but here it was, on his plate. He trusted himself to act fairly, which was something, and had acquired a little wisdom and experience along the way. After gathering the wrappings and putting them in a trash basket, he drew the portfolio closer, pulled out the first paper, and began to read.

Very soon, he knew more about several people of

his acquaintance than he wanted to know, most of it relating to sexual indiscretions and deviations of surprising inventiveness. He flipped through the next thirty or forty papers, consisting mostly of correspondence—probably stolen—and the testimony of those who had witnessed bad behavior. There were many detailed accounts, and it didn't matter if they were altogether accurate. The threat of having such excesses trumpeted to the world would be enough to terrorize the victims.

By the third hour, he felt as if he'd been swimming in a river of garbage. There were notes on the margins of the letters and witness accounts, and sometimes entire pages reporting information provided verbally, all in the former Duke of Tallant's jagged handwriting. Varden recognized it from signatures on Consortium documents.

After pouring himself another drink, he took up the last sheaf of documents, about forty unsigned letters bound with a length of rawhide. They were written by the same hand, and he recognized it as well. The late duke's fellow conspirator was the man he had suspected, the respected advisor and favorite courtier of His Majesty, King George the Fourth.

Charles, Lord Gretton, had sold his soul to the Beast.

His letters to the duke represented one side of a correspondence that had continued for several years, but the most interesting revelations began about the time Varden had been delegated to investigate Consortium losses in India.

It was Gretton's idea. "The Archangel," he wrote, "knows nothing of the business. He will believe what he is told. With care, we can direct his investigation, but you will need to provide false records and accounts of what the target has done." A letter dated two weeks later acknowledged receipt of the materials and praised their cleverness.

Later correspondence reflected the falling out of the conspirators. Varden selected two of the letters, locked the other documents in his safe, and went upstairs to change clothing. Not long after, a small pistol in a sling under his right arm and his new sword cane in his hand, he set out on foot for Gretton's unpretentious London residence.

Lord Gretton, seated behind a desk in his library, rose when the Earl of Varden was shown in. "I have been expecting you," he said in a quiet voice. "Are there constables waiting outside?"

"Not yet." Varden crossed the room, lit with colsa lamps against the oncoming dusk. Gretton looked tired, but he was smiling a little. "I wanted to speak with you first. How is it you expected me?"

"Well, not necessarily today." Gretton waved him to be seated. "But soon. Everything is going wrong, has been for a considerable time. When Reiver failed to report for—what is it? a week?—I knew you must be closing in. Do be seated, there's a good fellow." He sank onto his own chair and sat back, rubbing his forehead absently. "The last I heard from him, he had successfully engaged your carriage and was going after Tallant. Should I assume the duke killed him?"

"I did that," Varden said, watching Gretton's eyebrows go up. "Tallant fought the pair of hoodlums, who are also dead. Are there others?"

"Not that I am aware of. You are well, I see. And the duke?"

"Also well. You appear to be the only one Reiver actually harmed. Or was there ever an attack on your carriage?"

"Of course. The driver had to bear witness, didn't he? I cut myself a little with a penknife, wrapped the wound, and played victim for a time. You were supposed to conclude that Tallant was the gunman. Is it Reiver who put you on to me?"

"I tried to find out who employed him, but he refused to say." Varden drew from his pocket the two letters he had brought and laid them on the desk. "We have other sources, as you will see. This is a sample of the evidence in our possession."

Gretton put on his reading glasses, scanned the first letter, and laid it gently down. "You have found the documents I was seeking. The Beast was careless in many ways, but he never failed to keep records that gave him power over others. You will have most of the story by now, and certainly enough to see me hanged. So what is it you require from me?"

There was resignation in Gretton's voice, but no denial. "I should like to hear your account of what has occurred," Varden said. "There can be, you realize, no escape from the consequences of your actions. The one question remaining is—how far must the damage extend? Have you any concern for that?"

"Oh, yes. You will find this hard to credit, but my intentions have nearly always been benevolent. I am an ambitious man, certainly, but I have ever been dedicated to the well-being of my countrymen. When circumstances conspired to destroy me and everything I was trying to achieve, I reluctantly entered into a partnership with Beast Tallant. It has proven to be a disastrous choice, but early on, things went very well indeed."

Gretton glanced over to a tray set with several crystal-cut decanters. "Will you mind if I pour myself a drink?"

Varden pulled out his pistol and laid it on the plush arm of the wingback chair, placing his hand over it. "Go ahead."

"We formed the East India Consortium," Gretton said, crossing to the sideboard. "Tallant handled the opium deals while I kept the records. We had two sets of them, one for Consortium members to examine if they so wished, and the true records that show the considerable income we skimmed from the top. In early days, all the investors were making money, and with partners of your stature, they assumed the business to be entirely aboveboard."

"More window dressing than a partner," Varden said. "Does your profession leave you so in need of extraordinary resources?"

Gretton looked somber as he carried his drink back to the desk and slumped onto his chair. After a time spent staring into the deep red wine, he said, "It leaves me little time for anything else, including my dear wife. We made a love match nearly twenty-five years ago, and for the first decade, we were wonderfully happy. But as my status and influence grew, she, being neglected, sought entertainment elsewhere. Not with other men, although that would have been more tolerable than the consolation she found in gambling."

He took a long swallow and set down his glass. "At first it was harmless, but all too soon, she was in the talons of—of whatever it is that enslaves obsessive gamers. I hadn't understood that ladies could be so bewitched, or that they played for such high stakes. Her losses soon put us deep in River Tick."

"Was there no way to stop her?"

"I sent her to her family. I sent her abroad, guarded by people charged with keeping her away from her narcotic. And she tried, Varden. For months, and once for almost two years, she would shake free. But then she would decide a game of silver loo for chicken stakes could do no harm, or she'd place a small wager on a rubber of whist. The one step sent her plummeting back to where she had been, and the discouragement fueled her determination to win back what she had lost. I blame myself. She was too much alone when she began this, and had no idea what it would do to her."

Varden found himself feeling a little sympathy for Gretton, which was probably the man's intent. But there was an unmistakable note of sincerity in his voice. He had not meant to become what he was, any more than his wife had done.

"Profits from the opium trade kept us afloat for a time," Gretton said. "Then Tallant's brother began raiding our cargoes and making off with our boats. We had to continue paying investors, although at a lower rate, less they investigate what we had been doing. To cover the shortfall, we . . . diversified."

"Extortion."

"As it turned out, Tallant had been at it for quite some time. In my position, I had sources of information that served up more victims, and when Palazzo Neri became a gathering place, we were practically deluged with material."

In the documents, the Palazzo connection had been implied. "Beata was conspiring with you?"

"Ah, yes." Gretton regarded him sorrowfully. "You were her lover. She was careful not to speak of her friends, I assure you. Do you wish to know her role in this?"

"I think I must."

"She sold information, and went out of her way to get it. She knew, I am sure, how it was being used, but she was never involved in winkling money from the victims. The duke used to say, 'Beata Neri, cash and carry.' At the worst, she was greedy to expand her Palazzo and host ever more extravagant parties."

At worst? And what was he to do about her?

Gretton was speaking again. ". . . you see, it never felt as if I was doing great harm. The people from whom we extracted money were *guilty*. In many cases, they could be hanged for what they were doing, or had done."

Varden felt a rush of anger. "Castlereagh?"

Leaning forward, Gretton propped his elbows on the desk and knitted his finger together. "A sad case. Until then, I had no idea Tallant was deliberately setting up victims for entrapment. It wasn't that he needed to. He never bothered wringing Castlereagh for money. He simply relished having power over a powerful man. I wanted, then, to separate myself from him. But I still needed the money our association brought me, and I wasn't sure I had the courage to manage extortion on my own."

"You appear to have found it."

"After one has committed murder, all other crimes seem insignificant. I'll soon arrive at that portion of the story, but first you should know that I encouraged your mission to India. Had you got Michael Keynes locked away or executed, the revived opium trade would have again provided the funds to cover Mary's losses."

"I am sorry to have let you down."

Gretton gave him a surprisingly sweet smile. "A lamb into the tiger's lair. But you survived, and despite the circumstances in which we now find ourselves, I am glad of it. What is more, you succeeded in driving Keynes out of India and back to England, where I saw an opportunity to rid myself of the increasingly dangerous Duke of Tallant. When Keynes publically threatened to kill his brother, I contrived to do the business myself, knowing he would be blamed for it. Do you require all the details?"

"Enough to make sure the blame will not again fall on him, nor on anyone else."

Gretton took a drink of his wine. "The duke and I, engaged in devious activities for nearly a decade, had arranged a surreptitious means of communication. At Tallant House there is a secret door just beyond where the building joins with the smaller house on its eastern side. I have a key—"

Gretton reached down. Instantly Varden raised his pistol, finger on the trigger.

Seeing it, Gretton laughed and held out his empty hands. "There is no danger. Only a key in my drawer, but you can claim it later. The door opens to a private passageway that was used only by the duke, leading to his study on the ground floor and, by way of a staircase, to his bedchamber. He also leased the house next door, and his surreptitious guests came in through the garden there and . . . well, it doesn't matter. I was able to make a secret entrance and exit, as were the men I later sent to look for the very documents you found. Did you know that, last week, I hid a few documents there myself? Well, you couldn't, since they were still there when I returned to see if you'd found them. I had thought you would recall Wellington's riddle, and your answer to it."

Varden decided Gretton didn't need to know a trap had been set for him. "Back to the murder, if you will."

"Oh, indeed. The duke had been away, with me chafing for his return. I had by then hired two men he had sacked because they failed to murder his wife and daughter, or some such thing. They were watching the house and informed me when he arrived. I sent a message that I would come by the usual secret means, and we met that afternoon in his study. He was in a vile mood, looking to punish someone and easily distracted."

As Gretton reached into his jacket, Varden's pistol went up.

"I carry a flask," Gretton said. "Did I not show it to you? I can manipulate it without attracting notice. After I poured the duke a glass of wine, and one for myself, I tipped the contents of my flask into the decanter. The poison, sent me from South America, is tasteless, and I knew that the duke, once he began to drink, inevitably continued to do so. Shortly after, leaving with him the ledgers that showed the extent of our losses in India, I departed."

"A slow-acting poison," said Varden. "We tested what remained of it in the decanter."

"It depends on the concentration. I used it also on Phineas Garvey, and while it was working its way in him, he wrote—under duress—a suicide letter that included his confession to the duke's murder. In return I swore not to harm his family, and I have not done so."

"You had to find another candidate to take the blame, since Michael Keynes was away from London when the murder of his brother took place."

"Bad luck, that. I had verified by way of Beata Neri that he was at the Palazzo and intending to stay there for the day. The trouble with crime, Varden, is that the least little thing can spoil your carefully laid plans. I killed Garvey to halt the investigation, but how was I to rid myself of the new duke? What if he found the documents his brother had concealed? I had been told of their existence the afternoon I poisoned the duke, who threatened me with exposure if I tried to make trouble for him. And that, I hope, explains why I tried to make it appear that the new duke had taken up where his brother left off. Reiver's attack was meant to set you after him in earnest."

"And get me to do your dirty work. If convicted of a felony, he would be attainted. With his title and property forfeit to the crown, and no heir to petition for restoration, who would bother to search for missing records?"

"Bailing water from a sinking boat, I was." Gretton returned to the sideboard to refill his glass. "That's the devil of it. One transgression led to the next, each one more loathsome than its predecessor. But I could not find it in myself to turn back, or to stop."

" 'I am in blood stepp'd in so far that, should I wade no more, returning were as tedious as to go o'er.' "

"*Macbeth*. Yes. A cautionary tale indeed. Well, we should hurry this along. You'll not credit my good intentions, inadequate as they are, but I have tried in my way to make what amends I can. My desk, as you see, is overflowing with documents I have prepared

for you. There is a letter of instructions as well, which
I would have posted tomorrow morning. But as you
have come in person, we shall settle the business
now."

Gretton's face, pale when Varden had arrived, was
noticeably flushed. Perspiration beaded his forehead.
"I do not know how much you will elect to reveal to
the authorities, or to the public. For that reason, I
have prepared separate confessions to all my significant crimes, each containing information that could
only be known to the guilty party. Use them as you
see fit."

He drew his handkerchief from his sleeve and wiped
his face. "I have destroyed the records of the East
India Consortium, along with the extortion materials
in my possession. My financial resources are exhausted, but a few items of sentimental value have
been earmarked for friends. There is a list, and I have
written letters, which are not sealed, in case you wish
to examine them. I hope you will see that they are
posted."

Gretton's speech, near the end, had been slurred.
"Little time," he said, closing his eyes for a moment.
"I hoped that rather than expose my crimes, and
therefore my victims, in a public trial, you would give
me leave to depart this life as a gentleman."

"It would be best, if that is your wish."

"It is. But I couldn't be sure that you would consent. And besides, it seemed fitting to put an end to
my life in the same way I vilely ended three other
lives. I have drunk the poison, you see." Gretton
pulled out his flask again and after unscrewing the
top, upended it. "The contents are in that decanter,
the one I set apart from the others. Be sure to dispose
of it before a servant has a tipple."

Horrified, Varden jumped up and started to come
around the desk, halting when Gretton raised both
hands.

"There is nothing to be done. There is no pain to speak of, not until the very end. I have watched Garvey die, you remember. And my sweet Mary as well."

God in heaven. Varden backed away. "Where is she?"

"In our bed. I gave her the poison several hours ago, and held her in my arms until she took her last breath. Perhaps there is a hell waiting for me in the afterlife, but it cannot be so terrible as watching the woman I have always loved die at my hands."

Gretton was having trouble drawing breath. "It was for her that I did it, and for her family. She could not have endured the shame of my exposure. And even if my crimes were held secret, where was she to go? How was she to live? Her family would have taken her, but all too soon, her obsession and her grief would have drawn her back to the tables. Not wanting to, heart breaking as she did it, she would have bankrupted them. I thought it the kindest thing, to spare them all. She will . . . understand."

He opened a drawer that Varden could not see, fumbled about, and came up with a handful of keys. "You'll have to sort these. One is for the bedchamber door, which is locked. One for the secret door at . . ."

"What else do you want of me?" Varden said when Gretton did not finish his sentence.

"L-leave me. Don't watch. S-soon now."

Varden rose immediately and went into the passageway, closing the door behind him. He leaned against the wall, drawing harsh breaths, trying not to think of the man now drawing his very last breaths. After a minute or two, he became aware of a servant standing a little distance away, regarding him with concern.

"Is there something I can do for you, milord?"

Varden pulled himself together. "Thank you, no. I learned some bad news is all, and must think how to deal with it. Please inform the other servants that Lord Gretton does not wish to be disturbed for the rest of the evening. Go have your supper. As soon as I have bid him farewell and reclaimed my walking stick, I shall let myself out."

Sometimes, he thought as the footman smiled and left, there were advantages to being the Archangel Earl. No one expected trouble when he was politely issuing orders, even to another man's servants.

How long should he wait? Gretton was entitled to the dignity of expiring without an audience, but a pistol would have been a damn sight quicker. Varden could not help thinking that Helena might have become one of Reiver's victims at Beech Hollow. What Gretton had told him, and what the documents contained, barely began to encompass the evils he had done in company with Beast Tallant.

After giving it another five minutes, he reentered the library. All was quiet. Gretton had fallen forward, his head on his desk, a thread of blood from his mouth already beginning to dry on his chin.

After checking for a pulse at wrist and throat, Varden began to gather up the papers, taking everything on the desk for later sorting. He should have brought a portmanteau. There was a cloth draped over a round table by the window. He removed the lamp and vase of flowers from on top of it and began piling letters and documents in their place. The keys went in as well, along with Gretton's flask.

A search of his desk drawers revealed nothing else of use, excepting a loaded pistol. Varden left it there and went to deal with the decanter, still half-full of poisoned wine. The contents went out the window and onto the gravel beneath it. The decanter itself was stoppered with his handkerchief and added to the pile on the tablecloth.

Finally he thought he'd got everything that should be taken away before the authorities arrived. He made a bundle of the cloth, tying off the ends, and hoped no one of importance paid him any attention as he walked the short distance to his own house.

When he arrived there, he locked the documents in his safe, placed the other items in a chest and locked it, then locked his bedchamber.

By that time a horse was saddled, as he had instructed. He went first to Bow Street, surprised to learn that Sir Richard was still in his office. He had another bit of luck on the way upstairs, when he spotted Charley Trotter coming down.

"Wait by the entrance door," Varden said. "I need your services tonight."

"I won't—"

"Nothing to do with Miss Pryce. Double pay, Trotter, and trouble from me if I don't find you there in half an hour."

It took twice that to make Sir Richard agree to handle the explosive situation in what Varden had decided was the least destructive manner. Among the documents Gretton had left was a suicide letter, citing his ill health and that of his wife as reason for their mutual decision to end their lives. Varden had left it on the desk. The chief magistrate would have to find a way to avoid too intensive an investigation. They would speak again tomorrow.

"If word of anything other than what we agreed to release gets out," Varden cautioned just before departing, "I will know the source. And then, Sir Richard, you may wish to seek another profession, in another country."

Chapter 28

As the evening wore on toward midnight, Helena stopped looking toward the wide double doors that opened into the Sala dei Medici. Stopped looking every minute or so, anyway, and told herself that she was glad Varden had stayed away. What would he think, to see her now?

Wearing the costume Beata had given her, she was seated on a padded bench beside Signora Fanella, who was swathed in the voluminous black robes and veil of a nun. Because of the floor-to-ceiling mirrors interspersed with gold brocade wallpaper, she had only to glance up to find herself looking back at herself. The first few times, she was startled at the reflection. That could not be drab Helena Pryce.

Luckily, no one else paid her any mind. Who among this glittering assembly would wish to speak with a servant delegated by Beata to sit with her companion? Even the people acquainted with her, the ones likely to pay their regards, did not do so. But then, they probably didn't recognize her. All evening she had been careful to hold her elaborate mask, attached to an ebony stick, in front of her face, and the exceedingly odd headdress of her costume concealed the sides of her spectacles.

While watching for Varden, and trying not to watch for him, she had spent the evening describing costumes to Signora Fanella and speculating about the identities of the wearers. When guests moved close enough for their voices to be heard, the Signora recognized most of them immediately. She had superb hearing and could understand English, although she had not learned to speak it to any degree. *"Perché?"* she would say. "Nobody care my words."

Along with French and Latin, Helena had learned a little Italian at school, and a good deal more of it in company with Beata and the signora. If she decided to accompany the Devonshire party all the way to Italy, she would be able to navigate from there on her own.

They were to sail in only three days. Her few possessions, those that would not fit into a portmanteau, had been boxed up and sent along with one of Devonshire's conveyances to Dover, where the packets were being loaded. He traveled like a potentate, the sweet duke, taking with him everything he might possibly fancy to have along. The heaviest items, like his carriages and britskas and favorite horses, had been shipped to Calais the previous week.

She had worked for months on the arrangements, and the duke was delighted to add her to the party. In exchange for her services on the trip, he offered a salary that would provide for her needs until she chose a place to live and found a position.

It was all going so well. The prospect of travel excited her. Jamie, while he would miss her, was pleased that she was at last spreading her wings, or at least unfurling them. Her family would be spared the shame of her existence. So why were tears always burning in her eyes?

"Helena?"

In Signora Fanella's accented speech, it sounded a lovely name. Perhaps she would keep it.

"You have not told what *you* are wearing," she said in Italian, lifting a swatch of Helena's skirt and rubbing it between her thumb and forefinger. *"Provocante.* What are you meant to be?"

"A lion, I think. The mask, of silver accented with black and gold, is the face of a lion. Does one call it a face? And on my head there is a silver cap that covers all my hair, with bits of silver tissue cut into triangles that are intended to represent a mane. The gown is more like something worn by a Grecian lady than a jungle beast, and it, too, is silver."

And it clung provocatively to the parts of her that it covered, which did not include her arms or shoulders or a large expanse of her back and front. If not for a sort of halter that reached from her low bodice to tie around her neck, she would have been scandalously bare. There were silver gloves as well, to above her elbows, and silver sandals. All in all, she looked rather like the contents of a silverware drawer.

Alone among the revelers, Beata did not wear or carry a mask. She wanted to be noticed, recognized for who she was, and in her lush gown of deep red velvet ornamented with black lace and jet beads, she could not be missed. Her luxuriant hair, worn loose over the shoulders and halfway down her back, was her greatest ornament.

Helena, surprised that Beata had not stopped by as she usually did, remarked on it to Signora Fanella.

"I do not wish to speak with her," said the signora, anger in her voice, unhappiness on her face. "We have quarreled."

"I am sorry to hear it." More than most, Helena knew how it was for a servant to quarrel with her employer. "Is there something I can do to help?"

"We should never have come here. But, no, Helena. I think nothing can help us now. I wish to go to a place of silence. The loud voices disturb me."

Helena's Italian was not good enough that she picked up nuances in the language, but she perceived in the signora's tone more than a need for solitude. Determination, she thought. Urgency. "I shall gladly accompany you," she said. "The Limonaia, perhaps?" "I will choose later. Lead me through the crowd."

Taking her arm, Helena wove through the public rooms, trying to keep her mask in front of her face. In motion she drew a surprising degree of attention, all of it male, as heads swerved to follow her progress out the door. She hadn't thought how she might look when walking, and now that she did, she wished she had never left the bench.

When they finally arrived at a circular chamber, the signora tugged her arm loose and asked where in the Palazzo they were. Helena described the location, puzzled at the elderly woman's mood. "We are at the crossing place," she said. From here, one could select a passageway leading to any section of the sprawling villa.

"I will go alone," said the signora. "Tell me what places have no people."

"The meeting rooms in the south wing, the library, and the rooms near to it. For now, anyway. Later, guests will begin seeking privacy, as you are."

"I have time, then. Go, my dear. Leave this place, if you are wise."

Disturbed, Helena watched her move down the passageway, her gnarled hands tucked into the wide sleeves of her nun's habit, her veil swaying against her back. She might have followed for a time, but the signora's hearing was acute and her pride easily wounded. And of course, the Palazzo had been her home since its construction. When there were no crowds wearing costumes to trip over, she got around very well on her own.

Unwilling to expose herself to more ogling males, Helena went in the direction of the east wing and took the passageway leading to Beata's fanciful conservatory. She encountered no one on the way, and would have retreated elsewhere if the Limonaia had drawn guests so early.

But it was empty. The only sound, a musical splashing, came from the fountain where water streamed from whimsical lemons on the marble tree at its center. Lanterns in the shape of quarter moons shone silver and gold from the real trees—Spanish orange and lemon—illuminating their shiny leaves and globes of fruit.. The light reflected off the octagonal walls of stone tracery and stained glass, the enameled tile floors, and the tendrils of smoke wafting from copper braziers. She went to a marble bench set inside a small latticework pergola ribboned with vines, a location that gave her a good view of the door she wasn't going to watch.

Even if Varden made an appearance at the ball, there was no reason for him to look for her here. No reason to look for her at all. It was possible, although she had not yet come to terms with it, that she would never see him again.

It was better that way. A quiet escape, no fuss, no awkward farewells, no risk of betraying herself. She had last seen him, from a place of hiding, when he attended the political meeting on Monday night. It seemed a lifetime ago. Impeccably dressed, carrying a new ebony and silver cane that probably held a sword, he moved at ease among the great men of the country like the elegant aristocrat he was born to be. The world of shared adventures with a servant was behind him now. He had returned to the world where he belonged.

And she . . . well, she belonged to no world at all. What world could there be for a duke's daughter born to a whore? For a Rookery child with a proper-young-lady education? For a servant who didn't know her place because she didn't have a place. Her life had been to learn, to serve, and to pass the fruits of her service to those who could not do for themselves. It wasn't a life she would ever regret. She had been more blessed than anyone who grew up where she did, and had lived longer than most of them. If not for Varden, she would never have wished to change her circumstances.

She realized she was still holding her mask in front of her face, although there had been no one to see it for several minutes. Setting it beside her on the bench, she closed her eyes and breathed in the tart-sweet fragrance of citrus trees. Thought how bitter, and, yes, how sweet, it was to have loved.

And thought immediately that she must cease thinking about love, and Varden, and the wonder of having been, for a short time, a visitor in his life. No use watering a dead plant with tears.

"Helena?"

Her eyes flew open. She rose instantly, because it was him. Remembered she was supposed to curtsy.

"No." He lifted a hand. "No, Helena. Please."

She drew herself up again, digging her trembling hands into her skirts.

Because he hadn't moved from the doorway, didn't move at all, she had time to look at him. At his astonishing appearance, which she would never have expected. Above the mask of a Viking prince, his light cap of hair was uncovered. He wore a fawn-colored cloak, pinned at one shoulder with a large metal brooch, over a darker brown knee-length tunic embroidered at the neck. It was sleeveless. He had thrown back the cloak over one shoulder, revealing a bare arm and the golden band clasped on his tautly muscled biceps. A wide leather belt studded with medallions and slung with a large knife circled his waist. On his feet were soft leather shoes, and from them extended leather bands that crisscrossed his calves and tied below the knees.

Just then he pushed the mask, attached with a rib-

bon, up onto his head. Light from the braziers flickered over his face, teased at the golden hair on his
forearms and legs. A warrior, come to her from another place and time.

Speechless, she watched him stride toward her, his
expression unreadable. Stop directly in front of where
she held her ground, trapped by the bench at her back
and the curve of the pergola on both sides. He was
as tall as it was, and ivy brushed at his mask and hair
as he stood there in silence, gazing on her. Only gazing
on her, as if he had nothing else in the world to do.

"Is—is there anything wrong, my lord?"

"Only this." His voice was a whisper. "You take
my breath away."

And then hers went, and she sank onto the bench
with a whoosh.

A little smile, gentle and confident, curved his lips.
"I have missed you," he said. "You look glorious.
What are you meant to be?"

She fumbled for her mask, raised it in front of her
face. "Beata told me I was a fantasy for men who
lived commonplace lives while dreaming of lions. I
have no idea what that means."

"I do."

If heat translated as color, she had to be scarlet all
over. "And what are *you* meant to be?"

His smile became a self-deprecating grin. "I asked
for something simple, comfortable, and nonangelic.
This is what I got. Remind me to change my tailor."

He seemed content to answer questions and . . . and
feast on her. That was how it felt, being devoured by
his gaze, swallowed up in his desire. She had to put a
stop to this. Just when she had begun to detach herself, he swept in like a bore tide. Engulfed her. "You
said we could not meet. That it would be dangerous."

Like a snuffed candle, his smile vanished. "No
longer," he said softly. "Except for a great deal of

cleaning up and covering up, it is finished. But I cannot speak of this here, where we might be overheard."

Finished? She would have led him outside, except that she couldn't wait to hear the news. "I have spent days testing spyholes and acoustics at the Palazzo," she said. "If we speak softly, our voices will not carry from here. What has happened?"

He sank beside her on the bench, slumped over with his forearms on his thighs and his head bowed. "Carr's thieves found the documents hidden behind a stone in one of the secret chambers described by the duchess. They were delivered to me this afternoon. As you have always insisted, the duke did not follow his brother's path into murder and extortion. The Beast was partnered, then poisoned, and then supplanted, by Lord Gretton."

She swallowed a gasp. Held her voice steady when she could speak. "Has he been taken into custody?"

"There was no need. I confronted him with the evidence, but he had already accepted the inevitable. He had even prepared confessions and testimony to the most serious crimes. To make amends, he said, and perhaps it was true. Or he was merely painting over a corrupted reputation, salvaging what little he could from the disaster. And in his favor, he did spare us a trial and the outfall that would have resulted from public revelation of his misdeeds. Extortion is a filthy crime. In proving it, we necessarily hold the victims up to scorn."

"Are you saying he killed himself? And that you permitted it?"

"I would have done," Varden said after a time. "But before I knew what he was about, he had swallowed poison."

He shook his head, as if to clear away the memory. "I have sent word to the duke and duchess. There is one thing more you should know. The documents, and

Gretton's testimony, make it clear that Beata was involved. Not directly in the extortion, but she gathered and sold information, knowing how it would be used."

Helena could scarcely take it in. How deeply he must feel this betrayal. "You cannot permit Beata to come to trial either," she said at length. "What will you do?"

He glanced over at her, his expression grave. "I think Gretton may have advised her that the hawks were closing in. Before I went looking for you, I spent a few minutes in her company. She was much as usual—imperious, flirtatious, monarch of the revelers—but there was a sadness in her eyes, as if she was bidding farewell to it all. Or perhaps, in my preoccupation with her guilt, I only imagined it."

"Her companion has been behaving strangely as well," Helena said. "Signora Fanella told me that she and Beata had quarreled."

"That could account for Beata's mood. But it doesn't signify. She is being watched, and when the guests have departed, she will be taken into custody. I have some hope that she will accept self-imposed exile, even under the strict conditions I will lay out for her." A soft release of breath. "If she refuses, other alternatives will be considered."

"You wouldn't kill her, surely."

"I'm sure I could not." He rubbed the bridge of his nose. "Our earlier relationship makes this especially difficult. But as with Gretton, the first priority must be to shield the victims, however scurrilous their own behavior. We know that Beast Tallant was also manufacturing evidence and entrapping innocent people, and to distinguish the sheep from the goats is beyond my power. The ax must fall only on the criminals, whatever the degree of their guilt."

"Beata will go, I think," Helena said. "She made for herself a new life in a strange country when she came here. She can do so again, elsewhere."

"I pray you are right." Sitting up, he put his gloved hand, the one nearest her, on her forearm. "And now, Helena, will you greatly mind if we set this aside? I know you wish to learn everything I have learned, and no one has a better right. But I cannot tell you all of it, and I haven't had the time or the inclination to sort out what must be withheld. For now, the chief magistrate is dealing with the immediate problems. Can we leave it to him, please? At least until tomorrow?"

He didn't know what he was asking. Her plans were made. Tomorrow she would leave for Dover. "To be sure, my lord," she said. What else could she say? "In your hands, the disposition of this matter is in the *best* of hands."

His smile, somber and thankful, tugged at her heart. "I cannot leave the Palazzo," he said. "Nor can I bear to rejoin the party, and it will spread throughout the villa before the night is over. Is there somewhere we can be private?"

And she thought, immediately, that he might want to make love to her. It was often the first instinct of a man, to drown his anger and sorrow in a woman's body. Why should she not let him? A woman could give a gift as well. And steal one for herself . . . one last night in the arms of the man she loved.

"Helena?"

"M-my cottage, perhaps. But someone might see us go there."

"I don't mind. What are the uses of secrets and deceptions, unless they are contrived out of kindness? What we try to hide is so easily turned against us, and even if our secrets remain hidden, they bear a poison of their own. Do you not long for clear water, Helena? For truth, and for the company of people who are what they seem?"

With a rueful laugh, he rose and offered her his hand. "I sound like a chick still downy from the egg.

You would think that, at the end of a day filled with horrifying revelations about people I thought to be my friends, I would be stripped of my ideals."

He was driving knives into her heart. Mute with pain, she slipped her hand into his.

"But that is the nature of ideals, I suppose. They slither in when you least expect them." He pulled the mask down over his face. "At least from you I will always hear the truth . . . even if I don't like it. *Especially* if I don't like it. You are my clear water, Helena, and my wise counselor. I don't know what I should do, if you were not here with me tonight."

Chapter 29

So that she would always have company at the Palazzo, Beata had built several small residences along the wide stretch of land between the villa and the Thames. Helena, by coincidence or fate's perverse design, had been given to use the very cottage where Miranda Holcombe resided before marrying the duke. The irony of it was burning in her thoughts as she walked hand in hand with Varden across the sloping lawn.

First Miranda's castle, and now her cottage. There would be no escaping the shadow of the woman he loved.

Her own deceptions haunted her as well, although she would not undo the lies she had told. They were necessary when first put into her hands to tell, and while circumstances had changed, what purpose would be served by revealing her identity?

It would ease her conscience, she supposed. And Varden would no longer enshrine her on a pedestal of integrity simply because—with the insolence of a Keynes—she dared speak her mind to him. No, indeed. He would be politely enraged. Disgusted. Offended that she had played him for a fool. Then she would be gone, her brief presence in his life marked out by deceit and disillusion. No good, none whatever, was waiting at the end of a confession.

They arrived in silence at the cottage, which had a sitting room, two bedchambers, and very little else. Meals, baths, and other needs were provided from the Palazzo, and guests were expected to seek companionship and entertainment there.

Varden removed his mask and went to build up the fire while she lit candles from the lamp she'd left burning. "There is nothing of you in this room," he said. "No sign that you have ever been here."

"I know where the wine is kept. Will that do?"

He grinned at her over his shoulder. "Prove it."

"This is a temporary arrangement, you know. I brought only what I cannot do without, and that is very little. Books, writing materials, clothing." She took the decanter and a pair of glasses from a low cupboard, wondering what they would find to talk about. Usually they dealt with business, or discussed ways to handle a crisis, or quarreled. Now they had come down to the lack of knickknacks on the furniture and the reasons why.

A servant and an earl had no more in common than . . . than a Viking and an overdecorated lion.

When she turned, a glass of wine in each hand, he was standing in front of the fire with his arms folded behind his back, gazing at her with unsettling intensity. She remembered the looks of the men when she had walked through the public rooms, their eyes flashing from behind the eyeholes of their masks. The short distance she had to cross in order to hand him the glass seemed a long, long way.

But she did it, and was rewarded with a look of male appreciation so heated that she feared melting into a puddle of silver at his feet.

He took the glass, raised it in a silent toast, and drank. The way he drank wine should be made illegal, or there wouldn't be a chaste woman left in England.

"You have the look of a cat about to leap over a fence," he said. "What is it you fear?"

Myself. Weakness. Tomorrow. "That it was a mistake to bring you here. That I may have misled you."

"Meaning you fear I will try to seduce you."

Yes, and she had meant to let him. But while they were walking in the cold night air, common sense had its way with her. "It would not be a good idea, sir. I seem often to be with you in times of trouble, when passions run high. But stormy passions and proximity are a volatile brew. You must seek what you need from another woman."

"Making love with you, Helena, is always a good idea. The best I ever had. It is so good that it rarely leaves my mind. And what I need cannot—can *never*—be satisfied by another woman." He looked at her over the rim of his glass. "I won't lie to you. I want more than anything for this night to end with us in bed, and me inside you. Whatever occurs in the next hour or so, you may be sure that I will still be wanting that."

A shiver ran along her spine. "What is likely to occur, my lord?"

"Disaster, I expect. This is a poor time for me to speak. I am not at my best. A wiser man would find the discretion to wait. But of late, astonishing events have wrecked so many plans that I dare not put off the most important thing I have ever done. I think I must blunder ahead, my dear, even though I know you will disapprove what I say. Then the argument can begin."

Alarmed in earnest now, she backed unsteadily in the direction of a chair until she felt it against her legs. He stayed where he was, enviably straight and motionless, a fencer in control of his body. That left her with no choice but to remain on her feet as well, every defense she could muster snapping into place.

"There is no firing squad," he said, a little sadly. "I have always known a moment like this would come, but I did not picture myself wearing skins and leather.

And never once did I imagine my prospective bride bristling like a porcupine just as I was about to make an offer of marriage."

She dropped onto the chair like a stone.

"What did you think this was about?" The tone of sadness still vibrated under his words. "We have never experienced an ordinary time together, I suppose. There was always the bustle to accomplish something, and your unnatural docility when you remembered our difference in rank, and your headstrong lectures when you forgot them. Only when we were fencing did the barriers peel away. And when we made love, there was nothing separating us at all. I became part of you, and you welcomed me there, and we could laugh and take pleasure as lovers should."

She heard the crackle of the fire behind him. The distant sound of an orchestra playing a waltz in the Palazzo. The blood thundering in her head. "You speak of what occurs between a man and his mistress," she finally said. "An earl does not wed his mistress, or his secretary, or a woman who grew up in the Rookery."

"Not without difficulties. Perhaps some unpleasantness from sources I care little about. But you may be sure that this earl weds whom he pleases." He set his glass on the mantelpiece.

"No. I said that wrong. Try not to parse my stumbling speeches, Helena. I meant that if the lady is willing, this earl weds whom he loves."

If she hadn't been sitting down, she'd have fallen down. A banked fire in her heart burst into flames. Love. He had spoken of love, and spoken of it about her.

As quickly as it sprang up, the fire blazed out, doused with memories. With reality. She sat straighter. "Not very long ago—little more than a week—you were in love with another woman. She was the love of your life, you said. And though she would never be yours, you could never love another. You would marry for convenience. I was to provide a list of suitable conveniences."

"I cannot account for my behavior." A flush rose up his face. "I was mistaken."

"That's it? *Mistaken*? You tumbled into love with a woman you scarcely knew, tumbled out again because, well, you couldn't have her. And now you have scraped up the most unlikely Countess of Varden in all of England. Pardon me for asking this, my lord, but have you run mad?"

"It must seem that way. I was definitely off my chump when I bought the castle. But no harm done, except to my pocketbook, and I've thought of something good to do with my white elephant." He paused. Gave a little shrug. "All you have said is perfectly true. But is it so impossible to believe I have come to my senses?"

She desperately wanted to believe that, but one self-deceived lover in the room was enough. And even if she accepted his profession of love as true and enduring, it would not last beyond the moment she identified herself to him.

Which she had no intention of doing. There were plenty of incontrovertible arguments to throw against the marriage. What hope had love, if by some miracle it existed for them both, against such obstacles? He might surmount them, and she would ignore them, but there were other people to be considered.

"You cannot be in your right mind, sir, if you expect your family, your friends, and your peers to accept me as your wife, or welcome either of us into their company." She was pleased to have got control of her voice. And not carried it into briskness, which he could interpret all too well. "Even if I believed your declaration of love, I could not permit you to make such a sacrifice."

"I know. And it is that which gives me hope. It is

the nature of love—is it not?—to care more for the beloved than for oneself. All that remains is which sacrifice is to be accepted, mine or yours. We can't have it both ways, Helena. And in fact, I expect my family to close ranks around us. My friends, most of them, will do so as well. Does it really signify what others think of us?"

"It wouldn't, if we were suited. And if we loved. And if you were not an earl."

She wondered, trembling at the thought, if he would ask her to deny that she loved him. Deny it straight out, in unmistakable language, when he was standing close enough to read the treasonous language of her body. And what would she do then? What *could* she do?

It mustn't come to that. Better anything than such a lie. If he believed it, she would have betrayed him— and herself—beyond redemption. And if he failed to believe her, if he read the truth in her tension and her color and the very blood in her veins, she would be compelled to reveal the last truth of all.

In the deep silence of their alienation, she resolved that before she would deny love, she would make it impossible for herself to admit it. She would make certain that he stopped wanting her, or imagining that he did.

But it might not be necessary. Before it came to that, she had other, lesser truths to tell. Those should turn the trick. And why was he standing there, so maddeningly composed, so complacently *lordly*, leaving all the belligerence to her?

"Are you scheming?" He picked up his glass and took a drink. "Or have you run out of arguments?"

"There are too many of them to run out of. I was simply deciding how much to tell you of my life before we met. Since you refuse to accept that we will not suit, I must provide you some of the reasons why."

"It is not unprecedented for a man of high rank," he said, "to take a wife from the lower orders."

"To marry the daughter of a wealthy merchant is one thing, sir." Her chin went up. "To marry the daughter of a whore is quite another."

He blinked. His lips tightened, but only a little. Then he nodded. "That is not, I think, a detail we would choose to advertise. It does, however, explain your connection with an establishment that has been mentioned to me, one belonging to Mrs. Dora Teale. I heard that you once lived there."

"I was born there." Now she had to wonder how much Jamie had told him. Obviously more than the "nothing" he'd replied when she asked. Or perhaps Varden's hired Runner, the traitorous Tommie Trotter, had served up that tidbit. "Mrs. Teale was kind enough to allow me to remain there with my mother until she became ill. Then Jamie Carr took us to Lomber Court. She died on my eighth birthday."

"I am sorry. It must have be difficult for you. Is there more?"

She tore free of her chair, impatient with his calm. Confused by his acceptance of what would have driven any other man of his rank fleeing into the night. "What more do you need? Are the circumstances of my birth not sufficient to make you see reason?"

"They sadden me, for your sake. They do not change who you are. Is there cause to think a horde of unseemly relatives will sweep down on us? That happens in the highest of families as well. I just want to be prepared."

She went to the window. She went back to the chair, retrieved her glass from the side table, and returned to the window. Drank the wine. Found no way out. He would have the truth from her, because there was no other means of stopping him. Or might he do the stopping himself, if she told him all but what mattered?

"I once attempted to trace my mother's family. She said her parents left England, and perhaps they did, but it is more correct to say they disappeared. By that time, she had already taken refuge in London."

"With Mrs. Teale?"

"Not at first. I have most of this from Jamie, who probably left out the most unpleasant parts. Her parents were of moderate means, and they gave her what money they could spare. It was enough to provide for lodging and necessities until she could find work."

Helena, hearing her voice quaver, kept going with her story while she returned to the cupboard and refilled her glass. "She was only seventeen, but had been well educated. She could paint, embroider, sew, play the harp, sing, recite, and manage a small household—all the accomplishments of a proper young woman. But none of them would secure steady employment for a pregnant young woman. She did piecework for a mantua maker, worked in a laundry, scrubbed pots in a tavern. And along the way, she met Mrs. Teale, who took her in when she could no longer pay for her lodging. At some time after my birth, she accepted that we would both be more secure if she remained there and earned our keep in the time-honored way."

She paused, hoping she had said enough to satisfy him, and took a drink of the wine. It tasted bitter, like the story she had told. And the one she had not told.

"It must have provided a unique education for a young girl. Were there other children in the house?"

"I had no playmates. The ladies spoiled me as if I were their own, and I was kept well away from the men. But as you know, I learned rather a lot about . . . professional skills, and how to protect oneself." She had never expected to put that knowledge to use. An illicit relationship with an aristocrat, or with any other man, had been the last thing she would have chosen to undertake. Until she met Varden.

Leave me now. Please. While we can still part as friends. Before this ends in an explosion.

"Do you know the identity of your father?" he said.

"Does it matter? I never met him, and he never knew of my existence. He died some years ago."

"My dear, if I can accept everything else you have told me, why do you wish to withhold his name? I don't care if he was a felon, or a gravedigger, or a curate. It is only your reluctance to identify him that concerns me. We must be in all things honest with each other, don't you think?"

You are my clear water. And so it was come to it. Nothing had turned him aside. The man was as obstinate as she was, and no less determined. At least it would be over with. And when she departed, she would never be plagued with the temptation to return. That was something.

"Perhaps you are right," she said. "I could not have kept it from you in any case, if you persisted with the unholy notion that we should marry. The circumstances of my birth would be an impediment of the first order."

She had his attention entirely. And was learning to read in his body what he did not say. For all his profound control, there were telltale signs, visible even from across the room. So she looked away, because what she was about to do was already beyond her strength.

"You needn't have all the details, sir. I know some of this from Jamie, and some from my mother. In her version of the story, the family was on holiday at the seashore when she met a handsome man. She began stealing away to be with him, and although he was a good deal older, they fell in love. But when the holiday was drawing to an end, he confessed that he was married—unhappily, of course—and that to preserve the memory of a great love, they should vow never to meet again. It was a time out of time, my mother told me, for joy and pleasure, with no expectations and no regrets."

He frowned. "That is what you said to me at the castle."

"Like mother, like daughter." She gave him a cool smile. "But, for my mother, it was a fantasy. She found it easier, I think, to live in an imaginary wonderland."

"It wasn't true, then?"

"What I said to you, yes. That was true. Those words came to my lips because I had heard them a hundred times." She put down her glass before it shattered between her hands. "The point is, there was never a star-crossed love affair by the seashore. My father saw her walking alone, swept her away, and ravished her. If a man had not been passing by with his hunting dogs and a rifle, she would have been killed."

"Dear God." Varden mauled his chin with his good hand. "Was the . . . Was he caught and punished?"

"My father? Oh, no. But the man with the dogs was found dead that night. Her parents went into hiding. She thought that if she vanished, and if word went out that she had died of a fever or some such thing, they would be left alone. That's why she went alone to London. I don't know what became of them, and neither did she. From then on, her only concern was to protect me. My aristocratic sire was famous, it seems, for leaving no witnesses to his crimes. And since a child would be an incontrovertible witness, not to mention a nuisance, he made sure none of his by-blows were let to live."

Varden's composure was breaking. "You do know who he is, then?"

"Who he *was*. Years ago, he put a gun to his head. Or someone did it for him, most probably his son. When they're not killing their victims, the men of that family turn on one another. But let us put an end to this, my lord. Let me show you why, almost since the day I was born, my heritage has been concealed."

She moved a little closer then, to where the light fell on her. Saw the tension in his body, the look of apprehension on his face, the dawning awareness of what she was about to prove. The story had prepared him, but he was not ready to accept it. Not yet.

Pausing, she made a little prayer for strength. Said good-bye to him in her heart. And said to him, softly, "I am sorry, my lord."

With shaking hands, she took hold of her lion's mane headdress and tugged it off. Pulled the pins from her hair and ran her fingers through it until it fell in a thick black curtain that reached to below her shoulders.

She felt his reaction, but dared not look at him yet. Not until she could look him directly in the eyes. With both hands, she removed her spectacles and raised her pale wolf's eyes to his.

As if a bullet had stuck him, he jerked back, his shoulders hitting the mantelpiece. "My God! How could you keep this from me?"

Her pulse beat erratically. "I kept it from everyone. It was taught me before I could say 'mama.' Never show your hair. Never show your eyes. If Devil Keynes had learned of a child with this hair and these eyes, he would have killed me. Killed those who sheltered me. The Beast would have done the same. They always drowned their litters. They were famous for it."

He seemed to be trying to regain control of himself, this man who never lost control. "I do not question that. But they were both dead when you came to me in Richmond. Why continue the masquerade when the danger had passed? Or did you fear the last of the Keynes males?"

"Not Michael. He was a danger only to his brother. To *our* brother," she added, just to say the words. Even as the man who had wanted to make with her a family turned her away, she reached out to claim the family she had been born into.

It was like being tied to an anchor that had been thrown overboard, but in her pain, she needed something to cling to. After twenty-eight years, she had accepted who she was. And at the same time, revealed herself to the one man who would most despise her for it.

Brave girl, Jamie would say. But he had never revealed his own secrets, had he?

Her thoughts flew about like startled pigeons while Varden thought whatever he was thinking and not saying. She wished he would go. He knew everything now, except that she loved him. And of all things, that was the most insignificant.

"Does Tallant know?" he said like a whiplash.

Her hands twisted together. "In the carriage, when the fever made him . . . restless, his hands were flailing about. I had to remove my spectacles. He was delirious then, but later, he remembered seeing my eyes. I don't believe he will tell anyone. The decisions, all of them, were left to me."

"He didn't cast you off?"

"No." A tendril of joy curled up from her misery. "He seemed glad of it."

Varden cut away from the hearth, and she thought he meant to take himself off at last. His movements were ungraceful and full of anger, so unlike him that she drew back a step. But he went only to the window, as if he wanted to be outside without actually going there, and pushed aside the curtain.

Then an oath, one she hadn't imagined an earl would know. He took off for the door. "The villa's afire! Take word to Beata and get the evacuation underway."

She put on her spectacles, swept up her headdress, and set out for the front of the Palazzo, stuffing her hair under the silver mane as she ran.

Chapter 30

Varden sprinted across the lawn toward the villa. Nearest the river were two adjoined squares, each built around a courtyard. Rooms of various sizes and kinds, all with large windows, fronted the exterior. Passageways opened onto the courtyards.

Directly ahead, fire showed in most of the windows. It had begun about midway in the square to his right and was progressing rapidly in both directions. But more rapidly, he saw, in the direction of the south wing and the river. Almost rhythmically, fire sprang up in one window after the other, consuming the heavy winter curtains. Some were drawn open, and just beyond the latest window to go ablaze, he detected a black shadow and a smaller fire. A torch. It reached toward a new pair of curtains, and up they went.

Someone was setting the fires, and continuing to set them, although by now the wooden villa hadn't a chance of withstanding the conflagration.

He cut left toward the river, ran around the meeting-room square to where he knew there was a door, and came into the passageway. Smoke roiled along the ceiling, thickening as he made his way to where he last saw the arsonist.

There! At the far end of the passageway, a small figure, all in black. Carrying a torch in one hand, feel-

ing along the wall with the other. The hand reached
a door, opened it, and the figure disappeared inside.

He heard cries in the distance. Bells. The alarm had
been sounded in the north wing, where most of the
public rooms were concentrated. The guests would all
get out, unless they were stupid. Nothing for them to
do now but run.

He sped toward the room the arsonist had entered.
Halted at the door. The torch had ignited two pairs
of curtains and the arm was reaching for a third.
"Stop!" he shouted.

The figure turned in the direction of his voice, following the sound. Signora Fanella, her nun's robes
swirling around her, too close to the fire. Now she was
holding something in her other hand. A lamp, unlit.
He smelled lamp oil, knew how she had got the fire
raging so quickly. All the rooms had lamps on the
mantelpieces, on the tables. Even a blind woman
could easily find them.

"Signora," he said, as gently as possible. "Come
away now."

"Varden!" It was a snarl. *"Si Fermi!"*

Stop there. After two years with Beata, he understood
a little Italian. "Put down the lamp and come to me."

Oil was dripping onto the floor around her. Onto
her robes. One touch of flame and . . . Moving quietly
into the room and to his right, he unclasped the
brooch and pulled off his cloak. Her hearing was keen,
but the noise of the fire as it licked up the wallpaper
covered lesser sounds.

Smoke filled the room, cutting off air. She was little
more than a shadow to him, illuminated from behind.
The torch began swinging in great arcs around her, as
if trying to fend him off. She must have suspected he
would approach her.

Then a cry from the door. Varden looked over. Saw
Beata rush in, and Helena close behind, dragging on
her sleeve, trying to stop her.

"Mamma!" Beata cried. *"Perché, Mamma? Perché?"*

"La perdoni. È ammalata della gola e l'orgoglio!"
While the signora was distracted, he drew closer. Had to snatch the torch before it ignited her robes, pull her away from the fires at her back.

Beata broke loose of Helena and rushed toward the signora. "No, Mamma!"

The torch swung toward her. *"Fermati! Ah, figlia mia."* The signora's voice was sad, barely audible above the flames. "Brucio ora, che Iddio mi risparmi dall'Inferno."

And then, deliberately, she lowered the torch to her oil-smeared robes.

They caught with the force of an explosion. Flames engulfed the small figure. Like a torch, she blazed alone in the center of the room, beyond saving, beyond hope.

Screaming, Beata launched herself at the pyre, arms outstretched. Helena grabbed her hair, but she kept going. Fire lapped at her arm, catching a sleeve.

Varden dove toward her, his cloak held wide, and threw it over her even as his arms went around her shoulders. He dragged her back, out into the passageway, and snuffed embers on her sleeve with his leather glove. Then he ripped the sleeve from her arm.

She dropped to her knees, clutching her waist, rocking back and forth. Her brown eyes, dull with pain, looked up at him. "Nico. Oh, my Nico. Find Nico."

Her little spaniel.

"We have to get out of here," Helena said. "Help me take her. This way. The smoke is less."

Between them they got the moaning Beata to her feet and pulled her down the passageway to a door that opened into the courtyard. No flames there, except for a few Japanese lanterns hanging from the trees nearest the fire. The heat had set them ablaze.

They came out at the opposite corner of the courtyard and into a passageway near the crossroad. "Through that door," Varden said, pointing. "Take her down by the river, away from the smoke. Don't let her out of your sight. I'm going for the dog."

"You can't!" Helena called. "Come back!"

But he had already found the passageway he required, the one leading to the hidden staircase. The fire had not yet reached the front of the villa, although it was moving fast. There was smoke, though. His eyes burned with it. But he could see well enough to find the door, which looked to anyone else like a floor-to-ceiling painting of a Tuscan landscape. He had used it often enough, on his way up the stairs to Beata's lavish suite of rooms, and to her bed.

Smoke was seeping through floorboards and ceilings now. The storage attics must have caught quickly, fire racing along them, spreading out, devouring everything. Poor construction all through the villa, he knew, masked with splendid wall coverings and tapestries, carpets and trompe l'oeil paintings and plaster ceiling ornaments. If the light wind didn't shift, the cottages might be spared.

He entered the sitting room, heard barking from a small parlor to his right. Nico was a placid fellow, but he'd be frightened. Varden went into the bedchamber and pulled casings from two large pillows. Into one, he began throwing everything of value he could find. Beata had three drawers filled with jewelry. Many of the gems were paste, but not all, and there was plenty of gold. There was also a safe, but no time, and he couldn't open it anyway. Perhaps it would endure the flames. He found a stash of gold coins in an engraved silver box, three framed miniatures, and several jeweled timepieces. Lace collars and cuffs, embroidered shawls, and a box of expensive feathers took the last of the space.

He went then into the parlor, where Nico came to him warily, stomach low to the floor. Varden clamped a leash onto his collar and slid the pillowcase over his unprotesting body.

When he returned to the dark staircase, it was filled with smoke. He had stayed too long. One arm holding Nico to his chest, the heavier pillowcase suspended from his left hand, he made his way downstairs and out into the passageway. It, too, was full of smoke. He turned left. The other direction led to the Limonaia, but there was no way outside from there.

A fit of coughing doubled him over. When he came up, eyes streaming with tears, he was as blind as Signora Fanella had been. Taking a lesson from her, he navigated by swinging the jewel-filled case against the wall. If worse came to worst, he would abandon it. For now, it was useful. As he got closer to the fire, he didn't want to be rubbing his one good hand along the wall.

More coughing. Then the pillowcase met empty air. An open door, or the entrance to another passageway? He felt is if he'd entered the labyrinth of the Minotaur. Too wide for a door, he decided, stepping forward and swinging again. The crossroad? From directly ahead, he felt heated air coming toward him. Heard the sound of crackling wood. Falling timbers.

Cinders in his eyes. Smoke in his lungs. He was becoming dizzy. Disoriented. He would have to risk one direction and hope it led to safety. But which? There was heat coming from his right as well. Back the way he'd come would trap him.

Six passageways met at the crossroad, a small circular chamber with a domed ceiling. He moved around the perimeter, walking a little way down each passage in turn, excepting the two where the billowing smoke carried hot cinders and ash. No way to tell. Back in the chamber, he muttered a silent prayer and was about proceed along the passageway he'd chosen for no good reason when—

"Varden!" Distant, muffled. Helena's voice. "Varden!"

"Here!" he shouted. "Crossroad!" A fit of coughing overtook him.

"This way. Follow my voice."

Directly ahead. He'd thought that would take him straight into the fire. He heard "Varden. Varden. Varden." Followed it down a passageway he had rejected. Coughing too much to tell if it got louder. But he still heard it, kept hearing it, so he kept going.

And then it was to his right, but louder. Almost clear.

"This way! Through the room."

He found the door, entered another place of Stygian darkness, as dark as the room at the castle had been. He wondered if it was a fantasy. Helena calling to him, waiting for him . . .

"Varden? Are you there?"

"I'm here." But his voice was a bare croak. Then Nico barked, bless him.

"The fire is close. Next room. I'm outside the window, but can't get it open. Can you break it with a chair?"

By feel, he found the glass. "Back up!" He didn't know if she could see him. He could see nothing at all. "Back up!" a little stronger now. Setting Nico out of the way, he turned sideways, raised his bare arm over his eyes, and took a swing at the window with the bag of jewelry. A crashing sound. The case slipped from his hand and kept going. Glass shattering all around, hot air and smoke rushing out into the cold night. He heard more glass breaking, the sound coming from near the floor.

"Wait," said Helena's crisp voice. "I'm clearing the frame. Did I hear the dog?"

"I have him." He had picked Nico up and moved back to the window. Around it, the air was clearing, and he saw that the bottom sill lay only a few inches off the floor.

Hands and arms covered with filthy silver gloves

reached in. He passed her the bundled dog, made sure she had a good hold, and when she was out of the way, jumped through the window onto the grass.

"Come away from the building," she said. "Where the fire is intense, windows are practically exploding."

He grabbed the pillowcase of jewels and followed her down to the riverbank, where Beata, still wrapped in his Viking cloak, was standing with Tommie Trotter.

"You found Nico?" she said in a plaintive voice.

"Right here," said Helena, setting her bundle on the grass and drawing a shivering, reluctant spaniel out of it. She handed Beata the leash. "He's not injured. Only a little frightened."

Beata crouched down, gathered Nico in her arms, and gazed up at Varden's face. *"Grazie, angelo mio. Grazie."*

Nodding, he turned back to look at the villa. Like red-gold flags, fire streaked out the windows. Sparks shot into the sky. Most of the villa was fully engulfed, flames leaping across the roofs, blossoming from the courtyards. Only one small section, the one where Helena had led him, remained partly untouched. And even as he watched, fire darted into the room with the broken-out window.

Trotter moved up beside him. "Everyone got out. Most are in the streets, waiting for coaches and the like. The lady here bought no insurance for a fire brigade, but weren't nothing to be done anyway. No other buildings got caught. Out front, the Charleys are holding back the crowds. Word's gone to Bow Street."

"Is my coach where we left it?"

"So far as I know, milord."

"Very well. I wish to speak with the lady for few minutes. When I am done, I want you to take her, and this pillowcase containing some of her possessions, to my house in Great Ryder Street. She will be staying there for a few days, and you with her. The servants will make arrangements. She is not to leave, nor have any visitors."

Trotter took the pillowcase and went to stand a little distance away.

With one last look at the flaming Palazzo Neri, he turned back to Beata. She was watching it as well, the dog half under her skirts and curled around her feet. "Where is Helena?" he said.

A vague gesture toward the front of the villa. "To help organize the people, I think. You wish to ask me about Gretton, yes? And the Beast?"

"I know most of it. I'll have a few questions later, for clarification. The question for now is this. What is to be done with you?"

"I care nothing for that." Lethargy in her voice. "All I have is gone, save for Nico. If they hang me, *caro*, will you care for him?"

"I'd rather you cared for him, in some other country and sworn to silence about a great many things. I expect you can figure out what they are. Exile is a possibility, Beata, but only if you convince me you can be trusted. That won't be easy. Think about it, and we shall talk of this tomorrow."

"If you wish." A shudder as a large section of the building collapsed. "She was my mother. Signora Fanella. I did not want people to know I came from a poor family in a small village, so she pretended to be my companion. She listened to gossip, and told me of it. Nothing harmful, not too much harmful. But then I knew who to set my spies on, and they soon acquired information I could sell. All the money I spent to build this. And now it is gone."

"Do you know why she set the fires?"

"Gretton said we would soon be caught, but I did not believe him. He was always fearful. Mamma heard us talking. She had not understood until then what I was doing. Today we quarreled, and tonight—" Another gesture, despairing. "Did you understand what she was saying before she . . . before her clothing burned?"

"Only when she told us to stop. To keep our distance."

"She asked you to forgive me. *La perdoni*. She said I was sick with greed and pride. And it is true. I deserve no forgiveness. I cannot say what I would do in future, out of greed and pride. They rule me—have done since I was a child."

"You could never again achieve anything like this, Beata. But you might find some happiness, if you turn your hopes and expectations elsewhere."

"I must find repentance, Derek, if I can. They are not natural to me, the humble virtues. And how am I to be happy, when I have killed my own mother?"

"She turned the torch on herself."

"Yes. And do you know why? She told me, her last words—'I burn now, that God may spare me from hell.' I laid the guilt on her shoulders. She did nothing wrong, and then she punished herself when I should have been punished."

"She wasn't in her right mind. But I cannot help you to deal with this, Beata. If we find anything of her in the ruins, I shall make whatever arrangements you wish for her burial. No one need know that the fire, and her death, were other than an accident."

He gave Beata a few instructions, walked with her and Tommie Trotter along the river for a short distance, then up to the street where his coach and horses were waiting. When she was on her way, he went back to the villa, and to the cottage where Helena had been staying. Ash and cinders crackled under his sandaled feet. He let himself in, half expecting to find Helena there, changing out of her costume.

She was not, but from the sooty traces on the floor, he knew she had been there earlier. He went into the bedrooms and looked around. More black footprints, and a half-open drawer. The armoire was empty, except for a slipper in the back corner, as if it had been overlooked. An indentation on the bed, about the size of her portmanteau. Nothing in the drawers. It seemed she had packed up her belongings and taken them elsewhere.

Not unreasonable. Until the fire was altogether extinguished, a change in the wind could send it leaping from building to building. He was about to leave when a flash of color, silver and black, caught his eye. His lifted the counterpane and bent to look more closely. Reached down and drew out what he had seen. Her gown, gloves, slippers, and headdress, all of them silver and spotted with black, had been stuffed under the bed.

He put them in a drawer and was on his way out of the cottage when he saw her mask lying atop the cupboard where she kept the wine. Sweeping it up, he carried it with him to the street in front of the Palazzo.

As Trotter had warned him, several hundred people were milling about, some wearing their costumes, some in servants' garb, while the Charleys tried to direct traffic and keep order. The crowd also included curiosity seekers, newspaper reporters, neighbors come to see what had happened, hacks and carriages trying to get through.

Someone noticed him, and instantly he was surrounded by people shouting questions. He climbed onto a wagon so he could be seen and began answering them with diplomatic nonanswers, all the while scanning the crowd for Helena.

But there was no sign of her, not then, not through all the hours that followed. And as the sun came up over the smoldering ruins of Palazzo Neri, he had to accept that she was gone.

He had driven her away.

Chapter 31

Stone walls everywhere he looked.

In the days and nights after Helena vanished, Varden devoted every spare minute—the few he could squeeze out—to finding her. But the Gretton business occupied most of his time, and it wasn't a task he could pass on to someone else. Even the paperwork fell to him, for fear information would be sold to the newspapermen and broadsheet printers who surrounded Number 4 Bow Street like a pack of hooligans, clamoring for details of the double suicide. Sir Richard Burnie, overeager to get his name in print, required constant supervision.

Despair was nipping at Varden's ankles. It was all his fault. He should not have left her alone. But it had never crossed his mind that she would scarper.

The night of the fire, mind swirling with regrets and apologies, he had remained at the Palazzo for several hours, dealing with the authorities and making sure that what little remained of the villa was secured. There seemed an endless number of decisions to be taken, and with everyone looking to him for a ruling, he couldn't get away.

It was well after sunrise when he cut free long enough to return home for a wash and a change of clothes. Then he went directly to Sothingdon House, where he expected to find Helena.

He found only workmen, who said they hadn't seen her. But they let him enter and wander freely through the rooms, including her sitting room and bedchamber. Three or four of her plain dresses hung in the armoire, and a few items remained on the shelves, but little else belonging to her could be seen. He stopped short of rummaging through the drawers.

After ordering a pair of his servants to watch the house around the clock, he began to suspect that a long hunt lay ahead of him.

There was little use trying to find her in the Rookery before Jamie Carr returned from Somerset, so on Wednesday afternoon he rode north to Birindar's house. The duke and duchess had already left for Longview, somewhat to his relief, and Birindar assured him that Miss Pryce had not appeared there, nor sent any messages. Six more hours gone, Varden thought when he arrived again in London late that night, and no progress made.

Thursday brought the only piece of good news. Beata had arranged to join friends who were leaving for France, and within a short time, he had sent her in his own carriage to the departure point, where Tommie Trotter would make sure she got on the packet and didn't get off before it sailed. Another item scratched from his mental list of duties, and to his relief, he could leave the hotel where he had been staying and move back to his house.

In slightly better spirits, he decided to ride his luck. Early that afternoon, he took up his sword cane and went alone into the Rookery, where to his surprise, two of Carr's watchmen appeared from out of nowhere and quietly escorted him to Lomber Court.

Carr was there, a little drunk and in a strange humor. "I haven't seen her since the day you both came here, milord. More than that, I'll not say. Well, this much I'll say. If ever I learn you have hurt her, your life won't be worth a filed farthing."

"I did hurt her," Varden said without hesitation. "I didn't mean to. When she revealed to me her identity, I was unprepared. Stunned, really. I said nothing, but silence was not what she needed from me. Then the fire—you know about that?—and I have been looking for her ever since."

"To do what?"

"That is between the two of us, until she chooses to disclose it. Shall I expect to have an unfortunate accident on my way out of the Rookery?"

Carr shrugged and went to pour himself another drink. "Not if you carry a pair of cats."

"I beg your pardon?"

"The housekeeper at the castle sent cats for the Duchess of Tallant. They're descendants of her own cats, or some such thing. Helena had let slip that she was acquainted with the duchess, so Mrs. Culworth decided I was the one to see them delivered. They make me sneeze. Take them off my hands and you'll get safe passage. This once."

"Very well. I'll have them transported to the Tallant estate." He intended to call by Longview at some point, but tomorrow was for the country home of Lord Duran and Lady Jessica in Sussex. That was Helena's most likely bolt-hole, and no matter the demands on him in London, he could put off going there no longer.

"One thing more," he said. "I have been wondering if you might devise some beneficial purpose for the castle. It is of no use to me, but I dislike seeing the land and the buildings go to waste."

"As a matter of fact, I've been thinking along the same lines." Carr's voice sounded indifferent, but at Varden's offer, his eyes had brightened. "The men, particularly the young ones, did well in the clean air and away from temptation. They worked hard to find the documents, and were proud when they succeeded. One ran off, of course. The only surprise is that more of them didn't. Nor did they want to come back here."

"Well, you'll need to devise a plan and draw up a proposal. I don't mean to loose a slew of criminals in the Mendips. If your plans are sound, I am willing to make a financial investment to seem them developed, and so long as the property is being put to good use, it will be left in your hands for a peppercorn rent. Let me know what you decide. Now, where are those blasted cats?"

It was a tribute of sorts, Varden supposed, that Carr escorted him personally to where he had left his horse. And carried the basket holding two gray-and-white kittens as well. When Varden had mounted, Carr handed it over.

"Inform the duchess," he said, "that these were littered by Andy."

Varden gazed down at him. "I am in love with Helena. If you care for her as I believe you do, you will help me to find her."

"What makes you think I haven't?"

Varden was halfway home before he realized that Carr, who had carried the basket for a considerable time, never once let go with a sneeze.

Before dawn the next morning, with a basket of annoyed kittens attached to the back of his saddle, Varden began the long ride into southeast Kent. He knew, from the murder investigation, where the estate was situated, and by mid-morning, a bright sun and fresh breeze made the journey almost pleasant.

Or it might have done, if it hadn't given him so much time to think. The same few moments kept replaying themselves in his mind as if they were happening still. Helena pulling off the silver headdress. Pins dropping to the floor as she loosed her mane of shining black hair and let it spread over her shoulders. Lovely hands reaching to the spectacles. Removing them. And the look on her face as she tilted her head and gazed for the first time directly into his eyes.

Courage. Defiance. A glimmer of hope that, in his silence, collapsed into despair.

In the last few days he had thought a thousand times of what he should have said.

"It doesn't matter." But it did, and she would have heard the lic in his voice. He could not pretend that an alliance with the Keynes family, especially Michael, was a small thing to him. He would accept it, of course. The alternative was to lose Helena. And for her sake, he would accept it with as much grace as he could manage. But until the first shock had passed, there had been no coherent thoughts in his head. And by the time he had begun stringing thoughts together, it was too late.

Or, "I love you." But he had already said that, and she hadn't believed him.

Perhaps, "Do you love me?" But what if she had said "no"? What would he have done then?

He didn't know. But anything would have been better than what he had forced her to do. By rushing his fences, he had driven her from her sanctuary. And still he came at her, demanding she strip away, one by one, the last of her defenses, until she had nothing left but her pride.

And then he took that from her as well. He just stood there like the blockhead he was and stared at her. At the Keynes in her. He didn't really see Helena at all. That he'd felt as if a horse had kicked him in the head was no excuse.

Now, with the image burned on his memory, he saw nothing else but her. And with the opportunity to look closely, he began to decipher the language that had been speaking to him like flowing water while he ignored its message, listening only to her words.

By the time he came onto Tallant land and located the straight road, lined with tall elms, that led to the manor house, he knew what he would do when he found her.

*   *   *

"I am to tell you," Varden said, holding out the wicker basket to the Duchess of Tallant, "that they were littered by Andy."

"Andy?" She raised the lid, and her eyes lit up as if he'd handed her the moon. "Oh, my! They are exactly like her. It's Andromache. Or it was. Did Mrs. Culworth give them to you?"

"Indirectly. She sent them back with the men who found the documents at the castle."

"I have so missed my cats." She took the basket, set it on a table, and drew out one of the kittens. "Thank you for bringing them such a long way."

After the first glance, Varden had not looked at the duke, who stood by the window with his hands clasped behind his back, watching them. "It was my pleasure, Your Grace. But I can see that you are preparing to go out. Might I ask, before you depart, if I may have a word in private with the duke?"

"About Helena?" Tallant strode over to the basket and looked down at the kitten busily clawing its way over the high rim. "No need to send the duchess away. If ever you take a wife, you'll soon learn there's no use trying to keep anything from a female. Better to surrender at the starting line and get it over with."

"I am attempting to find her. Is she here?"

"No. What's the problem? Can't get along without your secretary?"

Expecting a rough go of it, Varden had put a check rein on his temper before entering the house. "Do you know where she is?"

"In fact, yes." Tallant picked up the kitten, held it on the palm of his hand, and studied it with a frown. "Do these have to live in the house?"

"Only if *you* want to live in it," said the duchess, unperturbed.

"See what I mean?" Tallant set the kitten on the

floor. "Welcome to Longview, cat. If you have to piddle, do it on that fellow's boots."

"Is there some ritual bloodletting involved," Varden said, "before I get an answer to my question?"

The duke laughed. "Perhaps later. If you find my sister, what are your intentions?"

"If she'll have me, I intend to marry her. If she refuses, I intend to persuade her."

"Without asking my permission? I am, to your displeasure, the head of the family."

"And she is of age. It would be better for her, of course, if the marriage was not unwelcome to her relatives. But since she managed to prosper for twenty-eight years without you, I doubt you can assert much control over her now."

"Probably none at all. But that won't stop me from looking out for her best interests. I don't think you are good enough for her."

"On that much," Varden said, "we are agreed. I will try to do better."

"You haven't made a promising start." Tallant dropped onto a chair and leaned back, fingers laced behind his head. "She came here two days ago. What kept you so long?"

"Serious matters I am unable to discuss. And there was a fire—"

"Right. You rescued a dog. And now you're trotting around finding homes for cats."

"All true," Varden said levelly. "On occasion, I even help to rescue a duke."

From the duchess, a musical laugh.

"Oh, ho!" said the duke. "Our angelic earl is growing teeth. You'll need them, if you expect to handle a Keynes."

"I am pleased that you are both female," said the duchess to the kittens, now curled on her lap. "Males can be *so* difficult."

Tallant raised an eyebrow. "You see, Varden. That's how it's done. But then, compared to my little sister, I'm a pussycat. She made me promise to tell no one where she can be found. Wrestled the same promise from the duchess. So you see, even if I wanted to, I couldn't help you."

Varden looked over at the duchess, who nodded. "In that case," he said, "there is no reason for me to take up more of your time."

"Easy on," said the duke. "Before you go, let's get a few things settled. That's in case you find her, and she doesn't toss you out on your ear. Which I'd like to see, by the way."

"If there's time, I'll send an engraved invitation. What can we possibly have to settle?"

"For one thing, the marriage settlement. She has refused to accept an allowance or any kind of support, which—being an independent cuss myself—I can't argue with. But if she marries you, there will be money. You are to persuade her to accept it, and you will not touch a penny of it."

"We won't need your money, Tallant."

"That's beside the point. Another thing. The duchess will insist you both be invited to family gatherings. Send her, but you stay home."

The duchess threw up her hands, startling the kittens. "He doesn't mean that, Varden. He's just being a swine."

"You wound me, Duchess." The duke was grinning. "I'm serious about the money."

"Is there anything else?" Varden said between his teeth.

"I'm thinking that in case we get stuck with you, the rest of the family ought to see what they're in for. But my brother's widow and her older daughter, the nice one, are heading out to Italy for the rest of the year. We're just about to go down to the docks in Dover and wave them off. It's only a short distance, ten miles or so. Why don't you come along? Maybe one of *them* will be able to stand you."

The duchess looked as surprised as Varden felt.

"Thank you," he said, itching to escape. "But as you have pointed out, I got a late start on my search for Helena. Nothing must delay it now. If you will pardon me, I'm on my way to call on Lady Jessica Duran."

"I don't think she'll be there," said the duchess, putting the kittens aside and rising. "It is the Duke of Devonshire's travel party leaving from Dover, and the two of them are great friends. She is bringing her new infant for him to see before he departs. Then she and Duran will stay here at Longview for a few days. If you wish to speak with her, you may as well come with us."

"Or go on ahead." Tallant rose as well, and went to stand beside his wife. "The duchess makes me travel in great pomp, which means a lot of flap and feathers when we arrive anywhere. Besides, I've had enough of you for one day."

Varden's heart, which had been picking up speed since their maneuvering began, seemed about to burst from his chest. Without breaking their word to Helena, Carr and the Tallants had been drawing him a map.

"Likewise," he said. "But I'll take your advice and swing by Dover, in case Lady Jessica is there. It's not that far out of the way. Your Grace"—he bowed to the duchess—"thank you for your kindness. Duke, I'll try to be gone by the time you get there."

He bowed to Tallant as well, and as he did, saw what was transpiring between one of the kittens and a ducal boot.

Varden had just reached the entry hall when a loud oath from the parlor told him the duke had seen it as well.

Chapter 32

"Two hours until the tide turns," said the Duke of Devonshire, bundled in a woolen peacoat against the freshening afternoon wind. "Can we possibly be ready to sail?"

Helena, standing in the prow of the smallest packet, one of three that would carry the party to Calais, looked up from her checklist. Devonshire's ruddy, worried face had hovered over her for much of the day, his nervousness growing as more wagons and coaches drew up at the docks with luggage to disgorge. She was assigning deck space now, directing the boxes and cases to be tied down, trying to make sure there would be room for the passengers.

"Females take too much with them," Devonshire said. "Italy is not the wilderness. They can buy most of what they require when we get there."

Since nearly all the excess luggage was the duke's, she smiled and nodded. "Why don't you slip into the tavern and warm up with a mug of hot spiced wine, Your Grace? I will soon need the spot where you are standing to put a crate of pineapples."

"Indeed. Indeed."

He went off, but when next she glanced over at the dock, he was pacing—or rather, weaving—around carts and crates and seamen. The duke was right about missing the tide, and the good sailing weather that might not exist tomorrow. Across the channel, vehicles would be waiting to transport them on the next stage of their journey. Traveling with Devonshire was something like marching with an army, especially when he chose to take with him an assortment of friends. She decided to add "quartermaster" to her resumé.

Some of the passengers were filtering over from the hotels where they had stayed the night. Behind them came servants with portmanteaus and personal items that would need to be onloaded. She saw David Fairfax escort the Dowager Duchess of Tallant and her daughter Corinna to a quiet spot where they could watch without being trampled. Nearby, Beata Neri sat alone on a box with her spaniel at her feet, wearing a cloak loaned to her by the duchess. She had arrived the day before, in Varden's coach, and when Helena saw it draw up, she had nearly fainted dead away.

Never mind. It hadn't been him in the coach, and she was *not* going to think about him. Not while she had work to do.

There was a small flurry near the end of the dock, and she saw a hand waving. Lady Jessica, with Duran standing beside her holding a bundle wrapped in a yellow blanket. Her namesake, Helena Duran. She wasn't sure she could bear seeing the infant, who was as close to having a child as she was likely to come. But she would have to greet them, she supposed, and smile while paying compliments to the happy parents. She waved back, knowing Jessica would understand that she could not free herself right now.

The pace grew more frantic. Piles on the docks shrank as the ones on the decks grew. Servants and seamen scurried back and forth, with Helena directing them as if she were conducting an orchestra. By now, no one questioned taking orders from a female. Devonshire wouldn't stand for it, and besides, there wasn't time.

She was nearly ready to direct the passengers to

start going aboard when another distraction pulled her gaze to the dock. People were turning to face the land-side end of it, and whatever was going on there.

None of her concern. She got the attention of a mustachioed dockhand and asked him to retie a stack of boxes that appeared unlikely to withstand a toss-ing sea.

Of a sudden, everything seemed quieter than be-fore. She heard the cry of gulls instead of the calls of workmen. The slap of water against the hull instead of the thump of luggage. She looked up again, and got a glimpse of fluttering capes as the wind caught a gentleman's greatcoat. The packet where she stood was at the farthest reach of the dock. Boxes and peo-ple cut off her view. But a thrumming in her veins told her who he was.

Then she saw his light hair, shining in the mid-afternoon sun. People moved aside to let him pass when he reached the gangplank. He never slowed, his stride swift and determined as he skirted the obstacles on the deck. Heart thumping, she took a backward step and stopped, the prow railing pressed against her waist.

He tossed his hat, which he had been carrying, onto a box. Cleared the deck of workers with a wave of his hand. And then he was standing directly in front of her, so close she could feel his breath on her face.

"I have come for you," he said.

She was shaking her head, her mouth open to deny him, when he raised a finger. "No arguments, Helena. The time for debate is over. Now we take a vote. But first, let us make sure of your credentials."

One hand reached up, plucked off her spectacles, and tossed them over the side. A small plink as they hit the water.

She hadn't time to react. He was untying the rib-bons of her bonnet. She tried to push his hands away, but the bow came loose and the bonnet went in the direction of his hat on the box.

His black-gloved hand slid behind her neck, holding her in place while he began wrestling with the pins that held her wig in place. She was beyond speech now, beyond protest. Dimly aware of people gathering along the dock to watch, she looked up at his face, at the taut lips and set jaw, at the intensity with which he worked.

He was, undeniably, master of this ship. And of her.

Two of the sausage-shaped forms dropped away and rolled across the deck. Finally the brown wig came loose and followed her spectacles into the sea. So did the pins that secured her hair. When the last one was removed, he slipped the fingers of both hands into her hair, loosened it, and like a cascade, let it fall around her shoulders.

"You have beautiful hair," he said. "When I felt it that night at the castle, I could not imagine how the hair I saw in the light could feel so lush, like tropical rain streaming through my fingers."

A hand went under her chin and lifted it. "You have beautiful eyes as well. Haunted eyes, deep with mystery. Burning with promise. Close them now."

She did, and felt his lips brush over each one.

"I love you," he said, "and I want to spend all my life with you. Our happiness, yours and mine, is in the balance now. Our children, waiting to be born, listen for your answer."

Her eyes flew open. "You know I cannot—"

"Shhhh." A fingertip over her lips. "There is only one way to vote, and it is not with protests. It's damn well not with reasons why you mustn't become the Countess of Varden."

His hands moved to her shoulders, resting gently there. "You have given me every argument you could muster, and I have found none that we cannot surmount together. Only one thing can keep us apart, Helena. I am not certain if I would accept a denial without trying—for however long it requires—to change your mind. But before I confront that dilemma, you must tell me if it is necessary."

"How can I?" She could scarcely draw breath. "What do you want of me?"

"Everything." Into his confidence crept a whisper of uncertainty. "Most of all, your love. If I do not have it, you may sail away with the others. But first you must look into my eyes and tell me, without sacrifice or dishonesty, that you do not love me and can never love me."

He removed his hands from her shoulders and let them fall to his sides. His eyes, a deep green, fixed on hers.

Not touching her, he surrounded her. Drew her into himself with a summons that vibrated in her bones. She resisted with all her strength. Pushed him away with her will. Her mouth opened to free him with the most unforgivable of all lies.

But the words lodged in her throat. Sent knives into her heat.

She could not deny him. Could not deny love. Her gaze lowered to a button on his greatcoat.

"I take it the vote is unanimous," he said, relief and joy singing in his voice. His arms wrapped around her, one at the waist, the other at her shoulders, and he bent her backward, as he had done at the castle, the ship's rail supporting her as his sword had once imprisoned her. And then his lips came onto hers, and her mouth opened to welcome him.

Dizzy with love and pleasure, she heard a sound in her ears as he kissed her, a sound like the rush of ocean waves and the ringing of bells. When they both had to seize a breath, she stole a glance at the crowd lining up along the dock. They were cheering.

He didn't seem to notice, seemed intent on returning to the kiss. But he didn't know about the tides. She put her hands on his shoulders. "My lord—"

"Make that 'my love,' and I'll listen to you."

"My love, any moment now, the Duke of Devonshire will swoop down on us in a panic. Or else he'll give the order to cast off while we are still aboard. Is that what you wish?"

"I suppose not," he said. "Time and tides and all that, right? Come along, then. I've a special license in my pocket, and if a Channel packet captain can't marry us, we'll find a clergyman who will."

"Let me see it," she said, pretty sure what she would find. "The license. Give it me."

A good-humored salute. "Aye, aye, Admiral."

A glimpse was all she needed. "The name is wrong. Helena Pryce is wrong. If we use this license, our marriage will not be legal."

He looked chastened. Disappointed that they could not be instantly wed, which erased the last shadows of uncertainty clouding her joy. Beyond the theatrics and the passion, he really did want her. Forever.

"What should I have put?" he demanded. "Ella Pryce? How were you christened?"

"I was named Leonie, for my mother's grandmother. She was French."

"Was she indeed? Excellent. That will swing Grandmere into our corner, and with both grandmothers supporting our marriage, most of the battle is won. But what of your surname? I know it ought to be Keynes, but I've no idea what happens when a child is unacknowledged."

"Nor did my mother. She wanted me baptized, so she arranged for it in an obscure parish. I don't know what lies she told, or how she brought it about, but I have seen the registry. It reads Leonie, followed by gibberish beginning with a *K*. I suppose that, even then, she did not wish to leave a trail for the Devil Duke to follow."

"A smart woman, your mother." He slipped his arm through hers and led her toward the gangplank. "We'll start over, and the first step is to get your name back. Then I can legally change it. What a bother you are, Ella Helena Leonie Keynes. And what am I to call you?"

" 'My love' has a nice ring to it."

Devonshire was waiting at the head of the gangplank. "I suppose this means you won't be sailing with us," he said with a flattering touch of regret. "Shall I have your luggage taken off?"

"Damn right," said Varden, glaring at her. "You were really going with them?"

"Not now." She bit her lip, raised the sheaf of records and lists still clutched in her hand. "I am sorry, Your Grace, for the inconvenience. Can you manage? I'll stay long enough to see you off—"

"The devil you will." Varden plucked away the papers and passed them over. "If Devonshire can't get out of Dover without you, he may as well stay in England."

Varden was starting to sound much like her brother, she was thinking as she waved to a smiling Devonshire and let herself be towed through the crowd.

Varden bowed when they passed Beata, but didn't stop. He had risked his life to bring her dog and her valuables—enough to get her started elsewhere—out of the fire. That was enough.

He did stop when they came to Lady Jessica, and released his hold on Helena long enough for the two friends to embrace.

"I am so happy for you," Jessica said. "Later, we shall have a row about eight years of deception and why you failed to attend the christening."

Helena looked over at Varden, who seemed mesmerized by the infant in Lord Duran's arms. "See this?' he said. "We need to produce one of these straightaway. That will bring every reluctant Leighton, if there are any reluctant Leightons nine months from now, into the fold."

"Not if they are holding out for an heir," she informed him.

"This is our daughter," Duran said. "We named her Helena."

"Ah. Well, we want plenty of daughters, too. Come along, my love. We have a notable obstacle to get by on the way to our carriage."

She looked ahead and saw her brother, flanked by the duchess, the dowager duchess, and her daughter Corinna. David Fairfax stood beside the girl, eyes round as dinner plates. It appeared her family had kept her secrets, even from him.

But not from Varden, she suspected. The gleam in the duke's eyes confirmed it.

"You promised," she said directly they came up to him.

Tallant made a dismissive gesture. "I only dropped a hint. And I didn't figure Varden was smart enough to pick up on it."

"Here we go," said the duchess, shaking her head. "Do behave, Your Grace, at least while I present the other members of the family to Lord Varden."

He bowed to each lady as she was introduced, and gave Cory a smile that banished her shyness long enough for a smile in return.

"So what happens now?" the duke said. "Will you make an honest woman of her, or must I call you out?"

"There is some difficulty," Varden said, not rising to the bait, "with establishing my bride's legal name. She would like to be acknowledged as a Keynes, if you can arrange it."

"I'll see the papers drawn up. What else?"

Varden looked down at her. "Is there anything else, my love?"

"I can't think very well right now," she said truthfully.

"Here's this, then," said the duke. "Varden, begin as you mean to go on. No back-corner ceremony with a drunken cleric and two church mice for witnesses. Post announcements in the papers. Cry the banns. Wed the lady proudly, in front of all the world."

"Done," said Varden. "Will you come to stand with her?"

"Will you have me?"

"Does anyone care what I think of this?" Helena asked.

"You said you weren't thinking right now, my love. And the duke is correct, for a change. You will be welcome at our wedding, Your Grace, and in our home."

"See that," the duchess said to her husband. "Good manners. That's how it is done."

"One more thing, Your Grace, before I carry your sister off to Devon and the Varden estate. Will you mind telling that Runner standing with Beata to take my horse back to London? There's a good fellow."

"Varden!" said Helena, shocked.

Laughing, the duke put his arm around his wife. "I will. Now go, before the ladies start ganging up on us."

A short time later, after Varden had given directions to the driver and joined her in his carriage, he pulled down the shades, lifted her onto his lap, and set about kissing her.

"Will we really wait so long to marry?" she said after a breathless interval.

"A month, I expect, to allow for the legalities concerning your name and the banns. But we'll return to London in a day or so, to meet with my family. And so that I can do my duty by Parliament."

"What about your duty by me? I do not wish, my lord, to be without you all that time."

"You mean in bed?"

She nodded vigorously.

"Then nothing to worry about, my lady." One hand

slipped under her skirts and began heading north. "I never said we would not anticipate our vows. In fact, we will start immediately. Have you ever made love in a coach?"

"Ooohh," she murmured as he reached his destination. "You know I haven't."

"Nor have I. But in this, as in all things, we shall begin as we mean to go on."

"With adventures," she said, offering her mouth for more kisses. "Lots and lots of adventures."

About the Author

Lynn Kerstan's Regency and historical romance novels have won a score of awards, including the Golden Quill, the Award of Excellence, and the coveted RITA.

A former college teacher, professional bridge player, folksinger, and dedicated traveler, she lives in California, where she plots her stories while walking on the beach or riding the waves on her boogie board.

Visit www.lynnkerstand.com for more about the author, her books, and the times and places in which her stories are set.